DEBORAH AND BARAK

IF GOD BE WITH US

TRUDY MORGAN-COLE

REVIEW AND HERALD® PUBLISHING ASSOCIATION
HAGERSTOWN, MD 21740

The author assumes full responsibility for the accuracy of all facts and quotations
as cited in this book.

This book was
Edited by Gerald Wheeler
Cover art and design by Jo Card
Electronic makeup by Shirley M. Bolivar
Typeset: 12/14 Bembo

PRINTED IN U.S.A.

10 09 08 07 06   5 4 3 2 1

R&H Cataloging Service
Morgan-Cole, Trudy J.   1965-   .
    Deborah and Barak.

        1. Deborah (Biblical character). 2. Barak (Biblical character). I. Title.
                                222.32

ISBN-10: 0-8280-1841-3
ISBN-13: 978-0-8280-1841-8

▲▲

Other books by Trudy J. Morgan-Cole:

Connecting
Esther: A Story of Courage
God's Positioning System

To order, call 1-800-765-6955.

Visit us at www.reviewandherald.com for information on other
review and Herald® products.

DEDICATION

In creating the story of Deborah and Lappidoth,
I relied on the truism that behind
(or, better yet, beside)
many a successful woman
stands a supportive man.
No one knows that to be truer than I,
and so this book is lovingly dedicated
to my wonderful husband,
Jason.

ACKNOWLEDGMENTS

Researching an unfamiliar period of history is always a journey into the unknown. I would like to thank my guides on this journey, Dr. Douglas Clark who answered many questions and did a thorough read-through of the manuscript, and my editor Gerald Wheeler whose painstaking attention to cultural, historical, and geographical detail compensated for my own lack of knowledge and thus made this a much better book. The errors that remain are entirely my own responsibility.

Thanks are also due to the many fellow writers who participated in National Novel-Writing Month 2003, during which I completed the first half of this manuscript. Would-be writers who wish to set themselves a challenge should check out www.nanowrimo.org.

Finally, as always, thanks to my family—my husband, my parents, and my children—for their continual support. When given a Mother's Day project to fill in with the information "My Mommy is good at _____" my son put: "Writing on the computer," an accolade that means more than any number of literary awards.

PREFACE

Deborah, a prophetess, the wife of Lappidoth, was leading Israel at that time. She held court under the Palm of Deborah between Ramah and Bethel in the hill country of Ephraim, and the Israelites came to her to have their disputes decided. She sent for Barak son of Abinoam from Kedesh in Naphtali and said to him, "The Lord, the God of Israel, commands you: 'Go, take with you ten thousand men of Naphtali and Zebulun and lead the way to Mount Tabor. I will lure Sisera, the commander of Jabin's army, with his chariots and his troops to the Kishon River and give him into your hands.' "

Barak said to her, "If you go with me, I will go; but if you don't go with me, I won't go."

"Very well," Deborah said, "I will go with you. But because of the way you are going about this, the honor will not be yours, for the Lord will hand Sisera over to a woman." So Deborah went with Barak to Kedesh, where he summoned Zebulun and Naphtali. Ten thousand men followed him, and Deborah also went with him (Judges 4:4-10).

Few books in world literature tantalize us as much as the Bible. It tells us so much and so little. The great story of the first woman to lead Israel, the military commander on whom she relied, and the second woman who enters the story later to strike the decisive blow in battle is of epic proportions, but it occupies only two chapters in the Bible, and the second chapter (Judges 5) is simply a poetic retelling of the events recounted in Judges 4.

As always, it's the unanswered questions that fascinate. How, in the extremely patriarchal society of Israel did a woman rise to such prominence? How did the men around Deborah accept her as prophetess and judge? What was the nature of her relationship with Barak? Why does Barak insist on Deborah's presence during the military campaign, and why does she take this as a sign that he is unworthy to win the victory?

The story that follows provides one possible set of answers to the questions that echo around the brief tale of Deborah and Barak.

List of Major Characters

Abigail, Barak's wife

Abinoam, Barak's father

Anna, Lappidoth's daughter by his first wife

Avi, Lappidoth's second son by his first wife

Azubah, Lappidoth's first wife

Barak, son of Abinoam, the liberator of Israel

Deborah, daughter of Ruel and wife of Lappidoth, prophetess and judge

Dina, Deborah's younger sister

Eleazar, Anna's husband

Eli, Lappidoth's eldest son by his first wife

Hananiah, a Hebrew field slave belonging to Sisera

Heber, a Kenite and husband of Jael

Isa, Deborah's younger brother

Lappidoth, Deborah's husband

Jabin, Canaanite king of the city of Hazor

Jael, cousin of Deborah and Barak, wife of Heber the Kenite

Japhet, son of Deborah and Lappidoth

Joel, son of Barak and Abigail

Josiah, a priest, husband of Tirzah

Keturah, Eli's wife

Micah (the elder), Barak's father-in-law

Micah (the younger), son of Barak and Abigail

Mirah, daughter of Deborah and Lappidoth

Miriam, Deborah's childhood friend

Nathan, a bandit and later soldier under Barak's command

Rahel, Deborah's childhood friend

Ruel, Deborah's father

Samuel, Barak's boyhood friend and fellow soldier

Senet, Egyptian steward in Sisera's house in Hazor

Shemiah, cousin of Barak's wife, Abigail

Sisera, Canaanite general and later ruler of the city of Harosheth Haggoyim

Tirzah, a young woman of Shiloh who seeks Deborah's counsel

Ziri, Deborah's cousin

PROLOGUE

"You think this edge is sharp enough?" A man's rough voice interrupted the dry scraping of stone against metal.

"If you sharpen it any more you'll wear it away to nothing. What does it matter, anyway? Sisera's army has spearheads of iron. Tomorrow's the day of our death—you know it as well as I do." The second voice was slurred. Deborah knew that some of the men had taken to strong drink tonight to dull the edge of fear and guarantee a few hours' sleep.

"Gods curse you, man, don't say that," a third, and younger voice, spoke up.

"They have cursed me!" the half-drunk man declared, and though it was dark and she stood on the other side of the tent, away from the opening, Deborah could almost see the reckless gesture with which the man raised his wineskin. "Baal, Astarte, even the One God of our fathers—I'm cursed, cursed down to the bone. Otherwise why would I be here throwing away my life at dawn tomorrow?"

"Shut up," said the first voice, that of the man sharpening the edge of his bronze sword. "I'm going to lie down. Don't know if I'll sleep, but I'll give it a fair try."

Deborah found her feet leading her over the stony, uneven ground between tents, around to the entrance where a flickering torch, thrust into the ground, burned between the three men. Her sudden appearance surprised them. She saw two men sitting upright and one half-sprawled on the ground, their bearded faces lit by the flickering flame. Scores of such small groups of men sat or lay this night around the encampment, under the velvet blanket of a sky whose sun had set two hours before. As she stood there she saw how they had first glanced to see if the intruder were a chieftain or a common fighting man like themselves, then noticed the cut of her robe, the way she moved. "'S a woman," the younger man said in a piercing whisper, jabbing one of the others in the ribs.

The man he poked—the one who'd obviously been drinking—let a slow grin spread across his sleepy features. "Well, hello, sweetheart," he said. "Come to cheer the men up on the night before battle?"

"Yes, I have," Deborah said, lowering herself to the ground beside them. Inwardly she cringed. The army of Yahweh ought not to have loose women as camp followers, but they were here nonetheless. Nor should it have drunkards or men who swore by the Canaanite gods or who believed their cause was hopeless—that they would surely die in the morning. But the Lord's army consisted of human beings. All these things were here, and a force so riddled with doubt and fear and sin would surely fail in the morning's huge and daunting task.

"Hold your tongue, fool!" The sword-sharpener spoke to his companion with a note of alarm in his voice. He had recognized Deborah, or more likely had noted her age and known she could not be a camp-follower. "This is no common woman—this is the prophetess, Deborah."

The prophetess, Deborah. She felt the title hanging on her like a weight, heavy as a sword at her side. Yet at times like this, it was useful to be able to command men's instant respect—a rare experience for any woman. "I am Deborah," she conceded, "though I am no more than a common woman, myself. But the Lord speaks to me, and the Lord tells me that the men of Israel need courage and strength tonight."

The older two men—the sword-sharpener and the wine-guzzler—looked as if they would deny their fears. She could see them buckling on manly bravado like breastplates. But the younger one—really, he was no more than a boy, no older than Avi was when . . . no, better not think of that.

The youngest soldier leaned toward her almost eagerly. His beard had only begun to sprout, a soft furring on his chin, and his eyes were wide and honest.

"It is true, we need courage, prophetess," he said. "The men say we are doomed. General Sisera has nearly twice the men we have, and they have the chariots of iron. We are poorly armed, and some of us have never fought before. Can you give us a word from the Lord to cheer us?"

From the way he said "the Lord," Deborah knew this man was faithful to the One God, and that in turn cheered her. She had received no vision, heard no voices, since they had started the journey to Mount Tabor, and that troubled her. Deborah had never needed God's voice this desperately—indeed, there had been times when she had wished that she could not *hear* it, that God would leave her alone and choose some other to be His mouthpiece. But tonight, and many nights since, she had longed for a word, a sign, a vision. None had come. Only the silence of night on the mountain, broken by the chirring of night insects. Now she reached into her own memories, to the certainty she had felt when the God had touched her and started this whole journey—she could hold to that, by faith.

"We will win," she said, not sure as she spoke the words how much she believed them. "Driving back the iron chariots, we will conquer. The hand of Yahweh is upon this army. If we are faithful to Him"—she allowed her gaze to become stern as she glanced at the man who had spoken of Baal and Astarte—"then He will be faithful to us. We are His people. Long ago he promised us this land through Moses and Joshua. His promise has not changed, though we are slow to take hold of it. Tomorrow we seize it. Tomorrow we begin to turn the tide."

It was a fine speech, a miniature of the ones she had given in Israelite towns and villages as she traveled north, rallying the men to Barak's side. Speaking the words made her bolder, gave her a little certainty. Until, that is, the sword-sharpener said, "I'd be a good deal more sure your God was faithful if He'd managed to stir up a bit more interest among the men of Reuben."

"Or of Dan," the drinker said with a derisive laugh. "If we're all the children of Israel, why won't the other tribes join us? You know why. Because they don't want to put their heads on the block along with ours."

Now her sternness was real, not feigned, as she turned to him. "This is no way to speak. Even the strong drink you hide behind gives you no courage. You are not worthy of the army of the One God. When we fight tomorrow, we do it without slackers and mockers. Go find your chieftain, and tell him that Deborah told you to stay out of the battle tomorrow." Rising to her feet, she turned back to the other two men. "I know you are afraid. There is no shame in fear, only in cowardice. May the God of Abraham, Isaac, and Jacob bless you. Now get some sleep."

Then she left them, walking between the rows of tents, no longer trying to stay hidden. Here and there she knelt on the ground beside the men, joining their conversations, asking what they felt, assuring them of God's presence. As though the words themselves had power, her own sense of certainty grew as she told them again and again that they would win this battle. But when she went back to her own tent, weariness dragged at her garments. By now it must surely be near the end of the second watch. Her tent was near the edge of the clearing, looking over the long slope down which the army would march tomorrow. In the darkness she could not see the Canaanite army camped below, but she could sense them. They were there with their iron swords and iron chariots and an iron general named Sisera who had held Israel's children in a grip of terror since Deborah had been a young girl. Could this ill-prepared and fearful army truly prevail?

Her servants were sleeping, having readied her bed and laid some food and drink out for her return. Instead of going inside and resting, though, she sat at the doorway of her tent, just as the men were doing all over the camp. She guessed, rightly, that she would not be alone long.

Barak appeared from the opposite direction. He had been doing the same thing she had, walking among the men at the other end of the camp. But he did not say anything until he sat heavily on the ground beside her and run his fingers through the thick, curling thatch of his graying hair. "I knew I would not find you asleep," he said then, looking up, his tired face creasing into a slight smile.

"No, I am awake. I visited with some of the men."

"How did you find them?"

"Frightened. Discouraged. They have little faith in our God, Barak."

"Some of them do not even worship our God, Deborah." He picked up a twig that lay on the ground and twirled it round and round in his fingers. "And even to those who pay Him tribute He is remote and mysterious. People like their gods with faces. A god they can set up on a table in a shrine and bring little offerings and bow before. Not a mighty stranger who will not show His face. I fight in His name, but I cannot know or love this God as you do. Few of us can. He speaks only to you."

Deborah gazed out at the black sky edged with silhouettes of blacker trees. Though the night was warm, the faraway stars seemed icy. "Even to me, He speaks but rarely, old friend. But having heard His voice, I hear more in His silences."

Barak shook his head. "As always, you speak like a prophetess. I can only talk, or think, like a soldier. We have occupied the high ground, so we have an advantage, it's true. But we are so few and our weapons so weak against theirs. It will need more than high ground to win tomorrow. The men need heart put into them."

"Only God can do that."

"But God does not speak to them, remember? They need you and me for that. And my own faith is not so strong. Sometimes I would rather have a God with a face, too."

"Don't speak or even think such words, Barak. You are Yahweh's chosen warrior, and you go into battle tomorrow for His people and His land. How can you fight with doubt in your heart?" Deborah felt the same anger rising in her that she had experienced with the cowardly drunkard—how could God's army defeat Sisera's when even their commander could not hold firmly to his faith?

Slowly Barak shook his head. "How else can I fight? I have the doubts—they are there. I fear dying on the morrow as much as my men do, but I will go down fighting. I wonder about this God who led our forefathers out of Egypt, but who now speaks to us so rarely. Yet I am here at His bidding, against my better judgment. Sometimes it's like shooting an arrow in the dark, but I make my best shot anyway. Doesn't your God honor that?"

She knew Barak's doubts, yet he rarely questioned God's ways to Deborah's face like that. Still she found her anger ebbing away. She had received no vision since leaving Shiloh two full moons ago. But she carried her memories of the words the Lord had once spoken and the tales of her ancestors, and these had to be enough to sustain not only her own faith but that of everyone who depended on her. Yes, she understood Barak's words about arrows in the dark.

"Be strong, Barak. The Lord does speak to us: He chose you and brought you to this mountain. Is it an accident that we hold the high ground? Tomorrow we will do His will and drive back our enemies. Be bold, and of good courage," she added in the words of Joshua who had brought them into the land at the time of their great-great-grandfathers.

With a smile he stood, strapping on the sword he had laid aside. "I will be bold, Deborah, never doubt that. Once a battle is in hand, I don't lack for courage. It's this cursed business of sitting around waiting that unmans me."

"Waiting is always the most difficult," she agreed. "Do you remember—" She broke off, not sure if this was the time for reviving old memories.

In the dark night, lit only by the stars and the flare of a torch, his dark eyes caught hers and held. "I remember everything, Deborah. Everything, from the first time we met."

His tone was so serious that she tried for a lighter note herself. "I was only thinking of the morning by the river, when we first heard the name of Jabin of Hazor. Twenty years ago. Could you ever have imagined you'd be fighting him and his general for so long?"

"I have spent my whole life fighting those two men: Jabin and Sisera," Barak said, in a voice very different from the tender one he had used a moment before. He sounded grim, and weary, and no longer young.

Deborah laid a hand on his arm: a bold gesture, for she rarely touched a man now that her husband was gone. "You are an arrow on the bow of the one God, whether shot in the dark or the light," she said. "He will see that you fly straight to the target."

"Thank you," said Barak. "Let's trust His aim is true."

He was gone, invisible in the darkness after only a few moments. Sitting down again on the hard ground in front of the tent, she wondered if she could sleep at all or if she would sit there till dawn. The mind of every man in the encampment was on the next morning, no doubt, but her mind was ranging far back over the years . . . through the time of her people's bondage under Sisera and Jabin, and through the years of her own life and the strange journey that had led her to an army camp on the eve of battle. Her thoughts returned to the first journey of her life, and to her first meeting with the man who tomorrow would be loosed on the enemies of God like an arrow from the bow.

CHAPTER 1

"Hurry now, girl, or the morning will slip past us!" Deborah's father called as she raced from the house with another bundle to tie to the donkey's back. She was going as fast as she could, but she would not say so to her father. Instead, she only made an effort to run a little faster.

Mother was handing little Isa, just weaned a few months ago, over to Aunt Tamar, brushing away a few tears as she did so. Isa and Dina, at 4 and 7 years of age, were too young to make the long journey north and would remain in the care of Deborah's aunt and uncle, with whom they shared the house. Her younger cousin, Ziri, emerged from the courtyard leading their goats out for a day of pasturing on the hill slopes below the village. He was Deborah's closest cousin, just two years younger, and now he looked at her with wide and longing eyes. "I wish I were going with you!" he whispered.

"So do I. Don't worry, I'll tell you everything when I return." She squeezed his shoulder in farewell, and he departed, walking ahead of them down the rutted narrow path through the village, the shaggy goats bumping and butting at his legs as he went. Other young boys from the surrounding houses joined him until the path was a furry, bleating mass.

Mother said her last goodbye to the little ones and, amid farewells from the rest of the family, Deborah, her parents, and their heavily laden donkey began the journey out of their village. The girl couldn't suppress a flutter of excitement. She had never been far from home before.

Her friends, Miriam and Rahel, stood waiting in front of Miriam's house to say goodbye. Both girls carried heavy water jars, having just returned from their morning trip to the village well. "Goodbye, Deborah! Tell us all about the north when you return. May the gods bless you!" Miriam called. Rahel caught Deborah by the arm and whispered in her ear, "Tell us about the handsome young men you see in the north!"

"Shh—goodbye!" Deborah whispered hastily, hurrying down the path behind her mother and father. Neighbors and friends all around called their farewells. It was rare for anyone from the little village of Ramah to go on such a long journey, and Deborah knew many villagers wondered if the family of Ruel would ever return.

Her father was one of the chief elders of the town, thus one of the few able to afford such a journey, but even so most considered it risky to travel so far.

Looking at the stern set of her father's jaw now, Deborah feared he might have heard Rahel's last, careless words. Perhaps not. More likely it was Miriam's thoughtless comment about the gods that had angered him. Though the villagers they lived among worshipped Baal and Astarte and the other gods of Canaan alongside the One God of Israel, Father was old-fashioned in his ways, strict and unbending in his insistence that his family worship Yahweh alone. "You shall have no other gods before Me," he would rumble in his deep voice when he heard the women talking about sacrificing to Asherah to ensure an easy childbirth.

By midmorning, the sun was high and Deborah was tired of walking. They had worked their way down the slopes of the hilltop on which the village perched, passing on the way the agricultural terraces where their relatives and neighbors were hard at work. The wheat harvest had nearly ended, and many farmers now tended their grapevines and olives. Deborah waved a greeting as she passed Ziri and the other boys with their goats and a few sheep. Sheep were something Deborah's father intended to bring back from his journey to the north, for Mother's family in the tribe of Naphtali, were herders with large flocks.

Down in the valley, where the trees and bushes were even shorter and more sparse, the sun beat down without mercy, and even Deborah's head covering could not shelter her face from its rays. She was glad when her parents stopped in a large clearing where a still-flowing stream enticed many travelers to break their journey. A tall, broad palm tree spread its shade over a good portion of the clearing.

"The Palm of Deborah," her mother said as they laid down their packs and tethered the donkey.

"A fitting place to take the noon meal on our Deborah's first journey away from home," her father said, giving his eldest daughter one of his rare smiles. The girl took the donkey's lead, bringing him to the spring for water.

"Our Deborah will be as good a woman as she for whom this tree was planted," the girl's mother said as her daughter returned. Unpacking their food from a small bag, Father said, "What do you know of the Palm of Deborah, daughter?"

The girl drew a breath of the hot air and searched her memory. The words were not hard to find, for she had been told many times of the woman for whom she was named. "'Now Deborah, Rebekah's nurse, died, and she was buried below Bethel under the oak. It was named Allon-bacuth, the oak of weeping,'" she quoted. Her father had repeatedly told the old stories of their people, and had encouraged the girl to memorize long passages from them. Now he was teaching them to her younger brother and sister, but the task did not come as easily. Deborah genuinely loved learning and remembering the ancient tales. But her younger siblings would rather play in the courtyard, though her little brother was already interested in learning to make clay pots, and her sister was begining to spin wool.

"Very good," Father said. "A woman remembered for her kindness and love to Rebekah, wife of our ancestor Isaac. May you be so remembered, my daughter." He sat on the ground and took a piece of the bread his wife was tearing into pieces. A hunk of goat's-milk cheese went with it.

Other families were also eating their noon meal nearby, and Deborah's mother spoke to several of the other women. The couple nearest them were a little younger than Mother and Father, and from their clothing and the bags they carried Deborah could see they were poor. She wasn't surprised when her mother invited them to share some of the family's food.

"My husband is Ruel, from the village of Ramah," Deborah's mother introduced herself. "This is our eldest child, Deborah. We are traveling back to the tents of my family, in the land of Naphtali."

"A long journey," the other woman, who had already introduced herself and her husband as Judahites from the village of Hebron, replied. "We are honored to break bread with you. Will you stop at Bethel tonight?"

"No," Deborah's father replied. "We will go to Shiloh, in hopes that we can be there in time for the evening sacrifice."

"Then we have the same goal in mind," the man from Judah said. He looked sad and tired, but he brightened a little at the mention of Shiloh. Deborah saw her father's approving nod: now he knew he was breaking bread with true Israelites, faithful to the One God.

As Mother, reminded of the need for haste, began gathering up their food and bowls, Father cast an eye at the tethered goat nearby. "You go to sacrifice?"

The man bowed his head. "Yes." But then he raised his chin as though he needed to look people in the eye when he told this story. "Some weeks ago I was out in the wilderness trying to bring down birds with my sling—a little meat for the family for the feast." He did not need to explain that his family was too poor to slaughter an animal: most people ate meat only on feast days, but the poor could not afford it even then, and often tried to catch wild game to supplement their diets. "I did not know that my neighbor, a kinsman of my wife's, was not far away gathering berries. One of my sling stones struck him on the head—and he was killed."

"Oh, how terrible," Mother said, casting a sympathetic glance at the other woman.

"So we go to Shiloh to sacrifice," the man said simply, saying nothing about what it must have cost him to slaughter the kid-goat, the sacrifice for an unintentional sin. The sad little story explained the weary, burdened look in his eyes, the sagging way he carried his body. Would he, Deborah wondered, look lighter, happier, after he had made his sacrifice?

"Come, brother," Deborah's father said, offering a hand. Although a reserved and solemn man, he still treated any fellow-worshipper of the One God as if he were kin. "Journey along with us, and we will all be at Shiloh for the time of sacrifice."

It was a long afternoon of walking, but well before they would have stopped for an evening meal they saw the cluster of houses and the sprawl of tents that huddled around the tabernacle of the One God at Shiloh. Seeing the long curtained wall of the tabernacle, Deborah felt as if a cool finger had touched her spine. She had never been here before, though her father, and sometimes her mother, made the journey on holy days. Here was the place where the One God Himself was said to dwell, though it had no image of Him before which worshippers might bow down. Instead, she saw the great altar, heard the chanting and singing of the priests in their brilliant robes, and smelled the stench of burning animal flesh that pervaded everything. Deborah, her mother, and the woman from Judah remained on the outer edges of the crowd while the men went forward to perform the sacrifices and join in the worship. Even from the periphery, she could sense the wonder, the holiness of this strange place.

As he led the man from Hebron through the crowd, the tied

goat trailing behind them, Deborah's father looked different. His face had lit up as if a lamp burned within. The priest's ancient, familiar words washed over the crowd, words Deborah had learned so long ago:

"Hear, O Israel:
The Lord our God, the Lord is one.
Love the Lord your God
with all your heart and with all your soul and with all
your strength."

Deborah saw her mother stand straighter, taller. Though they still had many miles to go before they reached the tents of her mother's family in the north, the girl thought both her parents looked as if they had come home.

The next morning they continued their journey along on a narrow winding road—more of a track in places—that snaked upward into the hills. Deborah's mind was still full of all that she had seen at Shiloh—the faces of the worshippers, the robes of the priests, the sound of the singing, the smell of the burning animals. As Father and the donkey took the lead, she fell into step beside her mother. "It means a great deal to you, doesn't it, to see the tabernacle of our God?" she began.

"It does, my daughter. I am glad you have seen it too. It is what every faithful child of Israel dreams of—being in the presence of Yahweh at His tabernacle."

"Is the One God really there? There were so many things to see, but no image of a god anywhere."

"Of course not. You know why."

Looking away, down the green valley, she recited, "I am the Lord your God, who brought you out of Egypt, out of the land of slavery. You shall have no other gods before me. You shall not make for yourself an idol in the form of anything in heaven above or on the earth beneath or in the waters below. You shall not bow down to them or worship them; for I, the Lord your God, am a jealous God, punishing the children for the sin of the fathers to the third and fourth generation of those who hate me, but showing love to a thousand generations of those who love me and keep my commandments."

"What a memory!" Deborah's mother said proudly under her breath. More loudly she added, "So you see we have no images, no idols of our God. But He is there. In His tabernacle, where He promised to dwell among His people. We cannot see His presence, but we can feel it when we are there."

"Rahel's mother says it's better to have gods you can see. She says our God is the same as El, the God of the Canaanites—He is the father of the gods, great above all the rest. But the others, she says, are like the younger gods, closer to us, and we can see their faces and ask them for favors. And she says it's easier for a woman to talk to Asherah, perhaps, about childbirth or marrying, because a goddess can understand a woman better than some great God high up in the sky." Deborah's heart raced a little as she thought about how she and her friend Rahel had often talked about such things. Although Rahel's mother was always ready to give an opinion as she sat weaving at her loom, in Deborah's home such talk was unwelcome. The girl would never have brought such questions to her father, but they burned inside, demanding answers.

Mother glanced up ahead at Father, then back at the girl. As always, she seemed to read her daughter's thoughts too well. "You fear to ask your father about these matters, Deborah, but he is the one who can answer you. I know only that the Lord our God is One God, that He brought us out of Egypt into this land, and that we are His chosen people. To talk about why he is better or greater than the gods of the Canaanites—I cannot do that. Your father can. If you wish to know these things, you must speak to him."

It was Father himself who broached the subject for Deborah while they sat around their campfire many hours later. "Did you learn much from seeing the sacrifices at Shiloh, my daughter?" he asked as he finished his meal.

"Oh, yes! It was wonderful to see it all at last. Though it is hard to watch, all the blood and the smell—"

"But it serves a purpose," her father reminded her.

"Yes. Sin is death, and in blood and death we see the price of our sins. But, Father—" she began, then broke off, glancing at her mother.

"Deborah had many questions after we left Shiloh," her mother said gently. "She is an intelligent girl."

"We have always known that," her father said with a smile. "What are your questions, Deborah?"

His daughter picked her words with greater care now. "Our way of worship is so different from the Canaanites, and even from our own people who worship their gods. I have heard some say that our

God is like El of the Canaanites, a great god above all others, but that people need smaller gods, deities whose images we can pray to for certain things, as— well, as a woman might pray to Asherah for a child, or some such thing. Why do we not believe the same?"

Father's brows drew together and for a moment she feared his anger, but then she saw that he was calming himself, focusing on her question rather than his own contempt for those who abandoned the One God.

"We are a special people, Deborah, and we have a covenant with our God. You know this, of course. When our God gave His name to Moses, His name was I Am, for He is all. Not just above all, like El—He *is* all, Deborah. Do you see?" His voice quickened now, and his eyes brightened, for this was what he loved—talking about the One God. "The Canaanites—they cut God up into small pieces, a god for this, a god for that. A goddess for fertility, a god for war. A god for crops and a god for rain. But this is not how it is with us, Deborah. Our God is one God. One—and all. It was He, not some pagan goddess in a grove, who gave our ancestor Sarah a son of promise in her old age. But not because Sarah came pleading to Him with a sacrifice in hand. No, why did He give the barren woman a son?"

Deborah thought a moment, scratching in the dust with her fingertip. "Because of His promise to Abraham?" she suggested.

"Exactly. Because of His own great plan. You see, these people" —he waved a hand at the silent evening hills to indicate the Canaanite tribes around, and his own wayward people—"they choose a god for this and a god for that. A woman prays to Asherah for help in childbirth, a man worships Baal when he wants his crops to grow. But our God chose us, Deborah. Not because we wanted children, or crops, or even a way out of Egypt. He selected us because of His own plan, my daughter! Do you see the greatness of our God? We do not crawl to Him, begging Him to do our will like these little gods the people of this land have. He comes to us and fits us to His will, for He is greater than we are—far greater than any little rain god or crop god. Do you see? His name, Deborah. His name is I Am."

Everything was silent except for the crackling of the fire and faint chirr of insects somewhere in the grass. Deborah saw her father, his eyes shining with excitement and joy and devotion to his God. For a moment she shivered, though she was not cold. She could almost feel the presence of the One God, though Shiloh was miles behind.

They journeyed many more miles in the days ahead, pressing always north through the hills and valleys, joining paths with other travelers for safety wherever they could. Passing other villages of the Israelites, such as Shechem and Jezreel, they climbed through the foothills of Mount Ebal, Mount Gilboa, and Mount Tabor. Far beyond the paths they had chosen, her father told her, lay the great walled cities of the Canaanites, still strong in the land despite the many generations that had passed since Joshua had led God's people into the territory they were supposed to have conquered. Although things had been relatively peaceful since the great deliverer Ehud had freed them from the Moabites before Deborah's birth, the Chosen People still lived in fear much of the time, never truly possessing the land that God had promised them.

After Mount Tabor, they entered the lands of the tribe of Naphtali, Mother's people, and when they passed the north shore of the Sea of Chinnereth they turned west, toward the place she had been born, the village called Ramah, just like their own.

Deborah had grown up hearing the story of how her father had gone north on a journey, dwelled among the tents of Benar the herdsman, and then chose to marry Benar's youngest daughter. Young Ruel of the tribe of Benjamin had no money for a bride price, but he worked for a year, married his bride, and brought her on the long trip south to his own Ramah. In all the long years since, Mother had not seen her own family. Indeed, their settlement had moved, and Father had to ask the local people to show him the way to his father-in-law's camp.

When at last they were in sight of the tents of Benar's family, they encountered young boys on their way home from a day with the flocks. One of the boys ran ahead with word of the travelers. Women emerged from the tents, their arms outstretched, embracing Mother and crying over her.

Soon they found themselves swept in among the tents, into the heart of the clan. The women exclaimed over Deborah and quizzed Mother about the two younger children, while Father and the donkey disappeared among the men. Deborah and her mother did not see Father again till the evening meal, when everyone gathered around a great fire. They had slaughtered some sheep for the feast, which Deborah knew was a tremendous sacrifice for her mother's family at shearing time. Yet the arrival of their daughter and her family after so many years away seemed to be such a great event that no one could possibly begrudge the loss of a few animals.

Deborah was hungry, and the tempting aroma of the roasting meat made her mouth water, even as it reminded her of the sacrifices at Shiloh. She wondered about her mother's people—did they worship the One God, the Canaanite gods, or both? Plenty of time later to find that out. Her head spun from introductions as someone presented her to this or that aunt, uncle, or cousin. "She has such a memory. You should hear this girl repeat the laws and the tales of the fathers," Ruel said proudly. "But who knows if she will be able to recall all these new names?" Her father was relaxed, almost laughing, glad no doubt that the long journey was over.

"Well, Deborah," someone said, "will you remember our names tomorrow?"

The girl turned to face the woman—her mother's cousin, she knew—but she had no idea what her name was. Shira? Miriam? "I will remember the names," she confessed honestly, "but I will have no idea which faces they belong to!"

"Never mind, here's another," the woman said, reaching into the crowd to draw a boy to her side. "My son, Barak," she announced.

Looking up, Deborah knew at once that she would not forget either the name Barak or the face of the boy who bore it. He was, indeed, more man than boy, though he was probably no more than two years older than she. It was impossible not to be reminded of Rahel's idle words about handsome young men, when she looked at this tall, bronzed youth—his muscular chest bare above his kilt, his tangled fall of hair a deep brown tinged with golden lights. His brown eyes were warm, and his strong chin was yet beardless, which was why she guessed he was not much older than she was. When he smiled at her, she wondered if it was just hunger and weariness that made the world seem to spin.

"Welcome, Deborah," Barak said.

CHAPTER 2

The bank of the stream rang with the shouts and cries of the young people and the children. Barak stood throwing stones into the ripples of the stream, challenging the others to throw farther or hit a target more accurately. He always won and was used to being the best at any feat of skill, though he praised the others when they did well.

His cousin Deborah let fly a pebble that splashed and then skipped lightly over the top of the water. "Well done, Deborah! A good shot—for a girl."

"A good shot for anyone!" she retorted. The stone flung from her sling had hit the dead center of the target. None of the others, including Barak himself, had done as well.

"Very well then, a good shot—leave it at that," he conceded, picking up a long, sharpened stick. "But you couldn't do as well with the spear. You lack the strength in your arms."

Another of the boys picked up a stick too and threw it toward the target. It went sailing past it into the brush. Barak's stick hit the target with a solid thud near the center. Deborah didn't even bother picking up one of the makeshift spears, nor did any of the other girls or younger boys, except for Jael, a wiry little child who hated to be told she couldn't do something. She was much smaller than Deborah and staggered under the weight of the spear.

"Come now, that's almost as long as you are tall, Jael. A good warrior knows when he's beaten!" Barak admonished her. But ignoring him, she launched the spear anyway with such force that she toppled over and landed in the grass.

A cry and a splash drifted up to them from the stream bank, where the smaller boys were splashing through the cool water. It was a rare hour snatched at the end of the day, when boys and girls who could spare a little time from their work with the herds or around the farmsteads gathered by the stream to bathe and play. Barak and two of his friends were the oldest here, with Barak the acknowledged leader, while many of the girls of the same age—14—were already married and barred from such childish pleasures. Deborah, who was 12, felt a moment's panic as she thought of how quickly womanhood would be upon her. Even now, in her busy days, an hour of pleasure and play felt like something precious, almost stolen.

Deborah was trying to separate two of the little boys whose wrestling match had turned into a fight. "Come, Barak," she laughed, "help me part these two!"

When Deborah and Barak finally held a scratching, scrabbling youngster, Barak wasn't really surprised to see that the one in Deborah's arms was no boy at all, but 8-year-old Jael, as ragged and muddy as any of the boys and just as fierce. "Come now, Jael," Deborah was saying, "that's no way to behave. Settle down, or I'll have Barak throw you in the water."

"Throw me in the water! Throw me in!" Jael insisted, and Barak rolled his eyes at Deborah. He took the feisty little 8-year-old in his strong arms and carried her to the shallow water, dumping her in with a splash.

"Come in, Deborah! It's nice and cool here!" Jael spluttered as she wiped her face.

"No, thank you!" Deborah replied. Like most of the older girls she would wade in just far enough to cool her dusty feet and ankles.

Barak caught himself watching Deborah as she stood ankle-deep in the water. He found himself watching her more and more these days. She and her parents had been here for some time now—since the beginning of sheep shearing, one full moon at least. The girl fit neatly into their lives, busily sharing the women's chores. Barak liked her—a lot. Deborah was clever and fun to talk to. Was she pretty? He stared full at her now while she wasn't looking. He and his cousins had begun noticing and talking about girls in the past year—how Rivkah's red hair, under her head covering, was the shade of the sky at sunset, how round and plump Abijah was and how that somehow made her look cozy and inviting. Deborah, he decided, was not one of the pretty girls in the camp. Too skinny, for one thing. But there was something about her—maybe it was her eyes. Barak couldn't put a name to it, but he knew that one night he had lain awake and heard his mother and father talking about Deborah's family.

"They may stay long enough to find a husband for the girl," his mother had said.

"Surely she's not old enough," his father had replied.

"No, but in a year or so she will be. I think her parents would rather she wed one of our own people than marry into the families around them in Benjamin, for many of them are not faithful to our God."

That new idea—that Deborah might stay, might be given as a bride to someone in their camp—had kept Barak awake longer than he liked to admit.

Now, though, she turned and caught him staring, and he looked away hastily, cursing the blood that rushed to his cheeks. "Let's gather up the little ones," she said. "It must be almost time for the evening meal." The older children pulled the smaller ones from the water. Clothes and hair dried in the warm air as they all ran back to the encampment.

Families gathered outside their tents. Around the fires, the women had pots of lentil stew slowly simmering and great flat rounds of bread ready to break and pass around. But tonight, something was different. Barak's family had hardly started their meal when they heard a shout: "A traveler! Welcome, stranger!"

The visitor—a ragged man of middle years—truly was a stranger, which was odd in this country where most of the families knew each other well. As he staggered wearily to Grandfather's fire in the center of the camp, all eyes followed him. Barak could see that the dark stains on his cloak looked like bloodstains.

"Hail," Grandfather said, rising from his place of honor by the fire. "Who are you, traveler, and what news do you bring?"

The man looked around, his eyes wild. "Hail, honored father," he said. "My name is Nathaniel, and I lived in Kedesh. But no longer. I come to tell you that Kedesh is no more. Jabin, king of Hazor, fell upon our city by night with horses and chariots, and put many of the men, women, and children to the sword. Then he burned everything left. I was one of the few who escaped."

Cries of alarm and ripples of shock ran around the camp as the news passed from one person to another. Barak had heard the name of King Jabin before. Rumor had it that the Canaanite king seemed determined to wipe out the Hebrew settlers, but this was the first real attack they had heard of.

"All? All slaughtered?" Voices around the fire echoed Nathaniel's words even as hands reached out to offer him a cloak, a bowl of stew, and a piece of bread. Barak heard the women's words rising out of the babble of sound: "My brother—my brother and his children were in Kedesh." "My mother and father." "I had two sisters in Kedesh." The tally of loss continued, the women's voices rising to a mourning cry, while the men asked hard, sharp-edged questions: "They attacked under cover of darkness, you say? What were their weapons?"

Now Grandfather spoke. "There is no time to discuss, or to debate," he said. "This news changes all. We must act quickly. Tonight we set a watch. At dawn we break our camp and travel toward Ramah. We must move into the town, help defend and fortify it. There we may have some chance—in a camp such as this, we have none. Who will keep watch over our tents tonight?"

Quickly, Barak stood. "I'll stand watch." He caught his father's look of pride.

Hours later, a hand on his shoulder awakened him. "Time for your watch," his father said.

The night was cold and clear, with stars sprinkling the sky as Barak and one of the older men slowly patrolled the perimeter of the camp. Barak kept his eyes on the east, where Kedesh had been, where Hazor was, and where Jabin's soldiers were on the march.

At dawn, another pair of sentries relieved them, and the camp began coming to life around them. Just as Barak was about to return to his tent, hoping to catch a few moments' sleep, he saw his cousin Deborah slip away from the women around the fire and head toward the river. Hesitating only a moment, he followed her.

She sat on a rock by the riverbank. Picking up a small stone, he curved it high in the air so that it fell with a splash in the water a few feet from her. She turned to look.

"Good morning, cousin," he greeted her.

"Good morning—if it can be called good. Everyone was so full of fear last night that I woke up afraid myself this morning." She looked away from him, to the horizon where the gray clouds blushed a soft pink.

"Every new day is good, Deborah," he said, smiling. Excitement rose inside him. "If our enemies are coming to fight us, that is good, for I can meet them with my spear, and fight like a man at last!"

"You are eager for a fight," she said. He could hear disbelief in her voice and read it in her eyes.

"I can't wait for the chance to try my skills. Shooting at targets or hunting birds is good training, but I'm ready to kill some Canaanites."

"Even if they come in iron chariots, brandishing weapons of iron?"

He sobered for a moment. "It will be hard, but our God will give us victory."

The sentiment was a familiar one—he had heard it on the lips of the men around the fire last night. But as he spoke it, Barak felt unsure. He could see that Deborah mirrored his doubts. "Will He really, Barak? Do you believe it? We are supposed to be God's Chosen People, and this our land of promise, but what are we chosen for? We live like sheep harried by wolves, always running away from this king or that tribal chieftain, always frightened. It's as if—" she hesitated, unsure how to put into words what she meant. "As if we made a mistake," she concluded. "Came to the wrong land. The tales of old say we were supposed to drive out the people of the land. Instead, they're always driving us out." The clouds had reddened to a deep crimson, almost the color of blood. She turned back to him "I'm so scared, Barak."

He put a hand on her arm. "Of course women and children are afraid when an enemy threatens. But men are made to fight, Deborah, and to protect you. That's what I want to do." His words lingered in the morning air. He wanted to protect her, in particular, but how could he say that? Their fathers had never discussed the possibility of marriage between him and her, and they were too young even to consider it. As they looked at each other, wordless, a sudden shaft of gold lit her features. Turning, they saw that the sun had slipped above the rim of the hills and was flooding the stream bank with its brilliance.

"Come, we must go back," she said quickly, standing and gathering her robe about her.

Together they walked back to the camp in the rosy light of dawn.

It was their last chance to talk together. By midmorning, as the families packed up their belongings and Barak and the other boys prepared to herd the sheep west, Deborah's father Ruel spoke to Grandfather. Barak overheard him. "While you go west to your village of Ramah, we will head south to our own Ramah."

The boy's heart skipped a beat. He had not imagined Deborah would leave.

"It will be dangerous—three travelers alone on the road in such times."

"I think we will not be alone—we will meet others fleeing south," Ruel said. "I would stay with you, but our other children are at home in Benjamin. If Jabin attacks, God alone knows how long it will be before anyone can travel south."

"Of course. God speed you on your journey."

Barak was busy loading packs onto a donkey when he saw the tiny procession say their farewells and take the long road south. He broke into a run, covering the rough and rocky ground quickly, and stopped awkwardly on the path just ahead of his uncle, aunt, and cousin. Uncle Ruel looked at him, a careful measuring glance.

"So, Barak, son of Abinoam, you have come to bid us goodbye?"

"Yes, I—that is, I wanted to wish you well." He looked at Deborah. She gave him a smile, then turned her eyes modestly to the ground.

"I hope you travel safely," he added.

"I pray we will," Ruel said.

"You are in my prayers. Perhaps—perhaps we will meet again," he finished lamely.

Deborah's mother raised her eyes to meet his. "Go with God, son of my brother. You and your family are in my prayers too."

And they left. Barak watched a moment, waiting for Deborah to look back. When at last she did, it was the tiniest of glances, but their eyes met. He ran back to his task, reminding himself that there was time—years and years ahead—to think of girls and marriage and such dreams. In the meantime, he had work to do. And the Canaanites were coming.

CHAPTER 3

As Deborah's father had predicted, the roads through the hills to the south were full of people hoping to escape the north before Jabin unleashed his full fury. The Israelite families banded together, keeping to the high roads as much as possible and avoiding the valleys, sleeping together in small encampments at night. Deborah was glad when they passed the heights of Mount Gerezim and Mount Ebal and the town of Shechem. After that, they were once again in the territory of Ephraim, where she felt safer.

And then they were almost home, passing again by the Palm of Deborah that marked the halfway point between Bethel and Ramah. This time they did not stop at the Palm but pressed homeward in the vanishing daylight, eager to reach their own house, to see the children, the aunts and uncles, and the neighbors again. Deborah looked back at the palm, though, as they passed it, and thought of her namesake Deborah. Only the woman's name had survived into history—that and her burial place, and the fact that she must have been greatly loved.

Will I be greatly loved in my life? Deborah wondered. *Will I marry, and raise children, and will people someday know the place where I am buried?* She thought of her friends at home, how eagerly they would listen to her tales of the cousins in the north—and especially of handsome Barak. Rahel would no doubt suggest they pray to Asherah or some other goddess, maybe make a small sacrifice in hopes the goddess would motivate Barak to travel south and offer a bride-price for her.

For a moment, the idea was tempting. In the privacy of her own heart Deborah had to admit how very much she would someday like to be Barak's wife—when the time was right. Could prayers to a goddess help make that dream come true? She remembered her father's words: *We do not come to Him begging Him to do our will. He comes to us and fits us to His will.*

The God of her fathers seemed so big, so mighty, and, in some ways, so distant. It was easy to petition Him for victory in war, to preserve His Chosen People against a foreign invader. But to ask Him for a particular marriage partner for one young girl in a tiny village in the tribe of Benjamin? Could a God so great even notice, let alone care?

I wish to do Your will, O God of my fathers, Deborah prayed silently, tentatively, as she came in sight of the little cluster of houses that made up the town of Ramah.

As they had expected, everyone in the village was surprised to see them back so soon, and shocked by the news of Jabin's raid on Kedesh. Here in the south, the tribes had enjoyed peace for so many years that the wars of past generations had become like legend to them. "Surely he will not come this far south," her uncles said as the family sat in their courtyard that night, enjoying the evening meal.

"His eye is on the north—on the tribesmen of Naphtali whom he sees encamped on his doorstep, building towns and cities that threaten his own and blocking the trade routes between north and south," Father said. "But I have heard that this Jabin is more than just the king of Hazor. The kings of Hazor see themselves as ruler of all the Canaanite cities, the ones to whom all must bow. If Jabin can wipe out the Hebrew invaders in the land, no doubt the other Canaanite kings will be more likely to pay him tribute and follow his lead. So if the northern tribes fall, we will not be left in peace for long."

"When are we ever left in peace?" another of the uncles demanded.

"We would know more peace," Father said sharply, "if we were faithful to our God. And to one another. If we banded together to resist the enemy, rather than every tribe, every village, caring only for its own needs. Our God brought us into this land as one people, faithful to Him, and that is how we will conquer."

As the uncles murmured, the aunts gossiped among themselves, eagerly pulling every scrap of northern news from Mother. In exchange, they told her everything that had happened in Ramah during the weeks the family had been gone. A fever had spread through town and two small children were dead: "One is the infant son of Lappidoth. His wife had it too, and is still sick. She pines with grief for her youngest child and continues to lose strength." The youngest of Shimei's sons had made an offer of marriage for Shirah, the daughter of Ram, and the community would celebrate their wedding before the time of the winter rains.

Deborah listened with only half an ear to the adults. Sprawled across her lap, her little brother and sister had fallen asleep. Her cousin Ziri was sitting in the shelter of her arm too, but he was beginning to doze off. Already she was glad she had come home. The encampment of her mother's family in the north had begun to seem like a distant, barely remembered dream that slips away as the day's duties begin.

And indeed, Deborah's duties kept her busy in the months ahead. Along with the everyday tasks of taking care of the house, she worked at the loom with her mother, weaving the wool they had brought from the north into cloth. She helped both parents make pots and jars from clay and taught her little brother Isa how to shape a simple pot, for Ruel's family took great pride in their skill at pottery and made extra vessels to trade with others in the village.

Village life went on too. The rains came, the crops on the hillsides ripened. Shifah and her husband celebrated their marriage and soon announced they were having a baby. It set the girls Deborah's age speculating about which of them would be first to receive an offer of marriage. The wife of Lappidoth grew sicker and then died, as did two old men who had lived so long that no one ever expected them to die. Then it was spring, the barley ripened, and Deborah's father went to Shiloh for the Passover.

He returned with guests: Adiel and Eber, two of the cousins from the north, had made the long journey south for the Passover too, and were coming now to stay a while with Ruel's family at Ramah. Deborah hurried about with her mother, making up extra beds on the upper floor of the house for the guests, collecting extra food from storage to feed them, and listening eagerly to their news.

"A good thing it was that we retreated to Ramah—our Ramah, in the north—when we did," Eber said over a meal of barley bread, figs, and dates that first night. "Jabin continued raiding the Israelite settlements all around Naphtali throughout the winter, and when he fell upon Ramah, we were able to resist him and drive him back, though we lost many men in the battle. But he holds Kedesh now, and many other villages too, while containing our people west of the waters of Meram. Since things have been peaceful for some time now, we decided to make the journey to Shiloh for the feast. But we never know when he will strike again."

"You live under a terrible shadow," Deborah's father said. "As do we all, if we but realized it. Our peace is fragile, and we do not yet possess the land. Many perished in the battles with Jabin, you say?"

Adiel began reciting names: he had a poet's memory, as Deborah herself did, and a poet's way with words too, for he wove the names into a lament. She heard the names of several of the men she had met during her visit, but the one name she listened for was absent, though she dared not ask about him outright.

Her mother did, though. "What of Barak, the son of my kinsman Abinoam?" she asked lightly, without a glance at Deborah, reaching forward to dip a piece of bread in olive oil.

Adiel, though, knew no such tact. He looked across the fire directly at Deborah as he said, "The son of Abinoam fought well indeed in those battles. Not only did he escape injury, but all men say he will be a bold warrior, though he is barely bearded yet. He spoke to me of making a journey south himself sometime. He said that perhaps next year at Passover he will come to Shiloh, and then travel on to visit his kinsman by marriage, Ruel of Ramah."

No one could mistake the import of this piece of news, not with Adiel's eyes so firmly fixed on Deborah and a teasing grin plucking at the corners of his mouth. Feeling her face flush, she pulled her

DEBORAH AND BARAK | 31

headdress over her mouth, hiding her flaming cheeks. She glanced at her mother, who smiled too, and at her father, who looked grave.

Adiel and Eber stayed with them a few weeks, leaving to travel north again as the wheat crop ripened. Deborah had passed her thirteenth birthday and was busy about the house and the workroom. Her father went to Shiloh again at the New Year, staying until the Day of Atonement. Although she asked permission to go with him, her parents could not spare her at such a busy time of year. "But I am glad that you wish to go, my daughter," he said. She could hear in his voice his pleasure, his pride, that she was choosing to worship the God of her ancestors rather than following Canaanite ways as many of her friends did.

She could not have explained herself why she longed to go back to the tabernacle. No, she did not expect to see Barak there until Passover in the springtime, if he came even then. Rather, it was something about the tabernacle itself—the sense of holiness, an awareness of the presence of the One God, that she had felt when she had been there before. It had left a strong impression, and its memory had only deepened with time. Sometimes, when her family gathered with others to pray on the Sabbath day, she remembered those hours at Shiloh and wished that she could feel as near to her God as she had felt then.

Father and the small group of faithful men who went with him to the Tabernacle returned after the Day of Atonement and settled back into their working lives. Deborah knew that the group included her father's friend Lappidoth, but she was unprepared when her father raised the man's name one day as she sat beside him in the workshop, carefully smoothing the sides of a newly shaped clay jar.

"You know it will soon be a year since the wife of Lappidoth died," her father said abruptly. "His mourning has almost ended."

"Yes," Deborah said, dipping her hands in water and spreading the water over the surface of the jar, feeling with her fingers for tiny imperfections and rubbing them smooth. She enjoyed the sensation of the clay beneath her hands, loved to see a piece of work taking shape. "His children are so sad, without their mother. I hope Lappidoth soon takes another wife."

"He will," her father said. An odd note in his voice made her look up, and she saw he was watching her carefully, but she did not guess what he was going to say. "Lappidoth has already spoken to me, Deborah. When his days of mourning are ended, he will come to our house to offer his bride price and ask for your hand in marriage. He would like to celebrate the betrothal after the winter rains, and the marriage at the time of Passover, when you have passed your fourteenth birthday."

That was all. He did not ask how she felt, but simply announced the arrangement he and his friend had come to, as was a father's right. Deborah felt the pit of her stomach sink. She had been such a fool to let her mind fill with dreams of a handsome young warrior. If Barak came south at Passover, she would be a married woman by then, the wife of a widower her father's age. Stepmother to his two children, both not much younger than she was.

"It is a good match," her father said. "You are a good housekeeper already, and your talent with pottery will be useful to him, for Lappidoth is skilled at the craft of making lamps. And he is faithful, Deborah. He worships the One God. You know I could not let you go to one who did not worship as we do."

Barak worships the One God! she thought rebelliously, though she bowed her head so he would not read anger in her eyes. Of course he would choose a neighbor, someone he knew and trusted, rather than a young man from the north who would take her far away into an uncertain land torn by war. It was a sensible and wise choice. After several minutes Deborah lifted her gaze.

"I thank you, my father. I am honored to be chosen by Lappidoth," she said, continuing to smooth the bumps and wrinkles from her clay jar, making it neat and perfect.

CHAPTER 4

Barak and Samuel crawled through the low-lying brush. Their bellies scraped the stones. Rough grass and branches scratched their faces and arms. The night around them was so still the insect noises rang harshly in their ears. With a grunt Barak pulled himself forward on his elbows, then bit his lip as Samuel shot him a warning look.

They were close now. Barak could smell smoke from campfires and the dampness of the nearby stream. But he could not yet hear the noises of the enemy camp. When he glanced at Samuel, the other boy shook his head. He could hear nothing either.

Then the wind caught a shout from well to the north of their hiding place. Without exchanging a word, Barak and Samuel again began wriggling over the wet ground, this time hugging the stream bank. Above their heads, the moonlight outlined the reeds with silver. *Curse the full moon,* Barak thought. On a cloudy night, spying was much easier.

At last they had slipped close enough to hear sounds on the other shore. Horses whinnied. Armor clattered. Most importantly, men talked. Some voices were too low to hear. But these were no doubt private conversations, not what Barak and Samuel had crawled all this way to eavesdrop on.

Finally their long wait was rewarded. A man's voice, one with an officer's authority, rang out above a babble of others. "Pay attention now, you worthless louts!" No chorus of protest greeted the harsh words. Yes, he had to be a high-ranking officer. "Tomorrow at dawn we strike at their north wall. Our archers will—" The wind carried his words away, but Barak didn't need the rest of the sentence. The next words he heard told him what the archers would do. "—the fire. Then our other wing will come from the south—"

They lay there a long time but heard little more. Finally the two boys exchanged glances and nods. The officer had finished with his orders and had moved on. The men's voices were a dull murmur. Now, before the Canaanites bedded down and their sentries grew more cautious, it was time for Barak and Samuel to go. Not daring to turn around, Barak instead began to crawl backward. Samuel followed his lead.

It was a long and uncomfortable journey back to the cover of trees below the town. Here the boys could walk upright, but still they moved silently and with stealth. Barak wasn't foolish enough to think that only their side could send out spies. Still, the makeshift wooden wall ringing the town was in sight now. They were almost . . .

Samuel, in the lead, jerked back suddenly. He looked as if he had tripped, but if he had, he would have fallen forward. Almost too late, Barak saw the bare arm of the silent man who had reached from behind the trees to grab his friend around the neck. In a splash of moonlight filtered through trees, Barak saw a glint of metal in the man's hand.

Like a cat leaping on its prey, Barak crouched and sprang in a single movement. He tackled the man from behind, pulling his knife-arm up and off course. When the Canaanite's hold on Samuel faltered, the boy turned to grab the knife from his assailant's hand.

It was over in a moment. Both boys crouched over the enemy, pinning him to the ground. Samuel handed the knife to Barak who pressed it against the man's throat. He hoped not to have to use it. A captured enemy was more useful than a dead one. Besides, he'd never yet killed anyone.

Then, lightning-swift, the man jerked his hand free and thrust it toward his own leg. He was very strong. Thrown off balance, Barak realized he must have a knife strapped to his thigh. His right arm moved of its own will, driving the enemy's own blade into his throat.

Blood spurted out, hot and sticky. Dropping the knife in shock, Barak sprang back. Hearing Samuel's cry, he motioned quickly to silence him. The man jerked, his mouth moving as if to speak. Samuel grabbed the bloody knife from the ground and killed him with a second swift blow.

The boys arrived back in the village a quarter of an hour later, shaken and quiet. They went at once to the village elders. Barak's father and grandfather sat in the circle of elders, waiting for the report.

"We spied on their camp and heard the enemy's counsel," Barak reported. "They will attack tomorrow at dawn, striking at the north wall with flaming arrows. They plan to use the confusion of the fire to launch another attack on the south end of the town while we defend the north and put out the fire."

Abinoam, Barak's father, nodded. "It sounds like the plan they have used in other places. We will be prepared."

"Was it Sisera himself you heard?" another of the men asked.

"I think so," Samuel said. The boys had never seen or heard the fearsome Canaanite commander, but who else could have spoken to his men with such authority?

"Good work," another man said shortly with a nod of dismissal. "You will sleep tonight and join the archers on the south wall at dawn. The boys hesitated before turning to go.

"You have more to tell," Barak's father said. "Your clothes are bloodstained."

Barak turned to him. "Sir. We surprised a Canaanite spy in the woods below the village on our return."

"You should not have killed him," Grandfather said. "A captive could be useful."

"So I thought, sir," Barak said. "Although we thought we had disarmed him, he had another blade and tried to attack us again. We killed in self-defense."

"Such a thing cannot be avoided in time of war," Abinoam sighed. "Well done. You may go now and rest."

Rest. As if he could rest, Barak thought, less than an hour after killing his first man. Not with an arrow at a distance, or with sword or spear in the heat of battle, as he'd always imagined his first kill. No, his bare hands, armed with only an iron blade, had dealt death at close range. He had plunged his knife into living flesh and felt the blood on his hands. Beside him, Samuel was silent too as they unrolled their sleeping mats beneath the south wall where the soldiers slept.

"It was strange, wasn't it?" Samuel said after a long silence.

"Not like I imagined," Barak agreed.

Another long silence followed, broken only by the snores of the men around them.

"Are you frightened?" Barak asked finally.

"About tomorrow?"

"Yes."

"A bit," Samuel admitted after a heartbeat's pause. Soldiers weren't supposed to know fear—or to talk about it.

"We could die tomorrow," Barak said, thinking of the man who had perished tonight.

"It's not that so much," Samuel said. "It's just—well, I don't think I'd mind dying. If it was fast. But all the things I'd never—"

"—get to do. I know." Close friends, they sometimes found themselves finishing each other's sentences. "If I died tomorrow, I'd die without ever being a man. Never to get married, or have a son of my own."

"You think about that, don't you?" Despite their sober mood Barak could hear a smile in Samuel's voice. "About getting married."

"Well, of course. Everyone does, sooner or later."

"Sooner? Are you still dreaming about Deborah?"

Barak shrugged, even though Samuel couldn't see him. "Deborah is far away. Maybe if we win tomorrow, if the Canaanites go back to Hazor and leave us alone, I can see her again someday. Go south, like I've been talking of doing. But who knows? It's in the hands of God. Now, I might worry more if I had my eye on a maiden closer at hand, as you do!"

"Hey, shut up, you two!" an older man's voice came from beneath a blanket. "Don't you know you've got to fight in the morning?"

Studying the stars, Barak lay awake long into the night. His father sometimes said that the One God lived beyond the stars, and had made them all with His own hand. Could such a deity really care what happened to people on earth? Father and grandfather believed they were fighting not just to survive as a people—to settle the land—but for their God. Tomorrow they might be dying for the right to worship the One God and not the Canaanite gods, though plenty of Hebrews here in Ramah bowed to Baal and Astarte. Could any god be worth dying for?

Protect me, God of my fathers, Barak prayed to the dark and silent night. And then, though he hadn't thought he could, he slept.

Morning came with the blast of a rams horn long before dawn. Barak scrambled to his feet and began rolling up his sleeping mat. All around him, men were doing the same. Samuel passed him a torn-off piece of bread and a handful of dates, which Barak munched while pulling on a leather tunic over his undergarment. "Any sign of the enemy yet?" he asked.

"All quiet on this side," one of the sentries on the wall replied. Just then a boy a few years younger than Barak came running from the houses behind them. He was a messenger, as Barak and Samuel had been when the Hebrew tribesmen had tried a disastrous raid on the Canaanite camp a few months before. Since then, while the survivors of that raid barricaded themselves inside Ramah, Barak and the other boys his age had trained every day at archery and at combat, waiting for their first battle. Waiting for today.

"They're marching on the north wall," the boy announced, almost out of breath. "They've begun shooting—and the arrows are on fire!"

"Well done, boy," the commander growled. "We hold here, men." The Canaanite enemy was hoping most of the men in the village would rush to defend the north wall and put out the fire, but the defenders on the north side were already prepared for such a move, and the job of Barak and the others here on the south end was to wait for the inevitable attack from the south.

The raiders were a long time coming. Barak heard the shouts from the north side of the village, followed by high-pitched screams. Acrid smoke drifted on the wind. He longed to be there, battling the invaders. Waiting seemed impossible.

Then the cry went up. "They come!"

Barak scrambled into position atop the wall. He had an arrow fitted to the string long before the line of Canaanites approached within bowshot range. He tried to keep his arm steady and his eye fixed on the target until the command came. "Fire!"

He pulled back, feeling the taut muscle in his upper arm as the bowstring let go and the arrow flew. It joined a hail of arrows from the other Hebrew defenders. Not waiting to see where it had gone, he reached back into his quiver for another.

Now the first volley of arrows from the enemy archers reached them, and Barak ducked below the wall, then straightened up to release his own arrow. The flight of this one he saw. It arched over the heads of the enemy. Dodging another Canaanite arrow, he again reached for another from his own supply.

Beside him on the wall, he heard a cry and a sickening thud as the man beside him took an arrow in the chest. Barak willed himself not to look, only to shoot. This arrow, too, he saw. The enemy soldiers were close now, and Barak's arrow buried itself in a man's body. The man jerked back and slumped to the ground.

He moved into a rhythm. Shoot, duck to avoid being shot, get another arrow, fit it to the string, stand up, shoot. He heard the screams of men around him. Then he reached back and felt nothing. His quiver was empty.

But the time for arrows was past. The enemy was close now, near enough for Barak to see their eyes peering through the slits of their metal helmets. "Charge!" came the command. Dropping his bow and quiver, Barak scrambled over the wall and dropped to the ground. He pulled his bone-handled knife from his belt as his feet hit the dirt on the other side.

Almost immediately he found himself in the path of an oncoming Canaanite soldier. The man was huge. His long sword seemed an extension of his arm. Barak dodged beneath the arm and managed a quick stab at the man's shoulder as he ducked away. Turning, he found himself face to face with a boy about his own age who wielded a short dagger much like Barak's own, though it seemed far sharper. The Canaanite slashed toward him. Barak blocked it and returned a cut of his own. The two squared off in a deadly duel as other men fought and died around them.

It was almost a dance. Barak thought of nothing but parrying the other boy's blows and driving forward with his own. They were well matched—better than at his practice sessions, when none of the other village boys could really test him. How different it was when it was life and death. Different, yet the same. Same moves. Same energy. Only the fear thrumming in the background made it strange.

His opponent gave ground, stepping back a pace or two. Now Barak saw fear in the other boy's eyes. Gradually Barak pressed forward—always forward. The young enemy kept busy blocking and defending, with no chance to make an offensive move. Seeing his opening, Barak plunged his knife with all his strength into his opponent. The boy buckled to his knees and collapsed. Barak had to pull his bloody knife free.

It wasn't like killing the man in the woods last night. Now he had had no time to think, to be horrified. Another Canaanite charged toward him, and Barak was tensed and ready before his mind could react. Battle left no time for thought. But a fierce, powerful energy surged through all his muscles. His senses were alert. Disarming his opponent, he moved at once to find another.

He was doing well, but gradually he became aware that more and more Canaanites surged around him. Fewer and fewer of his own men fought by his side. Barak had no idea how long the battle had lasted—it could have been minutes or hours. But with a sinking in his gut he suddenly knew that the Hebrews were losing.

He had taken a slash to his right arm—he didn't remember when, but he'd been blocking out the pain. Now it leaped hot to the surface as blood oozed from the wound. Barak needed that arm. For a moment he stood in a clear space, no enemy facing him. Dead bodies lay at his feet. Stepping over one, he looked down and saw Samuel.

Time and space suddenly became real again as the battle-lust drained from his veins. Samuel sprawled motionless, his eyes wide and staring. His wound was in the chest. The boy was beyond help, but Barak knelt by his best friend, unable to believe what had happened. "Samuel," he said, touching the still face.

It was just the hesitation his enemies needed. Barak looked up to find himself surrounded by five Canaanite warriors, their spears pointed at him. When he glanced around he saw only Canaanites standing. No, there was another Hebrew—an older man from the village. Two muscular Canaanites pinioned his arms. Looking back at his own captors, Barak slowly realized that to triumph or die were not the only fates possible. There was also capture—a life of slavery and a slow death. That's what would happen if he submitted quietly to the Canaanites.

Barak drew his knife again, though the effort seared his arm. Pointing it at the nearest spear-wielding enemy, he lunged forward.

ChAPTER 5

Deborah straightened up and reached back to rub the sore spot at the base of her spine. Making bread was not a new task to her. Her mother had taught her to mix and knead and pound flat the dough when she was no more than 6 years old. But how different being a young girl learning the household tasks was from being a wife whose job it was to bake all the bread for the whole household, every day of the week. And twice as much on the preparation day, for Lappidoth, like her father, was strict in his observance of the weekly Sabbath.

A stew of lentils and greens simmered over the fire in the central courtyard. Now she moved the cooking pot to the edge of the fire pit and shoveled some of the coals into the domed clay oven. When it grew hot enough, she slid some of the dough inside to bake. Her stepdaughter Anna came running out of the sleeping area in tears, babbling, "Avi hit me! He hit me!" The little girl launched herself into Deborah's arms for comfort, who just managed to move away from the fire pit in time before both she and Anna tumbled onto the coals. She stroked Anna's tangled curls and called over her head, "Avi! Come out here at once!"

The boy reluctantly crept out of the sleeping quarters, dragging a stick in the dirt behind him. He was 5 years old, and his dark brown eyes looked rebellious. "I didn't do it! It was an accident!"

"You must never hit your sister, Avi," Deborah said. She was amazed at how stern and grown-up her voice sounded. Of course she had cared for her younger brother and sister for years, and guided them through many such squabbles. But just like breadmaking, it was different when you were the mother and wife. Deborah had been the wife of Lappidoth for three months, and sometimes she felt responsibility as heavy as a yoke on her shoulders.

"I want to go out with Eli and the goats!" the boy said, kicking the dirt floor with his toe.

"In a few years, Avi, but you're too young to go now. You know what your father said." It was always best, she'd found, to remind them that Lappidoth was the ultimate authority. Ten year-old Eli, skeptical about a stepmother just four years his senior, had already squared off against her more than once, fists on his hips, saying, "Mother never used to say . . ." or "Mother always . . ." He wouldn't come right out and say, "You're not my mother!"—if his father ever heard such rudeness Eli knew he would be beaten soundly—but the accusation was in his eyes. As the oldest child, he remembered his mother the best, and Deborah knew she herself could never measure up to that memory.

Indeed, Azubah's memory was everywhere in that house. The first time Deborah made date cakes for a Sabbath meal, Lappidoth was delighted. But when he tasted them, he frowned. Azubah had employed different spices than those Deborah's mother had taught her to use. Almost every day she encountered some new way in which she felt she would never fill Azubah's sandals. Lappidoth didn't make her feel that way on purpose, of course. In fact, if anything, he went out of his way *not* to make comparisons between his first wife and his second. But Deborah couldn't shake the feeling that in this house she would always be "the new wife."

"It's almost time for Eli and the other boys to return home," she told Avi now. "Why don't you go down to the end of the road and see if you can spot them coming? Don't go past Sarah's house. Anna, can you stay with me and help me sweep the courtyard?" The child loved to be given small tasks around the house to do. She was the youngest, since her baby brother had succumbed to the same fever that killed their mother. Perhaps because of that, she reached out to her stepmother far more than the others did, and had quickly taken to cuddling against Deborah and calling her "Mama."

As the two of them swept the courtyard and then played a counting game with stones, the tension and turmoil inside subsided. By the time Avi returned with Eli and the goats, Deborah felt peaceful. Behind the boys with their goats came the village men who had worked all day tending their crops on the terraces below the village. Lappidoth walked close behind his sons and sat on the ground in the courtyard near the cooking fire, listening to the children tell him about the small events of their day as Deborah took the bread from the oven and the bowl of stew from the fire.

". . . and the spotted kid was gone!" Eli was telling his father, breathless. "I looked everywhere for him, and then I could hear him bleating, far off, and I had to get Gavriel to watch my goats—our goats—while I went looking, and I had to crawl through bushes and everything. I finally found him caught in the brambles, and he couldn't get his leg free."

"You did a good job," Lappidoth replied. "I'm glad we have such a trustworthy boy looking after our animals."

"Can't I go too, and learn to watch the goats?" Avi begged. "I don't like being stuck here all day with the *women.*" He cast a glowering look at his sister and stepmother.

"Not yet, Avi," his father replied. "You have much to learn here at home yet that Auntie Deborah can teach you." That was their compromise for the older children—they would not require them to call her "Mother," at least not yet. She was "Auntie Deborah" as most of the grown women in the village were "Auntie" to the children. "Perhaps tomorrow she will let you grind the grain. Won't that be fun?"

"I can do it all by myself! I'm *strong!*" Avi said proudly. "Stronger than Anna. Almost as strong as you, Papa!"

Deborah eased herself down on the ground beside her family. She never ceased to admire the way Lappidoth brought peace and warmth to the family circle. When he was here, everything seemed all right. In her own childhood, her father had been a respected, but somewhat stern and distant figure. Was it just losing their mother that had made these children so close to their father, or was it something essentially different in Lappidoth himself? He was a quiet man, but he had a gentle manner of seeing the best solution to every problem and presenting it in a way everyone could agree with. When his children were grown he would be one of the village elders, settling disputes between his neighbors, and Deborah thought he would be well suited for the task.

Now he lifted his hands in prayer, and Deborah and the children followed his example. "O God of our Fathers, maker of the universe, we bring you our humble thanks for this good food you have provided," he prayed. "Thank you for my wife Deborah, whose hands made this bread, who cares so well for our family. Thank you for my sons and my daughter. May they grow to know and worship only You, O Lord. Amen."

As Deborah tore off chunks of bread to hand around to each family member she wondered how many other courtyards in Ramah echoed with the same prayers tonight. Her father's household, certainly. A few others. But more and more households, it seemed, had little shrines to the gods of Canaan, and it was there that families gathered to give thanks, to make their petitions, to offer their small sacrifices. She was grateful to be wed to a man who worshipped only Yahweh.

Yet as much as she admired Lappidoth for his skills as a father and his loyalty to God, she still felt a little shy of him, once they were all alone with the children asleep. As she wandered around the courtyard cleaning up evidence of the day's work Lappidoth made sure the animals were secure for the night. She had grown up in her father's household, which, like most of those in the village, contained an extended family—three brothers and their wives and children—living in rooms around the central courtyard. Since Lappidoth's sister had married and moved into her husband's home, and his parents had died, this house contained only Lappidoth, Deborah, and their children and animals. At times like this it seemed oddly quiet. Deborah didn't remember much silence in the house she had grown up in. Once the children slept she had no other women for her to talk with around the fire. Instead, she was alone with her husband.

"Now, my Deborah, time we get ready to sleep ourselves," Lappidoth said, as he did every night. It was he who had suggested that they might sleep apart for the first little while if she were more comfortable with that. "You are still a young girl," he had said at the time, "and I understand it will take a while before you are used to the idea of being married to an old fellow like me." She understood, too, that he was still mourning for Azubah, whom he had loved very much. Even so, it was strange for a man to show such restraint.

Deborah recognized that his need for a mother to care for the children had driven him to remarry so quickly, and the necessity for more children would soon bring him to his new wife's bed. Three months had passed. The idea of having a baby of her own brought mixed feelings: childbirth was frightening, since women so often died. Her own child, on the other hand—hers and Lappidoth's— would make her feel more securely rooted in the family, less like an outsider and an intruder in her own home. *How would Anna react?* Deborah wondered. The little girl enjoyed her role as the baby in the family.

"How quiet you are. Are you lost in thought?" Deborah jumped at Lappidoth's voice so close to her ear. He had walked up silently behind her.

Glancing down at the last glowing embers of the fire, she decided it was time to act like a woman—a wife. She closed her eyes, drew a little strength from somewhere inside, and turned to face her husband.

"I was thinking of Anna," she said. "How she will feel if she has a little brother or sister. Will she be jealous, do you think, or will she welcome a baby?"

His expression of surprise turned to a slow smile. "She may be a little put out at first, but I'm sure she would learn to love a new baby even more than a new lamb or kid. Why? Do you think we should give her a little brother?"

"I think it is time to begin thinking of it," Deborah said.

Lappidoth took her hand. "I'm pleased to hear you say so."

Later that night, lying close to her in their bedroll, Lappidoth said, "Our God has blessed us both, bringing us together. At least, I think you are a blessing, for you are so good with the children and the house, as well as such a wise and lovely young woman."

He had just given her more compliments in one breath than Deborah ever remembered getting in a single day in her life before. She felt a warm rush of affection for him. "I feel blessed too," she said.

"Do you? I'm no fool, you know. I realize there are many young girls who are not happy to marry an older man with children of his own—someone with memories of another wife."

Deborah thought of her friends Miriam and Rahel. "Some girls go on and on about handsome young men," she admitted, "but I've never been one of those. Even those girls, when it comes time to actually make a match, are glad for someone kind and steady and reliable."

"Kind, steady, reliable." He repeated the words as if tasting them. "Well. I've been called worse. I'm sorry it's a bit late for you to see me as a handsome young man, though I might have been that, 10 or 15 years ago."

"I don't mind," she said, snuggling under the blanket. And really, she didn't. It wasn't that she never thought of Barak, of what might have been. But those were only dreams. This was reality—a girl's father made her a match, and she prayed to God or to her gods that it would be a good marriage to a kind man who could care for her, protect her, and not beat her harshly or needlessly. And, of course, that she would have children. Fond as she was of Lappidoth's children, especially Anna, she did want babies of her own.

It was true enough—though she'd never have admitted it to a soul—that images of a handsome young warrior, whirling his sling above his head as he defied the Canaanite soldiers, had danced through her head almost every night as she slept. But those were nights when she'd slept alone. Now she slept beside her husband. Deborah didn't think that dreams of Barak would trouble her from now on.

And indeed, they didn't. When she lifted Anna onto her hip and walked across the village square to her mother's house, she was able to tell her mother truthfully that she was happy in her marriage. When she met Rahel and Miriam at the village well, she listened without envy to Miriam's gushing rhapsodies about her upcoming marriage to a good-looking boy just a few years her senior. Rahel—still unmarried, with no match made for her yet—pressed her to share the most private details of married life, but Deborah just smiled. "Lappidoth is very kind to me," she told them, and meant it.

Kind Lappidoth was, and happy with his new wife and family, but he was less and less pleased with all that was happening in the village around them. When the family went out to the terraced hills to bring their grain crop in from the fields, he said, "We must praise God this Sabbath for His goodness to us!"

A neighbor, overhearing him, laughed. "Yes, and I'll praise Baal for his kindness to me! Look, my baskets are as full as yours—maybe a little fuller! Do you really think the God of our fathers is any better than Baal?"

"Better? Yahweh is mighty, great above all gods! I and my house will serve Him as long as we live," Lappidoth answered, mildly enough but with an edge to his tone. Only the mildness surprised Deborah. Her own father would have thundered out the commandment about worshipping the Lord God only and serving no other. Her husband was less likely to confront others, less quick to point out their wrongdoing. But the harvest celebration in the village square ignited his usually quiet anger.

Several of the families built a great fire and set up an image of Baal in the center of the village. Lappidoth's family, Deborah's parents, and a few others kept to their homes, but most of the villagers gathered in the square, either to participate in the worship or at least to watch and stare. There was plenty to stare at too. At first the villagers confined themselves just to dancing and singing, but soon—as Deborah's aunt, who stopped by on her way back from gawking, reported—some of the men began cutting themselves with knives, offering their blood as a thank-offering to Baal. "But that's not the worst of it," she said, almost relishing the news. "After a while I began to see couples—young people, not married—slinking off into the shadows. And then I saw a few married men going off with women who weren't their own wives. When I asked Avram what was going on, he said they were celebrating Baal's gift of fertility—that it was all part of the festival, and there was no sin in it! Can you imagine!"

"Peace, sister, we'll hear no more of this," Lappidoth growled, for Eli was still awake, though the younger children slept. Deborah's aunt left soon after, obviously hoping to see more shocking sights before she returned safely home. From the square, shouts and cries and drumming noises continued to echo long into the night.

"I do not know this place anymore," Lappidoth complained to Deborah in bed that night. "When I was a boy, most people at least went through the motions of worshipping our God, even if they might privately acknowledge other deities. But now it has become so open. Baals in our public spaces! People coupling with their neighbors in celebration of their pagan gods! This is not what God planned for His people, Deborah."

"I know," she agreed. "He sent us into this land to conquer it for Him, but instead it seems the land has conquered us. Even here, where we have remained free from the rule of the Canaanites, we have fallen under the spell of their gods."

Lappidoth raised himself up on one elbow and looked at her keenly. "You have a good mind, Deborah. It's a pleasure to speak of such things with you." He sounded a little surprised, and she wondered if perhaps that lovely and talented housewife, Azubah, had not been particularly clever. The thought made her momentarily pleased, but she knew that was sinful envy and tried to forget it.

"What would you say to leaving Ramah?" he asked suddenly.

"I—ah, I've never thought— Why, do you want to leave? Where would we go?"

"For a long time I've been considering leaving here," Lappidoth said, "and what happened tonight only seals it in my mind. This village is full of idolatry and wickedness."

"But isn't every village the same? It's sad, but that's what I hear travelers say," she pointed out.

"One village is not. One place at least we could go and know we would hear only the God of our fathers worshipped."

"Shiloh?" she asked in wonder.

"Yes. I have kin there—my mother's people—and I am thinking of taking us all to Shiloh. Would you be happy there?"

Deborah remembered her visit there, her glimpse of the tabernacle, of the songs of the priests, of the evening sacrifice. The people there had displayed the same level of energy, the interest in ritual, and the focused passion that now flowed through the village square—but dedicated to a higher cause, the worship of the true God. She imagined living near there, going regularly to the sacrifices, bearing a child in Shiloh.

"I would be very happy there," she said, "if that is your desire, my husband."

"Then I will begin making my plans at once."

CHAPTER 6

Barak heard the whip before he felt it. He knew its sound well: a whistling snap that ended with a stinging pain on his bare back. The worst thing was that by now his back was such a mass of healing, half-healed, and blistering sores that every lash opened up old cuts and made the pain worse. He imagined pain as a stone the size of his fist, and saw himself removing it from himself, placing it behind him. Pain was something the body felt. His mind would be stronger. Had to be stronger.

"Move along, sluggard!" the voice behind him growled. It was a Canaanite voice, and the dialect was a little different from the Hebrew tongue Barak spoke. But by now he knew a few Canaanite phrases well. "Move along, sluggard" was one of them.

Barak was shackled, wrists tied behind his back, to a line of captive Hebrews making the long march toward the city of Hazor. Ahead of him was his father, Abinoam, also captured at the battle of Ramah. He wasn't sure who was behind. The procession consisted of about 30 of them in all, mostly healthy, fit men who had been wounded and captured in the battle. Most of the women, children, and old people had perished, though some had probably escaped to the surrounding hills. Barak had not seen his grandfather among the captives. Probably the old man was dead. Mercifully, Barak's mother and sisters were gone too. It would have been far worse for them if they had been captured. Some women had been taken from the village, but most were dead now, after having been used for the soldiers' amusement for the first several days of the march.

By fire and sword, Sisera's army had wiped out almost the whole population of Ramah in Naphtali. The attempt to defend the village had been futile. The devastation was total. Barak's family had been wiped out and his best friend was dead. Countless other friends, too. And Barak himself was a prisoner of war—a slave.

Hoping for death—praying for it even—he had tried to go down fighting. All that earned him was the wound in his shoulder. It was healing badly, festering, and sore. But the wounds of the lash on his back were so fresh he almost forgot the knife-wound in his shoulder.

He wanted to speak to his father, but their captors would not allow the prisoners to talk among themselves. At night they slept surrounded by guards. They had no hope of escape.

One morning, a few hours after dawn, the Canaanite soldiers began shouting to each other. Barak recognized it as the cry of men seeing their home again after a long absence. Sure enough, off in the distance rose the walls of Hazor.

Barak hadn't seen the city before, though he knew the general area well enough from boyhood. But he'd never come this far north. Still, he'd heard tales of the walled cities of the Canaanites. Such tales didn't come close to the truth, though. He'd imagined something like the defensive walls they'd constructed on the north and south ends of Ramah—small, makeshift, and temporary. Hazor rose from the ground like a mountain, as if the gods themselves had built it there. How could human hands have raised something so powerful, so solid, so eternal?

Looking up at the vast wall as they drew nearer, Barak remembered the old tale of Joshua and Jericho. Had the walls of Jericho been like this? The story must be a fable, then. Such walls could never fall. Unless—

God of our fathers, he prayed—his first prayer since the battle. *If You still hear us, and care for us—can you break down walls like these? We need a new Joshua, O Lord—someone who can lead us, can win back this land for us.*

Once, the idea would have stirred his heart with joy and pride. He had even, perhaps, cherished a secret dream that maybe *he* could be the new Joshua. God had given him such strength, such skill. Men liked to follow him, to listen to him, even though he was still a boy. But those dreams were dead. He was a slave now. His life would be ugly and short. Indeed, he hoped it would be over as quickly as possible.

Once inside the city, the soldiers separated their captives into groups, herding the younger, healthier men together. Barak saw his father being led away with a group of older men. "Father! God go with you!" he shouted. A guard cuffed him hard in the mouth with the back of his hand. But Barak had caught the light that briefly glowed in Abinoam's eyes and wasn't sorry.

The city was like no village Barak had ever been in. Stone slabs paved the streets. Houses adjoined each other, and more people than he'd ever seen in one place before milled in the open spaces. Many paused to gawk at the Hebrew captives. The guards led the young men—about 10 in all—up through one of the narrow streets toward an open square.

The square, too, was like no village square in any Hebrew village. Barak stared at the throngs of people. Usually, in a town square, you might see women drawing water at the well, a few old men loitering, and the smallest children running and playing. Everyone else would be hard at work in the houses or fields. Here, men and women of all ages swarmed everywhere. Around the edges, people stood or sat by small booths that displayed fruits, vegetables, the butchered carcasses of animals, bolts of woven cloth, and stacks of clay pottery. Others were looking through the goods on display, haggling with the venders. They seemed to be offering to barter or trade goods, though it was hard to imagine so many people with extra goods available to trade, all at once. The square pulsed with life.

Moments later, Barak realized that food and household goods weren't the only things available for trade and sale in the square at Hazor. Their guards led him and the other young men up onto a raised platform, and a crowd quickly gathered. He dared a glance at the boy nearest him. Under the blood and grime on his face Barak could see it was Jonah, a year younger or so than Barak himself. A native of Ramah, he and Barak had begun training together when Barak's family had come to the village the year before. Jonah looked back at him with frightened eyes. He obviously had no idea what was happening.

"Slaves," Barak mouthed. "We're being sold."

The other boy's eyes widened, but he said nothing.

The guards missed this little exchange as they busily moved among the boys, separating them, tying their hair out of their eyes, and stripping off the rags they wore. Barak flinched but did not resist as a man tore off his ragged loincloth, leaving him exposed to the eyes of the crowd. Of course, potential slaveowners would want to judge the fitness of the young men they were buying.

The bidding began. Barak had never seen a slave auction, and he found it hard to understand the local dialect, so he couldn't follow most of what went on. Instead, he concentrated on watching the people who bought the slaves. Rich men, he assumed. What kind of masters would they be? And what kind of work, what kind of life awaited the slaves?

When his own turn came, a portly balding man near the front of the crowd muscled forward and called out a number. Another man, eyeing Barak with a cold glare that made him shiver, shouted as well. But then Barak saw a soldier step forward and place his hand on the shoulder of the merchant conducting the sale. Barak couldn't catch the words, but he was sure he heard the name "Sisera." The merchant nodded, and the soldier moved over to Barak and pulled him out of the line. Then he pushed Jonah forward, and the bidding resumed.

"Where are you taking me?" Barak asked, expecting another blow for his rudeness.

Instead, the soldier replied, "General Sisera owns you now."

Sisera. The butcher who had slaughtered the people of Ramah, who had destroyed his family—Barak belonged to him now.

Binding him again, the Canaanite led Barak to Sisera's villa on the west side of the city. Looking at the house, the boy felt awe surface through his anger and fear. He had grown up in tents and only in the past year had he become used to sleeping inside or on the roof of a mud-brick and rubble village house. This sprawling two-level villa was built around a central courtyard, like the village homes in Ramah, but there all similarity ended. The rooms were cool, clean, and spacious. The large, flat paving stones under his feet made the house seem far more elegant than a dirt-floored house could ever be. A ripple of soft music came from somewhere. It took Barak a minute to locate the slave girl playing a stringed lyre in a corner. Her fingers moved busily, but her curious eyes scanned the new arrival.

A well-dressed older man appeared and waited while the soldier untied Barak. Whoever this was, Barak knew it wasn't Sisera. The man didn't look like a Canaanite soldier. He was tall, and his head was shaven perfectly bald. His skin was darker and his accent different than anyone Barak had heard or seen before.

"I am Senet, Lord Sisera's household steward," the man said slowly. "Come with me. I will give you food and clothes." He spoke matter-of-factly, as though he had no hostility toward Barak. That made him the nicest person Barak had encountered since the battle for Ramah had begun.

"I would like some clothes," he said cautiously. He had come from the marketplace naked, just as he had been sold.

The bald man frowned at him. "Do not speak unless I have asked you a direct question," he said. "Your place in this household is to be silent and serve."

Barak raised his eyebrows but said nothing.

In a back room the steward gave him a length of coarse linen cloth to wrap around his waist, and handed him a piece of bread and a cup of beer. "When you are clothed and fed, Lord Sisera wishes to see you," Senet said, then withdrew, leaving Barak alone.

Quickly he scanned his surroundings, thinking first of escape.

The small room was obviously a storeroom for food, kept cool by lack of windows, though the walls had some small openings near the ceiling. Nothing large enough for a man to slip through. Rounds of cheese and bags of herbs hung from the ceiling. Shelves stacked with dried fruits lined the walls. Barak sat on a wooden bench, one of two that provided the room's only furniture. Senet had closed the heavy wooden door behind him when he had left.

Slavery. So this was to be his fate. He knew his body was healthy and strong and unless he fell prey to violence or a disease he could live a long time, even with limited food and hard work. Could he survive a life of slavery? Barak didn't think so. He remembered another of the old stories, about the forefather Joseph who had led the children of Israel into Egypt. Joseph had started out as a slave too, and proved so loyal and faithful that he had risen to be steward of his master's house and eventually overlord of the land of Egypt.

Well, Barak thought, *I'm no Joseph.* Serving this dog of a foreign general faithfully wasn't one of his big concerns. But if he could remain sharp and alert and look for every opportunity, maybe escape would someday be possible.

First, he needed to know as much as he could about this place and the people in it. Had Senet really gone away and left a captive slave unguarded in the room? Setting his cup aside, Barak moved silently to the door. He pushed it open gently, looked to the right and the left, but saw no one.

Perhaps luck, or God, was with him. Maybe he could get out of here without ever facing Sisera. He stepped outside the room.

The storeroom was at the end of a corridor that led off the central courtyard. Other servants would be in the courtyard, of course, but perhaps there was another way out. Barak took another cautious step out into the corridor.

"Freeze, Hebrew filth!" a rough voice accosted him. Barak did—not because of the words, but because the point of an iron spear jabbing his throat. Two guards lounged almost casually in niches on either side of the corridor. One held the spear.

Slow gutteral laughter came from the end of the corridor. But neither of the guards was laughing. Barak looked up.

A powerfully built man of middle height stood silhouetted in the sunlight that poured in from the courtyard. He was clapping his hands with deliberate mockery. "Well done, little Hebrew! I guessed your first thought would be to escape." In three swift strides the man stood in front of him.

Barak hadn't seen Sisera before, but he had no trouble recognizing the insignia of rank on the man's tunic or the arrogant air of command. The general was a man several years younger than Barak's father, with a thick black beard and a heavy thatch of black hair still untouched with gray. He was muscular and broad-shouldered, and his dark eyes pierced Barak.

For a moment the two faced off—Barak was a little taller—till Barak felt a wrenching twist on his upper arm. One of the guards had grabbed his arm and forced him to his knees.

"Kneel before your betters, Hebrew," Sisera hissed. "Today you begin learning who your betters are and why we rule this land. I'll make sure it's a lesson you won't forget."

Stepping forward, he took Barak's ear between his thumb and forefinger, and twisted hard. Barak kept his face still. It hurt, but he had endured so much worse pain. *He'll never hear me cry out or see me flinch,* he vowed silently. "Learn this lesson also," Sisera said, his voice quiet and deadly. "You will not escape from my house, or from my fields when I send you there to work long days under the hot sun. For the rest of your life you will never be out of my control or out of my power again. And your people will never, never rule this land. Do you understand?"

Barak remained silent.

"Do you understand?" Apparently this was one of those direct questions he was supposed to answer.

"I understand, sir," he said. Then his eyes rose to meet Sisera's defiantly. "Also, that was more than one lesson. Are you sure you can count?"

Sisera's arm caught him across the mouth at the same time the butt of the guard's spear jabbed him in the back. Biting his lip, Barak just managed to keep from crying out.

"Take him and flog him," Sisera said carelessly, turning to go. "As often and as long as it takes to teach him respect."

Barak let his body go limp so that it forced the guards to pull him to his feet and drag him along. As he hung between them, listening to Sisera's retreating footsteps, he made another promise to himself. *Respect. That's one lesson I'll be a long time learning.*

CHAPTER 7

Holding two willow branches high above her head, Deborah moved in the long snakelike line behind the other women. The ringing beat of the tambourines coaxed her feet into a dancing rhythm as the women circled outside the inner circle of men. The priests led the people in singing praises to the Lord as each of the men held up the branches of willow, myrtle, and palm bound together, with the etrog held in the other hand. "Praise to the Lord!" Deborah shouted. "Hallelujah!"

When the dance concluded and the men gathered to hear the reading of the law, most of the women drifted back toward their homes. Deborah stayed a little longer, eager to hear the sacred words. The children were asleep back at her tent, watched over by Lappidoth's aunt who lived near them.

"So beginning with the fifteenth day of the seventh month, after you have gathered the crops of the land," a Levite chanted, "celebrate the festival to the Lord for seven days; the first day is a day of rest, and the eighth day also is a day of rest. On the first day you are to take choice fruit from the trees, and palm fronds, leafy branches and poplars, and rejoice before the Lord your God for seven days. Celebrate this as a festival to the Lord for seven days each year. This is to be a lasting ordinance for the generations to come; celebrate it in the seventh month. Live in booths for seven days: All native-born Israelites are to live in booths so your descendants will know that I had the Israelites live in booths when I brought them out of Egypt. I am the Lord your God."

Deborah walked back to their tent after the festival feeling tired but somehow stronger, more full of life and hope. Slipping inside, she found the children all sleeping. Then she went back outside and sat down in the shelter of tree branches that her husband had made. The surrounding booths were quiet. Most of the men were still at the tabernacle service, while the majority of the women who had been there were already back and probably asleep. Deborah couldn't explain why she had felt such a need to stay longer. She only knew that being at the tabernacle was like being in God's very presence, and she needed that like a thirsty plant needed rain. Some days, going about the busy round of her daily activities, she would look toward the tabernacle perched at the center of the hill, and draw strength just from the sight of it.

Lappidoth had been wise to move their family here, she told herself. And yet, to others, it might not seem the best of choices. They had been here almost a year now, and the first harvest had been difficult. The wheat and barley crop they had planted last year had produced poorly, forcing them to endure many lean weeks, though neighbors had shared with them. Having now planted this year's crops, the family was praying for a far better yield.

But their salvation had been an accidental discovery she and her husband had stumbled across while struggling to establish a home for themselves and feed the children. Both Deborah and Lappidoth had been making clay pots, lamps, and other household goods to replace things they had left behind in Ramah, for they had wanted to travel light and not burden themselves with too many household goods when they moved. Both were skilled at these tasks. Deborah particularly enjoyed working with clay. The soft, responsive yielding of the material as she pressed it between her fingers satisfied her. All day she worked with things that were transitory—she baked bread and prepared food eaten in a few moments and cleaned clothes and dishes that quickly became dirty again. But when she shaped a pot or a jar she felt the satisfaction of knowing she was doing something permanent.

One day Lappidoth went to the kiln to fire a few clay lamps that Deborah had made, and met one of the priests from the tabernacle. The young priest had admired the lamps and asked if Lappidoth had produced them himself. Later, the priest stopped by their tent and asked if they had any lamps to spare. "A great many are required for the tabernacle," he said, "and we are constantly looking for someone who can supply good quality lamps."

Deborah had already noticed that the economy of Shiloh's village differed in some ways from that of Ramah. At home, every family provided for their own needs: growing their crops, spinning their cloth, making their own pots, and building their own furniture. At Shiloh, the needs of the tabernacle—for clothing, for food, and for lamps—was far greater than any household could supply, and the priests themselves were too busy with the religious rituals to produce everything required. The wives of the priests did much of the work, but the priests had also developed a system of trading extra crops with villagers who could manufacture vessels, priestly vestments, and other necessary items. So the lamps had been their salvation: the priests provided them with extra grain and seed for the new year's planting in exchange for all the lamps Deborah and Lappidoth could supply.

Unrolling her blanket, Deborah lay down inside the booth, looking at the stars through the lacy ceiling of leaves. Living in a booth for seven days seemed almost unnecessary when they had already made the move from a substantial village house to a tent. Lappidoth hoped to be able to build a house in Shiloh for them soon, but Deborah had learned to actually enjoy the simpler existence of a tent dweller. It was a small price to pay. Even less food and the absence of her family were small prices to pay for the privilege of living so near the house of God.

Until she came to Shiloh, Deborah hadn't realized how oppressive the constant presence of pagan worship back in Ramah had been. Shiloh reminded her of the joyful weeks she had spent with her mother's clan in Naphtali a few years before—a place where everyone worshipped the One God and no one spoke of the Canaanite deities at all. Oh, she was sure that even in Shiloh a few people privately said a prayer to Astarte or to Baal, but no pagan shrines dominated the streets here and no Asherah poles stood in the woods outside the town. Here, worship of Yahweh was central to every aspect of life.

Now she could hear the men walking back from the tabernacle. She listened among the murmurs for Lappidoth's voice. In the year and a half they had been married she had come to respect and even love her husband. Only one thing lay unfulfilled between them: the desire to have a child of their own. Deborah wondered why God delayed answering that prayer. Before she left home, of course, her friend Rahel had suggested a few quiet offerings to Asherah to ensure her fertility. Although Deborah wouldn't even consider such a thing, she now understood why women might resort to the fertility goddess. It was nice to imagine praying to a powerful woman who was especially interested in childbearing. If she'd remained back home in Ramah, Deborah might have been tempted. But here in Shiloh, it was unthinkable. After all, the One God also gave children to women—even barren women. Hadn't Sarah, the wife of Abraham, been barren but still gave birth to Isaac in her old age? *And I'm only 15,* Deborah thought. *There's plenty of time yet for God to bless me.*

Still, she hoped it would be soon. Maybe tonight, as she and Lappidoth lay together under the stars in this temporary shelter, in the middle of a feast of joy and celebration, God would see fit to quicken her womb and make her a mother.

The feast of Tabernacles ended, the villagers gathered the harvest in, and the winter rains came. By that time, Deborah knew the God of Israel had answered her prayer. She waited another month to be sure, and spoke to one of the village midwives before she told Lappidoth.

His face shone as if he had received a gift. "My Deborah! A child of our own! How wonderful!"

She still wondered how Lappidoth's children would feel about a new half-brother or half-sister. Deborah was much more comfortable with them now, almost two years after her marriage to their father. Anna simply treated her as her mother. She shadowed Deborah as she worked in the fields or around their tent, and Deborah couldn't imagine loving any daughter of her own more than she did Anna. Eli, almost 13 now, was absorbed in his own growing up, busy becoming a man. He was polite and pleasant to her, as he might be to a favorite aunt, and Deborah had never expected to supplant his mother's place in his heart.

Avi was the difficult one. Almost 7 now, he still called her "Auntie Deborah" and ran to his father rather than his stepmother whenever he needed an embrace, an answer, or a quarrel resolved. Lappidoth would try to steer him gently toward Deborah, but although the boy was never openly defiant or hostile, he resisted, and she didn't push. She knew that trying to force her way into his affections would only make things worse. But she worried about him. It was good that he was so close to his father, but even a boy at that age needed a mother's love, and Deborah felt sure Avi was still mourning his own mother.

None of the children seemed upset by the news of the new baby, though. Eli was politely interested, Avi seemed proud, insisting that it would be another boy, and Anna was excited. "I'll help you look after the baby, Mama," she said again and again. "I'll wash him very gently, with soft cloths, and I'll rock him to sleep when he cries. Or her. It could be a sister, couldn't it, Mama?"

"It could indeed," Deborah replied. Everyone assumed she wanted her firstborn to be a boy, and of course she did, but a daughter would be fine as well. She was just looking forward to the whole experience, to bringing a child into the world, a child who would seal the bond between herself and Lappidoth. It couldn't be as exciting for him, she thought—with three children of his own already. Yet he seemed pleased that his new young wife would bear his child, and throughout the winter months life in their tent was happy and mostly serene. Lappidoth began work on a small house for the family, insisting that they could not raise a new baby in a tent.

"Are you sorry now that I took you so far away from your family?" Lappidoth asked one evening as Deborah sat beside him on an unfinished wall of their new house. The sun was setting in the west, over the tabernacle, which they could see silhouetted in the dying light.

"No . . . well, yes, in a way. I miss my mother especially. I would love to have her here, to rely on her help and advice. But in another way, no. I'm so glad to be here. I feel this is the right place for us."

The midwife had told her to expect the baby in the heat of midsummer. As the months wore on, with the grape harvest ended and the figs and dates ripening, Deborah found it harder and harder to complete a day's work or get a comfortable night's sleep. She tired easily, and the children—even Avi—were carefully solicitous, helping lift and carry things for her. One day Anna tried making bread all by herself while Deborah sat on a low stool nearby, giving direction, shifting as she tried to find a comfortable sitting position.

"There! Now it's all nice and round . . . do I flatten it out now?" Anna asked, her dark hair falling forward over her earnest little face. She began patting the ball of dough into a pancake, when another voice said, "What good work, Anna! What a big girl you're becoming!"

Deborah looked up sharply. It seemed impossible, but her mother stood in front of the tent, carrying a small bundle of clothes. Beside her was Deborah's youngest brother. "Mother! Where did you come from?"

"From Ramah, of course. Your husband sent word that my daughter was about to have her firstborn child, and I could not imagine staying away." Putting down her bundle, she went to help Anna with the bread. Her mother was not a demonstrative woman, but Deborah felt as if she'd been enfolded in a warm embrace. Her joy and relief brought tears to her eyes.

So it was that on a hot morning a few days afterward, Deborah squatted on the birthing stool in her tent surrounded by the midwife, her mother, and two neighbor women who had become close friends. Deborah's mother pulled her daughter's hair away from her hot, sweaty face, tying it back with a strand of wool. "Now, you cry out if you need to," she told her. "Don't try to be brave."

Deborah couldn't have been brave even if she had been trying. The pain was excruciating. But the knowledge that she would hold her child in her arms, nurse a baby at her breast when all this was over, sustained her through hours of hard labor and delivery. At long last she heard the midwife cry, "The head! I see the head! Push again, Deborah, one more great push—"

Throwing all her strength behind the effort, she pushed the baby's head out through a fiery surge of pain that she thought would tear her in two. Deborah had attended other women's birthings. She knew the next sound she heard would be the baby's cry followed by the women's sighs of relief and admiration.

Instead, she heard silence. The midwife sucked in her breath sharply, and Deborah's whole body stiffened. "What is it? What's wrong? What's wrong with my baby?" She leaned forward, and saw a perfectly formed infant in the midwife's arms. Beneath the blood and mucus of the birthing, the baby's skin was white—too white, almost blue. "He's not breathing," she heard one of the neighbor women gasp.

"Hurry—make him breathe!" Deborah's mother ordered, but the midwife was already at work, blowing her own breath into the baby's mouth, trying to make the tiny chest rise and fall. "O Lord, God of our fathers," one of the women began, "look upon Deborah and her child with mercy. Spare this child, O Lord we pray, according to your great mercy . . ."

The prayer rose and fell, an unheeded babble behind the women's worried voices. Deborah felt her heart grow hard as a stone inside her. Her eyes met the midwife's and confirmed the truth. "It's no good," the midwife said. "He was dead before he was born. The cord may have been around his neck. I'm so sorry."

The atmosphere in the room changed from that of a joyous anticipation of new life to a solemn preparation for burial. Deborah's mother washed the body of her grandson and the midwife wrapped him carefully in white cloth. Deborah held the cold body for a moment, marveling at the perfection of his eyes, nose, and lips. So perfect, and yet he had never taken a breath.

Telling Lappidoth and the children was the worst part. He comforted Deborah, hiding his own grief, and Deborah remembered that her husband had already suffered the loss of one child. Anna threw herself into Deborah's arms in stormy grief. "I want our baby!" she cried. All Deborah could do was stroke her hair and murmur, "I know, my darling. I want our baby too."

When Lappidoth was allowed to lie with his wife again, he held Deborah gently in his arms. "Nothing can take away this loss," he said. "But you are young. We can have many more children."

"I know," she replied. She knew, too, that no other child would replace her firstborn, but she didn't need to say that to him. He understood.

Her mother, too, was sympathetic, stroking Deborah's hair and kissing her cheeks before she said goodbye. She had never been so openly affectionate, even on the eve of Deborah's marriage. "I lost three myself," she said softly. "Raised three, and lost three more. You never forget. Somewhere inside I still believe I have six children." Drawing back, she looked her sensible self again, and said, "Time moves on. When I see you again, you will be able to smile."

Deborah wiped away a tear. "I hope it will not be too long."

They moved into their new house at summer's end, though without the rejoicing they had expected. Deborah enjoyed settling her family in a proper house again, but it was hard not to think of the child she should have carried in her arms all the while she cooked and cleaned and wove her cloth. One night after the evening meal she slipped outside alone and sat in front of the house, looking again toward the tabernacle. "Oh Lord," she prayed in a whisper, "I know that bearing children and burying them is a woman's lot, but did it have to be my firstborn? I hoped so much . . ."

Her questions hung unanswered in the air, but she heard footsteps coming from the house behind her. Lappidoth, she wondered, coming to console her? Or Anna, wanting a last snuggle in her arms before bedtime?

It was neither. Avi settled down beside her, not quite close enough to touch but nearly. "It's a nice house Father built us, isn't it?" he said.

"It is, Avi. Your father takes good care of us all."

The boy did not look at her. His eyes were fixed, as hers were, on the far-off tabernacle. "I'm sorry about your baby, Mama. I really wanted a little brother."

Deborah reached out and slipped her arm over his shoulders, and he leaned against her. "I'm sorry too, Avi. But I'm so glad that I have you . . . and Anna, and Eli. God has been very good to me."

And indeed He has, she thought. *I lost a son, and I gained a son. Blessed be the Lord.*

CHAPTER 8

Sun fierce as a clay oven beat down on Barak's bare back. Its skin was a mass of scars now, hardened and baked in the sun. Occasionally the overseer's lash caught him again and made him bleed, but Barak was careful. He had become skilled at working just hard enough to escape notice—not doing too little, but not too much either. Sometimes he would do a little damage if he thought it would escape notice. Pull up a few plants and bury a few others so deep they would never sprout. If the overseer suspected it had been done deliberately, he would beat all the field slaves rather than waste time trying to identify the guilty man.

This was the second planting season that Barak had worked in Sisera's fields. When the early harvest came, it would be two full years since the battle of Ramah. Two years of slavery. Two years plotting a revenge he could never carry out. Two years of hatred growing like a thornbush inside him.

Before Ramah, he had hated the Canaanites in a cool, impersonal way. They were the enemy, the pagans whom God had said to drive out of the land. Because they threatened the peaceful lives of the Hebrew people, they had to be fought. But now it was different. His hatred was hot and personal. He was seldom in the city, but the previous winter Sisera had the field slaves brought back to build an addition to the upper floor of his villa. They labored like dogs while the general and his family lived in luxury that Barak had never imagined. He saw their soft clothes, the meat that regularly appeared on their table, their beds piled with pillows, the women's shameless display of gold and jewels.

Occasionally Sisera himself came to inspect the fields. Sneering at the slaves, he kicked them as he passed, sometimes using the over-seer's whip himself. He was hard on the Hebrews—Barak in partic-ular. "Have you tamed this one yet?" he asked the overseer as they wandered past Barak, bent double, scrabbling for weeds in the dirt.

Barak tried to keep his eyes on the ground. With the overseer he could usually manage to act servile and silent. But Sisera himself—no, Barak found he could not cower before the general who had or-dered the rape and murder of his mother and sisters. He looked up under the long unruly thatch of his brown hair and met the general's eyes with his own, letting his lip curl in a sneer. *You'll never tame me,* he willed his eyes to say.

"Not quite tame yet," the general muttered. That was one of the times he took the whip in hand himself.

Four of Sisera's slaves were Hebrew. Two had been captured at Kedesh several years before. The third was an older man from Ramah whom Barak hadn't known well before the battle. The oth-ers were mostly from other Canaanite cities. The field overseer was Egyptian, like Senet, the house steward.

Barak had tried to talk to the other Hebrews. "We can band together," he had hissed to Jacob from Kedesh as they plowed side by side. "If you and Reuben could distract him, I could slip up be-hind the overseer and throttle him with my bare hands. It would be easy. Then we could all escape."

Jacob had not even turned to meet his eyes. He looked away, dumb as an ox, pretending he didn't hear. That night as Barak lay in his bedroll, another slave—not a Hebrew—put his face near Barak's ear. "No foolish plans, no wild plotting," he said. "It's been tried before. The men who did are dead."

Wanting to know more, Barak turned to him. But the man had disappeared into the darkness. After that day, the overseers never teamed Barak with any of the other Hebrews again.

All that had happened more than a year ago. Barak still thought of escape—constantly. But he was losing hope. He had turned over a thousand plans in his mind but couldn't see how one man alone could ever get away. What would the future hold if he couldn't es-cape? Although he couldn't imagine living and dying as Sisera's slave, any other future seemed unlikely.

Sometimes he tried to pray. But without his family around him, without other worshippers of the God of Israel, it seemed futile. Where was Yahweh? What evidence existed that He had ever really cared for His so-called chosen people? Barak felt himself slip into despair.

He was unprepared for another whisper in his ear at night. The overseer stirred up such a spirit of competition and rivalry among the slaves that none of them trusted each other. At first Barak wasn't even sure who was speaking, though the man knew his native Hebrew tongue.

"We can go together. There is a way."

Barak knew he didn't dare turn and face the speaker. Around them in the open field where they slept, men snored and tossed in their sleep. But the noise wasn't enough to cover a suspicious conversation. Nodding, he hoped the other man could see or sense it. "Who?" was all he said.

"Hananiah."

He was the other man from Ramah. Although captured at the same time as Barak, another citizen of Hazor had owned him before Sisera bought him, so he had been working the general's fields for only one year. Neither he nor Barak had ever spoken to each other beyond the few words necessary in their daily duties.

Starting the following morning, Barak kept an eye on Hananiah like a hawk watching a hare. He sensed the other man also observing him, but they exchanged no signals, not even a nod. Nothing to make the overseer suspicious.

Finally Barak had his chance. They were digging a drainage channel to bring rainwater from some hillside slopes to the terraced fields below. It was backbreaking work, but simple and mindless. Hananiah was one of the men driving the cart full of dirt they had dug up to the lower field where they would use the soil to build up the terraces. Just after Hananiah set off with another load, Barak asked permission to go relieve himself.

"Be quick about it," barked the Canaanite slave who was serving as the overseer's deputy.

Barak headed for a stand of trees. As soon as he was within cover he sprinted through the trees, coming out just above the path that led down to the terrace under construction. He whistled a high, piercing note he hoped could be mistaken for a birdcall. Sure enough, Hananiah, returning with his cart empty, glanced around quickly and then, leaving the cart in the road, ran into the woods to join him.

"What's your plan?" Barak said. No time for pleasantries or preliminaries.

"When we finish digging the drainage channel, they'll take us to a project along the Jordan River. I've been there before—there's a tiny cave not far away. We can create a disturbance—a fight. One of us will get thrown in the river. I can swim a little—you throw me in. In the confusion, you run to the cave. I'll float downstream until I can safely come ashore. The river meanders through a papyrus marsh, and it's easy to keep out of sight there. As soon as possible I'll meet you at the cave. If we hide till after dark, when they've stopped looking for us we can go further downriver."

It was a crazy plan. Overseers didn't quickly give up looking for runaway slaves. They were too valuable, and because of that their owners would keep searching as long as necessary. Barak and the other man could get caught at any time. "Is the cave well hidden?"

"Very. I found it when I was working for my old master. I have to go now."

"I'm with you," Barak assured him.

Yes, it was risky—probably too risky. But Barak was past caring. Dying in an escape attempt was better than a life of slavery. If he was recaptured and brutally flogged—well, he'd been flogged before. Never trying to escape at all would be worse.

Now, for the first time in Barak's life as a slave, he worked hard. Eagerly tossing each shovelful of dirt, he never looked at or spoke to Hananiah.

But one day, on the way back to their sleeping quarters from the worksite, Hananiah deliberately pushed him. Barak tensed, thinking his coconspirator was about to deliver a message. Instead, Hananiah said loudly, "You worthless scum! Your father and all his family were traitors."

Quickly, Barak shoved back. "Traitors? If it hadn't been for your family, our village would never have fallen!"

The overseer swiftly moved to separate them. "Whatever quarrels your people had, there's no place for that here," he said, his tone bored and distant. Such disputes were common among the slaves. "Your old lives are over. Forget them."

Barak shot Hananiah a glowering glance, though he'd like to have embraced him. Now, if they quarreled on the riverbank, the others would remember and find it easier to believe that an old enmity existed between them.

Several more days of hard labor passed before at last they finished the drainage channel. A few of the men managed a weak cheer. Some of them really seemed to consider themselves part of Sisera's household, to care about doing his work well. *Like Joseph,* Barak thought ruefully, reminded of the old story. The faithful slave. *They won't be telling any stories about me,* he thought. He had always resented his master and done as little work for Sisera as possible. *Better to survive and fight again than to be a legend,* he thought. Joseph had trusted God, but Barak had his own kind of trust. The only thing he wanted from Yahweh was his freedom. He wanted Hazor's walls to vanish far behind him, and he hoped his dream would soon become a reality.

Once they had finished the channel, the overseer marched them to their new project along the Jordan. The men rested on the riverbank eating their noon meal—bread and a handful of dried figs. It was a more pleasant spot than the fields where they usually worked, ate, and slept. Everything was a little more relaxed than usual. The men occasionally talked among themselves, though the overseer still kept his eye on them.

Hananiah stood and walked to the river's edge, looking down at the water. Barak got up a moment later and grabbed his shoulder from behind.

His face a mask of anger, Hananiah spun around. "Take your hands off me, dog!" he shouted.

"Take back the name *dog!* If anyone here deserves it, it's not me!" Barak retorted. He could hear voices behind him. The others had noticed the quarrel, and undoubtedly someone was already tattling to the overseer.

"Hey you! Get them apart!" he heard the official order the other slaves.

Just then Hananiah shoved Barak. Lunging forward, his muscles tense with excitement, Barak pushed back, hard. Hananiah lost his footing—the fall was quite genuine, and he'd picked his spot well. He tumbled down the bank into the swiftly flowing water. Barak stood frozen for a moment as the others came up behind him. Then he dove into the nearest bushes. Behind him he could hear Hananiah thrashing in the water, calling for help.

"Someone after Barak! Don't let him get away!" shouted one of the other slaves, one of the overseer's toadies.

But Barak was already darting through the underbrush, zigzagging, avoiding anything that looked like a path. He cursed under his breath as branches snapped, knowing they would leave a trail for trackers to follow. When he broke through and found himself near the riverbank, he stepped onto a large flat rock where he'd leave no footprints, and from there lowered himself into the water. It was frigid, having warmed little since melting from the snows of Mount Hermon. Fortunately—as it was now wandering through a papyrus swamp—the current was not swift.

The papyrus reeds cut off the sound of any pursuit. Only the cries of marsh birds and the sighing of the wind through the papyrus stalks disturbed the silence. Suddenly he realized that he had no idea where this cave was, how far it was from where he'd pushed Hananiah in. This was insane, and doomed to fail. He'd never find the cave. Or maybe there were many caves, and he'd wait in the wrong one like a rat in a trap until they found him. *God of our fathers, don't let them be looking.*

By now he decided that he was well downstream from the area where the work detail had been resting. The riverbank was rocky here and it was easy to see that there might be a cave, or caves. Beyond that, he had no idea where to look or what to look for.

A few minutes later he saw Hananiah standing in the water not too far away. The man beckoned, and Barak waded to the shore. "Up here," Hananiah said, then pointed. Although he saw nothing but the rocky banks, Barak hurried after him. They scrambled out of the water, trying to leave as few traces as possible. Flattening himself into what looked like a narrow cleft in the rock, Hananiah then seemed to disappear. Barak followed his example.

The cave inside was certainly not large, but it was spacious enough for two men to sit close together. And from the outside most people would see no indication that it was there at all.

Barak sat curled up, his knees against his chest. Hananiah squatted facing him. "How did you ever find this?" Barak whispered.

"My old master was a smuggler. They sometimes use these caves to hide goods they're bringing into and out of the city."

"It was good of you—to bring me with you," Barak said.

"I don't know if I could have done it by myself. I thought about it, but one man alone is easier to follow. With two of us, they'd have to split up, and not everyone would be that eager to find us. The overseer will worry that some of them will try to escape themselves while they're searching for us. Sisera's a fool to treat his slaves so badly."

"He is," Barak agreed. "He's worse than a fool. Anyway, thanks."

"Thanks to you too. I saw you fight at Ramah. You were the only one I would have considered escaping with."

Barak did not answer. But he thought to himself that it was incredible that he'd worked beside this man for a year, saying nothing, knowing nothing about him. Now he felt as close to him as a brother—as close as he'd felt to his real brothers, or to Samuel or any other of his friends.

"I heard news of your father, but I didn't dare tell you," Hananiah added. "I learned it before I came to Sisera's house. My old master's slaves weren't so tightly guarded. I didn't have a chance to escape, but we did talk. I'm sorry, but I heard that Abinoam, son of Abinithar, died a few months after his capture."

The knowledge felt like a knife in his throat, and Barak swallowed hard. "All my family is gone, then," he said finally.

"Mine too," Hananiah said slowly.

"If we escape, I'll avenge them," Barak vowed.

The other man said nothing. In the silence, they both listened. After a while they heard the sound of splashing as someone waded downstream. Voices shouted, but they couldn't make out the words.

They waited in the cave till well after dark. Then Hananiah carefully poked his head outside. "It looks safe out here," he told Barak. "No sign of anyone, and the night is cloudy, so no moon."

"What do we do from here?"

"Walk where the shoreline is rocky and deserted, like here. Wade when we come to softer soil where we might leave footprints." Hananiah led the way.

Picking their way carefully downstream took the men several hours, but near dawn the river widened and Hananiah said, "I think we're safe here. We're well past the outlying farms. Look, you can see smoke from Hazor back there."

Barak glanced over his shoulder and saw thin columns of smoke from cooking fires rising in the north. "I'm glad to be well away from there," he said.

"We're not completely safe till we're back among our own people," Hananiah pointed out. "It'll be a day's walk till we get to Kinnereth. Anyone who sees us may want to earn a bounty for returning a runaway slave." Those who saw two strangers wandering by themselves would assume that they were either bandits or escaped slaves and would report them.

Still, Barak and Hananiah felt free as they headed southward on the road away from Hazor. "My old master lived in Hazor, but he smuggled stolen goods from Kedesh," Hananiah said. "It wasn't a hard life, but when he got caught I was part of the fine he had to pay to Sisera."

"Why didn't you speak to me sooner? After you came to Sisera's fields?"

"I was waiting. I could see you were hot-headed and would jump at any chance of escape. But I didn't want to offer you some half-baked plan and risk losing my only opportunity."

Barak smiled, recognizing the fairness in Hananiah's calling him "hot-headed." "I don't know," he said slowly. "This whole plan didn't seem fully baked to me."

"It was safer for me," Hananiah explained. "I knew where the cave was."

A wagon, drawn by a donkey, rumbled northward on the road toward them. "Should we leave the road?" Barak suggested.

"Maybe, though it will be harder going. But not right now. If we do it just as someone approaches, we'll look suspicious."

They walked on toward the small cloud of dust kicked up by the donkey cart. "What will you do when we get back to Hebrew territory?" Barak questioned.

Hananiah shrugged. "Try to trace who's left of my family, I suppose. Move farther south. Stay out of trouble." He paused and glanced at his companion. "That's not your plan, is it?"

Barak shook his head. "No. Whatever I do, I doubt I'll keep out of trouble."

The two men smiled at each other. Again Barak marveled at how quickly a bond of friendship had forged. After two years of trusting no one, of making no friends, it seemed strange to be at ease with another human being.

Bales of woven, dyed cloth filled the donkey cart. An older man drove the cart, while a younger man walked along beside. Barak noted that the younger man was armed with bow and arrows as well as a short knife in his belt. A sensible precaution for anyone carrying valuable goods on these roads, at constant risk from bandits. Still, it made him uneasy. The men were Canaanites. He lowered his head.

"A fine day for traveling," the donkey driver called as they came within earshot.

"Fine day, indeed," Hananiah replied.

The driver appeared inclined to pass without saying more, but the younger man slowed as he approached them. "Where are you bound today?"

"Going south, toward Kinnereth," Hananiah said, keeping his pace steady. They were level with the others now.

"We're bound for Hazor ourselves," the young man said. Then he added, "Not many of your people take this road to get to Kinnereth. Are you coming from Hazor yourselves?"

Everything about us looks suspicious, Barak thought. They were two men in ragged clothes walking alone with no parcels or burdens, on a road leading straight out of Jabin's city, a road rarely traveled by Hebrews. *If we get through this without being caught, we'll abandon the main road and go across country,* he vowed silently.

His heart hammered in his throat, but they were past now, and almost safe. Suddenly the man reached out and caught Barak by the arm. "Too proud to speak to your betters?" he growled, spinning Barak back to face him.

Fighting back panic and anger, he tried to figure out how to respond. To struggle out of the man's grasp, or to throw a punch, would be certain disaster. "Pardon me, my lord," he said in his most servile voice. "We are but poor travelers and will soon be off this road and out of your lands."

"My question has more to do with what you're doing *in* our lands." Barak lowered his head even further, but the man tightened his grip on his arm. "Father!" he shouted. "I think they're escaped slaves!"

"Run!" Barak yelled at Hananiah. When the other slave hesitated, Barak shouted again. *"Run!* One of us must get away, or it's all for nothing."

Hananiah darted away.

Refusing to be taken without a fight, Barak swung at the other man's jaw just as he reached for his knife. The Canaanite blocked the blow but lost his grip on Barak's arm as he did. Then Barak launched a kick at his captor's midsection and sent him staggering back a step or two. The older man was climbing down from the cart. Not waiting to see what happened, Barak used his momentary advantage to take his own advice and run as fast as he could.

Down the road a ways, Hananiah had paused, waiting for him.

"I doubt the old fellow can run much. It's two against one, and we have a head start," Barak panted as he caught up with Hananiah and both men veered off the wagon track and began to run across open ground.

A whistling in the air behind him reminded Barak of something he'd forgotten. The man on the road had a bow. An arrow thudded to the ground, missing the mark but landing frighteningly close. Without speaking, both men began to swerve and veer from side to side, presenting a more difficult target. Barak glanced back and saw the archer notch another arrow to his string as he ran.

Again the whistling sound. Suddenly Hananiah screamed in pain. The arrow had lodged in the back of his leg. His face suddenly white from pain, he sank to the ground.

"Run," he croaked weakly to Barak, who knelt on the ground beside him. "He's coming. Nothing you can do. Like you said—one of us has to get free. *Go now."*

Barak glanced up. The younger man was drawing closer, though the older one still waited on the road. Almost certainly the Canaanite would take his one sure catch—the wounded man—back to Hazor for the bounty, letting the other go free. "But I owe you my life," he told Hananiah.

"Then take it and make something of it. Go!"

"May the God of Israel watch over you," Barak said, springing to his feet.

He heard two more arrows, but they were wide of the mark, and he made good time over the uneven ground, calling into play muscles he hadn't used in two years of farm work. Air rushed into his lungs and past his ears. He didn't stop running for a long time, even though he knew he was far out of reach of the men who had shot Hananiah—who were even now probably taking the other slave back to Hazor to collect their reward. He imagined the fate that awaited his friend. A brutal flogging? Or would he be tortured and killed, his body left hanging in the square as a warning to other would-be runaways?

When Barak finally collapsed from exhaustion in some bushes next to one of the channels of the papyrus swamp, he had no idea where he was or what to do next. He splashed his face and body with water and drank all he could, then lay on the ground, staring up at the empty sky. It was a beautiful, clear blue, and he was a free man again—the thing he'd longed for every day and night for two years.

But all he could see in his mind were the bodies of the dead. Samuel, butchered on the battlefield of Ramah. His father Abinoam wasting away in a slaveowner's field. His mother, brothers and sisters, going to their unknown deaths at Canaanite hands. And Hananiah, the bravest man he'd ever known, bleeding in agony on the ground while facing the sure knowledge of a horrible fate.

Are you out there, God of my fathers? Barak said. *If You are, You have a lot of explaining to do.*

CHAPTER 9

"It's dreadful . . . I can't sleep at nights. I never thought it would be like this." The young girl clasped her arms around her knees as though hugging herself, rocking a little back and forth.

Deborah laid a hand gently on her arm. "It seems as though the pain will never ease, but it will, I promise you. I won't say it will go away altogether—at least, it never has for me. But it becomes easier."

"But you have another child now. I don't know if I ever will." Tirzah's pretty face was miserable beneath the white frame of her head covering.

"That is hard. I will pray for you, and you must pray yourself. Not just that you can have another baby, but that your heart will heal, and you'll be able to look back at this without so much pain. It happened for me, even before my Mirah was born. I know you, too, will also find such healing."

"Thank you so much, Deborah. Everyone else—the midwife, even my mother—told me I shouldn't grieve so, that losing a baby was a common thing."

With a smile Deborah took the younger woman's hands in hers. "Well, what I can tell you is that you are not the first to talk to me like this. Every woman grieves, though perhaps we believe we ought not to."

She watched the girl go down the path between the houses, back to her own family compound, walking just a little taller and straighter. But she didn't have long to stand and gaze. "Mother!" came Anna's cry from inside the house. "Baby's awake! Should I bring her out to you?"

"No, I'm coming in," Deborah said, returning to her own courtyard and climbing the ladder to the sleeping quarters above. Two-year-old Mirah had just begun to toss and whimper on her blanket, and Anna was scooping her up in her arms. At 9 years of age, Anna was very proud of her responsibilities as Mirah's caretaker. But there was one job an older sister couldn't do, and now that Mirah needed to nurse, Anna handed her over to Deborah and sat back with a contented little sigh. "She's so pretty," Anna marveled. "I love just watching her sleep."

"I know. I like to slip in and look at her sometimes too when she's asleep."

Anna rested her chin in her hands. "I wonder if my own mama used to look at me like that?"

Tears sprang suddenly to Deborah's eyes. It was sometimes a surprise to remember that Anna had never nestled in her arms or tugged at her breast as Mirah was doing now. "I remember your mother well, Anna, though I was only a young girl when you were born. I used to see her carrying you so proudly about the village. I'm very, very sure she looked at you in your sleep and loved you just as much as we love Mirah. And may I tell you a secret?"

"Of course," Anna said, eyes wide.

"Even though you are such a big girl, sometimes at night your Papa and I still look over at your bedroll and watch you sleep, and love you just as much."

The girl's face glowed. "I'll go start cooking the lentils for the evening meal" was all she said, but Deborah could feel the child's pride and happiness.

Mirah was too old and too active to be contented for long at the breast, and soon she was squirming free, grabbing handfuls of her mother's clothing and trying to stuff them into her mouth. "You'll get no milk that way," Deborah chuckled, pulling the coarse fabric away from the baby. "Come now, let's go down to the courtyard; there's plenty more work to be done," she said, lifting her daughter onto her hip.

In the courtyard, Anna was busy cooking the evening meal. Deborah sat down at her loom, enjoying the cool shelter of the workroom while Mirah toddled about, playing with bits of wool on the floor. As the loom fell into its familiar shuttling rhythm, Deborah studied the almost-finished two-room house that now faced theirs across the courtyard. Eli, with his father's help, was building it for himself and his soon-to-be-bride. When they returned from working in the fields today the men would put in several more hours' work covering the roof of the little house with branches and reeds. Then they would pack down a layer of clay. Meanwhile, Deborah and Anna were weaving and sewing blankets and cloths for the new home, though their work was light compared to that going on at the bride's home, where her family were preparing her wedding clothes.

Anna also stood looking at the house. Finally she came over beside Deborah, leaving the clay pot bubbling over the fire, and picked up some sewing. "It's so hard to believe Eli's really getting married," she said.

"I know," Deborah agreed. "It seems only a few months ago that he was a little boy taking the goats out to pasture." That was Avi's job now. And it hadn't been a few months. It had been six years since she had come to Lappidoth's home as his bride and mother to his children. Five years since they had moved to Shiloh, four since she had borne and lost her first son. And two years since Mirah had come to brighten their home. Deborah counted off the years, season by season, surprised to realize she herself was now 20 years old. How quickly time flew! Eli's new bride, Keturah, was just 14, while Eli himself was 17, a sturdy young man with a full-fledged beard. Deborah realized she was excited about a newly-married couple and the possibility of new babies. With two dwellings in their compound, they were becoming a real family, settled citizens of Shiloh at last.

Later in the day, after the men had returned from the fields and began working on the roof of the new house, Deborah left the baby with Anna and picked up her two large water jars—one on her head and the other on her hip. She usually let Anna get water in the morning, but in the cool of later afternoon she enjoyed the trip to the well herself, especially the opportunity to meet and talk with the other village women there. Several had gathered already, resting for a few moments under the shade of the trees that grew around the well.

"Hello, sister," an older woman named Hannah greeted. The mother of Eli's bride-to-be, she already considered Deborah a family member. "I passed your house and saw Lappidoth and Eli hard at work."

"Yes, they hope to have the roof finished tomorrow."

"I'll send Daniel over to help after we eat, then they'll be sure to finish by nightfall," the older woman offered.

"But when will the bride be ready to sleep under her new roof?" one of the other women asked. "Is she getting eager for her wedding day?"

"Now, she's a proper, modest young girl," Hannah said, smiling. "She's not over-hasty to be married, but she's prepared to do her duty to her husband and be a good help to her mother-in-law."

"Just hope she doesn't have a baby too soon," another commented. "My poor little Tirzah—she's barely 14, no older than Keturah—and she had such a hard time with that first baby. She's still heartbroken over losing it, and if you ask me, that husband of hers is too hard on her. Did you know he beat her because she let his firstborn son die?"

All around the women let out little gasps or clucked their tongues. Certainly it was a man's privilege to beat his wife if she were unruly or rebellious, just as he would do his children, but most decent men with good wives rarely needed to use that kind of discipline. To punish a young bride for something that was in the hands of God—that had never been her fault—suggested that Tirzah's husband was a brute. Deborah thought back to her conversation with Tirzah that morning. Yes, she'd known something was wrong, something more than the loss of the baby. The girl had almost confided in her, too. But "almost" wasn't enough.

"That man is trouble anyway," still another woman said. "I told you, Michal, it was a mistake to let Tirzah marry a northerner, knowing so little about his people and his family."

Michal shrugged. "He's a priest. What were we to think? They come from all over. My husband was sure any man pledged to the Lord's service would make a decent husband."

"That only shows how little your husband knows," Abira, the wife of a priest herself, muttered. "Priests are only men, when all's said and done. My Aminadab is a good man, but they're not all like that. Even if wives of priests don't talk about their troubles."

Deborah, who had been filling her jars, now set the second one down, brimful, and rejoined the women, whose conversation she had been following closely. Now she addressed Tirzah's mother, Michal, directly.

"Michal, the man may be a priest, but this can't be allowed to continue. Beating your daughter for losing a baby is cruel. The high priest must know if one of his priests is behaving in such a manner."

The women were silent. Some looked away. A few gave her challenging looks. Deborah knew what they were thinking. Husbands and fathers unjustly beat women every day. It might be a sin, but it was one no one but God and other women would ever care about, and only God had the power to punish.

"It may be the right thing to do, Deborah, but my husband would never go to the high priest with such a complaint. What good could he do?"

"The high priest has authority over his priests. He could talk to Tirzah's husband, see that he either stops treating her cruelly or gives her the authority to return to her parents' home."

"It won't happen, Deborah," Abira reasoned. "None of the men would speak out. Not even my husband. How would it look if one of the priests went tattling on another to the high priest?"

"It happens all the time," Deborah countered. "They're like a bunch of children, complaining about each other, jostling for position and ambition. It's nothing for a priest to talk of another behind his back, even to the high priest. What never happens is that no man, not even a priest, ever gets called to account for what he does to his womenfolk. That's wrong. Nowhere in the law does it say a man may beat his wife. Did you know that? If none of your husbands will speak to the high priest about this thing, I'm sure mine will."

Michal looked both ashamed and grateful. "I'm sure it would be a wonderful thing, Deborah, if Lappidoth could do it. I know my husband would never have the courage, but if someone would go to the high priest, perhaps Tirzah's life could be made a little easier."

"Ask Tirzah to come speak with me tomorrow morning," Deborah said. "We will see what can be done for her."

"I'll do that—I certainly will," Michal said. "And may God bless you."

Deborah walked home slowly, burdened not only by the heavy jars of water but also by her new knowledge and the step she had vowed to take. That night, when Lappidoth and the other men had finished working on the roof of Eli's house, she broached the subject to her husband.

"I know I did wrong to promise you would act without asking you first," she admitted. "I can be headstrong when I see someone being treated unjustly, especially when that person has no one to speak for them."

He smiled and took her hand in his. "I'll admit you're headstrong, but if my wife is headstrong in the cause of God, that doesn't trouble me. I feel just as you do, and I'm sure you knew that before you made a promise on my behalf. Also I'm sure that if I said I wouldn't speak to the high priest, you'd go talk to him yourself!"

"I would," she admitted, "but I'm experienced enough to know that a man's words will carry more weight than a woman's."

"Then you speak with Tirzah tomorrow, and the next day I'll seek an audience with the high priest and tell him what we know. He's a fair man and a good leader. I don't think he'll let this pass. And now, my wife, come to bed with me." The children were asleep, the animals fed and watered, the house quiet. Deborah had just finished her time of ritual uncleanliness, and she knew Lappidoth was eager to hold her in his arms again. Now that baby Mirah was nursing only a few times a day, Deborah's monthly courses had returned, and Lappidoth was already asking if she would welcome another baby. He loved Mirah, but Deborah knew he would be proud to have another son.

Tirzah came the next morning and, with tears in her eyes, confessed everything. As Deborah had suspected, the story involved more than a single angry beating. The girl's husband was frequently drunk and had been harsh with her since the day of her marriage. Indeed, as the story unfolded, Deborah thought it likely that the baby's too-early birth and death had been brought on by one of the priest's drunken beatings, though she didn't say so to Tirzah. Instead, she saved up all she heard and passed it on to Lappidoth, who went to talk to the high priest.

Meanwhile, as this small village drama unfolded, preparations continued for Eli's marriage to Keturah. The day came when her family led her from their compound across the village to the courtyard of Lappidoth's house, where Eli waited in his new robe, ready to welcome her into their new house. Lappidoth, Deborah, and their three younger children stood by with gifts for Keturah and her family as they, along with most of the neighbors, crowded into the courtyard.

"For this cause a man shall leave his father and mother, and shall cleave unto his wife," Lappidoth intoned as the pair joined hands. "And the two shall become one flesh."

Amid much laughing, clapping, and dancing, Deborah and several other women got the feast ready to bring out into the courtyard. The family had slaughtered two goats for the occasion and stewed them with greens and couscous. The pungent bowls of stew lay ready on the fire along with bread, raisin cakes, olives, figs, and cheese. The best wine available in the village flowed freely as relatives and friends embraced the new couple and wished them every happiness.

Later still, when everyone had eaten and drunk their fill, Eli and Keturah, along with their families and most of the wedding guests, walked to the tabernacle for the evening sacrifice. Eli had brought along a kid goat as a thank offering, and when he gave it to the priest, he asked for the priest's blessing on himself and his new wife.

"You are Eli, son of Lappidoth, are you not?" the young priest asked.

"I am," the bridegroom said.

"Wait a moment," the priest said, then disappeared.

Moments later, the high priest himself came into the outer courtyard, clad in his splendid robes. "Eli, son of Lappidoth," he said, "let me offer you God's blessings upon your marriage." He placed his hands upon Eli's head. "May your union be blessed by God. May you be fruitful and multiply, as the Lord said to Adam and Eve. May the God of Israel light your way and ease your burdens. Amen."

"Thank you, my lord," Eli said, a little in awe that someone as important as the high priest himself should offer this blessing.

A little later, when the sacrifice was over and some of the worshippers still lingered in the courtyard, Deborah, watching with the women from outside, saw the high priest approach Lappidoth and speak to him for a few moments. Both men glanced over at her, and then the high priest started toward her. The other women moved away a little nervously, leaving Deborah alone to talk to the impressive figure in his flowing robes and jeweled breastplate.

"Deborah, wife of Lappidoth," he said. "The woman who makes the fine lamps that shine by day and night in the house of God."

"I am honored, my lord, to be of service," she replied, bowing.

"Your husband tells me it was your intervention that caused him to come to me about Tirzah, wife of Josiah?"

"It was, my lord. Pardon my brashness, my lord, but the woman came to me herself speaking of her sorrow, and then her mother told me of the beatings she suffered at the hands of her husband, and Tirzah revealed even more with her own lips. I believed you would want to know that one of your priests was acting in such an ungodly fashion."

The high priest was a powerfully built man a little past the prime of life—perhaps in his early forties. His eyes were very dark and they drilled into Deborah with a forceful gaze. "Do you not know, Deborah, that God commanded Eve to submit to her husband, Adam, and said that he should rule over her?"

"I do, my lord. But I also know that God ordained husband and wife to be one flesh, and no man should treat his own flesh as Josiah has treated Tirzah." She kept her eyes lowered modestly as she spoke to him, but could not resist raising them at the end to meet his penetrating gaze full on. He did not look angry, only intrigued.

"Well argued, good woman. But what am I do to in such a case?" His shoulders lifted in a shrug. "The man is a bad priest. He drinks, and his language is careless, and he does his duties poorly. I have spoken to him about these things, and also about his treatment of his wife. In consequence he went home angry with her, and beat her worse than before. What good has it done?"

"I know of this, my lord," Deborah admitted, "and I feared something of the sort might happen. But Tirzah has now gone home to be with her parents, and for the moment is safe from his anger."

"Safe until he comes to claim her again. He will argue it is his right under divine law."

"The law allows a man to write a certificate of divorce for a woman who displeases him, and to send her from his house," Deborah countered. "How can Josiah say Tirzah pleases him if he beats her till she can barely walk? Clearly he does not find her pleasing. A man who has authority over him should tell him so, and explain to him that the best course—the only course—would be to divorce her and leave her at her father's house."

The high priest raised his eyebrows and nodded. "A cunning course of action—and one that makes good sense. If, as you say, there is someone with the authority to make the man see sense. It should be his father's responsibility, but his father is far from here."

"But he is a priest, under the authority of the high priest."

"In the meantime, I still have an unfit and unprofitable priest on my hands."

She smiled. "But that, my lord, is a problem I am sure you in your great wisdom can solve. Unlike Tirzah, you are powerful, and need no advocate to argue for you."

"Tirzah has a good advocate." The high priest was silent a moment. "I shall see the thing done. And I shall watch out for you, Deborah, wife of Lappidoth. Blessings on your house this day." And he was gone.

Deborah went home that night with a light heart. After all, she had many reasons for joy. Her stepson was married, and his wife was a good young woman who would be an asset to their home. All the children were well and healthy, and her husband loved her. Furthermore, she had done what she believed right in the matter of Tirzah, though standing up to the high priest took courage, and she had been rewarded—Tirzah would be freed from her cruel husband. And best of all, Deborah had a secret. The time for her monthly courses had come and gone, and she had not bled. She was almost sure she carried another child. As the family walked back to their home in the pink and gold brilliance of summer sunset, accompanied by the sounds of tambourines and flutes, Deborah felt so light-hearted her feet wanted to dance.

She remembered that light, joyous feeling a few weeks later when she went to lift Mirah from her bedclothes and found the little girl hot with fever. Fever had swept through the village during the past several weeks, taking many of the small children and old people who were too weak to fight it off. As she hugged Mirah's small, sweaty body her own heart chilled. *Oh God, not another one, not another of my children,* she prayed desperately. "Anna, quick! Go find a healer. Rachel, or someone else skilled with herbs and healing. Mirah has the fever!"

The healer came, but Deborah knew from the frown the woman gave as she bent over the child's body that the herbs and potions could do little for the child. The house went untended, the animals unfed as Deborah sat with her small daughter in her arms, pleading silently with God. Children were a treasure from the Lord, but a treasure He too often chose to reclaim, especially when they were very young. Deborah tried to coax her baby's dry, cracked lips to take the breast again, expressing a little milk and dabbing it around her mouth. She and Anna soaked rags in water and attempted to cool Mirah's little face, dripped water into her mouth, trying to get her to drink that. But she lay listless, her usually active little face a blank, her eyes glazed over. Before nightfall she had stopped breathing.

Deborah tore her clothes and began to sob loudly and passionately. Anna, too, wailed. It was left to Keturah to take the child's little body and wash it and wrap it, though Deborah came to help at the last, closing her baby's beautiful eyes for the last time. The courtyard filled with family and neighbors who joined in the mourning, though no one could stay for long. Everyone had much work to do, and other deaths to mourn. During the past weeks Deborah had comforted other women in their grief, but now she was alone at the heart of her agony. The pain was far worse than the loss of her first-born, for this was a child she had nursed and loved and cared for for two years—a child she had truly known. *Oh God, how could You take her from me?*

God was silent, yet Deborah felt a presence like that of another woman, older and wiser, sitting beside her and weeping with her, an arm around her shoulders. Like her own mother would do, if only she were here. Deborah's throat ached with longing for her mother, for someone who could take her in her arms as she herself had rocked Mirah such a short time ago. She comforted herself with the image of being rocked in God's arms, of a motherly God who wept along with women when children suffered and died.

Later, it was Lappidoth who sat beside her and held and rocked her. "I'm so afraid," she confessed. "Afraid for the new baby, the one still inside me. I have borne two children and lost both. I feel as if my womb is cursed."

"Hush now, no such talk. Not every child born on this earth is born to live—we have always known that. But all are precious in the hands of God our Father."

"Then why does He let us grow to love them, only to take them away?" she asked, dabbing at her eyes with the edge of her headdress.

"I think a great many things in this world are not as God would have them be," Lappidoth sighed. "Did God intend for children to die, or wives to be beaten by drunken husbands, or His chosen people to cower in the land He gave them for a heritage? This is not

Eden, my Deborah. God has a greater plan, and we see only a tiny piece of it. Some days, even God must weep."

"I do believe that," Deborah said, and felt again those strong, warm arms around her—arms stronger even than her husband's, arms that felt so real for a moment she thought that if she turned, she would look into the eyes of God Himself.

CHAPTER 10

"For this cause shall a man leave his father and mother, and cleave unto his wife. And the two shall become one flesh." The village priest recited the ancient words over the bowed heads of Barak and Abigail, and the onlookers burst into cheers and song. Barak tightened his grip on his bride's hands, feeling lost and desolate. She and her family were all celebrating. No one understood how those words filled him with despair. How could he leave his father and mother? He should be marrying from his father's tent, bringing his bride home to his parents' encampment. Instead he stood here, the orphaned bridegroom, without parent, grandparent, brother, sister, or anyone of his own lineage to stand beside him. The villagers of Hammath had welcomed him into their homes and into their lives, but none of them—not even Abigail—guessed how deeply the pain of his lost heritage cut into his soul. Of course, that could be because Barak took great care to be sure no one would ever guess his feelings or catch a glimpse of his heart.

Abigail turned her veiled face up to his, and he manufactured a smile for her as he led her toward the feast her family had prepared. Music and dancing filled the courtyard, as did the good aromas of cooked food. There was no smell of meat cooking, however. Once Barak would have considered that odd for a wedding feast, but he'd become used to life in Hammath. Instead of meat on special occasions, the villagers didn't eat it at all. A feast day was one in which everyone got enough to eat.

But men worked in the fields and women spun cloth and children played in the streets—and young couples still got married.

Village life in Hammath went on, rather than coming to a bloody end as it had in Ramah. Even here in Naphtali, living in the shadow of King Jabin of Hazor, it was possible for a Hebrew village to avoid the fate of Ramah or Kedesh. Everyday life could go on—at a price.

People pushed that price to the back of their minds now as the feasting and dancing continued. Abigail's sisters and the other young women, giggling and whispering among themselves, pulled her away from Barak. He let her go without protest. It was no secret that the girls were going off into the forest. In a sacred grove they would sacrifice to Asherah and ask the goddess to bless the marriage bed with fertility. The village took for granted the mingled worship of Yahweh of Israel and the gods of Canaan. It had always been there, of course. But since the town elders had chosen to bow their necks under Jabin's yoke it was far more widespread and open. At least, that's what the old-timers had told Barak. He himself had been here just a little more than a year. The conquest of Hammath—if you could call it a conquest when there'd been no resistance—had happened three years before, not long after the slaughter at Ramah, while Barak was a slave in Hazor. Barak had never known life in Hammath any other way.

Micah, his father-in-law, clapped him hard on the shoulders. "Drink up, my son!" he shouted, pushing a wineskin into Barak's hands. The man had three children living, all daughters, of whom Abigail was the eldest. Delighted to obtain a son, he didn't even mind the fact that Barak had no family. Indeed, an orphan son-in-law was all the better as far as Micah was concerned, for he would have no loyalty to any family but his wife's. Barak had lived in Micah's house and worked his fields with him since his arrival in Hammath, and though his position at first had been that of a servant, marrying Micah's daughter had been a natural step to take.

"You're the quietest bridegroom I've ever seen," Shemiah said, coming to sit beside him. Micah's nephew, Shemiah was a young man of about Barak's own age, who would be not only cousin but brother-in-law in a few years, for he planned to marry Abigail's younger sister as soon as she was ready. The man was the closest thing Barak had to a friend in Hammath. He knew Shemiah sometimes wondered why Barak kept his distance, why their friendship had never become closer. Barak couldn't let him know that he had sworn never again to have a close friend, never to trust anyone or to care too much.

"It's a big day. So much happening," Barak shrugged now.

"Yes, and a big night ahead," Shemiah said, digging him in the ribs with an elbow. "Maybe you're resting up for the hours ahead?" His laughter was coarse, but it was the kind of manly jesting that Barak had enjoyed when he was a boy. Now he felt cut off from all humor or enjoyment. Even at his own wedding. Somehow he managed a smile. "I'm sure everything will be just wonderful," he said. Then the smile disappeared like the light of a blown-out lamp, and his face became shuttered and dark again.

"Have another drink. Make yourself merry, cousin!" Shemiah suggested. "You don't want to look like the angel of death at your own wedding feast!" He leaned closer as he handed Barak yet another wineskin and said in a lower voice, "Are you happy with your choice, Barak? I know you had little say in the matter, but my cousin is a good girl and not bad-looking, either."

Again Barak forced a smile. It wouldn't do for Abigail's relatives to think he was unhappy with the match. "She's a lovely girl, and I know she'll be a good wife. Marriage is a sobering responsibility, that's all."

"Sobering! Well, join me in another drink, and we'll try to clear up some of that soberness!" Shemiah said, and Barak joined him, hoping that maybe a little more wine would blur his discomfort, help him to enjoy his own wedding.

Later, standing at the edge of the crowd of men, he wondered at his own reserve. *Why couldn't I just say this all makes me sad?* he thought. *Shemiah would have understood that I miss my own family on my wedding day, that I wish they could be here. That I can't help thinking about how they died.*

The procession of young women returned from the grove, accompanied by musicians. Abigail danced in the middle of them, the others holding a cloth over her head like a canopy, raining flower petals at her. She was unveiled, but before she returned to the house where the men waited, she replaced her veil over her pretty face and glossy curls. Yes, she was a lovely girl. Barak had lived in her father's house for more than a year and never had anything you could call a real conversation with the girl. But then it was natural that a young girl should be quiet and reserved before her father's hired man. Even before her own betrothed husband. And of course the reserve wasn't all on her side. Barak hadn't really spoken much with anyone since arriving in Hammath. Its people had accepted him and taken him in. They didn't have to do that. Micah's family had hidden Barak and protected him. Marrying their daughter was the least he could do.

Anyway, it was time he was married. No use wondering what he and Abigail would talk about once they were husband and wife. Soon enough she'd have children to occupy her, as well as her work. He'd labor beside Micah in the fields and time would pass. They'd live out a normal life and someday they'd die. End of story.

I'm going mad, Barak thought. *What kind of bridegroom stands watching his bride at the wedding feast and thinking about death? Even stranger, concluding that death won't be such a bad thing when it comes?*

Late in the evening, when they had eaten the feast and everyone was tired of dancing and most of the family had drunk more than was good for them, a noisy procession led Barak and Abigail to the couple's sleeping quarters. The bed had been covered with flower petals and leaves. When at last they were alone, Barak lifted her veil, thinking of the old story of Jacob, who went into his tent after the wedding feast and didn't discover till the next morning that the wrong woman had been underneath the veil all along. The thought made Barak laugh.

"What's funny, my husband?" Abigail said. She really was a pretty little thing, with soft curves and dimpled cheeks. He lifted her hair away from her neck to admire her smooth round throat.

"I was thinking of the tale of Jacob and Leah," he said. "Jacob must have had more than a few skinsful of wine at that wedding feast, not to even know he had the wrong bride!"

She looked puzzled. "I've never heard that story."

"Never mind. It's an old one. About a man who worked seven years to earn his bride and then received the wrong sister."

"Maybe Papa should have made you work seven years for me?" Abigail suggested. She reached down to take off her sandals and curled up her legs with her bare feet lying in Barak's lap. Her toes were like tiny polished stones, small and perfect.

"I've worked a year already, and I'm sure your father will get at least seven more years out of me, but I don't intend to delay claiming my bride," he said, putting his arms around her. Unlike Jacob, he had had just the right amount of wine. Not enough to blur his senses or make him stupid. Just enough to help him relax and stop thinking about his parents and battles and blood and fire for a little while. Long enough to enjoy this lovely young woman who gave herself so willingly to her fine, strong husband.

In the months that followed it seemed marriage hadn't changed his life much. He lived in the same house and did the same work. Abigail was less reserved and quiet with him, of course. In fact, sometimes it seemed she talked too much now. Or maybe it was just that so little she said interested him. Hers was the world of women—of gossip and babies and village life. Although she was a good wife, Barak didn't feel any special closeness or bond to her such as he imagined a man should feel for his wife. But maybe that would come later. When they had children, perhaps. Only a few months after the wedding she told him she was expecting a baby. After that, plans for the coming child seemed to absorb all her time—and all her conversation.

The baby was born after Passover, during the wheat harvest. Barak was working so hard along with his father-in-law, getting in the crop, that he didn't pay much attention when Abigail said the baby could arrive any day now. It was women's business, anyway, and she was surrounded by her mother, aunts, and sisters all day. One morning he left at dawn to work and was greeted at dusk by his mother-in-law running out of the house shouting, "It's a boy! You have a son, Barak!"

He stood for a moment rubbing his head with the heel of his hand, not quite understanding. "I what?"

"A son! You have a son, praise God!"

"Oh, the baby? A boy? That's—that's wonderful! Abigail—is she all right?"

"Yes, she's fine. What an easy birth! I've never seen a first baby born so easily, and such a big, healthy lad too. Come in, come in, see your son!"

Barak climbed the ladder to the sleeping quarters. Abigail lay curled in her blankets, her hair plastered against her face with sweat, her mouth slightly open, breathing softly. She was sound asleep. Curled next to her, in the crook of her arm, his slack mouth brushing against her bare breast, was a tiny, red-faced infant.

Abigail's mother lifted the baby out of her sleeping daughter's arms and handed him to his father. Barak took the small bundle awkwardly. The baby shifted and stirred, opening his mouth a little, but didn't awaken.

Barak walked away from the women, to the front of the room

that lay open to the courtyard. He perched on the low ledge there and tried to settle the baby into a more comfortable position in his arms. Then he looked down again at the sleeping infant and tried to think of something to say.

"Hello, my son," was all he managed. He didn't even know what they were going to name him. Abigail had chattered endlessly about names for the baby, but nothing had sounded right to Barak. He remembered her suggesting, "Is there anyone in your family you'd like to call him after?"

"No." That was all he'd said, shutting that conversation down as he had done so many others. He didn't want the baby to be a living, breathing reminder of everything he'd lost.

"Abigail said you'd probably call him Joel, after her grandfather," Barak's mother-in-law said, coming up behind him. Her approach startled him, but he managed not to drop the baby.

Barak stared down at the infant as names whirled through his mind. Abinoam. Samuel. Hananiah. "Joel is fine," he said, handing the child back to his grandmother.

Baby Joel was 8 days old on the Sabbath, and so everyone was free to attend his circumcision and the feast his grandparents held in honor of the occasion. It wasn't as grand as the wedding feast. If truth were known, Barak thought, Micah and his wife were much more excited about their grandson's birth than about their daughter marrying a landless escaped slave. But harvest was a busy time, and except for the wheat being brought in, food was in short supply. Another big feast was impossible.

This year's harvest was bountiful, but that wouldn't mean good times for the villagers. Soon the overseers would be here. Barak tried not to think about it—tried not to make his son's welcoming feast a copy of his wedding day, when he brooded in corners instead of celebrating. Having a firstborn son was something to celebrate. And didn't it make him part of this community, give him a connection? Maybe now that he had a son, his life meant something.

So Barak drank the wine, held his newborn son proudly, and tried to rejoice. And it almost worked.

Then the Canaanites arrived.

A breathless small boy darted into the courtyard from one of the neighboring houses. "They're coming!" he panted, and no one in the courtyard had to ask whom he meant. The Canaanites showed up every harvesttime, as well as unexpected visits in between. The soldiers collected as tribute a hefty portion of every crop gathered in the village. Sometimes they came on a whim to pluck young men and women from the village and take them to work in the fields around Hazor as slaves. Other times they appeared in the village for no reason at all except to make sure no rebellion was brewing, that everyone in Hammath remained loyal to their Canaanite overlords.

That was the price the village had paid to escape the fate of Ramah. Most of the other Hebrew settlements in the area had responded in the same way. Everyone here seemed to accept it. But Barak couldn't.

Not after two years as Sisera's slave and losing so many good people to his army. The idea that the people of Hammath willingly gave up their children into Canaanite slavery stuck in his throat.

"I'll go," Micah said. The head of each household was supposed to come to the village square and report to the soldiers how much grain they had harvested, and then turn over a large share—usually anywhere from a quarter to a third of it—for the soldiers to take back to Hazor as tribute. The king of Hazor was growing very, very rich from the Hebrew farmers.

Several of the other men left too. Abigail came over to Barak, clutching the baby and looking frightened. "Are you going to hide?"

"I don't want to." Every time the Canaanites came, someone pushed him into hiding in the back of the sleeping quarters. But it made no sense to protest, and he knew it. "I'll take the baby with me," he said abruptly.

Abigail looked confused. "The baby? But—why?"

Impatience battled with his nervousness. "You birthed him, you nurse him, you have him in your arms all day long. He's my son. Just this once, I want him with me. Is that so hard to understand?"

He could see a dozen protests rising to her lips, but she bit them back and obediently handed him the baby, who was awake but quiet. Barak took his son in his arms and climbed up to the roof above the sleeping area. He lay there with the infant beside him, looking over the roof edge toward the town square where the men had begun gathering.

"I hate this," he told the baby, who looked up at him with solemn dark eyes. "Hiding out here like a child or a woman. But what choice do I have? If someone recognized me, they'd have every right to haul me back to Hazor."

He snorted softly. "What hypocrites they are! They scramble to hide me. But when Jabin's soldiers come for slaves, they give up their own sons and daughters." Not willingly, he knew. Families sent older children into the wilderness or hid them in their houses. Yet the soldiers always went away with new slaves. Knowing what kind of life they were going to have enraged Barak. The villagers might try to evade capture, but they would not stand and fight. They would not band together to resist the oppressor.

The baby whimpered. He snuggled into his father, his small bud of a mouth moving blindly against Barak's chest as if rooting for the breast.

His father chuckled. "You'll find nothing there, my son. Here, try this." He offered his forefinger, touching the tip to the baby's mouth. Joel sucked at it eagerly and seemed content for the moment.

For a moment Barak smiled, only to have his brows draw together in a frown. "Someday they'll come for you. For my son. If we keep living this way, if we keep tolerating this. In 10 years, or in a dozen, those sons of dogs will march into our town and try to take you away from me."

The thought of his son as a slave laborer brought an unaccustomed feeling flooding back into Barak's body. It was rage. Rage had fueled him for two years in Hazor, then given him the courage to attempt escape. Rage had driven him on a weary journey to safety after the Canaanite's killed Hananiah. And rage had gotten him to Hammath. But once he was safe in Hammath, in Micah's house, the emotion had deserted him.

He'd been free two years now. Free as long as he'd been a slave—if you could call this freedom. Once he had vowed vengeance on Sisera and the king of Hazor. But for two years he'd actually been bowing his neck to their yoke. Now he had a son—a son they could take from him. The baby, now drifting off to sleep with his father's finger still clasped in his mouth—this small person changed everything.

After about an hour, Abigail climbed up to the roof. She sat down beside her husband and her sleeping son. "Everyone's gone home," she said, nodding down toward the courtyard.

"I know. I heard."

"The priest had to go too. I guess we'll have our son circumcised, but it won't be on the eighth day." She tucked her ankles beneath her. Only eight days after childbed, she already looked pretty and trim again, though she would be encouraged to stay secluded in her quarters with the baby for several more weeks.

"If the God of Israel doesn't mind your Asherah pole and your father's Baals, I doubt He'll get too upset about our son's circumcision being a few days late," Barak said drily.

His wife, he noticed, decided to pout. He'd never criticized their worship practices before. *So she's hurt, is she?* he thought to himself. *Feeling a bit guilty? Well, good. So she should.*

"I just came up to see if he needed to be fed," she said after a little silence.

"He's fine with me. The soldiers haven't gone yet, have they?"

"No, the men are still loading the tribute onto their wagons. I doubt they'll have any reason to come to the houses, though. You could probably come down."

"I think I will," he said, gathering Joel in his arms and standing. "I'm about finished hiding, anyway."

Abigail didn't question his last statement, or even seem to be aware that he meant anything beyond wanting to come down from the roof. He handed her the baby and watched her graceful form as she climbed down the ladder and crossed the courtyard. She was beautiful and obedient—what more could he ask?

But he did want more. Barak felt an almost physical ache for a wife with whom he could have shared his fear, his pain, and his anger. A wife who could talk with him about what it meant to live under an oppressor's yoke and what could be done about it. A memory he had kept tightly shut for years rose to the surface of his mind: his young cousin Deborah talking to him of why God's chosen people must cower in fear before pagan kings.

The Deborah he remembered—a thin girl with a narrow, intelligent face—wasn't half as pretty as Abigail. If he'd seen the two women side by side when he was 14, surely he'd have been drawn to Abigail. But when he was 14, he'd had the rare gift of knowing Deborah for those few weeks. It had colored his view of what a woman could be, or should be. He wondered what had become of her—if she was still alive.

Never mind. Abigail was his wife, mother of his son. That was what counted. Everything else he could endure alone.

But Barak knew that he couldn't do the work alone. He could get by without a woman to confide in, a woman to cosset and care for him. But he had to have other men, other hands to wield the swords that they would have to swing.

In the deepening twilight, family members began to filter back into the courtyard. Shemiah was there, complaining about the share of his crops he'd had to give the Canaanites. *How long will they go on complying and complaining?* Barak wondered. The yoke would only get heavier.

From the sleeping quarters the baby cried. Barak straightened his back. *I'll be cursed before I'll give my son back to Sisera as a slave,* he vowed. Then he crossed the courtyard to Shemiah.

"When you have a moment, cousin," Barak said softly, "I'd like a word with you."

CHAPTER 11

"Come, Anna, it's time to leave. We don't want to wait till the sun is high and we have to travel in the heat of the day," Deborah urged her daughter.

"I'm looking for Japhet's toy," Anna called from the workroom of the house. "He'll get fussy if we don't bring it." She came running out into the courtyard with the wooden rattle that Avi had carved for the child.

"That's very kind of you, Anna. But now we really must get started," Deborah insisted. "Is the donkey ready, Avi?"

"All ready. Mount up, Mama." He helped her onto the donkey's back, and Anna handed her 2-year-old Japhet, who was giggling from excitement.

"And you're not to worry about a thing here at home while you're away," Lappidoth assured her, squeezing her hand. "The crops will get planted, and Keturah will take care of everything in the house."

"Probably better than I could," Deborah agreed graciously. Her daughter-in-law was indeed a fine housekeeper, and as she had no children of her own yet, she would have plenty of time to devote to caring for the men while Deborah and Anna were away.

"I just hope our goats are safe with Lemuel," Avi said darkly. He felt torn between excitement at being the only man to accompany his mother, sister, and baby brother on their trip, and having to leave behind the job of caring for the family's animals. The boy was still young enough to consider looking after the goats a privilege rather than a burden.

As Deborah rode on the donkey's swaying back down the road that ran through Shiloh, she couldn't help remembering the journey she and her parents had taken when she was a girl of 12. This wasn't nearly such a long or arduous journey, of course—just the day's ride back to her hometown of Ramah. But the purpose was the same: to visit her parents and show them their new grandson. Age and ill-health had prevented Deborah's father from making the trip to Shiloh for any of the feast days since Japhet's birth, and neither of her parents had seen him. Deborah sighed softly, remembering that her mother had never seen Mirah at all. But this was no time to brood on what was past. She was a fortunate woman, with her healthy little boy riding in her arms and her two fine strong stepchildren walking on either side of the donkey. *God is good,* she thought.

A little way out of the village Japhet fell asleep, lulled by the rocking motion of the donkey's gait, and Deborah tied him in a sling and dismounted so she could walk a while. The donkey was not as heavily laden as theirs had been on that long-ago journey, but Deborah had packed as many gifts for her parents as she and Lappidoth could afford to spare. God had blessed their harvests the past few years, and she wanted to share what she could with her family. Avi led the donkey while Anna skipped ahead in the road, picking flowers and weaving them into her glossy black hair. The child was becoming a very pretty girl. *She's just a couple of years younger than I was when we went north,* Deborah thought, and remembered that on that journey she had met and been smitten with her cousin Barak and had begun entertaining thoughts of marriage. It was inconceivable that in a few short years Anna, too, might begin thinking about a husband. Inconceivable, but most likely true.

"What are you thinking about, Mama?" the girl inquired, dropping back to walk beside her and slipping her hand into Deborah's.

Not wanting to explain exactly what she'd been thinking, Deborah said instead, "I was just remembering that journey I took to my mother's family in the land of Naphtali many years ago, when I was not much older than you are."

"I remember. You told us about it. Whatever became of all the cousins you met on that journey? Have you ever seen any of them?"

Again, Deborah didn't want to say what came first to her mind. She had never seen any of her northern cousins in the 10 years since that trip, which wasn't unusual, as they lived so far away and travel was difficult. But she had heard no word, no news of them either, only reports that things were bad in the north. "I don't know what's become of them, Anna. I fear their lives have been much harder than mine. It was just at that time that the king of Hazor began attacking the Hebrew settlementss. Life in the north has been difficult and dangerous since then." Word had drifted south with merchants and traders telling of bloody battles, Hebrew men killed, women taken into slavery, villages burned. The worst horror stories, though, came from the early years of Jabin's campaign. More recently, they heard of Hebrew villages living under Canaanite rule—paying tribute to the king of Hazor in order to keep the peace. Peace at the cost of freedom. Deborah remembered her cousin Barak, still a boy of 14 in her memory, brave and fearless. What would he think about living under Canaanite rule? Was he still alive?

She'd made an effort not to think about him during the first years of her marriage, as she got used to her gentle, generous older husband. Thoughts about a handsome young cousin who might have one day made an offer of marriage seemed disloyal. Then, with her stepchildren growing up, her own children being born, and all the work of her home and village to concern her, life pushed romantic dreams from childhood far into the background. She hadn't thought about Barak for years. Now she wondered what had become of him.

"I hope they're all safe," Anna said.

"I hope so too," Deborah replied, but she doubted it.

At noon they rested in the shade at the Palm of Deborah and ate the food they had packed. Other travelers joined them, sharing names, news, and stories.

"Deborah, wife of Lappidoth, of Shiloh," one woman said thoughtfully. "Yes, I have heard of you."

"Heard of me? How?" Deborah wondered aloud.

"My sister-in-law lives in Shiloh—Penina, wife of Isaac the priest? You know her? Yes, she says you are the wisest woman in Shiloh." The woman, round and plump and browned by the sun, squinted at her. "Truth to tell, I'd expected someone a little older. You're very young to be as wise as Penina says you are."

Deborah felt her cheeks coloring. "I don't know where I got a reputation for wisdom. She is being very kind to say so, but I don't think—"

The other woman waved her hands and spit out the pit of a date. "Penina says all the women go to you with their troubles—with disputes they can't settle—and some of the men, too. She declares that you know the law as well as any priest, that you'll stand up for anyone who's in trouble, and that you can solve any problem."

"Oh, I fear that's greatly exaggerated. I try to help where I can, that's all."

"I'm only saying what Penina told me," the woman repeated. Deborah looked down to see Anna gazing up at her with shiny eyes. She wouldn't speak out in adult company, but it was clear she was eager to believe her stepmother was the wisest woman in Shiloh.

Probably just the most outspoken woman in Shiloh, Deborah thought. She found herself unwilling to sit by while she saw people mistreated, the poor oppressed, families and friends divided by quarrels. Proposing a solution was usually no more difficult than settling quarrels between Avi and Anna had been when they were children. A knowledge of the law helped sometimes, but usually a mother's common sense could see a way through most situations. *Any woman in Shiloh could do the same,* she decided. *Unfortunately, I'm the only one willing to intervene.*

Wise woman or not, she felt like a small girl again as she walked up the main street of Ramah that evening, leading her donkey and two tired children behind her, with a sleeping baby wrapped in her sling. Her father's household was still one of the largest in the village, but she didn't recognize the children playing in the courtyard and realized with a start that some of them might be her own nieces and nephews. Her brother was married with two children now, while the others were the children of her cousins.

Her mother rushed out of the house with open arms, looking thinner and frailer than Deborah remembered her. "We've been waiting ever since you sent word you were coming," she said gladly. Others crowded around: Deborah's sister, Dina; her brother, Isa; her favorite cousin Ziri. Aunts and uncles gathered her in their arms and exclaimed over Anna, Avi, and Japhet. Neighbors, too, squeezed into the courtyard, eager to see Deborah. That plump woman with the worried expression—could that be Miriam? And where was her other girlhood friend, Rahel? Deborah asked Miriam as the two women exchanged an embrace and a greeting. "Ah, poor Rahel, she died in childbed nearly two years ago," Miriam answered.

Other familiar faces were missing too, generally from the older generation. The most striking absence, though, was Deborah's own father, Ruel. In the busy hubbub of the courtyard it took her a few minutes to notice that he wasn't there. Fear knotted her throat as she turned to her mother to ask, "Where's Papa?"

"He's resting, Deborah." Relief at the fact that he was still alive was short lived, though—Deborah had never known her father to rest when he could be on his feet.

"Is he ill?" she asked quickly.

"He hasn't been well, these past weeks. Not for months really— he's going downhill. Be prepared, he doesn't look as you remember him. Much thinner, he looks very old."

Deborah knew she should have been prepared. Her father had sent word that he could not visit Shiloh because his health was poor, and he was, after all, more than 40 years of age. An old man. Still, she could only think of him as the strong and energetic person he'd always been.

"I'd like to see him now," she said.

Leaving Japhet in her mother's care, she climbed the ladder to the sleeping quarters. In the darkness she found it hard at first to orient herself. The small flickering light cast by her lamp didn't illuminate the dark corners of the long, narrow room. Then she heard a sound—the rasping breath of someone fighting for air—and followed it to its source.

He lay on a sleeping mat at the far end of the room, as far away as he could get from the noise and bustle of the courtyard. When the light fell on him Deborah had to bend down to be sure it was her father. The strong bones that had always characterized his face now stood out in sharp relief, making him look more severe then ever, for the flesh had fallen away and his eyes stared out of deep sockets. The hair around his face was thin and white.

"Father. Papa. It's me, your Deborah. I'm home."

He put out a frail hand to touch her. The hand trembled as he laid it on her head. She wondered if his mind was slipping away as his body was, but when he spoke, the words, though faint and feeble, were as clear as ever.

"Thank the God of heaven you have come. He has sent you to me in due season. Did you know that I was dying?"

"I—I did not hear it from anyone. But perhaps I knew . . ." She wasn't sure how to explain the deep certainty she had—that it was time to make this trip now and not delay another season. Perhaps it had just been intuition, a fortunate guess. Or perhaps not. "Maybe it was God who told me to come."

"Have no doubt, Deborah—he speaks to us. Not as clearly, perhaps, as He did to the prophets and leaders of old. We need another prophet, Deborah, someone who can hear God's words. His people are slipping away. Our people are being destroyed from within and from without, my child."

She knew what he meant. "I saw the altars on my way into the village. They worship the Canaanite gods openly now?"

"Shamelessly. If I were a younger man I would tear them down with my own hands."

Despite herself Deborah smiled at the image. "The people wouldn't like that, Papa."

"No, but I wouldn't care. But there's no one—I have no son, no nephew who has that kind of courage or conviction." He paused for a long, rattling cough. "You should have been a boy, Deborah."

He'd never said that in so many words before, though she knew he had always thought it. It was hard to know how to respond. In one way she agreed with him, had always envied the greater freedom and choices that men enjoyed. But on the other hand—she remembered giving birth to her children, even the two she had lost. The moment of passion and power when they burst from her body into the world, and the deep joy and strength she felt nursing them at her breast. What man could ever feel as close to God the Creator as a woman did when she took her part in the dance of creation? No, she could not truly echo her father's wish.

"I am only a woman, Father, but I will try to live as you taught me to."

"You'd best go now. They'll want you—down there. Your mother and all the rest. I'm—tired."

"I'll come talk with you again tomorrow, Papa."

Before she slept that night Deborah had made up her mind: she would stay until her father died. It wasn't really that her mother needed her aid so much. The household had plenty of people willing to do their part, helping with meals and cleaning and other work to leave her mother and sister free for the intimate tasks of caring for Ruel, bathing and dressing him, even feeding him on days when he was too weak to do so himself. But Deborah was eager to take her turn at those tasks. She knew she was her father's favorite, rightly or wrongly. He had left a mark on her life no one else could have, though she often feared him and occasionally disagreed with him. It was right that she be here at the end, part of his death as he had been part of her birth and her childhood.

Toward the end Ruel slipped into unconsciousness and only the slow rise and fall of his breath assured the family he was still alive. One morning, Deborah went to check on him before the morning meal and found that he was no longer breathing. It was that simple. No touching deathbed scene, no final words. She remembered the ancient tales of the forefather Jacob, blessing each of his sons with prophetic words before he died. *His must have been an uncommon deathbed,* she thought. Most deaths she had seen thus far were like her father's. By the time breath slipped away and the soul ceased to be, illness had robbed so much that the person no longer seemed to be himself or herself at all.

Two weeks after her father's death, Deborah told her mother, "I think it's time I returned home."

"Yes, your husband needs you, and the children should be in their own place. You know all is well with me." Deborah couldn't argue with that. Her sister Dina, her sister-in-law, her aunts—all were there to assist her mother through the loss. And Mother herself was strong. Deborah had never imagined her parents without each other. Her father's tall, commanding figure had cast a shadow that had always sheltered his quiet, placid wife. Now Deborah saw her mother standing alone, outside that shadow. To her surprise, her mother, though obviously lonely and sad, was capable of standing, perhaps even casting a shadow of her own.

"He was so proud of you, you know," her mother said on the

evening before Deborah's departure. "We both are."

With a nod, Deborah accepted the gift of her parents' pride in her even though she thought she had really done nothing to merit it. She had been a docile daughter, made the marriage she was bidden to enter, and had been a good wife to Lappidoth. That was all she had ever done; but then, that was all that anyone had ever asked of her.

On the homeward journey, Deborah and Japhet, Anna, and Avi again stopped for food, water, rest, and shade at the Palm of Deborah at midday. On this day the area was quiet, with only a couple other travelers present. Deborah was glad for the silence, and gladder still when Anna and Avi took Japhet down to a stream bed to splash and play in its remaining pools. For almost two months she had lived in the heart of her family, with neighbors and friends coming and going constantly. Soon she would plunge back into a similar life in Shiloh. A little peace, a few moments to be alone with her grief, would be a welcome respite.

And she did grieve. Her father had been the most powerful presence in her life as long as she could remember. So unswerving was his insistence on worshipping Israel's God that in her mind, she now saw, she had made the Lord in Ruel's image. She perceived Yahweh as loving but stern, immovable, and impeccably correct. In her imagination He even had Ruel's gray beard, though she wiped that image clean as soon as it appeared in her mind's eye. Surely to make pictures of God in her mind was the first step toward the unthinkable carving of a graven image?

Yet her image of God was graven, she realized, carved deep into the timbers of her heart and unmistakably molded in the likeness of her father. Now Ruel was gone, and with him his insistence on the One God as the center of the world, of all that was made. Deborah thought that in his lifetime she had put down her own roots deep enough into her faith in Yahweh that she no longer needed her father—but perhaps that wasn't true? Without her earthly father, what would happen to the heavenly Father?

Deborah looked to see that her children were still safe, happily playing in the water with the older two keeping a close watch on Japhet. Then she shut her eyes, trying to block out the world, and began to chant in a low voice:

"Hear, O Israel
The Lord your God
The Lord is one
And you shall love the Lord your God
With all your heart,
And with all your soul,
And with all your mind."

Suddenly it did seem that Deborah's whole heart, and soul, and mind, were flooded with God, for through the ancient words of the prayer broke her own inarticulate longing, her need for a Father, for someone who would guide her steps the rest of her life. Although she continued singing the same words, her voice broke and sobs, then tears, flooded through. She kept her eyes closed but behind them was a dazzling light. Deborah felt herself trembling, knew herself to be in the presence of something—Someone—entirely holy.

When she opened her eyes the landscape seemed flooded in something brighter than the light of noonday on a Canaanite plain. No longer did she hear the noises of the children or other travelers, no longer saw the donkey or her packages. Instead, the Palm of Deborah glowed in a strange radiance, and from the blue sky came two words, sung as clearly as if the singer stood beside her: *Beloved Daughter.*

And she felt it then, felt entirely beloved, entirely cared for and cherished in a way her father Ruel had never been able to do. Oh, he had loved her, but his love was cautious, measured, restrained, for to show too much love might invite weakness and indulgence. This love was lavish, even wasteful in the torrent of adoration it poured out on her. Deborah felt warmed from the inside out. This Presence, this God who glowed at her from everywhere, loved her the way she had loved Japhet and Mirah when they were babies, kissing their feet and little faces, nursing them at her breasts. Suddenly she recalled a sense of God's presence she had felt once after her first baby was stillborn. It had felt strong then, though now that she stood in God's very Presence she knew that it had been only a hint, only a whisper. That time, she had imagined God putting a mother's loving arms around her. Now, she was enfolded deep in those arms, taken straight into His heart, and now at last she understood fully why no daughter of Israel needed to bow the knee to Astarte or Asherah. A woman needs a goddess to worship, the other women had told her, but now she was inside the very beating heart of a God who was so far beyond male and female that Mother and Father and every other human relationship was taken up into that Godhood and given back to her a thousandfold. She was utterly certain that this God loved her as her mother did, as her father had, as she loved her children, as no human parent could ever love. This God had created her, a woman, and knew a woman's heart as intimately and surely as a man's, for both were reflections of His own heart. And in the singing joy of this presence, Deborah heard the voice again.

Beloved Daughter, it rang, *I bring you into My presence today not only to comfort you but to call you. I will speak to you again. Not for your own heart alone, but for your people. I will speak to you, and you will bring them my words, and teach them of Me, and do My work.*

"I, Lord?" Deborah said aloud. "But I—what can I do? I have no talent, no skill, no one will listen to me . . . just a wife and mother, a common woman of Shiloh."

Beloved Daughter, the voice said again. *Heed My call. Do not shut your ears.*

"I am listening, Lord!" she called, throwing her arms up toward the sky, and once again she was overwhelmed, shivering from head to toe as the bright glorious presence of God filled her. The world around glowed, shimmered, blazed.

And then the light faded. It was as if she had stared into a flame and then turned to look at the common world. She stood before the Palm of Deborah, which appeared as just a large, ordinary tree bathed in the sunlight of a summer day, nothing more. The children were running back from the stream. Everyday sounds and sights had returned. Nothing was changed—except Deborah herself.

Avi carried Japhet on his shoulders. Anna ran a little ahead and came up to Deborah's side.

"Mama, are you all right? You're shivering." The girl looked closely at her stepmother's face. "You've been crying," she said softly. "You must miss your papa very much."

Deborah nodded, though grief seemed an unreal and distant emotion now. She wanted to tell the girl what she had seen and heard and experienced, now while it still blazed inside her, before the joy and terror seeped away into ordinary life. But no, she must tell Lappidoth first. And then someone else, someone who would know what it meant, what she was supposed to do. She knew of no prophet among

God's people. The high priest, perhaps? He might be able to help her.

When she returned home, there was such celebration among the family, so much visiting of neighbors and sharing of news, that it was nighttime, and she lay with Lappidoth in their bed before she had a chance to speak to him.

"Something happened to me at the Palm of Deborah today, my husband," she said softly, not wanting to wake the children who slept around them. "I was alone, weeping for my father and praying, when I had a vision. I felt I was in the presence of God Himself, and He called me His beloved daughter. And then He told me He would speak to me again, and give me messages for His people." Lappidoth was silent, and Deborah gave a half-hearted little laugh. "I know, it sounds insane. But it was so real at the time, my love. Everything shone with a holy light, and I could see nothing except the tree and the sky and feel the presence of God—oh, it felt so real, and I was so sure. I wanted it to be real. It was like nothing else—no, it was like being at the sanctuary, in worship, feeling God's glory—but a thousand times more so. Closer. At the very heart of God." She broke off again. "I can't explain. Yet it was so real. Do you think I'm crazy, Lappidoth?"

Reaching out toward her in the darkness, he stroked her hair. "No, you're not mad, Deborah. I've lived with you eight years, and I know you're less mad than any woman I've ever seen. God has spoken directly to prophets and prophetesses in the past. Why not now? If He were to speak to anyone, why should it not be you?"

"Prophetesses? He has spoken to women, too?"

"Miriam, the sister of Moses. Was she not a prophetess?"

"Yes, she was," Deborah said slowly, then felt a rising river of excitement sweep away the barrier of doubt that had held back her inner certainty. "Could it really be, Lappidoth? Could the Lord have chosen to speak to me?" But even as she voiced it in the form of a question, she knew she had no real doubt. She had stood in God's presence that morning, had heard His voice. It was awesome and it was terrifying, but it was not to be lightly dismissed.

"You should speak to the high priest," Lappidoth suggested. "He is a wise man and will be able to guide you."

"Yes," she agreed, "I'll ask to see him."

It was a few days before she received an audience with the high priest. She had not spoken to him face to face since that day earlier in the summer when she had intervened on behalf of Tirzah. Would he remember her as an interfering busybody?

His smile was warm, though, as she approached him in the outer court of the tabernacle. "Deborah, wife of Lappidoth. Our skilled lamp-maker, I believe."

"One of many, my lord. I am honored that you agreed to speak with me."

"Your husband tells me you have had an unusual experience."

Carefully, she told him what had happened. She had thought her story through more coolly now, tried to frame it in words in a way that would capture something of what she had seen, heard, and felt more convincingly than the broken phrases she had used with her husband. The joyous excitement of that day had ebbed away by now, but she still felt the inner core of certainty, the knowledge that what she had experienced was real and enduring.

The priest listened silently, nodding a little. "And you heard a voice—an actual, audible voice?" he probed when she paused.

"I did. At least, it seemed audible to me at the time. My children were not far away but they heard or saw nothing unusual. But to me the voice seemed to speak aloud."

"What did it sound like?"

Deborah was at a loss to describe the voice that still rang so clearly in her memory. "It sang, I think, more than spoke. I really couldn't connect it to— I mean, I couldn't say that it sounded old or young, like a man or a woman." She saw the start of surprise in the priest's eyes: it wouldn't have even occurred to him, she supposed, that God' voice could be anything other than male. "It was— not human. But a voice. I could understand the words clearly." She repeated them for him a second time.

Again the high priest was quiet. He folded his hands behind his back and paced a few steps away from her. Then he turned back. "To whom have you spoken of this?"

"To my husband and to you only, my lord." She felt a wild panic. Was he going to tell her it was all a delusion, that she must never mention it to anyone? For a moment it seemed that loss would be as great as the loss of her dead children.

"I would be cautious, Deborah, for there are delusions, but you do not strike me as a woman to be easily deluded. I cannot be certain—for you see, I have never heard God's voice. I am no prophet." He looked sad. "I have certainly had experiences, here in worship, in the house of God, and especially in the Most Holy Place—well, I cannot speak of that, you understand. But I have felt myself in God's very presence, and it is as you describe. I could not find words for it, but I have felt the same things you speak of. I believe God has spoken to you, Deborah wife of Lappidoth."

She was silent, grateful, unable to say more for the moment. The high priest was only a man and not a prophet, as he had pointed out himself. Yet his assurance that what she had described was akin to the unspeakable things he had experienced beyond the veil in the Holy of Holies gave her the seal of certainty she needed. The vision was genuine. She had heard God.

Now he peered at her more closely. "Have you told me all the Lord said to you? Was there any particular message—a message for His people?"

"No, nothing. But He said He would speak to me again, and give me messages."

The high priest gazed at her with a long, level stare. "When He speaks to you again, come to me."

"I will," she promised.

CHAPTER 12

Barak rolled over and lay on his back. The ground was hard underneath him—rock barely covered by the faintest layer of moss—but the sky above was breathtaking. Thousands of stars punctured its blackness. A slender sliver of new moon shed almost no light. That was fine for his purposes. His 30 men had camped on the hillside across the valley from the city of Hazor, and darkness was their ally.

They would attack a few hours before sunrise, when all was most still. The small cluster of men and pack animals by the roadside below had set only one man as watch, for there was little danger. The king of Hazor and his general Sisera controlled the roads. In recent years there had been little to fear even from bandits.

Now, Barak thought, *the bandits are back.* He smiled to himself in the darkness, a feral grin that would have made anyone watching uncomfortable. Tonight was the final step in his transformation. In a few months he had gone from an ex-slave, a respectable husband and father and farmer in an occupied Hebrew village, to the leader of a band of outlaws. It hadn't been an easy journey, but he'd enjoyed every step along the way. And that was more than he could say about anything he'd done in the past five years—the long empty years since Ramah. In five years, the only time he'd felt this alive was during the day and night following his escape from Hazor. The same intense energy that had kept him honed then thrummed through his body now. He felt like a taut bowstring.

Four of the men in his company came from Hammath. His wife's cousin Shemiah was not among them. In fact, he thought Barak was insane even to talk about resisting the Canaanites, let alone striking back at them. Micah, his father in law, had tried to talk sense to Barak.

"You've lived among them, you've been their slave. Since you fought them at Ramah, you have seen what they do to towns that resist. Why would you suggest we commit suicide by drawing our swords and refusing to pay tribute?" Micah had reasoned.

"Because some things are worse than death. Living under Sisera's heel is worse."

The older man had given him a long look. "You think the fate of Hammath is worse than that of Ramah of Naphtali? In Ramah, the streets are empty. Here we farm our fields, build our houses, marry our women, and raise our children."

"Yes—raise your children to be handed over as slaves in Hazor!" Barak spat back. "I hold my son—your grandson—in my arms, and I am ashamed to live in a village that would even consider giving him up as a slave to our enemies!"

Micah sighed. "We do not do it willingly—you know this. But would it be so much better if we were all dead? I hardly think so."

"Everything you say makes sense, Micah, but there is a knowledge beyond sense. This is in my bones. It is time for me to stop bending the knee. A time to fight."

"And what will become of my daughter? Have you married her only to abandon her, and your son?" his father-in-law challenged. "Be sensible, Barak, as you have always been since you came to us.

None of us enjoys living in bondage. But we like living. Someday, our God will deliver us. Until then, we must be patient."

That was when the lid blew off Barak's temper. "And how exactly do you think our God will send deliverance? Is He going to thrust it in front of our noses? Men have to go out and fight before they can be delivered!"

"Oh, so you imagine yourself another Ehud, do you?" the older man shot back. "Are you sent from God to be our deliverer? Have you been receiving messages from on high?" As Barak stood silent he hammered the point home. "Or is this just your own rebellion, because life seems a little dull and you're afraid you'll die before you've had anymore excitement?"

Well, he was ready for excitement. And no, Barak thought, now glancing up into the night sky, he hadn't heard any voices from God. When Yahweh wanted to talk, Barak was more than ready to listen. The certainty he had now, which had driven him to recruit a handful of desperate, angry men from Hammath and other nearby villages, came not from a God outside but from a burning inside.

"Is it time yet?" a voice next to him growled, and Barak turned to find himself looking into a hairy face. This man had fled the town of Kinnereth after being accused of trying to murder one of the Canaanite agents who came to collect tribute. He was unbalanced, a little crazy, violence simmering under the edge—not a comfortable ally. But he was the kind of man Barak needed.

"Yes, get the men ready." There was little to do—no camp to break, no tents or bedrolls to put away. Their main camp was 10 miles away, in a cave in the mountains. They had marched here today with their weapons and what food each man could carry in a pouch at his side. No beasts of burden, none of the usual clutter that slowed an army down. But then they weren't an army—just bandits.

All day they'd waited for the tribute caravan, the wagons laden with summer fruit from the Hebrew villages, to wend its slow way north. Barak had picked the spot they were likely to stop for the night, and they had obligingly halted there. Their scouts had seen no sign of Barak's men, who had become good at hiding.

All around, Barak's men got slowly and quietly to their feet. The watchman on guard by the dying fire in the campsite below was looking in the opposite direction. Barak couldn't be sure in the dim light but he thought the man was nodding sleepily. Pulling his sling from his belt, Barak fitted a stone, readying it.

"Now," he breathed.

One young man—Nathan from Rimmon—stepped forward, his sling swinging slightly by his side. For a small band of outlaws slings were a better distance weapon than the large and costly bows and arrows. Stones were plentiful, slings small and easily carried—and extremely effective. Nathan moved down the hillside several paces ahead of the others, stopped on a small outcropping, and took aim.

The stone whistled through the still night air, curving a perfect arc as it descended down into the Canaanite camp. Barak would have liked to do this part himself. It galled him to admit the man was actually a better shot than he was. He told everyone he'd let Nathan do it because Barak himself would need to stand back and watch what happened, be ready to command the others. Everything depended on this shot, on whether it hit its mark, whether it killed or merely wounded.

It was perfect. Barak saw the stone hit the watchman squarely in the back of the head, and the Canaanite dropped without a cry. "Now," he commanded. "And silently!"

Quietly, the men swarmed down the hillside. The watchman had fallen without opportunity to give a warning, so everyone had time to spread out in a circle before Barak shouted. "Beware, men of Hazor! You are surrounded!"

Surrounded they were, and badly outnumbered, for there were no more than a dozen men in the tribute caravan. Shouts and cries rose from the tents as men began stumbling out. Barak himself took aim and hit the first man as he drew his sword, not killing him but knocking him to the ground.

Then battle was joined. Barak tucked away his sling and rushed forward with his sword drawn, goring the first Canaanite who approached. His opponent was little more than a boy, obviously poorly trained, and Barak scooped up his iron sword as the young soldier fell to the ground. They'd get a few decent weapons, and pack animals too, from this night's work.

Another Canaanite lunged at him—an older, tougher man. If Barak hadn't had the iron sword he'd taken a moment ago he might have been outmatched. For weeks he'd drilled his men and himself relentlessly, feeling his muscles toughen and all his fighting skills come back after the long years of disuse. Now, crossing swords with a real enemy who wanted to kill him, hearing the ring of iron striking iron and shifting his feet in the well-remembered dance, Barak felt something like joy. The Canaanite's heavily bearded face became Sisera's face, the face of every soldier who had fought and killed at Ramah. *"And you shall drive them out of the land, and possess the land,"* Barak thought, the words of the law singing in his blood. He thrust his sword into the other man's gut, and the enemy crumpled to the ground.

Barak looked around in the darkness and saw that the advantage of numbers was taking care of the enemy for them. Only a few Canaanites remained standing, and each one desperately fought off two or three Hebrews. Barak never got to draw his sword again. The battle ended within minutes.

All the enemy were dead. Barak had ordered even the wounded killed. No mercy.

Not till they explored the wagons did Barak's men discover three shivering, terrified Hebrew boys, none more than 13 years old, tied in the back of one of them. He personally cut their bonds. "You'll be going home tomorrow," he told them, "as free men." Of course, he knew all three. One was Abigail's young cousin. The boy's father had told Barak to his face that he was insane to rebel against Hazor, to refuse the tribute. The men of Hammath had practically driven Barak and his four allies out of town, telling them to cease their dangerous talk.

For a moment he felt tempted not to return the tribute—to take it to supply his own men, letting the three would-be slaves walk back on their own. But no. Returning as the conquering heroes, magnanimously bringing back both tribute and slaves—well, Barak knew what that would make him in the eyes of the people of Hammath. He saw himself riding back in one of the carts with the whole entourage in tow, presenting the boys and the grain to the village elders, and imagined Abigail looking up at him with shining eyes, her father glancing away shamefaced.

And the return to Hammath went as perfectly as if he'd rehearsed it. Behind him, his men led the donkeys and drove the other wagons. The boys who had been destined for slavery walked proudly behind Barak, almost giddy in their relief and excitement.

They traveled as slowly as the caravan had done originally, and they kept watch to the rear for armed men from Hazor, but apparently it was too soon for anyone to notice or question its late arrival.

Soon enough someone would find the butchered bodies by the road-side and the trail would lead to Hammath. But Barak would be ready.

At dusk on the second day they entered the village. The boys herding goats on the outskirts of town ran at their approach, no doubt wondering why the Canaanites had returned. Barak called out to one boy he knew. "Joshua! Go into Hammath and tell your fathers, all of you, that your tribute has come home again. And so has Barak, son of Abinoam, son-in-law of Micah!"

By the time they arrived there people lined the narrow street. The elders of the village waited by the well, Micah among them. "What has happened?" the oldest among them said.

Barak dismounted from his donkey. "What happened, honored father, is that we met the tribute caravan on the road to Hazor and slaughtered every one of them." He raised his sword above his head and jumped to the edge of the wall surrounding the well so he could better speak to the whole crowd. "Thirty Hebrew men went out and 33 came back," he shouted, "for we brought back your sons that you had given up to the oppressor! Not one drop of blood was spilled save the blood of the Canaanite dogs!"

A cheer started, and built in power. Barak beckoned the boys to step forward and show themselves before returning to their parents. Then he motioned to the other men who had joined him here in Hammath. All, like himself, had been branded as fools by their wives and families. Together they stood with swords upraised, and the crowd applauded them. When the noise died down, Barak spoke again.

"The animals my men and I will keep for our own use. The wagons and all they contain we return to you. Take back your own again! All I request is what I asked when I left here three months ago. Who will come with me? What men of Hammath will take up the sword against our oppressors? For this battle today is not an end but a beginning. Soldiers from Hazor will follow us here, and we will fight them—and again and again, till the enemy has been driven out and the land is ours as the Lord God promised!" Another cheer. He felt lifted on the rising tide of the crowd's enthusiasm. "Whether the village elders of Hammath choose to bow beneath the yoke and pay tribute again is their own concern. If you do not desire us here, we will go where we are wanted. But I ask the young men of Hammath, who is with me? Who will stand and fight rather than bend the knee?"

Men began to step forward, one after another. Shemiah, Barak saw, was among them, and met his eye with a steady gaze. A dozen men—no, more, a score—pressed toward him, and at last the oldest of the three boys who had been marked for slavery that morning joined them and stood before him. Barak heard the boy's mother cry "No!" as if her heart was being torn from her body.

Now Micah stepped from among the elders. "Barak, my son, we owe you a great debt. Tomorrow you may have to fight again, but you will have new hands to wield the sword with you. But tonight we hold a feast in honor of you and your men. Will you eat with us?"

Barak grabbed his hand. "Yes, my father, we will break bread together tonight." He had come crawling as a fugitive to this man's house and received shelter, work, and a daughter to wed. For years Barak had staggered under the weight of gratitude. It was good to know that the balance of power had shifted.

Within an hour the square was full of the smell of roasting food, of music and dancing. Abigail danced up to him. Her eyes shone, just as they had done when he had imagined this scene.

"You were wonderful!" she gushed. "A true hero."

"I did it for my son," he said. "May I see him?"

"He's asleep now, with my mother at our house. You'll see him in the morning; you are staying till then, aren't you?"

"We'll take the road again at first light," he said, raising the wineskin to his lips.

"So you'll sleep here tonight," she pressed, laying a hand on his chest.

Taking her hand, he covered it with his. "Yes. Tonight."

"I'll go home," she said. "I'll prepare our bed for you. Come find me when the feast is over." And she danced away from him, her face glowing.

Barak thought of her bitter farewell when he'd told her he had to go, of her tears and accusations. He would go home in an hour or two and bask in her admiration. In the bed she was preparing, Abigail would welcome him as a conquering hero. Her adoration warmed him, yet he recognized how easily it was won and lost. Having been three months without a woman, he wanted his wife again, but deeper than that was the old longing for someone who might truly understand what tonight meant, what it had cost, and what a long road lay ahead.

Tossing aside the wineskin, he wiped his mouth with the back of his hand. Every muscle in his body was weary. It had been a hard few days, but good. Again he replayed the scene of the fight, of seeing Canaanites die at his hands. Just as his father, his mother, his best friend had perished at Canaanite hands.

The musicians changed the beat. The men were forming a line for a triumphant dance through the streets. "Come, Barak!" they called. "Our fearless commander! Lead us in the dance as you led us in war!"

Barak threw back his head and laughed, then took his place at the front of the line. When the dance ended, he'd go home to Abigail. He'd go home and thank God for what he had.

CHAPTER 13

The rains had ended for the day and the air smelled as fresh as a child's newly washed hair. Deborah sat by the well surrounded by a group of women, all of whom had laid down their water jars. "My husband works so hard at the time of the barley harvest," one woman was saying. "And today is the preparation day. I know he'll find it difficult to come in before the sun sets, then stay away from the fields all day tomorrow."

"Mine, too," another woman said. "Deborah, is it really so wrong to go into the fields on the Sabbath? Those who worship the gods of Canaan have feast days and festivals every season just as we do, but they don't have to cease work one day in seven. It seems too much for our God to ask."

"Maybe it wasn't too much in the days of Moses," an older woman offered, "when the people dwelled in tents in the wilderness. My own people lived in tents when I was growing up, and beyond feeding and watering the animals it's no great hardship to take a day's rest. But things are different for farmers, people who live off the land. If it's harvesttime, say, and the crop has to get in, and a storm is coming or a swarm of locusts have swept out from the desert, are we really to cease work just because the Sabbath has come?"

All the women looked at Deborah, who had said nothing so far, only sat listening. Now she said, "Yes, the God of Israel does ask for one day in seven. It may seem that He requests a lot, and no, it is not always easy when there is so much work to do. Yet look at it another way. Our God is the only one who *gives* us one day out of seven."

"Gives it? I could use another day, if it meant another day to do my work, but not a day taken out of my work," said the same woman who had just spoken. "If God is going to offer me a gift, let it be more time to get everything done." The women around her laughed in agreement.

Deborah smiled too, but said, "What kind of gift would that be? One more day for you to labor and toil, to drive yourself into the grave with work. Our God offers us one day free from work, one day to say that we are something more than animals concerned only with food and survival. One day to lift our thoughts and our hearts to Him. It's a strange gift perhaps, but look what He is saying! One day to say we are more than our work. Though our fields and our crops and our cattle and our homes are important, they are not all that we are. Our lives are more than the total of the days we work. They are the Sabbaths too, the days God sets aside only for ourselves and Him."

"I never thought of it like that," one of the younger women commented.

"I see what you mean, Deborah," another observed. "On Sabbath, when I go to the services at the tabernacle with my husband and hear the singing and the words of the law being read, then I feel for a moment that there is something more to life than grinding the grain and making the flour and baking the bread, then eating the bread and washing the dish and starting all over again tomorrow."

"Exactly," Deborah said. "That's what I meant." Before she spoke, when the women were discussing how hard it was to refrain from working on the Sabbath, she hadn't known what she was going to say, except that she disagreed with them. And when they turned to her with expectant eyes, and she opened her mouth, the words were suddenly there. The whole clear idea, of Sabbath as a gift, a day to be something more than the sum of a man's or a woman's toil, came to here as a piece. It was an experience with which she was becoming more and more familiar.

As they left the well, young Tirzah fell into step behind her. "I spoke to the priest, as you said, about remarrying," the younger woman stated. Four years had passed since Tirzah's husband Josiah had put her away and she had returned to her father's home. Now Benjamin, another young man in the village, had asked her father's permission to marry her. Tirzah and her parents had come to Deborah for advice: the girl's husband had divorced her, but she had committed no adultery. Was her marriage truly broken, and was she free to remarry? On that occasion Deborah had received no sense that the Lord had a message for her to give, and had honestly told Tirzah the only thing she could—that the priests were the experts in divine law, and they were the ones to consult.

"What did he say?" Deborah asked now.

"He said the words of the law only made it clear that a man could put his wife aside and that the wife could remarry—though she could not marry the same man again. As if I'd ever wish too!" Tirzah added with a shudder. "But he said he thought the *meaning* of the law was that the woman would have committed adultery, so he could not assure me that I was free to remarry, and he certainly would not advise me to go out and commit adultery so I would truly be divorced!" Tirzah blushed a little. She was extremely fond of the man who had proposed marriage and eager to wed again. "Then he told me I should speak to you," she added.

Deborah raised her eyebrows in surprise but said nothing. She guessed Tirzah would have been unwilling to admit to the priest that she had actually sought Deborah's counsel first. But the priests seemed to accept the fact that the villagers—most of the women, but some men too—brought their disputes and their problems to Deborah, swearing that her counsel was so sound it must come straight from Yahweh.

But she didn't claim to have direct guidance from God on every question people asked. In fact, she had told no one except Lappidoth and the high priest about her vision at the Palm. In all the months since, she had not received another such vision. Her life as Lappidoth's wife, keeper of his home, mother of Japhet and Anna and Avi, maker of lamps, had continued much as before. Except that her reputation as a wise woman, a source of good counsel, had blossomed like wildflowers in spring. Suddenly people of all kinds were turning to her for advice and guidance. And more and more, that strange sense of certainty seemed to accompany the words that sprang to her lips and the thoughts that filled her mind at such times, as if God were giving her wisdom, not in the form of glorious visions and voices from the sky but in a quiet knowledge that grew from within.

They had reached the courtyard of Deborah's home. As Tirzah turned to say farewell, Deborah felt the word *Wait* imprint itself on her mind as clearly as if she had heard it. "Wait," she said, and tried to listen with her inner ear and see with her inner eye. Was this a message from God?

Wait, she felt again, and saw in her mind an image of Tirzah, flower-garlanded, a happy bride. From the blooms the girl carried Deborah realized that the barley harvest had passed and the wheat harvest had begun. And that was important—the time.

"What is it?" Tirzah asked. She didn't sound alarmed, so Deborah knew she had shown no signs of going into a vision as she had at the Palm. It hadn't been like a vision, yet it was something more than her usual quiet knowing.

"Tirzah," Deborah said slowly, "I don't know why, but I think the Lord is telling you to wait. Not for long—but wait till after the Passover, at least, before you say yes to Benjamin. Things will become clearer to you, I think. I believe you will marry, and happily—but you must wait."

Although she looked confused, the girl said, "I can wait. I will tell my parents—and Benjamin—that you think it best to wait. Perhaps the Lord will reveal more to you—or to us—before then."

Still a little awed by the trust others placed in her words, Deborah nodded. She could, after all, be making it all up, manipulating people with messages she claimed came from God. It wasn't hard to see how a false prophet might gain acceptance. In Tirzah's case, though, there would have been no desire to twist the truth. Deborah wanted to tell her to go ahead and marry, to be happy. And she felt that it might well be the truth, though the law was not clear about it. But for now, she was sure God's message was simply: Wait.

Inside her own compound, she found Anna and Keturah preparing the evening meal. Deborah brought them the water and then went to find Japhet, who was spreading clean straw for the goats who would soon return from the pastures with Avi. At 3 years of age, Japhet was proud to be able to do small things to help around the house. His mother helped him finish laying the straw, then scooped him up and carried him off to the courtyard where she scrubbed him down thoroughly with a cloth soaked in the water she'd just carried up from the well. He squirmed and wriggled while she washed him, then threw his arms around her. "I love you, Mama."

"I love you too, my son," Deborah said from the bottom of her heart.

Japhet was older now than Mirah had been, past the first three dangerous years during which so many children perished. Deborah was finally beginning to believe he would live; that this child at least would be hers to keep. He seemed likely to be her last. Though her monthly courses still came regularly and she and Lappidoth still bedded together, her womb had not quickened to life again since her son's birth. There was still time for another, of course, if God willed it. She was not yet 24 years old. But if Japhet was to be her last child, she prayed all the more fervently that he would continue to be as healthy and well as he was at this moment, careening across the courtyard from his mother's arms to those of his older sister.

Just then Lappidoth and Eli entered the courtyard, accompanied by Avi, the goats, and two strangers. "We met travelers on the road, Deborah," Lappidoth told her. "They told me they were looking for lodging in Shiloh, and I explained that there is always a place by our hearth-fire."

"Certainly," Deborah said, rising and going forward to greet the man and woman who stood by her gate. "When I said my wife was Deborah daughter of Ruel from Ramah," her husband continued, "this lady had a great interest in meeting you."

Deborah bowed to the strange man and to the woman beside him, whose head covering did not adequately hide an abundance of dark curling hair. Her skin was darker than Deborah's, and her dark eyes, fringed with long lashes, were vivid and lively. She was a small woman, much shorter and slenderer than Deborah and a few years younger.

"I knew a Deborah, from Ramah in Benjamin, when I was younger," the woman said. "I wanted to know if it was you; but I see it is."

Deborah had no idea who the visitor was, and when the man introduced himself as Heber the Kenite from Naphtali, she was no more enlightened. The Kenites were related to the Hebrews but not part of the 12 tribes of Israel. Their lands were in the southeast, and she had no idea any Kenites lived in Naphtali.

"My wife is Jael, daughter of Abiathar," the man continued. "She is a kinswoman of yours, I believe."

"Jael!" Deborah remembered her now, the little girl from her grandfather's encampment. The one who was so wild and always wrestled with the boys. She looked much tamer now, dressed as a demure young wife. But a grin that looked decidedly not demure peeped out at Deborah and for a moment the little girl was there again, dancing behind the young woman's pretty eyes.

They embraced, and almost at once Deborah drew away and became serious. "Jael," she asked as she led them to the fire, "what has become of our grandfather's family? I went home recently to visit my mother, and she has had no news of them. That visit 10 years ago was the last we saw or heard of our family in the north. Here in Shiloh word occasionally reaches us of the fighting up there, and of King Jabin's rule over the villages of the north, but of my own family—nothing."

Jael, too, sobered at once. "Oh, Deborah, what a tragedy it's been." She sat down by the fire and accepted the cup of milk that Anna pressed into her hands. "Our people moved to Ramah in Naphtali, of course, and tried to defend ourselves there. But when Sisera attacked that city, his troops slaughtered almost everyone." She closed her eyes as though trying to shut out painful memories. "My mother and sister and I, along with some of the other women, were sent away into the wilderness before the Canaanites attacked, for we knew what they did with women they captured. What an irony—we left our tents in the plains for the safety of a town, then fled the town to live in tents again! But we escaped the fate of those who stayed behind. Many of our menfolk—my father, my uncle Abinoam, his son Barak, countless others—were never seen again after the battle of Ramah. Either they were killed or they were taken captive, which would be a worse fate. Sisera's men put Ramah to the torch. When they had gone, long after, we returned and found some of the bodies—our grandfather, some of the other older ones, the uncles and aunts."

"How terrible," Deborah breathed. She felt Lappidoth sit down nearby and place a hand on her shoulder. While the deaths had happened so many years ago, yet for her they were fresh losses.

"My mother and sister and I went to Kinnereth and lived there for a time. The people of Kinnereth, like many others, learned a lesson from Ramah. When the Canaanites came to their gates they didn't fight—they surrendered."

Lappidoth nodded. "We have heard the tales from the north—how the Hebrew villages there are under the heel of Jabin and Sisera. How they pay tribute so heavy they can barely feed their children."

Jael's husband, the somber young Kenite, said, "We live that same life, my friend. My father, brothers, and I have extensive flocks and herds, but we give a large share of our animals and of the wool and milk they produce to Hazor."

"You are far from the lands where your people usually dwell," Lappidoth observed.

While the others talked, Deborah and her daughter-in-law brought the simmering pot of couscous from the fire and placed it in the center of the circle where everyone sat. Anna passed around bread and people tore off large pieces before passing it on. Heber now leaned forward to dip his bread in the bowl of couscous.

"Our lands in the south were overcrowded. My father took his three sons when I was still a young man and made the long journey north to the good grazing lands of your tribe of Naphtali. We have always been at peace with the Hebrew tribes, our brothers through your father Moses."

"Our family met Heber when we traveled north from Kinnereth to our old grazing lands," Jael said. "After several years in Kinnereth we were shocked when my brother Edam walked into town one day. He was one of the men we'd lost at Ramah, but we learned that he had fled after the battle and lived far in the south."

"Odd that he never came to find my family," Deborah commented.

Jael hesitated. "He was—he is—I cannot explain Edam, exactly. He was always a bit different from other boys, but the battle at Ramah scarred him badly. Now he doesn't like to be among people. When he came to Kinnereth, he wasn't searching for us—just seeking shelter on his way north. He had decided he wanted to return to the land of his birth. And I—well, I just decided to go with him." A note in her voice suggested there was more to that story, but Deborah did not press her. "We set up camp not far from Grandfather's old encampment, and Edam bought a few goats from our nearest neighbor, Heber the Kenite. After a time, Heber offered more goats to Edam—in exchange for his sister's hand in marriage."

She glanced up at her husband with a smile, and Deborah thought that little Jael seemed to have found a good match. Which she certainly deserved, after all her troubles.

"And how long have you been married?" Keturah asked.

A slight pause. "Three years now," Jael answered.

"That's just how long Eli and I have been married," Keturah replied. Deborah saw how the two younger women looked at each other. The silence around them grew a little uncomfortable, though nobody spoke the obvious, and Deborah quickly introduced a new subject by asking what brought them south at this time of year.

"My wife wanted to visit Shiloh for the Passover," Heber explained. "Like many of my people, I worship the God of Israel, though I am not of His Chosen People. I honor Jael's desire to come pray and sacrifice to Yahweh, so we are here."

Lappidoth invited the couple to stay at his home during the festival, and they gratefully accepted. That night, as the fire burned low, Deborah sat with Jael and Keturah by the glowing embers. She knew what the younger women wanted to speak about and felt that they desired her there as well when the painful subject surfaced.

"So, you say you have been married three years?" Keturah asked Jael, her gaze focused on the ground, after the small talk had died away.

"Three years," she confirmed. Then, after another little silence, Jael said, "I know what you want to ask—and no, I have not lost a child or miscarried. Three years, and I have never conceived." She raised her eyes to look at Keturah. "Is your story the same, or have you lost a baby?"

"No," Keturah said, "I, too, have waited three years, and not one child. I have gone to the midwives and tried all their remedies and all their potions. Eli and I have prayed, we have made special sacrifices—nothing has availed."

"It is the same for us," Jael confirmed.

"Is that why you came for Passover, Jael?" Deborah asked softly.

The girl looked down at her sandaled feet again. "Yes, I thought that perhaps if I prayed and sacrificed here, God would hear us and bless us."

"Don't depend on it," Keturah said, bitterness edging her voice. "We live right here on God's doorstep, and still he hasn't heard us."

Deborah put a hand over her daughter-in-law's. "The ways of

God are strange to us, Keturah, but don't let your heart become hard. Nor yours, Jael. I can assure you God always hears . . . He has heard every one of your prayers. I know that's hard to believe, for He doesn't always answer as we choose, and I don't fully understand why, myself. Nevertheless I believe He hears, and He cares."

The younger women were silent. Then Keturah said to Jael, "Mother Deborah knows what she speaks of. She has lost two children—one in childbirth and one to fever." Her eyes darted toward Deborah's. "I'm sure you said many a prayer for them."

"I did. And God did not give me what I asked for. We live in a hard world, and unlike the pagans, we are not assured that if we say the right words and make the right sacrifices our God will obey us. But He hears, and He is with us, even when all seems lost."

"Will you pray for us, Deborah?" Jael asked. "Tomorrow we will go to the tabernacle and make our sacrifice, and I will pray in my heart, and Heber will pray, and the priest will pray. But I want your prayers. I feel very close to God when I'm with you. It's the only time in years that I've felt God is nearby and not a thousand miles away."

Deborah took both women's hands in hers as she prayed that God would take pity on their barrenness and give them the gift of a child. She prayed, also, that they would receive strength to accept whatever life offered them. As she prayed, she felt a great warmth and light, and in her thoughts she tried to picture both young women with babes in their arms. She saw Keturah clearly, with a swaddled baby and a bigger child playing at her knee. But try as she might she could only picture Jael alone. No comforting image of her with a child rose before her mind's eye.

Later still, when Keturah had gone off to bed, only Jael and Deborah remained by the fire. Deborah wondered whether she should speak to her about what she had seen, but to do so required some explanation.

"Almost a year ago," Deborah said at last, "I had a vision, Jael. A vision in which God Himself spoke to me and told me He would use me as His messenger." She expected surprise or disbelief on the other woman's face, but Jael just nodded, her face grave. "I haven't had another vision like that since, but often I feel, especially when I'm at prayer, that God is speaking to me, telling me something. I've tried to pay attention to those messages. Tonight as we were praying, I tried hard to picture you with a baby, but the image would not come to my mind. I fear it may be the Lord's message saying that the task He has for you does not include bearing a child." The younger woman remained silent, and Deborah reached out to touch her. "I tell you this only because I believe that if that is God's will, you should be prepared to accept it."

"I am," Jael said, her eyes brimming with tears. "But I won't pretend it's easy. It's all the harder because—oh, Deborah, I didn't tell my whole story earlier. Even Heber doesn't know it all. Something happened to me—in Kennerith, when the Canaanites ruled us."

"Yes?" Deborah prompted.

Jael dug in the dirt floor with her toes and stared into the remains of the fire. "One day the soldiers arrived in town. They were always coming, of course, for the tribute, for slaves, or just to make sure we were docile and obedient. This time there had been some talk of rebellion, some resistance. A handful of men met them at the village gate with drawn swords. The solders quickly disarmed and hanged them, of course, but the Canaanites also decided to teach the rest of the village a lesson. They doubled what they had planned to take in tribute, seized a number of slaves, and burned a house. And they rounded up some of the young girls and— I thought we were going to be taken into slavery too. But no. The soldiers had had a lot of wine by that time, and the killing and looting and drinking had made them—well, anyway. Right there, in the village square, with our families looking on—the men used the women. Raped us. No one stopped them—no one dared. General Sisera himself was their commander. In fact, he was the one—he took me." She pressed the heels of her hands against her eyes as if trying to grind away the memory. "I'll always remember it—always see his face, twisted with hate and lust. It was terrible. I can't tell you. But that wasn't the worst."

Deborah held out her arms and Jael cuddled into them as if she were a child of Japhet's age. "My mother was wounded that day. She did try to save me when they were taking me away, and she received a sword cut that never healed properly. She didn't live long after that, dying before I discovered I was with child."

"Jael, how terrible. So you were all alone with no one to care for you, carrying the child of your enemy?"

"Some of the people in the village took me in. The baby came, a boy, and he lived only a few days. He was weak, and I found it hard to nurse him. I gave him up to another woman to wet–nurse, finally, but he didn't survive." The girl turned dark eyes full of pain up to Deborah. "The worst thing is—I was relieved, almost glad, when he died. I couldn't love him. I couldn't look in his face without seeing that man. That animal. I couldn't imagine how I would have raised such a child. I would have had to give him up to someone else. But I felt so guilty, then, that I had wished my own child dead. I'm afraid God has cursed me by never letting me bear another."

Deborah stroked Jael's hair. "There's no curse, little sister, no curse that could be greater than what you have already endured. And that was not God's curse but man's. Yahweh is the one who will help you heal from it."

"But why will He not give me another child?"

"I don't know that, Jael. The answer may have nothing to do with God and His ways. It may be a matter the midwives would understand. Maybe the rape, or the birth that followed, did some damage to your womb that makes it hard for you to conceive again. Or perhaps, since it is already clear that you *can* conceive a child, it is your husband who is barren. People do not speak much of men who cannot father a child, but all the midwives know that such things can be."

Jael sat in silence for a long time, then said softly, "You've given me much to think about, Deborah."

"Maybe too much. I cannot even be certain that God's message was that you would not bear a child. One thing I am sure of—God has a plan for you, and you have a place in His plan. Now, perhaps we both ought to get some rest."

Jael and her husband stayed at Deborah's home throughout the Passover festival, and she felt deep regret when it came time to say goodbye to the couple. In that short time together her childhood memories of Jael had knit together with the reality of the girl as a grown woman, and they had formed a bond that made her feel as if she really had found, and then lost, another little sister. Realizing that they might not meet again, Deborah wept as they parted.

"Bless me, Deborah," Jael said, and the older woman placed a hand on her head, feeling the weight of responsibility that came with her new role as God's spokesperson.

"The Lord bless you and keep you, the Lord make His face to shine upon you," she said. "The Lord watch between me and you while we are absent from one another. Amen."

The busy days flew by quickly after the festival, but happy news came to Deborah and Lappidoth's home. Keturah announced that she and Eli were expecting a baby the following year. "I have you to thank. It was your prayer that made the difference—I know it," Keturah told Deborah privately.

"You have the One God to thank," Deborah reminded her. "I am glad I could act as a channel for His power to bless you."

Less happy news arrived from another family in the town. One morning Tirzah came to Deborah's house, her face streaked with tears as if she had been crying.

"Oh, Deborah, it was terrible. Josiah came to my father's house last night. He was drunk again, as usual." Tirzah's former husband was drinking heavily now, and despite the high priest's best efforts to help him, he had been forced to dismiss the younger man from his duties at the tabernacle. "He was cursing and shouting, telling me I had to come back to him or he would beat me within an inch of my life. My father had to go out to him and drive him away by force. It was terrible. I'm so frightened of him."

"You did well to stay within the house and not to speak to him," Deborah assured her, but she felt some fear herself. How long would the troubled young man continue to haunt Tirzah's life? Even if she felt free to marry again, would he not still make her life miserable? The village was small, and it was difficult to avoid another person. Deborah had prayed for Josiah too, but she felt a deep impenetrable darkness when she tried to picture him in her mind, as if he had shut his mind to all influences from God. Now, after hearing Tirzah's story, she sent Avi with a message to the high priest. "Tell him," she said, "that Deborah says you must send someone in search of Josiah and bring him to you. Though he is no longer a priest, he is still sorely in need of your guidance."

Avi carried the message and returned to take the goats out to pasture. Lappidoth and Eli left for work in the fields. Anna went to the garden to gather some herbs for the noon meal. So Deborah was alone with Japhet, making bread in the courtyard, when a neighbor's small boy arrived with news. The high priest himself had summoned her.

When Anna returned to watch Japhet, Deborah made her way up to the tabernacle and the high priest's tent. She bowed low before him.

"Have you heard the news yet?" he asked.

"I have heard nothing today," she replied, puzzled, "save that this morning Tirzah, daughter of Elihu, told me that her former husband had come to her father's house last night, drunk and making threats. That was why I sent word to you to find him."

A faint trace of a smile flickered across his somber face. "Few women in Shiloh would so summarily send a message telling the high priest what he should be doing." But he waved away Deborah's apology. "I do not mind following your orders, Deborah, for you give them rarely, and I believe that when you do, they are truly God's orders. I sent men in search of Josiah. He was found—or rather, his body was. Dead, at the foot of the cliff on the edge of town. It is hard to tell if he jumped purposely or stumbled over it while drunk."

Deborah gasped. "I saw— I knew nothing of this."

"Nevertheless it is not quite a surprise to you, is it?"

She wondered what he meant, then understood. "Yes, a month or so ago, before the Passover, I told Tirzah she should wait before making a decision about her marriage. I felt strongly that God's message to her was to wait."

The high priest nodded slowly. "It seems to have been good advice. Now she is a widow by the law, free to marry with no questions even if her divorce is not valid."

"It seems a hard way to win her freedom," Deborah sighed. She looked away—out across the busy grounds of the tabernacle filled with hurrying priests and noisy animals. "I do not understand this gift, honored father. God shows me some things—He tells me that Tirzah should wait for her marriage day. Yet He reveals nothing that might help save Josiah. Not even a warning of his death."

The high priest frowned. "Other prophets have declared the same thing—that the messages of Yahweh are not always clear or easy to understand. Perhaps we must just trust that God tells you all He needs you to know. God Himself may have realized there was no more that could be done for Josiah. We cannot know."

"Or perhaps," Deborah said, "God shows us enough to see what the outcome might be, but still leaves room for our choices. I told Tirzah to wait a month. Perhaps in that month, if Josiah had used the time to better himself and change his ways, when he came again asking for her back, she might have wished to be reconciled."

"As you said, we cannot know," the high priest repeated. "We can only deal with what has happened. And it seems clear, Deborah, that God is speaking to you. I wish you to remain in close contact with me, so that I can discuss with you any visions or messages you receive."

"I am honored. I feel in great need of a guide."

"This morning I received a visit from Amram," the priest continued, seemingly changing the subject. Amram was the chief among the elders of the village. "He had a proposition to make, which I promised him I would think and pray about. After today's events I think I know my answer. He wanted to propose asking you to sit among the elders and give them counsel."

"I?" The idea left her momentarily speechless. Only rarely did women sit among the elders, and then they were elderly women, widows of prominent men who were respected for their wisdom and experience.

"Not you, Deborah, wife of Lappidoth, but you, Deborah, messenger of the Lord," the high priest said, a note of caution in his voice. "Amram felt, and I agreed, that if we have a prophetess in our midst, it would be folly for the village elders to conduct their affairs without her counsel. Will you agree?"

"I cannot say no," Deborah replied finally. She tried to imagine herself sitting with the white-bearded old men, giving them her advice. No, not her advice—God's message. Even so, it made an odd picture in her mind.

CHAPTER 14

Barak's muscles strained under the weight of a boulder as large as a kid goat. He heaved it up to the height of his own chest, laying it on top of the half-built wall. In the distance he heard Nadab yelling, "Hey there! Not like that! We need to fortify the wall there!"

Hebrew towns were rarely walled, but the elders of Kinnereth had agreed to ask Barak and his men to aid them in building a rudimentary wall for defense. Not a mere wooden barricade like the wall that had so poorly guarded Ramah, but also not on the scale of Hazor's walls or those of other Canaanite cities. Just a solid stone wall to provide the citizens with some security.

After two years of raids and ambushes, Barak's band had grown to about 120 men. Everyone—Hebrews and Canaanites—now recognized him as more than a bandit chief. The word was out that the king of Hazor had put a price on the head of Barak son of Abinoam. And Kinnereth was the first Hebrew village to decide they wanted to shake off Jabin's yoke. They had called on Barak and his men to use it as their base, to be their defenders. Thirty young men from Kinnereth had sworn allegiance to Barak and joined his armed band. Perhaps, Barak thought, he might begin to think of it as an army.

Then he laughed bitterly. Jabin of Hazor had 900 armed men in iron chariots alone. That didn't even include his thousands of foot soldiers. What were 120 desperate men—with fewer than a hundred weapons among them—against such a force?

But it was a beginning, he thought. A beginning.

When they had finished the wall, the men who lived in Kinnereth had to turn their attention to sowing the crop. Barak's band dwindled. Those who still maintained homes and worked the land in other villages returned home for planting. The remainder—landless by chance or by choice—stayed in Kinnereth, their tents pitched outside the new wall. They worked the fields in return for some of the food the village raised. But they also spent hours each day drilling and training: hand-to-hand combat with sword, spear, dagger, and bare hands, then target practice with bow and with sling. Barak saw those 50 landless men as his core group. He spared no energy in trying to mold them into a real fighting force, skilled and fearless.

Unfortunately, they had a long way to go.

The village elders were concerned. Three of them came to Barak one evening as he ate a solitary evening meal in front of his tent.

"We know we need you if we want to break free from Hazor," the first and eldest began.

His eyes narrowing as he took a long drink from his waterskin, Barak challenged, "And this is what you want—freedom?"

The elder shifted his gaze away and then back to Barak. "Not all agree on this. Some see you and your men as troublemakers. Many would rather bow the knee to Jabin and live in peace. Wait for God to send deliverance."

Barak spat on the ground, though he turned his head away so as not to be seen spitting at the man. "What if God's deliverance looks like me?"

"We know you believe that, Barak," another of the elders replied. "And we have chosen to trust you. Having set our feet on this path, we are willing to follow it."

"But that doesn't mean we must accept everything that comes in your wake," the third man interjected.

"What do you mean?"

"Women, for one," the oldest man said. "Fifty men without wives or families are camped in our midst. No man in Kinnereth wants to marry his daughter to a landless rebel, however noble he may be. But young men have their needs. Are we to watch our un-married girls become loose women, and our young wives be un-faithful to their husbands? Is that the cost of having you at our gates?"

Barak stirred uncomfortably. The knowledge that the elders were right only fueled his anger. He had heard the men's ribald jests, seen them come and go through the village gates late at night. After all, he was a man himself—if no longer very young, being near 30— and understood a man's needs, having last visited Abigail six months before. She was more than willing to welcome him back to her bed on his rare visits home. But even knowing that he would be based permanently in Kinnereth, she would not consider coming with him. Sharing a soldier's life was no part of her plan, and who could blame her? Anger choked him like a pair of hands about his throat.

"What if that is the price?" he said, leaning forward and draw-ing his belt knife, digging its tip into the dirt at his feet. "You had a choice and made it. On the one hand you can have Canaanite sol-diers running loose in your city, stealing your food, raping your women and girls at swordpoint. Dragging girls and boys alike off to a life—and death—of slavery. Or, you can have my men as a shield between you and the Canaanites, and share your food with us, and your homes if need be. And turn a blind eye when our men amuse themselves with willing girls."

The oldest man made as if to speak, but Barak bit off his words. "I have my rules. We are not bandits, nor do we demand food for a winter without offering to work. And I have told my men that any-one stealing bread or forcing a woman against her will, will be flogged." He stabbed the knife firmly into the ground. "That is all I give you. If you want more, you know your choice. I'm sure Sisera will be glad to come back when he knows what you prefer."

His anger was hot inside but cold and controlled on the outside. It left the elders stammering and stuttering.

"Have we exchanged one yoke for another?" one of them demanded. "Are these our only choices—to bend the knee before Jabin, or before Barak?"

Clenching his jaw and grinding one fist into the palm of his hand, Barak turned away. Then, taking a long breath, he faced them again. "I have no desire to be a king," he said. "I don't want slaves. Your choice is—my men to defend you against Hazor, or no defense at all. Take it or leave it."

They took it, of course. What other option did they have? Neither they nor most of the villagers were happy, but they were, for the moment, free. Barak went down to the archery range, as he did most nights, and hit the center of the target several times with arrows. Then he attacked it several more times with stones aimed from his sling. The exercise exhausted some of the anger. Enough, anyway, that he could sleep at night.

In the rare moments when Barak paused to reflect, he knew that he was too angry. He told himself that a man who led a rebellion against a foreign overlord had to be driven by such strong emotion. But even he wondered if he had to be so angry that the whole world looked sour and every word seemed like an offense. Most of all, he hated the pious words of priests and devout people. They assured him he was leading the army of the Lord—doing Yahweh's will.

Maybe I am, he thought. *It's a shame the Lord doesn't see fit to send me a word or two of encouragement, anything to let me know He still exists. But then again, I haven't had much to say to Him of late, either.*

The peace of Kinnereth continued as the crops grew. When the barley ripened, Hazor did not send out the usual team of tribute collectors. The villagers honored Barak and his men at a feast. Also they celebrated two marriages between Barak's men and daughters of the village. Suddenly marrying a landless rebel no longer seemed like such a bad idea.

The men were elated, as if they had won a battle. In fact, all they had done was to avert one by their presence. Barak lectured them in tones that stung like wasps.

"You fools! Yes, they're dancing in the village streets. Are you as naive as they are? Do you really believe Jabin and Sisera are sitting in the palace in Hazor, saying, 'Oh, Barak has 120 men guarding Kinnereth, so we'd better not attack and risk our 900 iron chariots?' You know what this is—he's trying to lull us into security, make us confident and careless so we're unprepared for his real attack. And judging by the looks of you, I'd say he's succeeding!"

Drilling continued at a heightened pace, though the men also worked long hours helping to bring in the crops. It tired them out, reducing their dalliances with village girls. The elders were happy. But not Barak.

He was right about the impending attack. Unfortunately, he was wrong about the timing.

Barak had guessed Sisera would wait until after the wheat harvest, demanding the largest tribute payment of the year. Losing that tribute would matter to Jabin of Hazor. As a result Barak calculated the attack would come when the wheat was in.

But he had forgotten what the wheat crop meant to the villagers of Kinnereth. Wheat was the difference between starvation and survival. And General Sisera meant to exploit the one great weakness that hit a city as soon as it hid behind walls.

They left from Hazor a fortnight before the wheat harvest. Barak's sentries brought back word almost as soon as Sisera's army was on the march. "About a day out from Hazor they'd be now, sir," the messenger told Barak.

"How many?"

"About 500, sir. A hundred charioteers, the rest foot soldiers."

Barak cursed. No chance his men could take on such a force. It would be a slaughter.

He called his captains for a hasty meeting. About 100 of his men were in camp at the moment. Some were still away in their home villages. "We'll take shelter within the walls and defend the town from inside," he decided. "But before we do we'll send messengers to every Hebrew village within running distance—west into Zebulon and as far south as Jezreel. Tell them we need reinforcements. We'll count on the men who carry the messages to organize whatever volunteers we get, bring them together, and camp at the mouth of the waters of Meram, where the river joins the Sea of Kinnereth." As he scratched his beard he realized that he had a great deal to arrange in an extremely short time. They'd have to devise some means of trying to send messages so that even within the village, under siege, he'd know when they had a force ready to attack Sisera. Then his men could march out of Kinnereth to join the battle.

"If we can get at least 300, we may be close to a match for them," one of the men said, excitement building in his voice.

"That is, if Kinnereth can hold out till we return with 300 reinforcements," another put in.

"Leave that to us," Barak said. But surviving a siege involved more than having walls with archers mounted on them. "Send to the village elders," he told yet another messenger. "They'll need to go into the fields and see if any of the wheat is ready to be brought in early. We have a day, no more. Tell them to gather everything they can before we barricade the gates."

The officers sent teams of men to fortify the wall, while the captains selected watchmen and drew up rosters of duty. The runners left at once after a brief discussion with Barak about codes and messages. He wasn't happy with what they'd arranged, but they didn't have time for anything more detailed. And he cursed Sisera's planning. Two weeks before the grain harvest. Barak understood all too well now, and wondered why he hadn't thought of it before.

By nightfall 100 men were billeted in the homes of the villagers, and the elders began drawing up plans to ration the meager supplies of food inside the village to withstand a siege. How long a siege, no one knew.

The gray light of dawn saw Hazor's army approaching on the road from the north. Not having slept, Barak paced the walls. Few if any of his commanders had. He wondered how Sisera had slept and if the general was leading his army himself. Barak felt sure, somehow, that he was.

The Canaanites camped north of the town, setting up their tents with an air of planning to stay. Later in the day their supply wagons arrived from Hazor, traveling more slowly with food, extra weapons, even camp followers. The slow movement of supplies didn't matter to a besieging army, of course. Unlike forces going to meet another army in the field, Sisera's had all the time in the world.

Sisera and his men were patient, Barak granted that. For two full weeks they camped there within sight, making no attempt at an assault on the walls. All they did was to drill every day. They knew the protracted wait, the fear and uncertainty, would begin to wear away at those within the walls, increasing the tension to an unbearable level. By the time the fortnight had passed, everyone was beginning to feel the effect of food rationing. And Barak also knew that disease would soon break out in the overcrowded city as sewage and garbage accumulated in the streets and sanitation broke down. A siege was often a race between whether disease would first wipe out the people inside or the army waiting outside.

But Barak also knew that a trained and disciplined army, brought within sight of the enemy and then forced to remain idle for weeks on end, became uneasy and discontented. Sisera would have to give his men something besides drill and practice to do. When he did, Barak intended to show them that they could not easily take Kinnereth.

The assault came in the third week. Scanning the Canaanite battle line, Barak saw no battering rams, no indication of heavy siege engines at all. A forest of archers marched ahead of the charioteers. This, then, would be a straightforward attempt to overwhelm Kinnereth's defenses and scale the walls.

Barak watched them advance, his own men ready and waiting for the enemy to move within shooting range. He wondered for an idle moment about the messengers he had sent out. What reception had they met—in Hammath, in Madon, in Rimmon? Were reinforcements even now on the march?

Or are we alone, to face this enemy and die? he wondered. *Well, I'll make sure of one thing—it won't be quick. No easy victories for Sisera. I owe him that much—and more.* He thought of the God of Israel, that mighty and distant figure who had supposedly drowned the Egyptian army and toppled the walls of Jericho. *You've been very quiet since then,* Barak challenged the empty sky. *Now might be a good time to take some action.*

Just then he heard the shout of the Canaanite commander, and raised his own arm at the same moment. "Fire!"

Arrows flew through the air like hailstones in the midst of a fierce storm. Barak's own bowstring sang again and again as he let fly, relying on his helmet and breastplate to protect him from the oncoming arrows. And a good thing, for one struck him a direct hit on the breastplate. For a moment he reeled at the blow, but fitted another arrow to the string even as he did so.

He heard a scream as a man beside him fell from the wall, his body tumbling out into the sea of armed men below. Now the charioteers began dismounting, running past the fallen bodies of

Canaanite archers. They carried scaling ladders and grappling hooks and rope. Barak watched one man throw his hook toward the wall, and took great pleasure in sending an arrow into his throat.

It was chaos—controlled and planned chaos, but chaos nonetheless. For a horrible moment Barak was back on the walls of Ramah, 12 years before, watching Sisera's approaching army. But no. This was not Ramah, and Barak was no green boy but a commander who had trained his men for such a battle. Even as his archers in the first rank fell, new men scrambled up from within the walls to take their place. Barak had held back some of his best archers for this task, along with some men skilled at the sling. Their job was to pick off the men rushing the wall, cutting them down before they ever scaled it.

And they succeeded. After a bloody melee, the Canaanites fell back. Only one man had managed to get a grappling hook into the wall, and a stone felled him seconds after he'd begun climbing.

Although Barak was grimly pleased, his own losses were heavy. He had 20 men dead and more than 30 wounded. And though the walls held and the enemy had retreated, the situation had not changed. Sisera still camped outside the walls, and food continued to run short within.

Every day the rationing got stricter. The fighting men were the first and best fed. Women, children, and the old were the hungriest, for being expendable they received the least food. A month after Sisera's army arrived, Barak got the first reports of death from starvation—two children and their grandmother, in one of the village's poorest houses. Others were coming down with fevers and other sickness.

"These deaths won't be the last," the elders told him.

"What do you want? To surrender?"

"If we surrender, are we worse off than we were before?" the man challenged him. "Under Hazor's rule we had at least enough to live on."

Barak laughed in his face. "Are you worse off? What do you think—that you will open the gates, Sisera will march in and say, 'Very well, everything will go back as it was before'? You don't believe he might want to punish, to make an example of a village rash enough to defy his king's rule?"

The elders blanched. "What have you gotten us into, you rash fool?" one sputtered.

"Nothing you shouldn't have expected, if you had counted the cost," Barak replied.

"Whether we open our gates or keep them closed, we die. Our only choice is a slow death or a fast one," the elder retorted.

"Unless perchance you can keep your people calm and fortified long enough for my reinforcements to arrive. Then we might just hand you a victory, little as you deserve it."

"Oh yes, your reinforcements!" another of the elders sneered. "Even the priest has given up praying for them to arrive."

Every day Barak had men watching the lake shore south of the town, their attention on the river mouth from which his runners had agreed to send a signal. But none appeared. And any messenger who tried to get past Sisera's men would probably be dead by now.

Meanwhile, Sisera's army had not been idle. While Kinnereth starved and Barak waited for reinforcements that never came, Sisera made two more attempts to scale the walls. The defenders repelled both of them, but the cost was high. Many of Barak's original band of men were dead or crippled by now. Every able-bodied man in Kinnereth—from boys of 13 to old men of 50—found themselves pressed into duty on the walls. Some were good shots. Others clearly showed their lack of training, not to mention their weakness from hunger. On the last attempt on the walls, Barak had given the order to use an effective but costly weapon. His men poured boiling olive oil down onto the attackers. Watching a man already in the act of climbing the walls scream in agony as the hot oil hit him, seeing him fall from the wall to the ground below, made some of the defenders queasy. Barak personally found it rewarding, but he was fast realizing that he wasn't a normal man anymore. He was nothing but a warrior, and not a very successful one. Oil was a precious commodity in a starving and besieged town, and repelling that attack had taken everything the village could spare.

A week later heavy wagons crawled along the road from Hazor. When Barak saw the battering rams and siege towers, he knew it was over.

"If you plan to surrender, the time is now," he told the elders tersely. "Once the walls fall, Sisera will show no mercy."

"What mercy will he show anyway?"

"You can claim that I took Kinnereth by force and held it against your will—that you never intended to defy King Jabin," Barak suggested. He knew the elders would think of this ploy themselves—perhaps already had. The least he could do was offer it to them.

"Will he believe us?"

"No, of course not. But just making the gesture will appease him a little. You may get away with only half the men in the village hanged instead of all of them."

As the siege machines moved into position, Barak ordered the best archers he had left onto the walls. Their only hope now was to try to pick off the men manning the devices, but it was unlikely they could disable enough to stop the attack.

When the first battering ram pounded against the north wall, an entire section collapsed at once. Designed to batter the stone walls of Canaanite cities, the rams were invincible against the rubble and mud brick walls the villages had hastily thrown up. Barak ordered the main force of men to guard the gap, making it too dangerous for the enemy to attempt to enter that way. Sisera's men didn't even try to charge. Instead, they pulled the battering ram back and wrestled it to another part of the wall.

Soon they had smashed down another part of the north wall some distance from the first. Barak's remaining men divided to cover both gaps, but it was a futile gesture. Barak joined the men at the larger of the two gaps just as he heard the trumpet call to charge. The attackers rushed both gaps at once. Barak ordered his archers to fire on the Canaanites. A few fell, but more and more advanced in the ranks behind them, swarming like insects up the rubble that lay where the wall had been. Then Barak found himself caught up in deadly hand to hand combat. Screams, the clang of swords, the crash of yet more of the wall falling—the noises were only a background to the frantic struggle to stay alive, to take as many of the enemy down with him as possible.

Driven down from the wall, back through the streets, he had killed four men, or five, before three Canaanite soldiers surrounded him and he took a spear in his thigh. Even as he buckled to the ground he managed to slash one of the three soldiers in the belly. The remaining two were ready to strike again when one dropped suddenly, felled from behind. As the second turned, Barak dispatched him. He looked up to see who had saved him and discovered himself face to face not with one of his own soldiers but with the oldest of the town's elders—the one who had doubted the value of Barak's force being there in the first place.

"Flee," the old man said. "Toward the river. They are burning the town. None of us will escape. But you must."

"No," Barak gasped. "Stand—and fight. To the last—"

"Those are a fool's words, and you are no fool, whatever else you are. You are fighting for something bigger than Kinnereth. Go, and may God preserve you to fight another day."

Barak gave himself no time to grapple with any moral dilemma. Was it cowardice or prudence to run when men were dying all around him? He didn't care. The old man had given him a moment's respite, and he used it to run toward the gate in the south wall. Behind him he heard a cry as the elder collapsed from a single blow of a Canaanite sword.

A wall of flame blocked the west gate. Men were fighting in the streets, but the resistance was short-lived. The Canaanites vastly outnumbered the Hebrews, and villagers fell to their knees in their eagerness to surrender. In horror as he dodged past, Barak saw a soldier drive his sword through the heart of a kneeling man who had been begging for mercy. He wanted to go back, to avenge the villager. But no—he must live to fight another day, if he could get out of there alive.

He actually got through the gate and only had to overpower one more man to do it. The town was an inferno already. He remembered Ramah. How many more times in his life would he flee from Sisera's swordsmen and leave behind a burning hell of death and destruction? At least this time he wasn't running into slavery. If he was captured, he'd fall on his own sword before they took it from him. *I'll fight to live as long as I can, but I'll die before I go back to Hazor in chains,* he told himself.

Barak almost fulfilled that vow. A handful of Sisera's men still ringed the town, keeping guard to prevent runaways from escaping. Barak watched them intercept two men and a woman trying to reach the forest. They left them to die on the ground. Still he kept running toward the enemy line, hoping he could fight his way through.

Sisera's men saw him and converged on him: five of them, well armed and fresh since they had not participated in the attack on the town. Barak was bloody, wounded, exhausted. He looked at the five swords pointed at him and knew he had no chance. They moved to circle him.

Then he heard a trumpet cut the air. It was the sound he'd

waited a month to hear. Beyond the Canaanites, a score of Hebrews came tearing out of the trees, swords drawn. Too late to save Kinnereth, but in time for Barak.

He gripped his own sword to fight again, unable just to stand there and be rescued. Sweat and tears blurred his vision and he swung wildly, but he managed to disarm his opponent. Then it was over. All five Canaanites were down and strangers surrounded him—strangers who spoke his tongue. Among them was Nathan of Rimmon, one of the runners Barak had sent to the south and west with a plea for help.

Rather than heading toward the burning town, the small band of men, with Barak at the center, made their way across a nearly dry wadi into the hills. A few Canaanites pursued, but good archery deterred them. Soon Barak found himself stumbling up a rocky path, climbing higher and higher, hidden by the woods. Time was meaningless as they fled deeper into the forested hills. He only knew it was near sunset when he collapsed on the ground at the mouth of a cave and someone poured cold water over his face.

Sputtering, Barak sat up. Someone thrust food into his hands: a piece of dry bread. Out of the maze of faces he turned to the one he recognized. "Nathan? We waited for your signal . . . why didn't you come? Where are the rest of the men?"

The courier hung his head. "These are all the men I could muster, Barak. Twenty from Rimmon. I went to Madon, to Hannathon, to Gath-hepher, and none of them would send aid. They said that Naphtali's problems were not theirs, that Yahweh would look after Kinnereth if it was His will."

Barak felt the familiar slow anger burning inside. Fear and panic had banked the fires these past few hours, but now the embers glowed again. Anger not just at the Canaanites, but at his fellow Israelites. One nation, one people, one God—indeed!

"They said that, did they?" He looked down through the clearing to where a smoky haze hung in the sky above the village of Kinnereth. "Well then, it seems this wasn't the Lord's will, was it? Perhaps Yahweh has forgotten us and left us to ourselves."

A young man with a thin, nervous face leaned forward. "Lord Barak, sir, do not speak so. I have heard of your exploits these past years and have prayed for your success. I believe God is leading us, though most of our fellow Israelites are too cowardly to aid us. They must be made to see the danger. If Naphtali is overrun, the same fate looms over the other tribes. They do not believe this is truly the land of promise, and they risk losing it. You must make them see!"

"Make them see?" Barak echoed. The man was spouting the usual pious platitudes, and, to tell the truth, he hadn't been listening. What responsibility of his was it to make men see things? He was a soldier.

"We've been talking, sir," Nathan interrupted. "The defeat at Kinnereth is devastating. I don't know if any of our men will survive. You're starting afresh, with a handful of men, as you did before. And we have to flee south—Sisera will have patrols out searching these hills by tomorrow morning, as soon as he realizes you've slipped through his net. Maybe you need to go yourself into Judah and Benjamin, tell them of our plight, explain to them that Israel must stand or fall together."

Barak couldn't grasp the import of his words, couldn't focus on them. He heard only one thing: *flee*.

"You may be right," he admitted. "But all I can think of now is sleep."

They set a watch and let him fall exhausted to the ground, where he slept for several hours. Finally he awoke in darkness, the night air chilly around him. He lay on bare ground with a cloak wrapped around him. The watchmen were silent.

Barak tried to guess where he might be this time tomorrow, or a month from now. The future was as impenetrable as the night.

God of Israel, he sent out into the night, *are You truly there? Do You truly care for your so-called chosen people? Have You called me to lead them, or am I deluding myself?*

The night gave no answer. He felt completely alone and without direction. When he looked around, he saw only a hostile world with no God in sight. And when he looked within, he found a core of hardness and hate so bleak that it made him turn away. He didn't recognize the person he had become.

All I can do is live to fight again, he decided. *I'll bring down that son of a dog, Sisera, with my own hands. If it's the last thing I do.*

In the distance, a ram's horn sounded. The watchmen looked at each other, and Barak was on his feet almost before the echo died away.

"I'll go to the lookout post," someone whispered.

"It's Sisera," Barak said. "He's not waiting till dawn to send out a search party. They're on their way."

"Then we must be on our way too," the watchman said, bending to wake Nathan.

Barak grabbed his sword and strapped it on. His unfinished prayer echoed down the empty corridors of his heart. *If there was ever a time I needed You, God, this is it. Show Yourself now, or never.* "Let's be on our way," he said, waking the man nearest him.

CHAPTER 15

Deborah sat up with a start in the darkness. She had been dreaming confused and troubled images of battle and conflict. In her dreams she had found herself back in Naphtali in her childhood, in her grandfather's encampment. Jael was there too, a little girl with wild unruly dark hair, weaving in and out among the legs of adults. And Barak. Deborah had not dreamed of him for years, but now he was there, laughing, handsome, and muscular. Then the dream swerved on a different path from history: the Canaanites were coming, but Deborah and her family did not leave in time. Instead, they were trapped among the tents as men with iron swords wreaked havoc among the women and children, and the Hebrew men valiantly attempted to stop them. She saw Barak, standing his ground as a huge Canaanite held him at swordpoint . . .

That was when she woke up, sweating, her heart pounding. She sat up on her sleeping mat, Lappidoth sound asleep beside her. In the darkness of the sleeping quarters she could see other huddled shapes: Japhet close by, Anna a little farther away, Avi on the other side of the room, enjoying the solitude of a boy who was nearly a man. A warm night breeze blew in from the side of the room that lay open to the courtyard below. Deborah stood, slowly crossed the room, and leaned over the low wall, looking down. She could hear the noises of the animals as they, too, slept or stirred restlessly below.

Suddenly she was aware of something different. A change in the air, a feeling as if a note of music had sounded, though she heard nothing. She stood, tensed, eager to know what was happening and afraid at the same time. And then she knew. She was again in the presence of the God Most High.

How she knew, Deborah could not have explained, except that it was the same as her experience at the Palm three years before. The very air tingled with the presence of something more than human. Knowledge and certainty flooded her. It was very different indeed from the hints and intimations she sometimes received in prayer or when giving counsel to another. Those came mediated through her own finite human mind. This—this *was* God. No mistaking it.

She looked around the room to see if anything visible had changed. The sky was moonless, yet the bodies of her sleeping family seemed touched with a silvery light, and she felt an intense sense of love and of loss, as if they were about to be taken from her. But no— no, she probed further into the strange reality of the vision. The loss was not hers. Someone, somewhere, was weeping bitterly for van- ished sons and daughters, husbands and wives. Was that strange? Every night in every town, someone was dying. But this loss was huge. She felt the suffering hit her like a wave. Somewhere, something terrible had happened this night. Smelling acrid smoke on the air, she knew with certainty that no one in Shiloh had lit a late-night fire. This smoke came from too far away for her bodily senses to perceive it, yet she was there, in the midst of fire and blood and suffering.

Then she heard it: a voice, clear as if Lappidoth had risen and spoken. And she knew, too, that it was not the voice of God that had once thrilled her spirit when she heard it. This was a human voice, but one removed from her daily reality. A voice carried to her in vision, one coming from far away. A man's voice, driven and des- perate with exhaustion.

"Help me," the voice croaked. "If you're there, if you ever wanted to help me, help me now."

Turning in the direction that the voice seemed to come from, she saw a man on the other side of the low wall, someone who, if he had really been standing there, would have been hovering in mid-air five cubits above the courtyard. His hands gripped the mud brick wall as if he had been running and only now found himself within shelter. As she stared at him, heard his cry, suddenly she knew who he was.

The dream, of course, had been her preparation for the vision.

This man was the boy Barak, no more than 14 years old as she had seen him last, except that the hunted, harried eyes were those of a much older man who had seen and experienced unthinkable horrors. The old eyes in that young face—the matted, filthy hair, the ragged clothing. But it was Barak. He caught and held her gaze, and repeated his plea in a voice that was little better than a croak. "Help me. If you're there, if you ever wanted to help me, help me now."

Realizing that it was futile, she still reached out to him. Her hand touched empty air, and the vision vanished. But the air still felt charged with Presence, with power, with possibility. Aloud she said, "Is this Your call, O Lord?"

Yes! the very air shouted. Deborah found herself filled with certainty, with unexpected energy. Barak was alive and in desperate need. Somewhere, many people had suffered horribly, and he had escaped that disaster and reached out for help. And God had brought his plea to her in the most direct fashion possible. She must respond.

"Yes," she replied, again aloud. "Yes, I will help." And the air in the room shimmered and grew brilliant, and she was full of joy and hope despite the pain she had just experienced so intensely that it was almost as if it had happened to her. She was alive, the whole world was alive, for Yahweh was in her and in all, and Deborah wanted to cling to this moment, to the presence of God—to never, ever let it go.

And upon that thought, it was gone. The air in the room no longer shimmered and danced, nothing was lit with silver on this moonless night. She was alone in her family's sleeping quarters on a dark night—that was all. The everyday world had returned and once again she stood by the low wall staring into the courtyard. Only her inner certainty that God was with her, that Yahweh had called her, that Barak and perhaps countless others needed her help—only that remained.

And with it lingered a question she couldn't answer. She had not heard of Barak for almost 15 years. She had no idea where he was, nor what his need was. How could she possibly help him?

The next day, Deborah asked to meet with the village elders at the well, and invited the high priest to join them. Dusk, after the day's work had concluded and people had eaten the evening meal, was the only time everyone could get together. The day dragged for Deborah. The message from Barak had been so urgent that any delay felt like a mistake.

When the men finally assembled, she immediately told them, "I have had another vision from the Lord."

"Another vision!" exclaimed the high priest. "Tell us of this, my daughter."

"I will, but first I have a question. Have any of you had word from the north, any news of what is happening there?"

"How strange that you should ask," the chief of the elders said. "Just today a man—a kinsman of Shimei, son of Haran—arrived from the north to attend the feast of Pentecost. He told us that the town of Kinnereth in Naphtali is under siege. The army of Sisera, the general of Hazor, has camped around the town, threatening to destroy it. Men from Kinnereth had visited his town when the siege began, asking for help, trying to raise an army to come to Kinnereth's aid."

"Why, I heard the same thing a fortnight ago," another man put in. "Messengers went to Gath-hepher in Zebulon, asking men to go to the aid of a town in Naphtali that was under siege."

"Jabin of Hazor has the north in a cruel yoke," the high priest observed. "But what has this to do with your vision, Deborah? Did the Lord reveal something to you of what is happening there?"

She took a deep breath, remembering the terrible sense of suffering that had assaulted her the night before. "Yes. From what the Lord showed me last night, I can guess that Sisera has taken the town."

The high priest sighed and shook his head, but then he looked up, his brow wrinkled. "But why should Hazor attack Kinnereth at all? From all I know, Kinnereth, like all the villages of the north, pays tribute to King Jabin and has sworn loyalty to him. Did they break that oath?"

"Yes," said the chief elder. "For the past few years, a band of rebel bandits has staged raids on Sisera's army. Some months ago, these rebels took over Kinnereth and refused the tribute payment. They say their leader is a fierce warrior, and even Sisera fears him."

"We have not heard of any such leader among our people for many years—not since the days of Ehud," Deborah said. "Who is this man?" But she was sure she already knew.

"I can't recall—was it—Bani? Benjamin? Or—no—something like that . . ."

"Barak, son of Abinoam?" Deborah asked.

The high priest and most of the elders stared at her with surprise and curiosity, but the chief elder said, "Yes! Barak! I do believe that was the name, though I cannot recall his father's name."

"Barak is my kinsman," she explained. "The son of my mother's brother. He lived in Naphtali. I met him there when I was a child. I have not seen or heard news of him since. But last night he came to me in a vision. I saw him clearly, and he begged for help."

"Tell me exactly what you saw and heard," the high priest said.

Deborah related the whole vision. It was not difficult to recall. As with her first vision, every detail had engraved itself into her memory.

"But what are we to do about this, Deborah?" the chief elder said when she finished. "We have heard that this Barak sent out messengers asking for help to break the siege, but none came as far south as Shiloh. And if your vision is true, the siege has already ended and Kinnereth has fallen. What could we do, even if we were close at hand?"

The men talked among themselves, but Deborah remained silent, trying to listen to a voice she could not hear with her ears.

"Even if Kinnereth is taken, Barak still lives," she said suddenly, her voice cutting across those of the men. "Yahweh would not have sent me the vision otherwise. Barak, as I saw him in my vision, was desperate and frightened. The Lord has not made this clear to me, but does it not seem possible that Barak and perhaps some of his men have escaped and are seeking shelter?"

The men nodded and murmured agreement. "If he has fled Kinnereth with Sisera's army at his heels," one of the elders reasoned, "then he may be hiding in the mountains west of the sea of Kinnereth. If we could find him, it might be possible to send a small force of men north to rescue him."

"If this man is as dangerous as we have heard, and we intervene and offer him refuge here in Shiloh, we risk drawing Jabin's wrath down upon ourselves," another man protested.

"If Jabin has the north in as tight a grip as we hear—especially if he has now overwhelmed these rebels at Kinnereth—he will be looking south next anyway, whatever we do," the high priest observed.

"Yes, but must we draw his attention? Is this really our cause?"

Another voice cut in—a younger man, who had so far remained fairly quiet. "And another thing," he said. "Are we to commit men to go off on this quest—to aid a rebel we know nothing of—without even being sure he's out there? Not only is this not our fight, we have no surety that anyone even needs our aid—nothing save the word of a woman who claims to have had a vision!" The scorn in his voice was obvious.

A few men murmured agreement. The chief elder looked troubled. But the high priest stood.

"Whether this is our cause or not, we must decide," he said, his eyes fixing the men with a stony gaze. "The Lord has seen fit to send a vision to our prophetess, a woman of Shiloh, and He must have had a reason for doing so. As to whether she is a prophetess, whether her word is truly the word of Yahweh—have no doubt of it. For I have no question myself." His words fell with all the weight of the tabernacle's authority, and for a frightening moment Deborah wondered what her life, her calling, would be like if the high priest had doubted her, if she did not have that authority behind her. It certainly stilled the others. They looked at her now with a deeper respect.

Still the practical problems remained. Deborah stayed late into the evening, taking counsel with the elders and the priest, and at dawn the community summoned the young, able-bodied men of the village to hear the elders' decision. A band of men would head north to Mount Tabor to seek out the rebel band from Kinnereth and guide them to safety in Shiloh. More than a few scratched their beards and looked skeptical when they found out that only Deborah's vision guaranteed even the very existence of the rebels, and that the Lord had not seen fit to grant her any information about the precise location of the men they were supposed to save. But again, the high priest's authority backed the venture, and in the end 30 men volunteered to go.

Lappidoth, Avi, and Eli all volunteered. The elders chose Lappidoth and Avi, but turned Eli away. "It is wrong for all the men in a single household to go," the chief elder decided, "even if it is the prophetess' own family. Lappidoth, you are the eldest, perhaps a little too old for such a perilous task, so I might send you back, but Eli's wife will bear him a son soon, and he should remain at home."

Deborah took her husband's hands in hers. "Thank you for believing me," she said. Knowing that he would risk his own life—and Avi's—for the sake of a vision the Lord had sent her, touched her deeply. She knew that Lappidoth, unlike most of the other men, would not have required the high priest's assurances before going on such an unlikely journey.

"It never occurred to me to doubt you," he told her, kissing her hands.

The men departed the following morning. Again, the delay was necessary. Thirty men leaving the village during the wheat harvest was a heavy blow, and Deborah felt humbled by the responsibility of having passed on a message that had caused such an upheaval. The village had to make arrangements for the women and the remaining men to get in the crops. In Deborah's household that meant herself, Anna, and Keturah working alongside Eli. Still, she chafed at the delay. The vision had been urgent, and days of travel still lay ahead before the men could reach Mount Tabor and even begin searching for Barak and whatever followers were with him. She was sure he was there, and in need, but were they responding quickly enough?

She could not know. At dawn she stood by the well watching the men gather, ready to march north. Lappidoth held her hands again and promised to do his best. She gathered Avi in her arms and, looking at her husband over the boy's shoulder, mouthed "Take care of him."

At a command from their leader, they started slowly out of town. Too slowly? Deborah knew there was no point in troubling herself further about their speed, about whether they would find Barak in time, or at all. The One God had given her the vision, she had shared it, and the men had responded. Everything else was in Yahweh's hands.

Standing silently there, she watched till the group dwindled to tiny dots on the horizon, and finally vanished from view.

CHAPTER 16

Entering Shiloh was the strangest thing Barak could remember doing in a long time. They reached the town at sunset, their shadows spilling long and dark across the landscape. And as they passed the outlying tents and houses, he found it was like walking into the past, into a world he only dimly remembered from childhood.

All around him people spoke the Hebrew tongue, yet they walked their streets without fear. They went about as free people, not glancing over their shoulders for the Canaanite overlord or soldier. On a hill at the center of town stood the tabernacle, and within those curtained walls men sacrificed to the God of Abraham. Without fear. Without hiding. And without compromise.

Barak wondered if he'd wandered into a dream.

It was a different world, here in the south. His whole existence in the north had centered around fear and hiding and fighting. This was a different life—one of planting and building and worship. Somehow he couldn't connect the two worlds in his mind.

He had no idea how many days had passed since his fleeing, terrified band of men had encountered the warriors from the south on the slopes of Mount Tabor. When the Canaanite scouts from Kinnereth caught up, the combined force of Barak's men and the band from Shiloh outnumbered and slaughtered the Canaanites. Then Barak learned that the Ephraimites had come, not in response to his requests for aid, but because their prophetess had had a vision from God.

The whole thing was hard to believe. He didn't put much stock in prophets and visions. And a prophetess—a woman? Who'd ever heard of such a thing? Barak almost laughed.

But the men were there. They had come to the right spot, at the right moment to save his life. And now they were taking him south to Shiloh, to meet the high priest and the prophetess.

The night after his rescue, one of the Ephraimites sought him out. "My name is Lappidoth," the soft-spoken older man said. "My wife, Deborah, is the prophetess who saw you in vision. She knew you, for she says you are a kinsman of her mother's family."

Deborah. He remembered her—the girl by the river in a morning sunrise. The girl who had haunted him all these years. Deborah, a prophetess? But then, he himself had been a soldier, a slave, and a bandit during those same years. Life took odd turns.

Now they were here in Shiloh. Back when he was young Barak used to think he'd visit here someday, maybe for Passover or the Feast of Tabernacles. He had never pictured arriving on the heels of a battle, running for refuge.

The high priest must be coming to greet them. The man in the richly ornamented robes of blue and gold and purple walked at the head of a curious gaggle of priests and townspeople. "Barak, son of Abinoam," the religious leader said. "We have heard of your struggle against this Canaanite king—Jabez?"

"Jabin." The name came out like a bark. Barak cleared his throat. He was in a Hebrew town where they weren't even sure of the name of Jabin, king of Hazor. If Jabin had his way, that name would be etched on their paving-stones—and on their hearts—before five more summers had gone by. "Jabin, king of Hazor. His general, Sisera. We men of Naphtali have been fighting them for—" he paused. "Ten years. Or more."

"The One God has granted you courage and determination," the priest said, his brow creasing into a frown.

Barak let out a harsh laugh. "Too bad He hasn't seen fit to grant us victory."

Quickly, the man called Lappidoth stepped to Barak's side, took his arm. "You are weary and weak from hunger and thirst, cousin. Come to my home where we will offer you rest and refreshment. Later, you can meet with the priests and elders of the town and talk of events in the north." He quickly hustled him away, eager to erase the embarrassment of Barak's blunt words. How dare he speak so to a priest of the Most High God?

Maybe the sun, the weariness, and the hunger really are starting to turn my brain, Barak wondered to himself. They'd ridden day and night with little rest or relief since the men of Shiloh found him with his band of rescuers in the mountains. The men had then scattered, many back to their own homes in the south. Only a few had accompanied him here to Shiloh. Villagers offered to take them in for the night. Barak walked beside Lappidoth toward the house where he would meet Deborah, the prophetess.

At first he didn't recognize her. That is, he knew the tall woman taking bread from the oven in the courtyard had to be Lappidoth's wife. She gave orders to a clutch of younger women—daughter, daughter-in-law, servants. Her loud, clear voice rose in the tones of someone used to command. Not unlike himself, he thought.

But when the woman turned, when Lappidoth strode toward her and took her in his arms in a restrained embrace, Barak found himself looking at a stranger. Middle age and childbearing had broadened her angular figure without softening it into womanly curves. A large woman, she seemed made of sharp joints and edges.

Her skin had weathered since girlhood, and the little hair he could see beneath her head covering was graying. The ungainly features that had once been gentled by girlish soft skin now stood out harshly in a woman's face. Noticng Barak, she moved toward him, hands held out, with a confidence he didn't recall. She had been—what, 12 or 13?—in those few weeks he'd known her. She must be near 30 now. Deborah, the prophetess.

Clasping his hands in her own large, work-hardened ones, she said warmly, "Barak, my cousin." Her eyes searched him quickly. She had an intense gaze. He wondered what changes she saw in him. Her voice and face betrayed nothing of what she thought. "What a terrible time you have been through. I am glad you can come to our home to rest."

Slowly he laid down the sword, the bow, and the quiver of arrows he had carried all the way from Chennerith. He felt strange without weapons. Like a totally different person. "I am glad you— that you somehow knew to send men looking for us."

She glanced away briefly, then back at him. "It must seem strange to you, that God would send me a vision. Sometimes it still seems strange to me."

"Not so strange. It happened. You saved my life."

"God saved it, then."

"He did not save the village I was defending." Why this sudden need to tell everyone that God was to blame? He had nurtured bitterness inside him for years. Yet, now that he was in a place of peace, why did it suddenly spill out?

Perhaps because here in Shiloh, everyone believed. Believed in the old tales of the One God, of the Chosen People, and of the Promised Land. All those fine-sounding ideals that meant so little when Canaanite slave traders hauled you away to a life of bondage and whips. *God sends you messages,* he wanted to tell Deborah. *Couldn't He use some of that power to strike down Jabin and Sisera and set His people free?*

But he said none of that, because Deborah gave him no time. Briskly she clapped her hands. "Bring bread and cheese and wine for Barak, son of Abinoam! He is our guest tonight! Avi, show him where he will sleep, and fetch water to wash his feet and face and hands. Come, everyone, let's have the evening meal now. Father is home safely, and my kinsman Barak has come to stay. It will be a celebration!"

Her voice rang out like a bell across the courtyard, sending family, servants, even animals scattering. Letting go of his anger and bitterness, Batak found himself borne on the tide of family. It reminded him of being back in Hammath with his wife's family. Even more, it brought back long-forgotten memories of the tents of his father and grandfather. When they bowed in prayer before the meal and Lappidoth addressed the God of Abraham, Barak felt briefly humbled. Something here was bigger than his doubts, even greater than his anger.

Later, with the meal finished and the family going about their evening tasks, Deborah sat beside him in the dying light of the fire. "Sometime you will tell me of all you have suffered since I saw you last," she said. "I feel sure, though, it is not a tale for tonight."

"Not unless you want to be awake till dawn," Barak yawned. "And I know I won't be." He shifted to look in her steady dark eyes. There was, after all, still something there of the girl she had been. "Truly, cousin, it's not much of a story. We fought for our lives and lost. I was a slave in Hazor. Escaping, I tried to make another life, but found I couldn't live under Canaan's yoke. And I've been fighting ever since." He forced himself to make his voice light. "Not so long a story, after all."

Lappidoth, who had been overseeing his sons as they fed the animals, came to sit across the fire from him. That was proper: even though Deborah was a close kinswoman, it was not seemly to sit talking so with another man's wife. "Not a long story, perhaps, but a sad one," Lappidoth observed. "And I suppose one that many of the men in Naphtali could tell."

"Our lives have been hard," Barak sighed.

Deborah stood. "This story you tell so tersely has left you scarred, Barak son of Abinoam. You are not the same man you were once—and I do not mean only the changes that time has brought to us all." Her voice had a strange note to it, as if it were not Deborah his cousin, wife of Lappidoth, speaking, but Deborah the prophetess, the woman who heard God's voice. "I see the pain and the anger inside you. I hope that here in Shiloh you find healing, before you go out to do what God has in mind for you." Then she left, retreating back to the world of women, doing their countless chores before darkness fell.

Barak looked across the fire at Lappidoth.

"She's like that sometimes," the other man said simply. "I think she sees further into people than the rest of us do, and she speaks more freely."

"Another man might want to curb his wife's tongue," Barak, who was also accustomed to speaking his mind, observed.

Lappidoth nodded. "Another man might," he said, "but I believe the Lord speaks through Deborah. Come, I'll take you to the sleeping quarters. You look ready to drop. Plenty of time for talking tomorrow."

CHAPTER 17

Deborah lay awake. Around her she heard the breathing and snoring, tossing and turning of her family at rest. In the courtyard below the animals grunted and snuffled. With a sigh she closed her eyes, but they fluttered open again. Sleep simply refused to come.

What a strange day this had been. Ever since her vision, ever since Lappidoth and the other men left on their rescue mission, she had been thinking of Barak. She had remembered him, of course, as a 14-year-old boy with golden lights in his hair and eyes, with a laughing voice and a readiness to take on the world—or a Canaanite army. Fourteen years had passed. She had thought little of the boy she had once hoped to marry. Then into her home today came this weary, hardened warrior whose eyes and voice were dark, who had spent years fighting without hope or without faith. Whatever remained of the boy she had known he had sealed away inside a locked box so small and so tight she could not imagine what might break it open.

Barak is the one who needs to hear Your voice and see Your glory, my God, she prayed. She had become accustomed to speaking to Yahweh in this way, almost casually, a constant interior conversation. Once it would have felt strange, irreverent, to speak so to the Creator, the God of Abraham. Now it was as natural as breathing. That's what she ought to be doing: praying for Barak. Not lying awake thinking of him like she had as a moonstruck 12-year-old girl.

But that was the problem, the one thing she hadn't expected. She had expected nostalgic memories, a rekindling of old friendship. On the other hand, Barak might have returned as an alien stranger, so changed she hardly knew him. Deborah thought she'd prepared herself for every possibility. But she hadn't anticipated desire flaring up again like flames from the last embers of a dying cooking fire. Lappidoth's faithful and happy wife for many years now, she had never glanced at another man with eyes of desire, even though she had far more contact with men outside her family than most women did. Never had she expected the possibility that she would look at Barak son of Abinoam—travel-stained and exhausted, scarred and lined from battles she knew nothing of, embittered and hardened—and find herself weak at the knees with her longing to touch him, to be in his arms.

God in heaven, take these wicked thoughts from me, she prayed, and reached out in the darkness to lay her hand on her husband's back.

Morning made things easier. Caught up in the busy bustle of the household, Deborah thought of Barak, for the moment, as just one more mouth to be fed. She had the sheep and goats led out to pasture, the bread started, and the morning meal prepared. The men readied themselves to go out in the fields. A hard days' work lay ahead as they tried to make up for time lost on the journey. Barak went to the fields along with Lappidoth, Avi ,and Eli, and returned weary and hungry at day's end to find that the high priest had sent a messenger for him.

"I need supper and a good night's rest, not a priest," Barak told Deborah. "Send word to him that I'll come to him on the Sabbath and not before."

"I will send the message, but I will soften your words somewhat. To speak so bluntly to the high priest would cause offense." Catching him before he voiced his reply, she added, "You may not care about offending the priests, but it matters to your cause. If you wish to convince people here in the south to aid those in the north, you cannot risk alienating the priests."

Barak stared at her hard for a moment, then nodded reluctantly. "Dress it in whatever words you wish," he said, and turned to go wash before the meal.

It was harvesttime, and everyone was busy. Barak did see the high priest on Sabbath, but he brought back no word of what the man had said. When Deborah met again with the elders of the village, no one mentioned Barak or of the cause in the north.

But after a few weeks, news from the north trickled in to Shiloh. Travelers told of the revenge Sisera had carried out on Kinnereth, the town that had dared to defy him. He had ordered every male in the town above the age of 12 years old to be hanged at the town well. Canaanite men had moved into the city, harvesting the crops and taking the women and children for themselves. Sisera's message couldn't have been plainer: to defy the king of Hazor was to risk annihilation.

Barak's mood grew even darker. Nobody in Deborah's household pressed him to talk about Kinnereth, but one night after everyone had eaten the evening meal and fed the animals, while members of the household went about their duties, Deborah came and sat near him as she had done on his first night in the household. Her keen inner senses, so open to the pain of those around her, ached every time Barak was nearby. So much anger, so much bitterness filled the man, and she longed to help him heal. Being as honest as possible with herself, she admitted that her attraction for him as a man had also not disappeared. Even beaten down by defeat as she saw him now, Barak was still a handsome man. Something in her did crave to touch that well-muscled arm, a kind of longing she had not felt since she was a girl. But another part of her recoiled from him. A core of darkness at the heart of Barak made her feel bleak and desolate. She wondered if anything could ever restore his faith in God.

Yet she could not allow a man hurting so badly to live under her roof without trying to help him. Nightly she prayed that her motives would be pure, that not even in thought would she betray her husband as she tried to bring healing to her cousin.

"Soon the harvest will be in, and we will celebrate the feast of Pentecost," Deborah said to him. "You know you are welcome to stay in our home as long as you wish, but have you given thought to what you wish to do?"

Barak looked up at her in the firelight, his eyes hooded and suspicious as always. "I had plans. I was going to celebrate Tabernacles in Chennerith with my men and with the townspeople we had liberated. We were going to proclaim the fact that one Hebrew town was free from the oppressor. Seems I've had a change of plan."

Every human instinct told Deborah to say, "I'm sorry," but that other voice inside her, the inner sense she was coming to trust as the voice of God, sounded a sterner note, and she obeyed it. "We know your plans have changed, Barak. What I want to know is, have you made a new plan? Have you given up hope of trying to defeat Jabin and Sisera?"

"Hope?" His laughter was like a cur's bark. "Haven't had that in a long time. But even without hope I can't stop fighting them. I tried once—to stop. Did the sensible thing. Settled down, married, had a son. But I couldn't get it out of my head that this is not how my people were supposed to live."

"We are agreed on that, Barak. The way our people live in the north—the way we here in the south lived in the days of Ehud—is not what God planned for His Chosen People. But now that your first attempt has failed, what will you do next?"

He met her eyes. "You're a bold woman, Deborah, wife of Lappidoth. As free to speak as when you were a young girl. Not everyone finds that seemly in a woman."

She fought down her annoyance and tried a wry smile. "Like you, I have had my times of being silent and seemly. For many years I was a proper wife and mother. But God called me. And when God summons, we cannot say no."

"Can't we?"

"No. Or if we do, only at great cost. After all, you yourself have not said no. You have been obedient to God's call to lead your people against King Jabin."

He raised an eyebrow. "That's your opinion. I know you see this as a holy crusade, God summoning me to lead the children of Israel. I don't view it that way. God hasn't given me much reason to believe He's concerned about our people. Maybe this is just my own crusade. I don't feel led by God, or called by God, or whatever it is you feel."

"What we feel is not the important thing, Barak," she said, settling herself more comfortably on the ground, hugging her knees with her clasped arms. "What matters is what is, whether we feel it or not. When you camped in the woods above Kennerith, fleeing the enemy, you prayed for help and felt nothing." She saw his fleeting look of surprise. He'd not told her that he had prayed. Anyone might have guessed he would have, but she hadn't even thought the words over before speaking: it had come to her with certainty that on that very night Barak had asked God to deliver him and had thought the heavens had been silent. "Yet even before you said that prayer, God sent me a vision, and my husband and the men of Shiloh answered God's call and came to your rescue just at the moment you needed help."

Although he nodded slowly, he still would concede no more. After a long silence, he said, "I need to go along with you when you meet with the village elders again. The high priest should probably come too. I'm going to ask if Shiloh will commit men for an army to go north. Only if the people of Israel unite will we ever drive out these scum."

The very next day Barak accompanied her to a meeting of the elders. Tersely he explained the plight of the northern tribes. "We need men. More men than we can raise there. We must have an army."

Silence greeted his words. "And you ask us to send you these men?" the chief of the elders responded finally.

Barak looked at the man with something like desperation. "You've got to."

The older men were already shaking their heads. "How can we risk the lives of our sons to fight against a king who has never troubled us? We are no match for an army with iron chariots, as they say Sisera has."

"And when we lose, all we will have earned is Jabin's wrath," another put in. "He will look south, and conquer us." Others nodded agreement. No one spoke in favor of Barak's request.

Deborah leaped to her feet. "Fools!" she exploded, the word sounding oddly harsh in her mouth, like a bad taste. The words tumbled so quickly to her lips that she felt as if they were flowing through her, as though she were only a mouthpiece, though every one reflected what she believed in her heart. "Jabin is not blind, that he cannot see beyond the territory of Hazor. He knows these southern lands are here. Already the other Canaanite kings pay tribute to him, along with the Hebrew tribes in the north. Where else will he look if not south? Whether or not we rise against him, his iron chariots will eventually swarm over the hills like locusts and devour everything in their path."

The men stared up at her as if transfixed. Yet they were not fools, even though she had called them so: surely they knew this? "And why will they devour us? Because they will do as they have done in the north, coming to this village and that encampment, picking them off one by one as wolves seize the weakest lambs from the flock. Because Israel, the people of the One God, are not a people. We are a collection of tribes, fighting among ourselves, disloyal to one another and to our God! If we do not stand together, in 50 years there will be no more talk of Hebrews in this land. No more of our villages and our tents! Those of our people who survive will dwell in Canaanite cities and worship Canaanite gods. There will be no prayers to the One God, no tales of Moses and Joshua and the Promised Land—and no tabernacle at Shiloh! The Shekinah will have departed this land, for the Lord will find no dwelling place here!"

The words rolled out of her like poetry, like a vast wind that stirred the desert sands. When she finished, the high priest was the first to rise to his feet, joined by all the elders. After a moment, Barak stood too.

"Truly, the Lord speaks to us through this woman Deborah," the high priest said formally. "The words you have declared are true, Deborah, wife of Lappidoth."

"The fear I felt when Barak son of Abinoam spoke to us is still there," the chief elder stated. "But I know now it is cowardice that holds me back from saying what I should. Deborah is right—for the Lord speaks through her. Do you not agree with me, men? Must we not send an army north to fight Jabin of Hazor?"

"Yes!" cried a chorus of voices. But it was not unanimous. As Deborah and the men sat down again some raised questions and doubts. But the force of Deborah's words had convinced most of them.

"But we cannot go alone, we men of Shiloh," one of the elders pointed out. "Barak is right when he says he needs an army. This message must go out—not just here in Judah, but among all the tribes."

The high priest looked at Barak. "You must take some time to go to other towns and tell them of the need, rally them to your cause," he suggested.

Barak looked terrified. "But what good will my words do?" he asked. "When I urged you to come, you refused. Not until Deborah spoke did you agree!"

"Truly, it was when we heard the voice of the Lord through the prophetess that we felt our hearts stirred," the chief elder agreed. He glanced at the high priest. "Could not the prophetess go too? Barak could tell them of the need, and she will stir them up to fight!"

The day was hot, but Deborah felt suddenly cold. Go with Barak? How could she leave her home? And how could she travel with this man for whom her feelings were so complex and contradictory? Would it not be improper to travel without her husband—or might Lappidoth come too? And would the One God speak through her if she rose to address the people again—or would she be left alone, relying on her own words?

A thousand doubts and questions flooded her mind. She wanted to say no, but knew she could not. This was her calling, just as she had summoned the men to theirs. Although she had no idea how it might come to pass, still, "I will go, if God wills it," she told the assembled men.

CHAPTER 18

R ise up, men of Asher! The day is coming when you can no longer sit safely on the shores of the sea, tending your nets. The enemy presses at your back. He nips at your heels like a dog. Your only hope of safety is to join your brothers, take swords in hand, and battle Jabin of Hazor. The people of the living God, the Chosen People, must rise and stand together!"

"She sounds a little hoarse," Barak commented to Avi.

"Her throat was sore last night," the younger man said. His eyes were on his mother, who stood on a low stone wall so that the fourscore men grouped around had to look up to see her, and her usually strong voice reached clearly to the back of the crowd.

They were in the seaport of Acco, in the southern part of Asher. The past several weeks they had spent visiting the villages and encampments of the tribe of Manasseh on the west side of the Jordan. Earlier they had celebrated the Passover festival at home in Shiloh after months of traveling through eastern Manasseh, Gad, and Reuben, urging the people to rally in defense of Naphtali.

A year and a half had passed since the elders of Shiloh had decided to support Barak and his tribe in their struggle for freedom from Jabin. In that time, Jabin's grip on the north had grown even stronger, though he had not yet pressed westward to the sea and these villages in Asher. Nor had his armies ventured south. Israelites in the southern tribes still felt relatively safe. It had not been an easy task trying to convince them to send men and weapons to fight a war in the north.

All these long months, Deborah and Barak had visited one town after another, accompanied by Deborah's stepson Avi. The young man was devoted to his stepmother and just as devoted to Barak and the cause of freedom for all Israel. His ardor and enthusiasm led to long conversations with the young men his own age in the villages they entered. Often these same young men would encourage the village elders to come to Barak's aid. Barak himself sat with the elders and told what was happening in Naphtali and described his own experiences as a slave in Hazor. Trying to make them see why Israel must shake off the Canaanite yoke once and for all.

But it was Deborah who was the center of their appeal. When they arrived in a town, the elders were usually surprised to see that a woman accompanied them and even more startled to learn that she would be the one to address the townspeople. But once Deborah started speaking, none of them doubted that she was a prophetess of Yahweh.

Leaning back against the rough-barked trunk of a tree, Barak watched her speaking, her arm upraised, her face intent. A cynic might say there wasn't much divine inspiration in it. Deborah gave nearly the same speech everywhere they went, adjusting it a little to fit the local situation. But she had the ability to hold a crowd in the palm of her hand. For a woman to have such a gift at all, when most never spoke to any man outside their own households, might in itself be an indication that the Lord was with her. But Barak had known Deborah as a girl. She had always been clever, strong-willed, and high-spirited.

He wasn't sure himself what had convinced him that it really was God who spoke through her. Most days he still had trouble believing Yahweh cared enough about His so-called Chosen People to even remember where they were, much less send them messages. But Barak had talked with Deborah. Knowing her doubts, her own fears, he realized that what happened to her when she stood up to speak in front of a crowd didn't come from within herself.

Wherever it originated, it was taking a toll on her. She had been truly reluctant to leave home again after returning for the feast of Tabernacles. Her youngest, Japhet—the only birth-child left to her—was growing up without her, tended by his half-sister Anna. Anna herself was married now, and her husband had joined Lappidoth's household. When Deborah was home, she was the center of a busy, happy family life. Standing here above the heads of a crowd of strange men with rough seacoast accents, her face slapped by the salt wind, Deborah not only sounded but looked weary.

She was near 30 years of age now, as Barak himself was. Both of them were no longer young. He would have pitied her, but she wasn't the kind of woman you pitied. Besides, he could no more pity her than he might pity his own sword. Deborah was his best weapon. Though many towns turned them away, many more had committed themselves to the cause. They could raise a real army soon, and smash Jabin and his general Sisera to shards beneath Israelite feet. That was what Barak lived for—revenge.

"How is this one going to go?" he asked Avi. "Have you talked to the young fellows?"

The young man nodded. "The elders say Jabin will never encroach as far as the sea, but the boys don't agree. They're on our side—stop Jabin now. Of course he wants to control a seaport like Acco. Any king would. If it's up to the young men, Acco will fight with us, and so will most of the tribe of Asher."

"Maybe they'd like to sit down and talk it over for a year or two, like the men of Reuben," Barak suggested with a bitter laugh.

But the men of Acco were more decisive. When Deborah had finished speaking, the chief elder announced that the council of elders would meet at sundown to discuss what they had heard. Barak checked the position of the sun, already slipping down in the afternoon sky. He, Avi, and Deborah now had a couple hours to talk privately with the men who had heard them speak publicly. They would use whatever arguments they could to persuade the men to commit soldiers and supplies to defeating Hazor.

In the end it proved fruitless. At sundown Barak sat on the dry, hard-baked ground near the village well and listened as the elders gave their judgment. It didn't take long.

"You have tried to persuade us that we must band together with men from the other tribes to drive the Canaanites out of Naphtali," the chief elder said. "Some of our young men agree with you. But we have decided that our strength is better used to fortify our own towns and prepare to defend ourselves if the enemy does advance toward the sea. We do not borrow trouble, and will not fight to save others from a threat that does not trouble us."

Silence fell. A thousand arguments leaped to Barak's lips, but he shut his mouth. He was used to this. All over the south they'd heard the same story. Yes, many had agreed to join them, but many more were shortsighted. If Jabin of Hazor wasn't camped on their doorstep, why go looking for a fight?

"We are honored that you have come to speak to us," the chief elder said, bowing just slightly in their direction. "You are welcome to stay with us this night, to share our food and sleep under my own roof. Also we will provide you bread for your journey on the morrow."

"He couldn't have made that much clearer," Barak commented to Deborah as they followed the chief elder down the rutted path to his home. "Food and shelter for the night, and make sure we're gone by morning."

"Nor did he say they were honored to have the Lord's prophetess in their midst," Avi pointed out.

"He could not have said that," Deborah sighed. "If he acknowledged I was a prophetess, he would have to explain why he would not obey the word of Yahweh. It's easier if he just believes I'm a deluded woman spouting words she thinks are the Lord's." She passed a hand over her face, and looked up with a hint of a smile. "If only I were. It would be so much easier to lay all this aside, to return home and be as these people are—blind and deaf to the needs of the rest of Israel."

Blind and deaf. That about sums it up, Barak thought next morning as they set out on yet another seacoast road, heading north along the coast. By evening that day they were in Achzib.

Here the mood was different. Not far away, west of the inland village of Abdon, Canaanite raiders had massacred several camps of Israelite herders. Some of the survivors had fled to Achzib. Acquainted with life under Jabin's iron fist, they were ready to listen.

Deborah didn't speak that night. She left it to Barak to tell his own story. Avi contacted the young men, both singly and in small groups. The next day, Deborah addressed the men of the village. Her voice had regained a little of its strength, though she still looked tired. The inhabitants of Achzib listened.

The women listened, too. "We've heard of this prophetess of yours," a man told Barak. "My wife wants to speak to her. We have a son who is lame. I'm sorry, but my wife believes the prophetess could heal him."

Barak knew what Deborah's answer to that would be. He had seen the same scene played out in dozens of villages. After the speech, while the elders talked among themselves, the woman brought her lame son to Deborah.

"I cannot heal," she told the mother. "The Lord has given me no gift of healing. I cannot lay hands on a sick person and raise him to health. All I can do is pray for him—and for you." Taking the woman's hands in hers, she prayed aloud. When Deborah prayed to the God of Heaven, people fell silent. Even Barak bowed his head. He'd never seen a sick person walk away miraculously healed after one of her prayers. But once or twice it had happened that they went back to visit a village where they'd been before. Each time, women and children came to Deborah with stories. "After you left, the weakness in my chest . . . the pain in my back . . . the aches in my head . . . it seemed to grow better. After you prayed for me, I conceived a child—this child. . . . After you prayed for me . . ."

Deborah believed her prayers had power, because she believed God had power. Barak still didn't pray, except to repeat the sacred words when Deborah or a priest led the people in prayer on Sabbath or at the time of sacrifice. Such prayers were important, because that was what it meant to be an Israelite. He would never bow the knee before the gods of the Canaanite tyrant. But before his own God, Barak found himself with little to say.

The men of Achzib eagerly agreed to join any army Barak might raise, but it was a small village, and they had not 50 able-bodied men among them. Avi, who was clever with numbers, was keeping count. That night, in the courtyard of the chief elder's home in Achzib, he said, "I think we might raise 5,000 men, maybe 6,000, if all those who said they would stand with us will come."

"Five or six thousand?" Barak doodled in the dust with a broken stick. While he couldn't figure sums or write out tallies, he could visualize pictures in his head. He could see a plain with 5,000 or 6,000 Israelite soldiers—on foot and poorly armed—camped there. Then the scene in his head shifted to the approaching armies of Jabin of Hazor, with Sisera at their head. Accompanying them were the armies of Jabin's allies, the other Canaanite kings they would rally to crush Israel once and for all. "Impossible," he said as images of iron chariots, iron swords, and spearheads of iron flashed through his thoughts. "We would be crushed."

"How many, then?" Avi asked, flinging down in exasperation the clay tablet on which he had scratched his figures. It cracked in two on the hard-packed earth. "Already they rule all the territory north of Mount Gilboa. All the towns of Naphtali, Issachar, and Zebulon pay tribute to the Canaanites—those towns that haven't been burned to the ground. Here in Asher the Hebrews hold the coast, but barely. In a year all these towns will fall, and we will have no land at all north of the mountains. It's the same story in much of the east—beyond the Jordan. How long will we wait to rise against them?"

Deborah's voice came softly from the darkness. "'When you cross the Jordan into Canaan, drive out all the inhabitants of the land before you. Destroy all their carved images and their cast idols, and demolish all their high places. Take possession of the land and settle in it, for I have given you the land to possess. . . . But if you do not drive out the inhabitants of the land, those you allow to remain will become barbs in your eyes and thorns in your sides.'"

"The words of the Sovereign Lord to Moses," the gutteral voice of the chief elder said, from across the dying fire. The group lapsed into silence.

"Well, Moses knew what he was talking about," Barak said. "They're thorns in our sides, true enough. But what are we to do about it now?"

"Drive them out," Deborah said. Her voice sounded certain, the way it sometimes did when she felt sure the Lord was speaking through her. Barak didn't know how she could tell, but she said it was just something she knew. "Drive them out, as our fathers ought to have done. Five thousand or 6,000, Barak, it's not enough. Ten thousand wouldn't be enough. But it has to be done. Avi is right. How long can we wait?"

Barak began to feel a growing excitement. The picture he'd had in his mind before—an Israelite army overwhelmed by Canaan's forces—changed. Now he saw swords flashing in the sun, arrows flying true to the target. Canaanite bodies littered the battlefield. Sisera—he visualized Sisera's dead body, and his own hand plunging in the sword. Shouts of victory filled his mind's ear. Avi was right.

It was past time to drive them out, to do what should have been done 200 years before.

"This is it, then," he said. "We will go back to the towns where we've been before, but with a new message this time. A time and a place to assemble for war. And that our hour has come!" He looked at Deborah in the firelight, searching for that certainty in her eyes that would tell him this was the right decision. But she stared into the glowing embers, and he thought that he saw a frown creasing her brow.

CHAPTER 19

An empty space lurked in Deborah. Lodged below her ribcage, the size of a clenched fist, it felt almost painful.

She knew what was missing: the sense of God's presence. The feeling of certainty. The God-breath that blew into her vital parts whenever she knew that the words she spoke, the thoughts she held, were not her own. Sometimes God's message was so clear she could hear the words audibly. He had given her the words to speak the first time she had tried to convince a crowd of men to join Barak's struggle against the Canaanites. In the long months since, every time she'd spoken, she had been trying to recapture those same words God had filled her with that day.

Other times, God's voice wasn't so obvious. But she still felt sure about things. She knew that a wisdom greater than her own guided her. When she reached into herself she found depths of knowledge and certainty that couldn't have come from her own limited experience. It had to be God working through her.

Now, there was nothing. When she searched inside she encountered only emptiness.

Barak and Avi both burned with the idea that the hour had come to bring the battle to Jabin of Hazor. Now, they were sure, was the right time to rise in revolt. She herself recognized that it was the right thing to do. Why else had she given up nearly two years of her life to tramp around the villages and towns of Israel with her son and her cousin, urging men to take up arms and fight? But was this the right time? Deborah had been sure that when the time arrived, God would tell her. Then she would be able to assure Israel that God's moment had come. Instead, Barak and Avi huddled by their campfire and drew up plans and strategies, while she remained silent. To her frustration, she had nothing to offer them. No certainty, no assurance that this was God's chosen time. No warnings, either. All she could sense inside was emptiness and silence.

That emptiness and silence drove her to her knees. As they traveled south through the villages of Asher, she stopped more frequently to pray. *Show me if the time is right, oh God,* she begged. *I need Your voice. I cannot tell them to go forward if I do not know.*

But she received no answer. And both men assumed her silence meant consent to their plan.

It was good to see them excited, ready for action. The long months of travel had begun to wear away even at Avi's youthful energy and enthusiasm. As for Barak, she was so sick of his smoldering anger and despair that she sometimes found it hard to be around him. Yes, she knew he had suffered terribly. His life had been hard and unfair. But whose life wasn't? Most people managed to carry on. Barak's suffering had twisted him in some way she didn't understand.

Once she had believed that she might be God's instrument to help him, to heal him. Now she knew that whatever healing God had in mind for Barak would have to come from another source. Even working together as closely as they did, Deborah seemed unable to lead him to any deeper faith or trust in God. And she was constantly aware of the danger, the impropriety, of spending much time alone with him. A married woman, she had been away from her husband for long months at a time, in the company of a man whose spirit she found disturbing and depressing, yet whose body was still virile and attractive. She was grateful that other people were almost always around—especially Avi, who had so willingly accompanied them on this mission. The little boy who had once resented his young stepmother had grown into a young man who was her pride and delight.

"Is supper ready, Mother?" Avi asked now, loping back toward their camp with long, easy strides. He and Barak had gone into the nearest village—a tiny cluster of single-story houses—to talk to the men. Now Avi's face was alight with excitement. "They are with us, down to the last man. One of the few towns in Asher where I've seen men so dedicated to fighting."

"Pity it's one of the *smallest* towns in Asher," Barak said, squatting by the fire beside him and taking the bread Deborah offered. She was cooking fish over the fire, fish that someone had given to them that morning as they left the last settlement. The people in these seacoast fishing villages had been friendly, had welcomed them. Some even seemed to believe she was actually the Lord's prophet: they asked her to pray over their sick, or to judge the right and wrong of some local dispute. But when it came to heeding the message the Lord had sent them—well, they were frightened. They lived close to the lands controlled by Hazor and knew better than people in the south did, what it meant to feel the wrath of the king of Hazor. When Jabin decided to push to the sea, most of these villages would sink beneath his heel without even putting up a fight. He would become king of all the land north of the Kishon River and the Plain of Esdraelon.

And what then? Then he would turn south. And in time, if they continued to bow and bend, the people of Israel would cease to exist altogether. No tabernacle at Shiloh, no Chosen People, no children of Abraham. No one at all who still remembered that Yahweh had promised this whole land to their ancestors. Deborah was slow to anger, but an ember deep inside her smoldered. She lifted the fish, roasting on a cleft stick, off the coals and passed the stick first to Barak and then to Avi. Each man took two small fish and wrapped his piece of bread around them.

"It tastes especially good when you've been walking so long," Avi said, taking a huge bite.

Deborah smiled. "Just as our own soft beds will feel good after many nights on the hard ground."

"A family in the village said we could stay there for the night," Avi offered. "But their house was very small. The people slept in the same room with the animals. I told them we had already made camp out here. Tomorrow, they want you to speak to them, Mother."

Deborah looked away from their camp and toward the west. The Great Sea was a blue line in the distance, steady and unwavering, constant as the promises of God. "What am I to say to them?" she wondered aloud. "It's no longer a question of just asking whether they are willing to fight. We know they will. What do I tell them now?"

Barak put the last pieces of bread and fish in his mouth and wiped his lips with the back of his hand. "You tell them that in three months' time, when the sowing of wheat and barley is done, our army will rally at Jezreel and march toward Kedesh. Under my command. Every man who calls himself an Israelite will be there with sword or sling or spear in hand."

"Kedesh?" Avi asked.

"It's the first city they took from us, and Jabin has held it for 15 years. It's on the road the leads to Dan, the only city in the north our people still hold. If we can take it, we strike a direct blow to his power in Naphtali."

"Kedesh is a good choice," Deborah agreed. The city's significance was more than military, more than economic. By striking at the first Israelite town that Jabin had conquered, they served notice that they planned to undo all he had done. Israelites would rally to that cause. "And the end of sowing is sensible. It gives us time to send word to all the towns we have visited. We can make one more visit to the head elders of each tribe, in hopes they'll give us our full support. Meanwhile, the word will go out to the towns, and whoever choose to fight can ready themselves for battle."

"How many do you think we can muster? It seems we could have five or six thousand, from the counts I've kept," Avi suggested.

"Remember, now, not all who say they're eager to fight will actually take sword in hand," Barak cautioned. "And some may not have a sword at all. They'll need all of three months to prepare themselves to go—to make sure the men are armed and shod and provisioned."

Despite herself, Deborah felt a little of the men's enthusiasm flowing into her own veins. Doing something would be so much better than endless talk. But neither of them had asked if the plan met with God's approval. Avi was simply too young and eager, too caught up in the excitement. As for Barak, she knew that he didn't really care whether it was God's plan or not. It was his plan, and he didn't wait for any higher authority.

After praying long and intensely, she went to bed greatly troubled. Although she had hoped for a vision in the night, or even a dream—something that would give her a hint they were pointed in the right direction—she awoke feeling as empty as ever. She simply did not know if they were meant to go to battle now or not.

Yet it seemed impossible to wait any longer. Faced with the

Lord's silence, were they supposed to move forward or stay still? Deborah had no idea. And neither Avi nor Barak raised the question.

So it was that in the early morning hours she stood by the well in that tiny village and said what they had agreed upon the night before. "Three months hence, when the sowing of wheat and barley is done, Barak son of Abinoam will gather the men of Israel at Jezreel, to march north and conquer the city of Kedesh." She could leave the military strategy and planning to him. Her job was to inspire the people. "At last we have a leader sent by God, a weapon in our hands, to strike at Jabin of Hazor, the oppressor of God's people! This is the land God promised to your fathers, yet your brothers in Naphtali live under the heel of the Canaanite, and the king of Hazor looks west to the sea. Rise up, before he trods you underfoot! Rise up, in the name of the God of our fathers, and fight with Barak son of Abinoam!"

The men—a handful only, for it was a tiny village—sent up a ragged cheer. "We will go!" a few voices promised. But one of the elders stepped forward and fixed her with a keen dark gaze.

"We have heard of Barak son of Abinoam," he said. "Many years now he has tried and failed to drive out the Canaanites from Naphtali. While he is a brave man, we have not heard before this that he is God's appointed deliverer for our people. Yet you come to us, Deborah wife of Lappidoth, as the sign of God's approval. We know your fame as well—as a prophetess and a wise woman. Are you here to tell us this is God's call to us now? Is this the time when Barak of Naphtali will finally succeed?"

Deborah said nothing for a moment. She could feel the silence, dry as the hot wind off the desert, all around her. When she spoke, her voice lacked the usual ringing confidence. "I am come to tell you that the Lord's hand is on Barak. I have come to tell you that it is God's will that we rise up against this oppressor, and claim the land He gave us." This much she was sure of. This much she could truly say.

But it wasn't good enough for the old man, whose white beard was the color of the purest lamb's wool and whose eyes glittered in a lined face. "And what is God's word for this hour, prophetess? Our numbers are few and our strength small. We will not throw them into a venture that does not have the Lord's leading." Until she began her journey Deborah had never realized that pockets of such deep faith still remained in the land. It came to her that her father would have been pleased to meet such a man. But her father was gone, and Ruel's daughter stood before these people of faith as the mouthpiece of Yahweh. The old man was not finished with her. He could not have put the question more plainly: "This army that will march in three months' time—is this the Lord's will, or the will of man? Have you received a message from God that we must proceed with this?"

The very questions she had been putting to herself and to God— the questions Barak and Avi had not asked. She saw the same questions in the eyes around her. Unable to march off to battle in doubt, they needed assurance and certainty. Even though she had no word from God, she was His chosen prophetess, and Barak His chosen warrior. If God did not deign to give a direct word, they must do their best with their own wits.

"Hear the word of the Lord!" Deborah said. "The Lord has appointed this task, this man, and this time. In three months the Lord God of Israel summons you forth to battle!" Her hand pointed toward the sky, and her voice rang. Only in her own ears did the words sound hollow. She saw the light of hope leap into the old man's eyes—into the eyes of those around him. *Hear the word of the Lord.* It was all they needed to ignite their spirits.

That night, sleeping again on the cold and stony ground, she trembled at the thought of what she had done. *Forgive me, oh God,* she prayed. *But You were silent, and they needed a sure word. What else could I have done?*

She could, perhaps, have done many other things, but when they came on their southward journey to a village that had earlier pledged support for their cause, she found herself standing before them again, repeating the same ringing words. The lie came more easily this time . . . and each time afterward. The first few times Deborah gave people her own words and claimed them as those of Yahweh she feared lightning from heaven would strike her where she stood. But the Lord did not strike, and He did not speak. Perhaps she was doing the right thing. God had given her and Barak wit and wisdom of their own, after all. Was it so wrong for them to make their own decisions, particularly when the Lord remained silent?

Not so wrong to make them, but to make them and claim they are God's sure words . . . her inner voice chided. She told it to be silent. As silent as God was when she addressed her prayers to Him each day. Once

He had been with her constantly, her daily source of strength. Now, she felt, He had withdrawn, leaving her to walk alone, to draw on her own strength. Which was running out. Yet day after day she stood before the people and told them that God was summoning them to battle after the sowing of the wheat and barley.

Chapter 20

Rain drizzled from a gray sky. The fourth rainy day in a row. The winter rain was a blessing, the gift of the gods or God. It gave life to the crops in the fields, to hungry people watching the wheat and barley grow.

But to Barak, commander of the Hebrew forces besieging Kedesh, rain was a cursed nuisance. It was the symbol of everything that had gone wrong with his war.

The timing had been perfect. Gather at the valley of Jezreel on the fifteenth day of Kislev. March north to Kedesh. They would arrive as the Canaanite settlers at Kedesh were sowing their vegetable crops, and an advance party would fall upon the men as they worked the fields. With the able bodied men surprised and slaughtered, the Hebrew army that followed could surround and besiege the town. If they could stop spies from getting out to Hazor with news of the attack, Barak knew Kedesh would fall in a fortnight. He and his men could occupy and fortify the town. It would be a base from which to defy Hazor, to start reclaiming the north.

Nothing had gone according to plan, however. When they assembled at Jezreel, less than half the 5,000 men he and Avi had counted on showed up. Messengers came from the tribal elders of Reuben: wait for the men of Reuben. They are coming. But from Asher, Gad, and Manassah, neither men nor messages arrived.

Two weeks they camped at Jezreel, waiting for the Reubenites, though the time wasn't wasted. Barak trained and drilled the men— farmers and herdsmen whose hands had little practice with sword or bow. Avi took charge of finding or making weapons for the many who arrived unarmed but willing. And they waited.

"The longer we camp here, the better chance someone will get word to Hazor," Barak grumbled. "They'll find out we're raising an army. Sisera will march out to meet us and mow us down like hay. Surprise is the only advantage we have."

"Can you march without Reuben?" Deborah had asked him.

"With 2,500 men? Hardly!" he snorted. "If they bring 500 men, perhaps we can start. But I need them here—" His eyes scanned the empty horizon. Then he turned away and shrugged. "I needed them here two weeks ago."

Finally 50 ragged-tailed men from scattered villages of Reuben's tribe arrived, shame-faced with the message they bore. "Our elders send word that they cannot risk men in this venture. We few came, because we wished to fight. But the elders would not send out a call to arms."

"But they told me to *wait!*" Barak exploded. Two weeks lost, for the sake of 50 men.

The Reubenite messenger—18 or 19 years of age, with bristly brown hair and a thin face—looked at his toes, scraping them in the dirt. "They debated it," he said. "One said to send men, another said to stay home. They could not decide, till the very last."

"When they decided to betray us," Barak spat.

The Reubenite took a step closer, holding out a crude weapon with wooden hilt and chipped bronze blade. "Such as we are, lord Barak, our swords are yours."

Barak stared at the blade, then at the young man and his sorry companions, and walked away without a word.

So they marched north, three weeks late and with half their an-ticipated force. The night before they left, Barak stopped Deborah outside her tent. He gripped her wrist, as hard as he would hold a man's. "Tell me, Deborah," he said. "Is your God really in this? Is it His will that we march?"

Her gaze, usually so clear and direct, slid past him like a fish slip-ping through a boy's bare hands. "It is our God's will that we fight to regain our land," she said finally. "You called for men, and these are the ones who came. What can you do now but march? What can I do, but pray?"

Improper as it was to touch another man's wife so, he continued to cling to her arm. He'd long stopped seeing her as a woman. "I could use more certainty, Deborah."

"So could I," she said, meeting his eyes at last. The next morning, when the men started north, Deborah kissed her stepson goodbye and bid farewell to Barak. She headed south to Shiloh and home.

When the men got within a day's journey of Kedesh, Barak led the raiding party. He left Avi in charge of the main force. Fifty of his best fighters approached Kedesh by stealth, creeping overland, avoiding the road. They came to the terraces where the crops grew. But it was too late for the sowing and too early for the barley harvest. On the hills were only boys tending sheep and goats. Boys and girls both. An ambush against grown men was bad enough, but fighting an enemy who had no chance to arm and face him in clean battle . . . Barak could not order a massacre of children.

So the advance party reunited with the rest of the army and continued on toward Kedesh. The boys on the hills saw them coming and retreated behind the walls. Barak had his men blow the ram's horn as they approached the town and surrounded it. He had issued his challenge—open your gates or prepare to be taken by force—and the defenders had rained arrows and stones from atop the walls. Sadly he remembered how years ago he had crouched on the wall of Ramah, aiming his sling at Canaanites outside. Now the Canaanites were inside Kedesh—a town that had, in his boyhood, been a Hebrew one—and he, Barak, was on the outside, attacking.

Besieging was the word, actually. But they had not come prepared for a siege, having no battering rams, nothing to beat down the walls or gates. Kedesh was stronger, better defended than he'd realized. So far he had lost 100 or more of his men in futile assaults on the walls. If they couldn't get through the gates, they would have to do it the hard way—starve them out. Sit down and wait outside Kedesh, until the barley ripened, till enough people inside were dead. Till the city leaders grew desperate enough to surrender.

They caught six spies, at different times, attempting to leave the city. Each had been bound for Hazor, for the city elders of Kedesh paid tribute to the king of Hazor and looked to him for protection. Jabin, king of Hazor had become in the past 15 years something quite different from most of the Canaanite city-kings Barak had known of in his time. The ruler now controlled the majority of the territory from his own city of Hazor west to Asher on the seacoast, and south as far as Mount Tabor. His vision was to rule the whole land—the land the Hebrews' God had promised them. Sooner or later, even without the spies, he would find out that a Hebrew army was besieging Kedesh. Barak knew he had to get behind those walls before Jabin's army arrived.

The siege dragged into a third week, then a fourth. The late rains continued. The men were wet, cold, and disgruntled. Several of them caught coughs and chills, and Barak feared that sickness would burst into flame and spread through the camp. He'd seen it happen before. For now, he faced a worse plague than ague or the flux—discontent and despair. Once those took hold, no army could triumph.

One full cycle of the moon after they had first made camp around Kedesh, Barak woke to a warm, dry dawn. He had slept perhaps three or four hours. Late into the night he had sat with his captains, trying to find a strategy that would end the siege and open the gates. It would have been easier had he felt they were all on his side. But they echoed their men's doubts. The tribesmen of Benjamin wanted to return home. They had almost convinced the few from Judah to agree with them. These southerners were far from home, and as they watched the barley grow on the terraces around Kedesh, they thought of their own crops in their own fields. Barak had to plead with them, then threaten, in order to keep them quiet. As he did so he wished he had Deborah's gift of speech. Better yet, he longed for Deborah herself to persuade them. But this was no place for a woman.

Still, even without a prophetess, one of the captains the previous night had had a decent idea. One that might work. It involved a spring that flowed out of the town on the north side. The officer believed that if a group of men staged an assault on the main gates, a smaller group could take advantage of the diversion to dig out the ground around the spring, weakening the walls and breaking through.

"It's risky, and we'll certainly lose men, but it's time to try something new," Barak concluded. If there were no danger of reinforcements coming from Hazor they could sit outside Kedesh all summer, but any day now he expected to hear Jabin's soldiers at his back.

The plan worked. By nightfall the next day Barak's men had overrun the town. The Canaanites put up a fight, but the battle was short. The men of Kedesh were soon dead or on the run. Barak had little stomach for killing fleeing refugees, but he gave the orders. He didn't want word of his conquest reaching Jabin any sooner than he could help it.

But some slipped through the net. Some always did.

Barak remembered the night, 15 years ago, when he sat as a boy by his family's fire and saw a bloodstained, weary refugee stumble into camp with the news that Canaanite invaders had captured and burned the Hebrew town of Kedesh. The same scene would repeat itself tonight by some Canaanite campfire. Some horrified man would blurt out the news that Barak, son of Abinoam, the landless bandit Hebrew, had taken Kedesh with an army of 2,500 men and slaughtered all its people.

He hoped Jabin of Hazor would pause at the news that Barak had marched from the south with a force of more than 2,000. If only the king concluded that all the tribes of the south had united to drive him out of the north, that thousands more men waited to follow Barak over the mountains. But Barak wasn't fooling himself. He was an upstart facing a strong, entrenched enemy, one who ruled the land with a fist of iron and chariots of iron. Within weeks, maybe days, those chariots would cross the plains from Hazor to Kedesh, and his men would march forth and fight them.

Whatever happened, he hoped he could hold Kedesh. He wanted to strike a hard enough blow at Jabin and Sisera to give them pause, to make them fall back to Hazor. But he had no illusions about ultimate victory. His force was too small, too weak, and no more men were about to pour north. The most he could hope for now was to fortify and hold Kedesh, to make it a base from which to begin to reconquer. But first, he faced a bloody battle.

CHAPTER 21

Deborah awoke to the sounds of donkeys braying, children crying, and men talking. It was early—she always woke early—so the noises must be those of travelers making an early start on the road. Throwing off her blankets, she climbed slowly to her feet, rubbing her sore back and stooping her head until she reached the center of the tent where she could stand upright. On the ground, Lappidoth still snored softly. Dim golden light seeped in around the tent flap. Japhet stirred in his sleep and flung one arm out over his blankets.

Wrapping a cloak around her shoulders, Deborah stepped out into the cool morning air. The departing travelers were the family from Bethlehem who had stopped there for the night, breaking their journey to Shiloh for the feast of Pentecost. The woman and her older daughter were first going to the spring with their water jars, filling them for the day's travel. The younger man was strapping packs to the backs of the two donkeys, humming under his breath as he did so. The old grandfather, white-haired but still straight-backed and strong, saw Deborah emerging from her tent and crossed swiftly to meet her.

"Prophetess, I hoped you would wake before we left," he said, holding out his hands. "Will you pray for my family, and bless us before we go to sacrifice?"

"I will," she assured him. "And will you carry a message for me to my daughter, Anna, wife of Eleazar the priest? Tell her we will not attend this feast, but will come soon, before her child is born." She could not explain why she would not make the short journey to Shiloh: it just seemed important right now to stay here at the Palm of Deborah, where she had camped ever since she returned from seeing Avi, Barak, Eli, and the others off on their march north. Lappidoth had not questioned her decision. Leaving their home in the care of Anna, her new priest-husband, and Eli's wife and children, he had taken little Japhet and pitched a tent here at the Palm. He said he would stay with Deborah as long as she felt she should remain.

While she had no idea why God had led her here, she was sure of His guidance, and that alone was a thing to gladden her heart. Deborah hadn't confessed to anyone yet the terrible sense of abandonment she had felt before the army departed, when she had sought for a word from God and received none. Nor had she admitted her own sin—that she had given Barak, and others, the clear impression that God *had* spoken when in fact He had been silent, as far as she could tell. She had sent more than 2,000 men into the teeth of battle with only her own assurance that it was the right thing to do—cloaked in words that made it seem as though they had God's blessing. Though she had repented of her decision to God, she had told no one about what she had done.

In response, she had received her first clear direction in months.

Now she knew, without doubt, that God wanted her to go to the Palm of Deborah, the place of her first vision, and to stay there. Stay there until He told her to return to Shiloh or go elsewhere. And Lappidoth accepted that without question, made arrangements for the care of their house, animals, and crops, and followed her. Truly, she was blessed to be married to such a man.

The family of travelers gathered around her, and Deborah prayed for them, laying her hands on their heads. People routinely asked this of her now, and when she prayed for them she felt a flood of assurance, a certainty that she was a channel through which God could bless them. They asked her to pray for healing and for barren wombs, and they sought her advice in settling disputes and resolving problems. At first she had received only a handful of such requests, mostly from those who were passing by the Palm on other business, but now people sought her out. Just the week before, two of the village elders from Ramah had arrived to ask her to settle a land dispute that had the town divided and the elders wrangling among themselves. The solution had seemed simple to Deborah, and when she proposed it, the elders agreed. It was clear, it was uncomplicated, but they had not been able to find it on their own. The incident had surprised her. At that time she had not felt any special sense of God's leading. Her proposal had seemed the right and obvious thing to do. She told them that it was not God's word, but her own, yet they seemed pleased with it and later sent word that the quarrel had been resolved and both sides were satisfied.

I do not understand this task You have called me to, O Lord Most High, Deborah prayed privately under the spreading branches of the great tree, after the travelers had gone about their business. *Sometimes I hear You speak, and sometimes I sense Your leading. Other times You are silent, but I feel confident with the wisdom You have given me. Only that one time—when I told Barak to march—did I feel I was stepping outside Your will. Perhaps because I did not tell the truth? I want to serve You honorably, Lord, yet I do not always know how, nor what You demand of me.*

She watched the road all day as she went about her chores, waiting for merchants or other travelers on the southward route into Judah. Anyone traveling from the north might have news of the army. Their fate was much on the minds of everyone who visited the Palm these days, for almost every village in Ephraim and Benjamin had sent someone north to fight. More than three months had passed since they had gone, and no word had come back. Again and again, people asked her if she had had a vision, if the Lord had shown her anything of what had happened to the army. But the Lord revealed nothing. She would have to rely, like everyone else, on a message carried by human tongue. Day after day passed, and no word came.

But this day was different. Near noon, Deborah was washing clothes and spreading them out on the rocks to dry. On the road to the north she saw a cloud of dust that quickly resolved into an unfamiliar sight: a rider on horseback. So few Hebrews owned horses, and so few Canaanites traveled this road, that Deborah straightened up at once and watched more closely.

The man headed straight for the Palm and her tent pitched there. Lappidoth was working outside the tent, molding a clay pitcher, and she saw him stand up to greet the rider. "Come, Japhet," Deborah said, leaving the wet clothes. She wanted to find out who the solitary rider was and what news, if any, he brought.

In moments she was close enough to see Lappidoth's face, though not the visitor's—the man had dismounted, but his back was turned toward her, though he seemed familiar. Lappidoth's face was what stopped her, though. He appeared shocked. Suddenly, he looked aged. Then his bleak eyes met hers, and he shook his head.

The man speaking to Lappidoth turned. It was Eli, her eldest stepson, who had ridden off to fight beside Barak. His face was grim. Deborah stumbled forward into his arms.

"Mother Deborah," he said, the old name he had called her ever since she had come, a girl three years his senior, to play stepmother to his family. "Mother Deborah, I bring sad news. You and my father will have to comfort one another."

She turned to Japhet to tell him to run and play, but Lappidoth had taken the boy in his arms. He was 6 years old now, so she supposed he was old enough to hear bad news.

"What is it, Eli?"

"We fought Sisera's forces on the plains south of Kedesh, north of the lakeshore, a fortnight ago. It was a terrible defeat. We lost many men—one of them Avi."

"Avi!" Deborah and Lappidoth cried out at the same time, and reached for each other. Eli stared down at the ground, looking weary and older.

When the first shock passed, they brought him into the tent and Deborah gave him some bread and dates. He told them the whole story: how Barak's forces had captured the town of Kedesh, then marched out from there to fight Sisera's army only a few weeks later. Outnumbered, they had fought bravely, but finally had to retreat in disarray back to Kedesh.

"What then?" Lappidoth asked. "Did Sisera's force set siege to Kedesh? How did you escape?"

Eli forced a tired smile. "No, God was with us that far. Though we lost the battle, Barak's men fought bravely. We did enough damage to Sisera that he did not press on to try to take Kedesh, but returned to Hazor. He is building up his strength and will no doubt launch an attack on Kedesh again soon." The brief smile vanished, and he sighed as he took a cup of wine from Deborah. "Thank you, Mother. Barak sent one man from each tribe back to bring news of the battle—and to recruit more men, if possible. I have been riding south through the villages of Manasseh and Ephraim. It's no easy task, telling old men their sons are dead and women that they have lost their husbands. With such news, no one is eager to volunteer for more fighting."

"Did you have time to see the family in Shiloh?" Deborah asked.

"One night only, with my wife and children. After I eat I must ride on from here to Ramah with the news. Fifteen men from there fell in the fighting, and it is a small village. That news will hit them hard. Your brother lived, though," he added as an afterthought to Deborah.

They were the lucky ones. Eli told them that of the 2,500 men Barak had taken north, nearly half had fallen on the plains south of the town. A small force, left behind to guard the town, had also survived. With just a little more than 1,000 men, Barak might hold Kedesh, but he could surely do no more toward retaking the north unless reinforcements came.

"Tell us about Avi," Deborah pleaded as Eli grew quiet, the important news all told. "Did you see him during the battle? Do you know how he died?"

Her stepson shook his head. "What am I supposed to say—that he died bravely? That's what soldiers tell people, isn't it? But we were not soldiers, Avi and I. Most of the rest weren't either. Ordinary men, cut down like grass in the field; it's terrible to see, terrible to be in. I didn't feel brave. I don't know what Avi felt. I know that the night before the battle, he was afraid. He didn't want me to see it, but I could tell. So young—not yet 20 years old—he was afraid life would be over before it was begun. And he was right."

"What will you do now, my son?" Lappidoth asked after a painful silence. "After you finish delivering word to the villages?"

Eli's eyes met his father's but avoided Deborah's. "I will go home to my wife and my children and my house and fields," he said. "I will not go north to throw my life away again. I'm sorry. I know this is a good cause—the Lord's cause. Avi would have gone on fighting, I'm sure. He truly believed it was right. I believe the same, and yet I cannot see much hope in it. Avi is dead, and your son Japhet and my own son are just little boys. I cannot see throwing away the future of our family for something that seems so unlikely to prevail."

Deborah felt a flicker of anger inside. He was right—his brother had had more faith. Avi would have fought on. *You have taken my best son and let the coward live, Lord,* she thought, and then was ashamed of herself for thinking it. Eli was a good man, but his concern was for home and family and the simple work of flock and field. No doubt most of the men who had died outside Kedesh had been much like him. She reached out and placed a hand on his head.

"Go in peace, Eli. It may be that this mission was misguided from the start—that this is not God's time to deliver Israel. Or it may be that a greater victory than we can imagine still awaits us. I am sure you do no wrong by going to care for your family and home."

Eli bowed his head under her blessing. Lappidoth, too, laid his hands on the younger man's head and said, "You have brought us heavy news, my son. But I rejoice that you, at least, were spared. Losing two sons would have been a blow too great to bear."

When Eli had gone, Deborah told Lappidoth and Japhet she was going to pray. She went to sit beneath the Palm, and only when she was alone there did her tears begin to flow. Memories flashed through her mind. Avi as the stubborn little boy who had resisted having a stepmother . . . as the boy a few years older who had first leaned his head against her arm and called her mother . . . as the fiery young warrior stirring up the youth of Israel to follow God's call to arms. He was dear to her in a way she could not express, and now he was lost, his youthful life blown out like a snuffed lamp. Worse yet was the burden of her secret knowledge: perhaps, in allowing the men to march with the belief that God had commanded it, she had doomed the mission and sealed his death. Could she ever forgive herself that? Would Lappidoth ever forgive her, if he should learn?

She felt tired, as tired as Eli had looked, and she longed for some clear guidance and direction from the Lord to tell her what to do next. But all she received was the same message she had received for months now: *Stay here. Pitch your tent here, at the Palm that bears your name, where I first spoke to you.*

And so she did, though she made one brief trip back to Shiloh to be with Anna when the younger woman's baby was born—a fine, healthy boy. Together, the family mourned Avi's death. Then Deborah, Lappidoth, and Japhet returned to their camp at the Palm, leaving the household in the hands of their son and daughter and their families.

Two months passed before further word came from the north. At the time of the grape harvest a messenger arrived with news. Barak still held Kedesh, strongly defended by the remnant of his army. Hebrew settlers from other towns and villages in Naphtali were coming there to settle, drawn by the hope of living in a place where they could escape the rule of the Canaanites. A community was growing there. Barak's forces were strong enough to make Kedesh virtually impregnable to assault, but too weak to carry the battle to any other of the cities of the Canaanites. They had fought a few skirmishes but no major battles. In a sense, Barak had returned to being a bandit chieftain, but now he had a sizable town for his headquarters. Word was, his messenger told Deborah, that King Jabin of Hazor and his general Sisera were amassing a sizable army, far larger than the one that had mown down the men of Israel on the lakeshore south of Kedesh. He might be planning a full-front assault on Kedesh, but spies said the Canaanites were provisioning themselves for a long march. It was possible Jabin of Hazor had decided the time had come to expand his control southward.

"I must alert the elders of the tribes," Deborah said. "Come and dine with us," she told the messenger. "We will give you a good meal, a bed for the night, and silver in payment. Then we must use you as a messenger again, to go to the chief men of the tribes of Manasseh, Ephraim, Benjamin. If there is a threat from the north, they must be prepared to meet it."

Deborah sent messages, but before the elders could respond to her summons, more news came. A Canaanite army led by General Sisera had marched past Mount Tabor and captured the cities of Shunem and Jezreel. The Hebrews put up little resistance and the towns quickly fell. Now Sisera stationed a Canaanite garrison in each town and began collecting tribute for Jabin of Hazor. The rest of the Canaanite army retreated back to the north. The campaign took no more than a fortnight.

At the end of the feast of Tabernacles, after the grape and olive harvests, the tribal elders of Ephraim, Benjamin, Manasseh, and Judah arrived at the Palm of Deborah, pitching their tents and turning the usually peaceful spot into something resembling a small and rather contentious village.

"This is what comes of our sending men north to fight," one of the elders of Manasseh complained. "Before Barak son of Abinoam sought our help, Jabin of Hazor was content to rule the land north of the Jezreel Valley. Now he has begun to march south and is on our very doorstep. Where will he stop? He will rule the land from Dan to Beersheeba before we are gathered to our fathers!"

"What nonsense!" another man, from the tribe of Ephraim, put in. "Our mistake was not in sending men north, but in sending too few! If we had given Barak a strong army, he could have broken the power of Jabin of Hazor once and for all."

"You would have us send *more?* I lost two of my three sons at Kedesh," cried an old man from Jezreel. "And for all that, my city is taken, and I barely fled with my life. If my sons had lived, they might have defended Jezreel!"

The babble of their voices rose around Deborah. Sitting in a circle upon the ground with them, she had said little since she opened the meeting by praying that the spirit of the One God would be upon them. So far, it was conspicuously difficult to see any evidence of a divine spirit in the gathering. Now, as one man after another spoke, their voices weaving together like the wrong side of a tapestry, Deborah raised her hands.

One by one, the men fell silent, looking at her.

"My brothers, my fathers, the elders of Israel, I have this to say to you," she began slowly and formally. She had not rehearsed these words. She had prayed fiercely through three days of fasting for God's Spirit to enter her and speak through her, and now she felt certain her words were God-breathed. "I beg your forgiveness for calling your sons and brothers to fight with Barak. Though I believe our cause was just, and the taking of Kedesh was a great good, still I fear that the time was not yet right for that battle. In my haste to see our cause prevail I gave counsel that ran ahead of the Lord. But today I have fasted and prayed, and I have asked for the Lord's words, and He speaks to you through me. This is His message: Stand fast! Resist the invader. Throw your lot in with Barak son of Abinoam and the men of Kedesh. Call together the flower of Israel's manhood, and assemble them to overthrow the Canaanite and free the cities of Jezreel and Shunem. Then march north to Kedesh, and see what the Lord will do there!"

The men were silent while she spoke—as silent as the dead bodies must have been when the sun rose high in the sky over the plain south of Kedesh. She felt the rush of the Spirit departing as she finished. Now she was only Deborah, with nothing but her own wisdom to guide her as the temporary spell shattered and the men became, once again, a gaggle of contentious tribal leaders.

"We cannot do that!" the man from Manasseh protested. "Prophetess, do you not have another word from the Lord for us? This is certain death—to defy the invader."

"Indeed not! She speaks wisely, for the Lord speaks to her," protested an elder from Shiloh.

"How do we know that?" another man, who had previously remained silent, now asked. "She has just admitted she gave false counsel once before. How do we know she will not do so again?"

"Because this is the word of the Lord!" another replied. "Dare you doubt the Lord's prophet?"

"I would not, if I saw a prophet," the same man replied. "But I see only a woman. When did the Lord ever send His word through a woman? She ought to be in her tent, doing the work to which she is called, not seeking to meddle in the affairs of men!"

Voices rose first to murmurs and then to shouts at these words. Deborah could hear some defending her while others agreed with the last speaker. "What woman has ever set herself up as judge and ruler among our people?" one man bellowed loudly, and no one could answer, though another fellow shouted, "Can't the Lord do a new thing if it pleases Him?"

"If ever it pleased the Lord to call a woman as judge over Israel, it would not be at a time of war," said the man who had first spoken against her. "We need a strong sword arm, not a mother hen! Call this woman's husband, and see why he lets her shame him by speaking before men like this! Perhaps he needs to beat her and teach her obedience!"

Several voices protested at this, but Deborah heard others mutter approval and agreement. With a sigh she gestured to a nearby young man to summon Lappidoth.

The high priest from the tabernacle at Shiloh was speaking. "In time of war what we need is wise counsel," he said. "The Lord has raised up a warrior in Barak son of Abinoam, but in Deborah wife of Lappidoth He has given us a judge and prophetess who can speak wisely. We in Shiloh learned that long ago, but now it is time for all Israel to discover it."

The young man came running back from Deborah's camp. "Hear the words of Lappidoth son of Nahor," he said in a clear ringing voice. "I told him that this company of elders wished to speak to him, and he said to me, 'Tell them I will not come. I am not an elder of the tribe, and I have no need to add any words to what my wife Deborah speaks, for she is the mouthpiece of the Lord!'"

Again, the group of elders took opposing sides. Deborah herself had said nothing throughout the debate, though she had risen to her feet when most of the men got to theirs and now stood there alone, unmoving. She had no plan but only waited to see what would happen. For several moments the men continued to throw arguments and insults back and forth at each other, with no sense emerging from the babble. Deborah surprised even herself when she finally raised her hands for silence and was even more startled when the quarrelling men, even those who questioned her authority, actually fell silent.

"Peace, my brothers, my fathers," she cried. "I am the Lord's handmaiden, but I will not set myself up as judge over Israel unless you will have me willingly. The Lord will make use of me whatever you do. I ask only that in this assembly you speak with a voice of order and not of chaos. Make your arguments in peace, and listen to one another, and I will sit quiet here and listen to you all. But for the sake of the God of our fathers, let this not become a brawl!"

A few shamed chuckles greeted her comment, and the high priest took charge of the council, with the other men deferring to his authority. A few stubbornly held that they would not have a woman lead them, but others—including the high priest—insisted that they could not disregard the voice of the Lord, even if it came to them by a woman's tongue.

The sun rose high in the sky, passed its zenith, and began to sink behind the branches of the Palm. Servants brought water and date cakes. The elders talked and argued, but at least no brawls broke out. One by one, the voices questioning Deborah's authority fell silent. But even of those who supported her most strongly, many still doubted the wisdom of rebelling against Jabin of Hazor.

Finally, in late afternoon, the high priest stiffly got to his feet. The men—and Deborah—were weary and hot from sitting so long.

"As the Lord's anointed priest, I take it upon myself to speak for my brothers here, the elders of the tribes of Israel," he said formally. "All day long we have debated and discussed. It seems to me that the fruit of our deliberations is that we acknowledge Deborah, daughter of Ruel, wife of Lappidoth, as a prophetess sent from the Lord. In these dark times we have need of a prophetess—and of a wise ruler as well. The will of most men here is that we should look to the prophetess Deborah as our leader, place ourselves under her guidance, and spread the word throughout the tribes that she is the judge of all Israel."

His words left her both relieved and frightened, as if she had been plucked from drowning in the ocean only to find herself perched on a narrow cliff edge. But the high priest had not finished. Murmurs, mostly approving, greeted his statement, but he raised his hand for silence.

"It is also our decision," he continued, "that to rise in revolt against the king who has taken Jezreel and Shunem is too great a risk at this time. Nor can we afford to send an army into the north to aid Barak son of Abinoam at Kedesh. Though we honor Deborah as prophetess and judge, she is still a woman, and in matters of warfare the men of Israel must judge as men. We conclude that we cannot now go to war."

The cliff edge had suddenly become narrower, and a sharp wind was blowing, threatening her balance. Deborah, too, rose to her feet. "My brothers, my fathers, elders of Israel, and my lord the high priest," she added, looking warmly at her old ally, "you have made a strange decision this day. I do not say it is strange for you to acclaim a woman as your judge, for as the high priest has rightly said, you have recognized the voice of the Lord, and it is that voice, not my humble self, that you have honored. Yet even as you say you will listen to me, you disregard the very counsel the Lord has given me for you. What am I to make of this?"

Their faces blank, they stared back at her. They had chewed over this decision as much as they were willing to do, and though the conclusion made no sense, she could see that they were going to cling to it. Again she sighed.

"I will try my best to do both your will, and God's will," she said finally. "I tell you now that God is calling us to rise up, but if your counsel is to wait, I cannot raise an army in my own strength. We will bide our time, and in such time as we have I will act as your counsellor and guide and judge. Only beware— I could rule you better if I knew you would obey all God's commands and not just those that pleased you."

They were harsh words to end on, and Deborah wanted to find something gentler, something to soften her disapproval. But the impulse she had learned to attribute to the Lord stilled her lips. It was right that these men—these elders—should go from here with harsh words ringing in their ears. It was a harsh time.

The camp had slaughtered several goats that morning, and the smell of the roasting meat was now so tantalizing that every man there was eager for the evening meal. They feasted together that night on meat, date cakes, and olives, and throughout the evening the elders came one by one to Deborah as she stood beside Lappidoth, and told her they were glad the Lord had sent them a prophet and a judge again at last. In the morning everyone bid farewell with kind words and blessings ringing in their ears. But Deborah knew the harsher warning of those other words had not been quite erased. And she was glad of it.

CHAPTER 22

"Good day, my lord!" a woman called, walking down the path from the well with a water jar balanced on her head.

"A fine day it is, Kezia, wife of Benjamin," Barak replied. He saw the girl's eyes glow a little just before she lowered them modestly to the ground. It paid well, this business of remembering names, taking a moment to speak kindly to people. Benjamin, husband of Kezia, was a simple young man who was better with a sling than with a sword, but still more skilled with a plough than with either weapon. But tonight his wife would tell him that Lord Barak had remembered his name and greeted her in the street, and when next Barak called for volunteers for a raid into Canaanite territory, Benjamin would volunteer quickly and fight hard.

Which might mean that young Kezia would be left a widow before she had even borne a son. Barak sighed. Commanding men was a hard business. Living among them and their families month in and month out made it far more difficult. They were no longer bodies, but husbands, sons, brothers.

As he continued down the main street through Kedesh, Barak greeted others: two boys leading a herd of goats, two men going out to the fields with their pitchforks and hoes, ready for a day of backbreaking labor in the hot sun. A woman sat in the courtyard outside her home shaping small clay pots. Watching her engaged in the task reminded him of Deborah. He hadn't seen her for two years. And he had never had a chance to tell her how sorry he had been about Avi's death.

The potter woman raised a hand in respectful salute, too far away to call out a greeting. Barak returned the gesture.

Two years ago, not one of these people had lived in Kedesh. It had been a Canaanite town. The Canaanite settlers had fled or been slaughtered after Barak captured the town. After the disastrous battle on the plains south of the town, he had barely managed to hold Kedesh. But he still controlled the city, despite several more attacks by Jabin of Hazor. Of the 2,500 men that had marched north with Barak two years ago, more than 1,000 had died and hundreds had returned to their homes in the southern tribes. A core of about 500—mostly young unmarried men, men like Avi had been who were willing to throw their lives into a risky venture—had remained with him at Kedesh. They were a fighting band, something bigger than a bandit pack but smaller than a true army, and hopefully the beginning of a force that might someday retake the north for Israel. At the same time they tried to rebuild Kedesh as an Israelite town, one in which Hebrews could live in peace, free from Canaanite overlords. Hebrews from other villages had come to settle in Kedesh, and many of Barak's soldiers had taken wives and started families. During these past months the place had finally begun to feel less like a garrison and more like a town.

He came to its gates, better manned and fortified than they had been two years ago. The guards saluted him as he approached. Old men sitting in the busy square just inside the gate bowed their heads respectfully to their leader as he passed. A group of small boys, too young yet to take the animals out to pasture, tossed stones at a target. They hushed and gazed in awe as Barak raised his hand in greeting.

Outside the town, men were hard at work in the fields. As Barak bent over the grapevines, his callused hands hardly even feeling the rough scrape of thorn and bramble, he heard a shout from the distance. He glanced toward the men on the neighboring terrace, but they were absorbed in their tasks. They had not called to him. Looking farther, to the road that led away from the town and was always guarded by a band of his soldiers, he saw a runner loping with a steady, easy pace up it. Having passed the sentries, the man now approached Barak.

"My lord!" It was Nathan, one of his most trusted messengers and spies bringing a report from the outside world to the enclosed community of Kedesh.

"Nathan! What news?" Barak dropped an armload of weeds onto the pile and wiped the sweat from his forehead with the back of his arm.

The messenger halted before him and gasped a few ragged breaths. "Sisera's army is indeed on the march again, my lord, just as our last reports told you. But they are definitely heading south, not toward Kedesh."

"South." Again. During the last year Sisera's raids into the south had become fiercer and more frequent. Jezreel and Shunem in Issachar had been the first towns south of Mount Tabor to succumb to the forces of Hazor. Now, King Jabin controlled all the territory between his own city and Mount Gerizim in Manasseh. He had pushed west, too, into the tribe of Asher, and now ruled several fishing villages. Gradually, he was becoming something more than just a local strong man as he acquired a growing kingdom. It was clear now that Jabin's dream was of an empire. "What is his target this time?" Barak asked.

"It seems to be Shechem."

"And he will prevail?"

"Doubtless. The city is mounting a defense, but although Deborah has called for the southern tribes to support them, the result is the same as always—100 men, no more, are willing to go. Sisera has 1,000. Shechem will collapse as all the others have."

Barak nodded. With strong walls and 500 men constantly drilling and training under his own iron leadership, he had barely managed to protect Kedesh for two years. Most Hebrew towns had little or no defense against the kind of force Sisera could mount.

"More news?" he asked shortly. No doubt Nathan was eager to be dismissed, to return to the town for rest and refreshment. Barak's messengers worked hard, ran hard, and faced great danger. He relied on them as lifelines, and treated them well.

Now it was Nathan's turn to nod. "My lord, I met with Avram on the road. He is going on into Asher, to see what he can learn there. But he had word that King Jabin has made a treaty of peace with the clan of Heber the Kenite, whose camp is less than a day's journey north of here. Heber and his men have sworn not to rise against Jabin, and to allow his army safe passage through their territory."

Barak swore under his breath. While the Kenites were not Hebrews, they were close kin and had traditionally been allies. In fact, he knew the wife of Heber the Kenite—his first wife at least. He might have taken another since then, as Barak's cousin Jael was barren. Still, there were family ties. He had hoped for more support from Heber, had even sent envoys to bargain for an alliance. Whatever Jabin had offered, it must have been thicker than blood.

Just as he was about to dismiss the boy, Nathan said, "Still more news, sir—from Hammath this time."

"Hammath?" Barak was alert at once, remembering the village where he had once lived, married, fathered a son. He had not returned there for seven years, knew nothing of the fate of his family.

"Yes, my lord. They have grown very bitter against King Jabin since the last harvest. The Canaanites took so much of their crop in tribute that several people—mostly children—starved to death during the winter. When the village elders complained to the Canaanite soldiers and asked for help, the soldiers hanged them in the village square as a lesson."

"God of Abraham," Barak swore half-reverently, and spat upon the ground. After being a slave in Hazor himself he was rarely shocked by tales of Canaanite cruelty, but this one was particularly offensive. He wondered who the old men were, thinking of his father-in-law Micah. But Nathan had more pressing information to report.

"Some men of the village asked me to send you a message," he went on. "One of them, my lord, is named Shemiah son of Eliab. He asked me to speak of him by name, for he said you were a kinsman. He asks for your support in throwing off the yoke of Hazor and setting his village free."

Well, this was unexpected news. For a moment Barak stood lost in thought, wondering what it might mean. In two years, not one Hebrew village had tried to rise in revolt, nor looked to Kedesh for protection. If Hammath was successful, others might follow. He thought again of Abigail and of his son. He counted back in his head, trying to think how old the boy would be now. If he even lived. Children had died, Nathan said, starved to death by the Canaanite tribute.

"Permission to dismiss, Nathan," he said, recalling himself with a start. "Go into the town and get a meal and a bed. Thank you for your reports."

That night Barak met with his council. All were in agreement. Hammath's cry for help was the opportunity for which they'd waited two years. Within three days a force of 300 men prepared to march to Hammath. Barak took command of the mission himself.

As they left Kedesh, he wondered what would it feel like to cross this land without fear, without watching for an enemy, and with the knowledge that he was traveling through Israelite territory. He hadn't done that since he was a boy. Then he had walked long miles believing that he was journeying through land God had given his ancestors. Twenty years later, he was a mighty man of war. But he was not free. He was leading his men through the mountains like the bandits they were, skirting a wide ring around Hazor until they were clear of the Canaanite stronghold and could join the main road again along the shore of the Sea of Kinnereth.

Strong, but not free. *And I'll never rest until I am,* he vowed.

But at least the expedition to Hammath was a start. After two years of waiting, of defending his one holding, Barak was more than ready for action.

What action they saw was swift. Within a half-day's ride of the village they met and eliminated the first of the Canaanite sentries. Barak commanded his men to fan out and circle the village. In that way, they made sure no runner brought news of their attack to the village. Barak caught the Canaanite garrison there—a mere handful of men—by surprise. Overwhelmed by Barak's numbers, they put up only token resistance. Within the hour all had perished by the sword. Only the commander survived. Barak captured him and brought him to the village square.

Memories of the place flooded his mind. The well sat underneath a spreading oak, and the steep rutted path ran from that spot down between the two rows of larger homes. At the end of that path was the house he had lived in, the home of his father-in-law Micah.

During the swift and bloody fight, the villagers had hidden inside their homes. Now they began to emerge into a blinding noonday sun. A group of men—the elders, no doubt—approached Barak. He recognized Shemiah, though his wife's cousin looked older now, with gray in his beard.

"Men of Hammath!" Barak called in a clear ringing voice. "I am Barak, son of Abinoam, ruler of Kedesh. Today my soldiers have taken this town in the name of Yahweh of Israel. The Canaanites who ruled you are no more. From this day forth my men will defend this village against the King of Hazor or anyone who seeks to place his yoke upon you."

After a moment's silence, a ragged cheer went up. Barak recalled how in his bandit days villages had been less than happy to see him come as liberator. Some would rather live under Canaanite yoke. But Hammath had sent word to him, asking for deliverance. Would they welcome it, now that it had arrived?

It seemed they did. The cheering built in volume and energy. More people—women and children—poured out of the houses and into the square. Shemiah stepped forward from among the men.

"Welcome home, Barak, son of Abinoam! Truly, you have delivered us today out of the hand of the king of Hazor. We will gladly be ruled by you!"

Barak stepped up onto the low rock wall surrounding the well. He gestured at two soldiers who held the Canaanite commander captive between them.

"What is it your will that I shall do with this son of a Canaanite dog?" he called.

This time, no hesitation. "Kill him!" the crowd roared.

Something had changed here during the past six or seven years. These people, once so placid under the oppressor's heel, had turned. Not enough to save themselves, but enough to welcome a savior. If only more Israelites would do the same!

"Hang him," Barak said almost casually to the elders. "My men will assist you. But do the deed yourselves. Hang him outside the village, near the road that leads to Hazor. Let his body rot there as a warning to the king of Hazor that this village is no longer his!"

Another cheer. "Lord Barak!" some called. "Our deliverer!" other voices added.

The cheers rushed through Barak's veins like strong wine. Fifteen years ago he had crawled into this village as a runaway slave. Five years later he had slunk away as a would-be bandit, unable to stir even his kinspeople-by-marriage to follow him. But today he returned not just as victor, as hero, but as ruler. Welcome home, Shemiah had said. Hammath had never felt like home, and Barak knew it never would be. But he had come back in victory, and victory was sweet.

Now it was time to find out what other unfinished business he had here.

The townspeople got busy at once with preparing a feast. Barak pitied them: feeding 250 men was no easy task for a village as poor as Hammath had become. But he had no bounty to share with them. Kedesh could feed itself but that was all. In fact, he would have to exact a tribute from Hammath and from any other towns he captured—but he would take care to see that it was a light tribute, one that would come as a relief after the harsh taxation of Hazor. For this one night, they would not mind emptying their storehouses. Tomorrow he would lead most of his men back to Kedesh. He would station— oh, perhaps a few dozen here. A stronger garrison than Hazor had left. But as for himself, Barak would return to Kedesh. There was no question about it.

Shemiah found him on the outskirts of the village, watching the hanging with professional interest. "There is one who would speak with you, my lord," he said, bowing as he spoke.

Barak felt something tighten in his gut. He hadn't thought much about Abigail and his son these past years—not as much as he should have. But now that he was here, he couldn't pretend he felt nothing at all. "This business is done," he said. "I will come with you."

He followed Shemiah down the familiar path to the house he remembered. Its outer courtyard wall looked worse for the wear. Plaster had tumbled off and not been replaced. A wild bush had sprung up and was climbing the wall. It had the look of a house of women, children, and old men. A house whose man had gone away and not returned.

She was waiting for him in the courtyard, standing with her hands clasped in front of her. His wife, he realized, was frightened. A young girl no longer, but a woman in the prime of her life now, Abigail's soft girlish curves had grown plumper, her face more rounded. Still she was very pretty. Her dark-brown eyes looked up into his, and he tried to read her expression. Beneath the fear lurked something that resembled anger. Well, she had every reason to be angry.

"Abigail," he said, stopping before her. With another man, a different wife, this might be a moment to take her in his arms. Neither of them moved.

She bowed her head. "My lord husband."

"Are you— have you been well?"

She raised her eyes to his again. Yes, definitely anger there. "As well as anyone in this village, my lord. As well as a woman can be without a husband to protect and care for her and her children."

"Cousin." Shemiah's warning was low, but Barak caught it. So they were both afraid of him. Barak guessed that Shemiah had tutored Abigail, warned her to be cautious, to bridle that sharp tongue of hers. She fought back her irritation and lowered her gaze again.

"Your—our son—does he live? Is he well?" If she wanted an apology, she wasn't getting one.

"Our two sons are well, my lord. On your last visit here, you left me with another child in my womb, who has grown up without seeing his father's face." She raised her voice. "Joel! Micah! Come and meet your father!"

How strange, that two half-grown boys should clatter down from the second floor of the house, running like kid goats, then stumble to a stop and hang back behind their mother. The younger boy, named for his dead grandfather— Barak had not even guessed the boy existed. But Joel—yes, he remembered now. The rounded face like Abigail's, the light eyes resembling his own. Barak thought of the baby who had wrapped a fist around his father's finger.

"Come to me, my sons," Barak said.

They obeyed—slowly. The littlest stopped at his mother's skirt and clung there, but Joel, though he paused for a moment beside his mother, approached his father and bowed before him. Barak dropped to one knee so he could look into the eyes that mirrored his own. The boy faced him with a clear gaze, obviously still nervous but standing his ground.

All the love that had not been stirred by the sight of his wife, now burst out as he looked into his eldest son's eyes. For a moment he struggled to find the right words. "Joel— you look as I remembered you, only you have grown up so much." He put a hand on the boy's shoulder and saw at once a spark of warmth, of welcome in those eyes. "I have been away so long, I have not seen you grow up. I am sorry for that. I have been fighting a war, and still have much fighting to do. But I have a home now, a safe place where you and your mother and brother can live with me." Then he glanced up at Abigail. Vaguely he realized that he had just made an apology that had not been his intention when he had entered the courtyard.

The boy smiled but said nothing, glancing at his mother. He was well brought up, then. Abigail had done her duty. As she would do now, Barak realized when she looked at him. There was no warmth in her expression, but there was something else. Relief? She still needed him.

"We will go with you, as you command," she said.

"I didn't mean it for a command," Barak replied sharply. "You have a home here—a family. I know there will be much to decide, to talk of. I only meant— it's an invitation, not a command, wife. I would be glad to have my family at my side in Kedesh."

Once more she bowed her head. She was as submissive as a wife should be, but he had not forgotten that her submission always had a sharp edge to it. Barak realized he had never really liked this woman very much. If they had lived together all these years, it might have been a hard marriage. On the other hand, they might have grown to respect, perhaps even love each other. No telling what might have happened. And to think about it was pointless. All that mattered was today, and what happened from now. Hearing a rustle beside him and feeling something, he looked down. The boy Joel had edged closer, slipping his hand into his father's large, calloused one.

Barak tightened his fingers around his son's.

CHAPTER 23

The town is divided, Mother. Truly, we do not know what to do. I begged them to make no decision till we sought your counsel."

Deborah searched the face of the man who stood before her and called her Mother. He was older than she was, with a serious, heavily lined face. Gradually, during these past years, the people who came seeking her counsel had adopted the title "Mother" in addressing her. Deborah, who had seen three of her children die before her, felt at ease with the term. The Lord had never before called a woman to lead and judge his people, so she had no forms, no rules for how she ought to proceed. Men seemed to find it easiest to approach her with their difficulties if they believed they were seeking the counsel of an old wise mother or grandmother.

It suited Deborah's purpose to look and act older than her 32 years. She was past the time of childbearing, though her hair had only just begun to gray. Still she kept her hair covered, and sometimes felt 50 years old. Especially as now, when she found the burdens of a land under enemy occupation laid at her feet.

Before answering she took a deep, slow breath. "Let me guess at what you have not said, my brother. Those who wish to withhold the harvest tribute are your young men, hot-headed and eager to shake off the foreign yoke. It is the older ones, and the women, who fear the conqueror's fist if the tribute does not get paid."

The man, a village elder of Bethel, nodded. "You see rightly. The younger women are divided, because they fear their children will starve if we give the tribute. Last winter was extremely hard. The Canaanites left us with next to nothing. Yet we know what happened to the people of Shechem when they tried to withhold their tribute."

"They did that against my counsel," Deborah pointed out. Every harvesttime a few towns and villages faced this dilemma as some of the men decided they would be better off refusing to pay the tribute. "Hide your crops if you can—if you must—but pay the soldiers what they demand. Until all Israel is willing to stand together and throw off the cloak of oppression, you can gain nothing by taking a stand alone. Sisera will turn and crush you as he did the men of Shechem."

"You counsel wisely, Mother Deborah."

"Because I have agreed with you, you think so." Already she had guessed that he was one of those advising caution in his village. "But I would have said the same even if you were bent on withholding your crops. Now, you must have an answer to give those young mothers who fear their children will die. Only fools will defy the king of Hazor to his face, but a prudent person may do a great deal behind the conqueror's back. Some of the villages harvest their crops under cover of darkness, finding out-of-the-way places to thresh the grain, so that if soldiers come they will not see how great the crop is. Hide and store all you can. I believe that if you are faithful, the Lord will provide for your children."

"Ahh—if we are faithful. There is the other matter," the man said, shifting uncomfortably from one foot to the other. Deborah waited. She knew what it would involve, of course. Visitors from every corner of every tribe came to her here at the Palm, and she heard what was happening in most of the towns. Bethel's story was a familiar one in these days of unrest and occupation. But she let the elder tell it himself.

"Those who worship the gods of Canaan have become very bold in these days," he said. "They have erected a Baal in the center of the town and bow down at it openly. Then they tell those of us who are faithful to the God of Abraham that if we tear down their shrine, we will incur the wrath of the Canaanites. Meanwhile the altar of our God is crumbling into disrepair, for no one will openly offer sacrifice there."

"They demolished the Baal and the Asherah-pole in Shechem, you know," Deborah said. "When the soldiers hanged the town elders, they said it was for defying the gods. Of course withholding the tribute was their real crime, but tearing down idols gives them a good excuse to vent their wrath upon you. Yet such idols are an abomination to our God. No city of Israel should have one."

"Then we should tear it down?" As the man's voice trailed away weakly she hid a smile. This fellow was not going to welcome any counsel that goaded him to take action. He would rather cower and hide in fear than face up to his enemy.

"The time is not right," Deborah said. "Just as the time is not right to withhold your tribute. Until we are ready for a full revolt, such half-measures will serve nothing but to bring suffering to your wives and children. Yet on one count the Lord will not have you sit idle. You should not neglect His altar. Whether the Canaanites and those who worship their gods like it or not, you must continue to sacrifice to the true God. Rebuild His altar, and lead those of your people who are faithful in worship there. You have priests and Levites in Bethel, have you not?"

"We do, but not all are faithful, and some are afraid, Mother Deborah."

She paused a moment, waiting. Finally she said, "You are a Levite yourself, my friend."

Fear flickered in his eyes. She could have put it to rest. She did not need a divine voice to whisper in her ear to give her such knowledge. Bethel was close at hand, and she knew its families well. It was not hard to guess the situation there. But if he believed the Lord had whispered in Deborah's ear, so be it. It reminded him that the Lord's eyes were always upon him.

"Y-yes, Mother Deborah. I have neglected my duties, I fear."

"Neglect them no longer, and fear not. Kneel, and I will pray for you." Resting her hands on his shoulders as she prayed, she felt the Lord's power flowing through her, a tingling sensation in her palms. They lived in a time of fear, yet when the Lord gave her the words "Fear not" to pass on to a fellow Israelite, she herself felt the power of those words. Yahweh of Israel was stronger than Baal and Asherah, and He would triumph. In her own strength, she sometimes doubted. But when she laid her hands on another to bless and pray for him, the Spirit filled her.

"Come," Deborah said to the man when they had finished praying. "Share a meal with my family in our tent before you begin your journey home."

"I thank you," the Levite said. "My servant has brought a small gift. We have little to offer, but—"

"We are grateful for whatever you bring," Deborah said. She lived almost entirely on the generosity of those who came to seek her counsel. In their first year here at the Palm, she and Lappidoth had tried to raise some of their own food. But Lappidoth was growing weaker, Japhet was not yet old enough to care for the crops alone, and she herself was busy nearly all the time with the affairs of the village and tribal elders, as well as individuals who sought her help. Such help was free of charge, of course, but she was grateful for any gifts people could spare. Yahweh always provided.

Lappidoth was sitting in front of the tent. He looked pale and tired, and Deborah hoped he had not been exerting himself too greatly. She presented the man from Bethel to him and then went inside the tent to bring out food for the men.

As the Levite ate, Deborah said, "When you return to Bethel with the counsel I gave you, remember what I said—that the time is not right *now* for withholding tribute or tearing down idols. But the moment will come. Tell those hot-headed young men of yours that soon the Lord will summon them to battle, and they must be ready to take up arms."

The Levite nodded, obviously uncomfortable with the idea that he would be carrying a message of armed revolt. "Wh-when do you think this might be?"

"I have no idea. The Lord has not told me. I am impatient, but I have learned to wait on the Lord's timing. Four years have passed since Sisera's armies pushed south of Mount Tabor. The King of Hazor controls many of the cities and towns of Israel now. His soldiers terrorize our villages and patrol our roads. We are strangers in our own land. I do not know when Yahweh's call will come, but I know we must be ready." She felt a fierce certainty of that. Even though she hated to see the suffering of her people, hated giving the cautious and careful counsel she had presented today, she was determined that this time she would let the Lord set the hour. It must be no half-hearted effort like the march on Kedesh.

In the north, Barak still held Kedesh. She had word from him occasionally. He had driven the Canaanites out of a few of the surrounding villages, but other attempts to reclaim the land of Naphtali had been rebuffed in bloody skirmishes with the forces of Hazor. Four years had passed since she had seen Barak face to face, but Deborah was beginning to wonder if he was still determined to fight for his land. Perhaps he was content to remain a local chieftain, to hold Kedesh in defiance of the king of Hazor. But it was not enough. God wanted more for His people.

When the visitor had gone, she sat beside Lappidoth. "How are you today, my husband?"

He smiled. "Not so bad. The pain is a little less today, I believe."

You may believe it, but I don't, she thought. Although he spoke lightly of his illness in order to spare her worry, she could see the lines of pain around his mouth and eyes. She saw how he picked at his food, trying to eat a little to please her, but the flesh was wasting from his bones. The knowledge that her husband would not live to see another winter lay like a stone inside her heart. Now she took his hand.

"You should rest. Japhet has gone to gather some wild fruits and berries for our evening meal while he tends the goats."

"Good—good boy. Yes, I think I will just lie down for awhile."

As he slept in the cool of the tent, Deborah sat beneath the shade of the Palm and watched the road. When she had first come here to live, the Palm had been a busy place, with travelers frequently camping there for the night. People were constantly passing on the road. Now, the roads were nearly empty. Only merchants and those who truly needed to go somewhere attempted the journey. It was safer to stay at home. Few came to the Palm, or passed it, except those seeking Deborah herself.

It was not a particularly safe place for a sick old man, a young boy, and a lone woman with just two servants. Deborah thought of their comfortable home back in Shiloh. Lappidoth's son and daughter and both their families lived there now. It would be a better place for him to die. She could not cloud the truth to herself, even though she and her husband might never speak of it openly. He was dying, and she could not keep him here, camped at a lonely crossroads in territory patrolled by enemy soldiers.

Canaanites also occupied Shiloh. The people there huddled under the same cloak of fear as did most of the other villages of Israel. In the past two years there had been no Passover or Pentecost feasts at the Tabernacle, though the priests still conducted some sacrifices and services. Shiloh was not a safe place. No place was safe. Yet Shiloh might be, for a time, a more comfortable abode.

Regardless of that, she was reluctant to leave here where God had called her to be. And since it was Lappidoth's comfort she was considering, and he would never admit he was dying, she had no one to talk it over with. No one but God.

"What would you have me do, my Lord?" she said now, aloud. "I want to serve you faithfully, and I know that you have called me to be here and judge your people. But I have made vows to my husband, and I must be with him when he dies. Should I return with him to Shiloh?"

As was so often the case, God remained frustratingly silent. She had lived with the voice of the Almighty in her ear for eight years now, and she was becoming accustomed to the fact that He spoke only when and as He willed. He did not always answer when she called. But she was learning to listen to His silences, too. In them, God called her to make her own choices, yet remain open to His leading. It was far more difficult than obeying a direct command from Him.

"Very well, then," she said. "Be it according to Your will. I am the Lord's servant." She bowed her head, then went back to Lappidoth. When he awoke, and Japhet returned with the goats and a basket of mulberries, she told them that she would like to make a journey to Shiloh.

"We have not been there in nearly a year," she said. "It is time to see our children and grandchildren again." Their son's eyes brightened at the thought of playing with nieces and nephews only a few years younger than himself. It wasn't good for him to be so much away from other children, Deborah thought. Perhaps when she returned to the Palm, she should come alone, sparing her family members the isolation of her difficult call.

They made the short journey slowly, walking beside their laden donkey. Deborah urged Lappidoth to ride, but his pride would not allow him to do so for more than a few short periods. He wanted to walk into his old home, she saw, upright and strong, even though the pain was tearing him apart within. They approached the gates of Shiloh at dusk. In the old days they would have heard the singing of the priests and people from the tabernacle at this hour, the time of the evening sacrifice. Now the hilltop was silent, and one of two Canaanite soldiers leveled an iron-tipped spear at them as they neared the gate.

"Who goes there?"

"Lappidoth, a citizen of Shiloh. My house is within the gates."

"I do not know your face, Hebrew," the soldier said.

"My son Eli dwells within, and my son-in-law Eleazar the priest."

"Eli and Eleazar I know," the soldier growled. "But before you go in, we search your packs."

"What?" Lappidoth said. The spear swung toward his belly.

"You bring no weapons into this town," the other soldier said as he began tearing their carefully packed bundles off the donkeys back. "Hebrew dogs may not carry swords."

"I have no sword," Lappidoth protested. But he stepped back, as did Deborah and Japhet. Deborah's heart beat a little faster. She was glad her own name and face were not better known. Sometimes she wondered if that was why God had chosen a woman to lead His people at this time. As long as she was only the wife of Lappidoth, she might be overlooked. If a man had been acclaimed as prophet and judge, the Canaanites would take more notice.

The soldiers tore through the packages. They found no weapons save the small working knife Lappidoth wore at his belt, which they took from him. They also seized a cake of dates and a bolt of fine, dyed blue cloth, both of which Deborah had received from visitors to the Palm. She had intended them as gifts for the family here in Shiloh, but of course she made no protest when the soldiers confiscated them. When the two men had finished, they walked back to the gate, sharing the dates, leaving Deborah and Japhet to repack the bundles. Exhausted and looking gray, Lappidoth sat down on the ground to wait.

It was full dark by the time they walked down the silent streets of Shiloh. Most people were abed by dark anyway, but in the old days there would always have been a few keeping late hours, coming or going on business of their own. Now, nobody liked to be out after sunset. Deborah had heard far too many tales of what Canaanite soldiers did to women—and even men—who walked alone in the village streets. As she passed the quiet houses of her former neighbors and the dark silent bulk of the tabernacle, anger burned inside her. Like Lappidoth, she carried a pain inside that was eating away at her. Only hers was a disease not of the flesh but of the spirit.

The family was asleep when the trio reached their home. As they entered the courtyard, Deborah heard a scurrying up in the sleeping room. A lithe figure scrambled swiftly down the ladder and crossed the court toward them, picking its way through the sleeping goats. "Who goes there? What do you want with us?" Fear edged Eli's voice.

"Peace, my son," Deborah said, seeing that Lappidoth was too weary to reply. "It is your father, mother, and brother. We were delayed on the way, and at the gate, and are sorry to arrive so late."

"Father! Mother!" All his tension gone, Eli instantly reached them. He took Lappidoth in his arms, and Deborah saw even in the dim light the worry that creased his face when he looked into his father's eyes. She remembered her own journey back home to Ramah, years ago, to visit at her father's deathbed. A father was the cornerstone of the family, the foundation of one's world. Watching your father die was a terrible thing. For a moment she regretted bringing Lappidoth home. She could have spared Eli and Anna this ordeal.

But by the next morning she knew she had done right. Lappidoth was comfortable in the best bed in the house, close by the courtyard wall of the sleeping quarters so that he had plenty of light and air. Anna and Eli's wife, Keturah, tended him lovingly, leaving little work for Deborah to do. "You must rest too, Mother," Anna said. "After all, you have cared for Papa all by yourself these long months. I wish you had brought him home sooner."

"Perhaps I should have," Deborah admitted. It was hard to explain to her stepdaughter why her own work seemed so pressing. Though her family felt honored that God had called her and proud that the elders of Israel looked to her for leadership and guidance, they were awkward, too, with the knowledge that their mother was so different from other women, that she moved in a world so remote from the common concerns of a woman of her age. For the moment, Deborah found it comfortable simply to be in a place where people called her "Mother" because she was their mother. Being a mother to all Israel was wearying. Right now, all she wanted was to be a mother to her own family, and most of all, a wife to Lappidoth in his final days.

She sat beside him for long hours, letting the younger women bring broth and bread and herbs that would supposedly relieve pain. The food and drink did not make him stronger, and the herbs did not dull his agony for long. Deborah sat holding his hand, feeling it clench more tightly when the pain was bad.

"What can I do?" she asked repeatedly. "Is there anything I can do to help?"

"Talk to me. Always loved—to hear you talk . . ." Lappidoth said between clenched teeth.

An odd thing for a man to like in a wife. Most men complained if their wives chattered too much, and a silent woman was the ideal. But it was true. He had always listened to her. So he listened now through his pain. She hardly knew what to say, so she began talking about their life together, how frightened and unsure she had been to come into his house as a girl of 14 and attempt to replace the first wife who had been the mother of his children.

The flicker of a smile played around his lips as she retold those stories, and his hand squeezed hers—not with pain this time. "And when I lost the first baby," she continued, "then you were so good to me. And our little girl—my Mirah, do you remember her? How pretty she was, with her curls and her big dark eyes? She was just beginning to talk . . . I thought I would die then, when she died. I didn't know how I could bear the pain. But you were always there. And all I want, now, is to be here with you."

Finally she ran out of her own words and began reciting the stories of the ancestors—the tales of Abraham, Isaac, and Jacob, and of Joseph in Egypt. As Lappidoth drifted into and out of wakefulness, she tested her memory by recalling the blessing of Jacob to his sons, reciting it word for word as her father had taught her so long ago:

> "The scepter shall not depart from Judah,
> Nor a lawgiver from between his feet,
> Until Shiloh comes;
> And to him shall be the obedience of the people.
> Binding his donkey to the vine,
> And his donkey's colt to the choice vine,
> He washed his garments in wine,
> And his clothes in the blood of grapes.
> His eyes are darker than wine,
> And his teeth whiter than milk."

"Is Father awake?" Anna had come in so quietly that Deborah had not heard her.

"No. He fell asleep while I was talking. But I kept going. He sleeps so fitfully, sometimes he likes to awaken and hear the sound of my voice."

"You should rest yourself."

"It won't be long now. I'd like to be with him at the last. There'll be plenty of time for me to rest afterward."

She was right. Lappidoth lived till sunset that evening. He did not open his eyes again, and his breathing at the last became more ragged and shallow. Unlike Jacob, he spoke no dying words to his children or grandchildren. Deborah remembered thinking the same thing at her father's deathbed: how rare that one actually had a chance to give blessings and say farewells at the time of death! And how fortunate were the families of those, like Lappidoth, whose entire lives had been a blessing.

She continued to sit holding his hand even after it had already grown cold. He looked so peaceful now that he no longer struggled for breath.

Anna placed gentle hands on Deborah's shoulders. "You said you would have time to rest when he was asleep. Go now and rest. I will sit with his body through the night."

Deborah lay on a pallet, a thin blanket pulled over her against the chill of the night, but she did not sleep. As she lay awake she tried to imagine life without Lappidoth. She had traveled so far, done so many things a good wife was not expected to do. Many husbands would have been angry, forbidden her to speak out, denounced her. Never Lappidoth. He had always believed her call was from God, always supported and defended her. Even when she left him those long months to go with Barak and Avi, preaching about the need to overthrow the oppressors. *Avi.* She thought of him, too, with a pang of pain. He should have been here in this hour, helping to lay his father to rest. Instead his own bones lay cold in the earth, in a spot she had never seen.

And she thought, too, of Barak. Was it wrong to wish for another man's consolation over her husband's grave? Wrong to imagine him placing strong arms around her as Lappidoth had so often done, shielding her from the pain and emptiness? Deborah didn't know if it was right or not, but she knew the dream was an illusion. The man in her imagination was a Barak she had created from fantasy, a picture of the grown man painted over the kindly 14-year-old boy he had been long ago. The real Barak would have had no consolation, no kindness to offer. He had suffered too many griefs of his own, and though he was a mighty warrior, she knew he was no source of strength. In the most essential way, Barak was a weak man, for his faith in God was fragile. Hers was stronger. She knew where she had to turn.

Lappidoth was dead. Avi was dead. Her own father was long dead. Barak was far away and no good to her. While Eli was family, she had never been as close to him as to Avi and Anna. If Deborah needed a strong man to lean on, she had but one choice.

God of my fathers, God my Father, be with me now. You called to me once, and I have followed You ever since. Now my husband is gone, and I do not know what to do.

Perhaps her call from God had ended with Lappidoth's life. Might she finish her days here at Shiloh, a widow among her children and grandchildren? At the moment the thought greatly appealed to her. She relaxed into Yahweh's loving arms as she once had into her husband's, and finally sleep came.

Lappidoth's family buried him, then mourned for the full seven days. When the period of mourning ended, Deborah asked Eli to take her to the tabernacle to make a sacrifice. She wanted to give thanks for her husband's life, to mark his passing with a public declaration of her loyalty to the God who had brought them together.

Eli frowned. "It is a good thought, Mother, and something we would have done in the old days. Now, people give sacrifices rarely . . . only at the feasts, or when they have committed a grievous sin. Most of us avoid going to the tabernacle."

"Is this true?" She turned to Anna's husband, who was, after all, a priest. He looked embarrassed and glanced down to the dirt at his feet.

"I wish it were otherwise, Mother, but it is true. I myself still go to the tabernacle each Sabbath, as you have seen, but most people in Shiloh rarely visit it. Many of the priests even stay away. The Canaanite soldiers harass the worshippers and often demand portions of the sacrifices. They desecrate the services. We cannot carry them out as the law says we should."

"What does the high priest say? What does he do about this?" she demanded.

"He says nothing. What can he? He does not wish to earn the wrath of the soldiers."

"Take me to see him," Deborah insisted. "I must speak with him—this day." A few moments ago, she had thought of herself as nothing but a grieving widow. Now she stood tall, feeling the Lord's anger inside her. Bad as things were, she had not realized that here in Shiloh, at the tabernacle itself, the Canaanites' influence had managed to bring a halt to the daily sacrifices and the worship of God.

Quickly, the two younger men readied a young kid goat for sacrifice while Deborah washed her face and put on her cloak. She strode through the streets of Shiloh ahead of the men and the animal. Her old neighbors peeked curiously from their courtyards as the little procession passed, but no one greeted them or asked where they were going.

As she climbed the tabernacle hill, Deborah realized something was wrong. What she heard was more than just the disturbing silence that had bothered her ever since returning to Shiloh. The tabernacle was not silent now. In fact, she heard shouts and commotion from inside. The rough voices coming from beyond the curtained wall were not all Hebrew ones.

"Take it away! You shall not bring this abomination in here!" It was the high priest, Deborah saw as she entered the outer court of the tabernacle. He stood, a frail and aging man, with a clutch of frightened priests and Levites huddled behind him—no more than half a dozen men in all. Like a fragile dam trying to hold back a river, they blocked the entrance to the holy place against several burly Canaanites and a number of Hebrew villagers from Shiloh itself. The larger group was trying to enter the holy place with a gilded Baal on a platform. "Lay it on the table of shewbread!" urged one voice. "No, over here!" another suggested. Then one of the Canaanites shouted, "What is in this place? Let us bring it here!"

"Not in the Most Holy Place!" the high priest protested in horror. *"No!"*

Deborah raised a hand, meaning to stop the priest. Let the Canaanites bring their idol into the Most Holy Place. She knew what would happen if such a person, bearing such a thing, set foot in the same room as the ark where Yahweh's Shekinah glory rested. Let them challenge the God of Israel, and taste His punishment themselves.

But clearly the Hebrews among the Baal-worshippers also feared the Most Holy, for they quickly said, "Out here is good enough. Here, on the table with the bread."

The high priest sagged as if air had rushed out of him. He turned to Deborah, whom he had just noticed. "Do you see this, prophetess of God? What is the Lord's word for us? They are setting up an idol in His very sanctuary."

Deborah was a woman and not a priest and had never even set foot into the Holy Place. But suddenly her vision was transformed, as if with one pair of eyes she viewed the old priest looking defeated in front of the curtain, while with another pair she saw the curtain torn apart so that she looked straight into the Most Holy. She gazed at the ark—something her human eyes had never seen—and the golden cherubim above it. They were dazzling with light, a radiance not their own but reflected from the shining Being between them. Although she saw no face, no body, only the overwhelming light, she knew God was there. His Presence was around her and blazing out from the tabernacle in a way she had never experienced—never even guessed at—before. Her first vision at the Palm and every vision of her life since had been only a prelude to this. Deborah had not imagined such glory.

The Voice that took possession of her thundered so loudly she wondered that everyone in the tabernacle and courtyard was not looking about in terror. But this Voice spoke to her alone: the others heard nothing, saw nothing out of the ordinary. In the background she could still hear the crowd, unaware, prattling away about their little metal god.

Deborah, my daughter, rise up! It is time for the men of Israel to rise! You must cower under their feet no longer! Send for Barak, the son of Abinoam. Tell him that the hour has come!

CHAPTER 24

Barak twisted to meet his attacker's spear, thrusting his shield between them just in time. The impact threw him back, almost off his feet, but he quickly regained his balance and turned again, slicing hard with his sword. The short, burly man he was fighting put up his own shield, but he wasn't fast enough. Barak's sword cut across his bare upper thigh, opening a deep gash. Howling with pain, the Canaanite staggered back. Barak would have moved in to finish him off, but another assailant appeared on the right, and he spun to meet the new threat. His spear had broken early in the battle, but he was quick with his sword, and it gleamed red with the blood of at least a dozen enemy soldiers.

"Retreat!" Barak heard the command ringing clear through the clanging and shouts of the skirmish. A sharp blast on the ram's horn followed. He took some satisfaction in knowing that over the years he'd become very familiar with the Canaanite signal for retreat. After all, he'd heard it enough.

"Pursue them!" he yelled at the top of his lungs as the Canaanites fled toward the village. Winning this fight wasn't enough. He wanted to slaughter every one of these dogs of Hazor. Only then could the people of the village know that Barak of Kedesh was their lord, and that they were safe from the king of Hazor. Only then could he send a clear message to Jabin and Sisera: *This is my land, and you do not challenge me here.*

It took another hour before they put the last of the small band of soldiers to the sword, but Barak's men were hard, trained, and efficient. Their own losses were few—five Hebrews dead, a dozen injured. The elders of Abel-beth-maachah set their healers to caring for the wounded while they hosted Barak and his victorious band at a feast in the center of the village.

At the end of the celebration, Barak summoned the elders. In the sight of all the people of the village, he said, "We have driven out the Canaanites who tried to win back this land. Your homes and your crops are safe. What do you give us in return?"

The chief elder went down on one knee. "We give you our allegiance, Lord Barak. We are loyal to you alone. We give tribute from our crops to you only, and we will not allow the Canaanites to set foot on our soil."

Until the next time, Barak thought. These village people were such sheep. But who could blame them, living in terror as they did? He did his best to keep them safe, but nobody was really safe in times like these. "Ready two wagonloads of wheat and barley to return to Kedesh with us as tribute," he responded. "In return I vow to protect you against any foreign lord, and to fight your battles for you." He hardened himself to ignore their looks of worry when he mentioned the wagons. The king of Hazor would have demanded more—much more—in tribute. These were lean times in the villages, but lean times in Kedesh too. Barak needed to feed his soldiers and their families.

The trip back to Kedesh the next day was slow. The wagons of tribute slowed them down, as did the wounded men who were well enough to return to Kedesh, and the bodies of the dead who would be buried nearer to Kedesh, where their families could mourn them. Barak made the most of the plodding pace, riding on his donkey in a wide arc so that he could survey more of the land he controlled, seeing the villages and the camps of herdsmen who relied on him for protection.

Nearly five years after his capture of Kedesh, Barak was secure in his position, so far as that went. He was unchallenged chieftain of the city itself and the land around it. Beyond that, a score of villages acknowledged him as their overlord, paying him tribute and relying on his protection. All together he controlled perhaps a third of the territory of the tribe of Naphtali, though each year he still fought numerous small battles with Canaanite forces for control over those lands. Some villages he held, others he lost. It was a long way from his dream of reconquering the north for Israel. Indeed, now that Jabin of Hazor ruled most of the southern tribes as well, Barak was well aware that his little island of authority gave him a very fragile grip on power. He'd ceased to dream about gaining more. Now all he thought of was holding on to what he had.

At dusk the men passed through rolling hills thick with sheep. Those in front cleared paths through the milling flocks, and before long the herd boys appeared, helping them. "Who is your master?" one of his men called.

The question made Barak wince. If he'd been closer, he'd have shut the man up before he had a chance to finish it. Barak, son of Abinoam, lord of Kedesh, knew full well whose herds these were, whose encampment he would find on the plain of Zaanaim, over the next hill. He made it his business to know everyone and everything in his lands, and he liked people to remember that. It would have been better for the herdsmen to realize that his master's name—and allegiance—were already well known.

But totally unaware of that, the herd boy—a gangly lad of 12 or 13—replied, "These are the herds of Heber the Kenite, sir."

Several at the head of the column glanced back at Barak somewhat nervously. The men, especially the wounded, were talking about stopping for the night. While they could make Kedesh by midnight if they rode hard, Barak knew they would all prefer to stop. "Will we rest in the tents of the Kenites, my lord?" his herald asked him.

Probably they were thinking that he might have planned the journey better. He could have arranged to arrive at a friendlier camp or village to spend the night. But Barak had known all along they would end up near the tents of Heber the Kenite. It wasn't his first choice of a place to stay, but the encounter could prove useful.

When Heber had left his family's holdings in the south and moved north to the land of Naphtali, he had taken Barak's cousin Jael as a wife. The ties were close enough that Barak had assumed Heber would be a natural ally in his quest to drive the Canaanites out of the south. But the man had surprised him. Refusing to ally himself with Barak, he had instead made a treaty with Jabin of Hazor. For five years now, Heber the Kenite had allowed Hazor's forces to pass freely across the plain of Zaanaim on their way to plunder and pillage Hebrew villages. Furthermore, he had offered them provisions on their way to fight Barak's armies. Barak had first attempted to strike his own treaties with Heber, then had threatened him. The Kenite stood firm.

"I offer you the same thing I offer the king of Hazor," Heber said. "I care nothing for the gods of Canaan or the God of Israel, but just want to graze my flocks in peace. Your armies may pass through my lands unmolested. I will offer you shelter and provision when you need it. But I will fight neither for you nor for him. I will not take up a sword in this quarrel."

It was an infuriating stance, and the thought of Heber the Kenite had bothered Barak for years. Unfortunately, he didn't have the time and forces to waste against a neutral kinsman. Even now, though, he hoped to win Heber more firmly to his side.

Jael herself came out of the tents to welcome them and offer them a meal for the evening. Barak greeted her warmly.

"My lord husband is a half-day's ride to the south, seeing to the shearing," she said, holding out her hands in welcome. "But your men may camp in the fields to the north of our tents, and may kill as many sheep as you need to feed you this night."

"I thank you," Barak said. He looked down at her with some pleasure, for he had always been fond of Jael. A few coal-black curls peeped from under the gray fabric of her head covering. Jael had matured, not into a beautiful woman, but into one who despite her nearly 30 years still looked girlish—or perhaps boyish—and bright. He thought of other women—Deborah, his own wife, Abigail—who had become stout, stately, and sedate after years of childbearing and care. Perhaps because she was unable to bear children, Jael was still slender, her little face unlined and her eyes bright. But what a price to pay for eternal youth! Heber the Kenite had a fertile second wife who had borne him several sons and daughters. The other wife cared for the family, while Jael oversaw the business of the camp and the herds.

As the men made camp and Jael's servants set about slaughtering and preparing the meat for the evening meal, Barak pulled his cousin aside from her work. "You must speak to your husband for me," he urged. "I fight for every cubit of soil. If he would stand beside me and defy the king of Hazor, I could offer my soldiers to protect him. We could be far stronger together."

Jael shrugged, a pretty but helpless gesture. "What can I do, Barak? I am but a woman, although I have as much cause to hate Jabin and Sisera as you do—perhaps more." She looked away. Barak knew little of her story, but he was aware that like many women she had been ill-used by Canaanite soldiers in a conquered village. Unlike many others, she had survived to nurse a burning hatred for the Canaanites. "If I could hold a sword, I'd drive them from the face of the earth. But standing in my husband's sandals, his view makes sense. He does not want you for his lord, Barak. He wants no lord at all, only to be his own man in his own land. And he can do this only by staying neutral, by making treaties with both sides and keeping his own kind of peace."

"The people of Abel-beth-maachah didn't like his kind of peace very much," Barak growled. A servant offered a basket of bread. Barak took a large piece and tore at it with his teeth. "I know Sisera's men camped here the night before they rode in to take the village," he added when he'd finished chewing.

Jael looked down. "I can do nothing about my husband's decisions, my cousin. Surely you must see that. I am a woman, and no soldier. I can strike no blow in this war."

"But your heart is that of a Hebrew."

"Of course. Far more than yours, perhaps. I still pray to the God of Israel, and dream of the day He will drive our enemies out before us. Do you pray or dream, Barak?"

He laughed. "You remind me of someone."

"Of Deborah?"

"How did you know?"

"Even before she was a prophetess, she had that gift of seeing into people, of speaking her mind. I don't have it. I wish I did. I wish I could speak to my husband the way I've done with you. I used to be brave when I was a girl. Now I'm angry, but not brave. There's so little any Hebrew can do in times like these—much less if she's a woman." Jael got to her feet gracefully. "I'm a barren wife past the age when my husband might hope for sons from me. I was born to have only one purpose in this life, and I failed at it. Why should he listen to me? Excuse me, but I must go see to those girls roasting the lamb. They waste so much if I'm not there to watch them."

She walked away. Barak stared down at the rest of the bread in his hand.

Jael was right, he decided later that night, lying awake. Not about herself—well, she might have been right about that too—he didn't know. But about him. While he had never had much faith, once he had had dreams. Now he was a practical man. He didn't believe in God, and he didn't believe in himself as the deliverer of Israel. As Barak, the lord of Kedesh, he had a small and simple job to do and a good sword arm for doing it. Life had become much simpler. It helped that that unsettling woman Deborah was far away in Ephraim, muttering prophecies. On the other hand, it didn't help that their mutual cousin Jael had proven today to be such an uncanny echo of Deborah.

Heber the Kenite didn't return before Barak left the following morning. Barak had to ride away without a further opportunity to try to persuade him into an alliance. It probably wasn't any use anyway. Another thing Jael was right about.

Before noon they saw the walls of Kedesh, sentries perched on top. Barak had spent a lot of labor these past years reinforcing those walls and training those sentries. Kedesh would be a hard city to take. But the gates opened joyfully for the chieftain and his victorious men, and Barak allowed them the pleasure of a small parade up through the main street. He made the most of every victory, no matter how small. Victories were good for morale. Also he made time, too, to speak to the families of the men who'd fallen. That was a dispiriting duty, but helped morale too.

Then, at last, to his own house, where his sons were returning from the fields with the goats and Abigail and her maidservants were busy weaving cloth. His wife managed the household capably and was skilled at all womanly tasks, but she took special pride in spinning, weaving, and dyeing cloth, and often made more than her household needed, trading some for additional luxuries. They lived well, far better in these past years then they had done before Abigail came to Kedesh. She had taken the commander's large but spare house and made a home of it.

The boys rushed into his arms, and Abigail emerged from the workroom with a more stately greeting. "Lord husband. God is gracious to bring you home safely again."

"Indeed," Barak replied.

"We have a visitor," she continued. "A courier from your kinswoman Deborah in Shiloh."

"Really?" He brightened at once. It had been nearly a year since he'd had word from her, though he often heard of her in other news from the south. The elders of all the tribes sought for her advice and spoke freely of her not only as prophetess but as judge of Israel. What had happened to motivate her to send word to him directly?

The young courier bowed low. "My lord Barak, I am sent from the house of Deborah, the widow of Lappidoth of Shiloh."

"Yes, I—" Barak broke off. "Did you say widow?"

"Yes, my lord. Lappidoth of Shiloh is dead. He was gathered to his fathers a fortnight ago, in his own house at Shiloh."

"At Shiloh, you say? So they are no longer living at the Palm?"

"They returned to Shiloh when my lord Lappidoth was in the last weeks of his illness, my lord," the boy said politely.

"I am sorry to hear it. He was a great man. Is there other news from Shiloh?"

"Yes, sir. The Canaanites there have set up an altar to Baal in the midst of the tabernacle of Yahweh. The prophetess Deborah and the high priest both spoke out against it, and there was some fighting between their followers and the Canaanites. Blood was shed in the sanctuary, but the altar of Baal remains, and the high priest has left the tabernacle."

"Bad news," Barak commented. He found himself wondering which had shaken Deborah more—her husband's death or the desecration of the tabernacle. Both occuring together must have been a double tragedy. But the tabernacle—that was a blow to all Israel. Barak had little faith himself, but he knew the importance of Shiloh, of that tent shrine brought all the way from the desert wanderings. It was the final symbol that the Canaanites had at last grown strong enough to crush Israel's hopes of ever calling itself a nation.

"You have traveled far to bring bad tidings," Barak said. "I am sure my wife and servants have made you comfortable. May I welcome you in our house until you are ready to return to Shiloh."

"My lord, all this I told to your wife and to others who have come into the house since I arrived two days ago," the boy said. "But there is another message I was to deliver for your ears alone. Mother Deborah did not send me only to bring you the latest news of the family or the town. She has had a word from the Lord."

A word from the Lord? Barak was ashamed to realize that his instant inner reaction was, *oh, no.* It could mean only one thing—trouble.

"The prophetess Deborah, mother and judge of Israel, says that the Lord has told her the time has come to rise up and bring battle to Jabin King of Hazor and Sisera his general," the boy said in the singsong manner of one repeating a message memorized by rote. "You are to rally an army from all Israel, and meet Sisera in battle, and the Lord will give you victory."

The courtyard of Barak's home was completely silent for half a minute. The message was for him alone, but it was no secret. The boy's clear tones had carried, and everyone—Abigail, their sons, the servants, the soldiers who had accompanied Barak home—heard his words.

Into the silence, Barak son of Abinoam laughed. A dry chuckle at first, but when he ran the words over in his mind, it became more of a laugh. "Very good!" he declared. "Well memorized and well recited! Tell your mistress the prophetess that I am lord of Kedesh, and the day before yesterday I lost good men trying to defend a village of farmers and goatherds. I fight all day, every day to hold the little land I have. Once in my life I summoned men from all Israel to fight Jabin of Hazor, and the ragged-tailed few who bothered to come were soundly whipped. I will not call men to die again in such a venture. Deborah may think the time has come, but she has been wrong before."

The boy looked shocked, but he stood his ground. "She said that if you doubted, I must tell you there is no doubt this time. It is not like the time before, she says. The Lord came and spoke to her in the tabernacle itself. He promises victory to you, Barak son of Abinoam, the deliverer of Israel."

Turning, Barak walked several paces away. He held up a hand and called over his shoulder, "I have given you my reply. You may stay until tomorrow and then return to Deborah with my words. I've nothing more to say."

Everyone else had plenty to say. The news spread all over Kedesh by nightfall: Deborah, prophetess and judge, had summoned Barak forth to war, and he had refused to go.

"What do the gossips say at the well?" he asked Abigail as he settled down to sleep that night.

"Half say you are— that you may be wrong, my lord husband. Some of them truly believe it is a word from the Lord and that you put yourself in peril to reject it."

"And the other half?" He watched as Abigail took off her head covering and unpinned the long dark hair that tumbled down her back, making her look younger. Something of the pretty, laughing girl he had married still remained in her. But she had grown wiser. She chose her words with care. Deborah's or Jael's unbridled tongue was not for her.

"The others say what I say, that you are a wise man and a good ruler. Most of the soldiers know we cannot win in the field against Sisera—not in a full-scale war. They say the other tribes will not rally to support you—that it will be another slaughter."

"And you agree?"

"Of course." She had stripped down to her inner garment and lay down now, pulling the blanket over them both. Her body warmed the bed and the smell of the spices she rubbed into her skin perfumed the air lightly. "I am proud to be wed to the lord of Kedesh. No woman wants to be married to a dead hero."

"Even if the Lord truly has called me?"

With a shrug she rolled onto her other side so that her back faced him. "I have always doubted this woman Deborah could be a true prophetess. Why would the Lord send His word to a woman? She has lost her husband and perhaps, crazed by grief, she just imagines she hears the voice of God. Isn't that right?"

Barak was silent. He could see Deborah in his mind's eye, standing before the men of Israel, telling them that God was calling them to go fight for their land. Strange, but when he was in her presence he had never really doubted that Yahweh spoke to her.

It might help if You spoke to me once in a while, he prayed into the darkness and silence. In response he heard nothing but the words the boy had brought today, words direct from Deborah, words she believed had come from God Himself. The Lord God had sent a message, not to him, but for him. That was the best he would get.

When he thought Abigail had fallen asleep, she suddenly said, "You are not thinking of obeying her summons, are you, my husband?"

"To fight? No. I don't see how we can win. But I'm going south to see Deborah myself. You're wrong about her, Abigail—she's more than a lonely widow speaking out of her grief. If she thinks she's had a word from the Lord, I need to discuss this with her face to face."

He heard the catch of her breath. "So you're going to Shiloh?"

Barak nodded in the dark, realizing he had come to a conclusion without even thinking it out. "Yes. I'm going to Shiloh."

CHAPTER 25

Deborah was in the workroom of her house, shaping clay into a small lamp, taking pleasure in the task as she always did. In these weary weeks after Lappidoth's death, Anna steered her stepmother toward tasks she knew Deborah found easy and rewarding, and Deborah did not protest. Anna and Eli and their families cared for her. It was an unfamiliar experience, having others care for her daily needs. But it allowed her to rest.

Rest was the very thing she needed. The long months of nursing Lappidoth through his final illness and the great chasm of emptiness that had opened upon his death would have been painful enough. Seeing the desecration of the Lord's sanctuary had shaken her to the core. And on top of all that, the compelling message she had received from God had warned her that she was not about to enjoy a quiet widowhood. God was preparing to toss her back into the maelstrom of conflict and warfare just when she had so little strength and courage to offer. She was exhausted.

But she was not thinking of these things as she squeezed the clay between her fingers. Actually, she wasn't thinking of much of anything at all. Her attention was focused on the clay, on the heat of the day that sent trickles of sweat down the back of her neck, on the voices of the small grandchildren who played at the other end of the workroom. She was completely unprepared when her oldest granddaughter, Leah, who at 6 years of age had been entrusted with the task of watching the younger children, said, "Grandmother, a man is here."

Leah had lived all her life in a small community in which she knew the name of any relative or neighbor who might enter their courtyard. Few Hebrews traveled outside the boundaries of their own towns and villages in these times, for the roads were no longer safe. If a stranger had come to their house, Deborah thought, the man must be a Canaanite soldier. She rose to her feet, quickly pulling her head covering over her damp hair. Anna and Eleazar, Eli and Keturah were all out in the fields, and Japhet was gone with the goats. Apart from the two maidservants, Deborah was the only adult in the household. Cautiously she went out to meet the visitor.

For just a moment, he was truly a stranger, and she did indeed think it was a Canaanite. He was a man of war, tall and broad and bronzed, wearing a leather breastplate beneath his travel-dusty cloak and carrying a long sword at his hip. Then she saw his face, and five years—no, 20 years—dropped away.

"Barak!" she cried, and darted toward him, her hands outstretched.

He hesitated a moment, then opened his arms to her, and she went to his embrace. "I was so very sorry to hear of Lappidoth's death, cousin," he said to her as she drew away. "He was a good man."

"The best. He suffered terribly at the end, and I am glad he is at peace." Then her mood shifted abruptly. This was not merely a meeting with her cousin, with—most dangerously—a man she had once been deeply drawn to and who, despite the years and the burdens he carried, was still treacherously attractive to her. This was an encounter between the prophetess and judge of Israel, and a prince of the tribe of Naphtali—a warrior chieftain who had come at her summons. Taking a step back and straightening, she spoke more formally.

"I have had a word from the Lord, Barak. He came to me, His very presence, and spoke with an audible voice in the sanctuary, saying *'The hour has come.'*"

Barak nodded. "The boy you sent told me you had word from the Lord."

She could see that the details she'd added—the palpable sense of God's presence, the sound of His voice—meant nothing to Barak. The whole world in which she moved, the realm of prophecy and messages from the Almighty, was perhaps comprehensible only to a man like the high priest who spent all his days in the worship of God. To an ordinary, devout Hebrew that world was barely perceptible, something one might catch a fleeting glimpse of at prayer or during a holy day. To a man like Barak, his faith shriveled and twisted by his own long battle, she might as well have been speaking a foreign tongue.

Still, she had to explain. "That was all He said—that the hour had come, and I sent a messenger for you at once. But in the days since, He has revealed more. Not through voices or visions, but daily, almost hourly, the Lord has been sending messages. I see His plan taking shape. This is nothing like the last time," she added. "Then, we were making our own plans, and the Lord gave us no assurance. It was a mistake to allow you to go forward as I did, trusting in my word instead of God's." Although Barak's eyebrows raised slightly he made no other acknowledgement of her confession. "This time the hour is the Lord's, and the plan is the Lord's. He commands you to raise an army of 10,000 men and march to Mount Tabor. He will draw Sisera and his army to the Kishon River and deliver them into your hands."

Barak stood silent for a long time. Finally he said, "The Lord's message is very detailed. Ten thousand men? And the Lord Himself will lure Sisera to the Kishon? I don't need to worry about that part of it?"

Deborah felt he was trying to bait her, but she did not rise to the challenge. "The Lord will go with you, Barak. This is his leading."

"The Lord may go with me, but the men of Israel won't." He raked his hands through his hair and paced away from her, across the courtyard. Deborah raised her hand to signal a servant to bring food, drink, and water for him to wash. Barak had endured a long journey. Then she dropped her hand, checking the gesture. She could play hostess later. Right now she was the Lord's mouthpiece, and all other business must wait until she had delivered the message and was sure Barak had heard it.

"Five years ago I could raise less than 3,000," Barak said. "Now—after five years of Jabin extending his power, taking more and more of our land into his grip—now you want me to assemble 10,000? They won't come, Deborah. They're used to living as slaves and cattle."

"I think you're wrong," she challenged, crossing the courtyard so she stood in front of him again, her arms folded across her chest, like a stone in his path. "I hear their cries, Barak. They are weary of oppression and eager for God to send a champion to deliver them. What happened here in Shiloh at the tabernacle was a final blow. The people of Israel have had enough of the Canaanite sword and of the Canaanite gods."

"Oh, and there are no Hebrews going up to the tabernacle to make sacrifices at the altar of Baal? Believe me, Deborah, I have seen them. Our people are not as faithful as you'd like to think."

"Nor so faithless as you believe!" she shot back. "Believe me, Barak, the Lord has His faithful, and they *will* respond if you call them. But it's not me you need to believe. It's the Lord. This is His word, not mine."

Again Barak turned away. He put his face in his hands and rubbed his face vigorously, like a man trying to awaken after a long sleep. "The Word of the Lord," he repeated slowly, and looked up from his hands, away from her. Although he could see nothing but the plastered stone wall enclosing the courtyard, Deborah thought he gazed as if he were viewing all the land of Israel, its plains and mountains, the rutted roads over which honest travelers no longer dared pass, the empty villages whose inhabitants had fled to walled cities, the fields of crops stolen as tribute by the king of Hazor.

Finally he once more faced her. "I will go. I believe you. I believe this is God's word. I don't see how I'll do it, but I will go. But you have to come with me."

"To battle?"

He laughed. "I can't see carrying a woman into battle, though it may come to that. But you return to Kedesh with me to rally men to our cause. If I am going to the men of the north to say that God has called us to war, I want His prophet beside me. I want you to be able to tell them this is the word of the Lord."

"I had never thought—" Deborah hesitated. She hadn't really envisioned what her role might be, beyond delivering this message.

Perhaps she had assumed that she would be staying here in Shiloh or returning to the Palm, continuing her role as judge. But she had never imagined riding north with Barak.

"I can't do this without you, Deborah. But if you come along, I will do it."

Deborah opened her mouth to say yes, that she would accompany him. She didn't plan the words that followed: they were on her lips as if they'd never passed through her mind. It wasn't entirely an unfamiliar sensation. Sometimes the Lord's messages came this way.

"I will go with you, Barak. But I warn you that because you hesitated over this, you will not have the glory you have dreamed of since you were a slave in Hazor. Your own hand will not cut down General Sisera. The Lord will give that honor to a woman. A woman's hand will slay Sisera."

"What?"

Deborah looked as blank as he did. "The Lord gave me the words," she said. "I can see it—a woman's hand slaying Sisera—though I know not how it will come to pass."

Barak laughed nervously. "You think to take a sword into battle and kill Sisera yourself?"

"I do not know, Barak. If it's Yahweh's will, perhaps I will do just that. But the Lord has promised you victory in this battle, and you do right to obey his command. We will have to wait and see how He brings it about. Now, will you sit and take food and drink? I will call a servant to wash your feet."

"I thought you'd never ask," he said with a smile.

A week later, Deborah headed north out of Shiloh, accompanied by Barak and 20 men of Shiloh who were going to fight in the Lord's war. Already she had sent messengers to the chiefs of the tribes of Benjamin, Reuben, Ephraim, Issachar and Manasseh, recruiting men for the army. She and Barak themselves would stop in several towns on the way north, spreading the word.

But this was a far more difficult task than it had been five years earlier. Canaanite forces now garrisoned virtually all the towns. The same soldiers patrolled the roads. Just getting Deborah's messengers, and later their small party of men, out of Shiloh had been difficult. The two of them slipped out of the town in the hour before dawn, hoping darkness would cover their escape and prevent questions. They avoided the main road, hiding in the forest outside the town until dawn. Later in the day they met up with the rest of the 20 men, who had left the town singly and in pairs during the previous few days. The Canaanite soldiers were well aware that something was afoot. Three of the men for whom they were waiting never arrived, and Barak finally gave the order to march north without them, guessing that Sisera's men had questioned and detained them when they attempted to get out of Shiloh.

It was a rough journey over rugged terrain. They had to stay well away from the roads. Deborah and Barak departed the main group several times to enter towns and villages, disguising themselves as a merchant husband and wife with a bundle of goods to trade. Once inside the town, they managed to contact the chiefs and elders. As Barak had predicted, most were skeptical about raising a force to fight against Sisera.

"You see that we cannot even walk freely in the streets of our own city," a Hebrew leader in the city of Jezreel told Deborah. "How can we march out of here with an army? There would be bloodshed long before we ever reached Mount Tabor. We would have to fight the Canaanites in our own streets first."

"Then perhaps that's what you'll have to do," Barak interjected, his face a stern mask.

The man raised his eyes to the warrior's. "My lord, you have done great things in Kedesh, but even you have been unable to liberate the whole tribe of Naphtali. Why do you now dream you can retake all the lands of Israel, and overthrow the king of Hazor?"

Barak's face showed nothing of the doubt that Deborah knew churned within him. "I have Yahweh's prophetess beside me, and I march at His command. Deborah has told me that she has a sure word from the Lord. That is enough for me. It should be enough for you too."

The chieftain's eyes went to Deborah. She knew the man: he had come to the Palm seeking her guidance when Sisera's forces had first captured his city. A proud individual, he hated living in subjection to a Canaanite king. "Mother Deborah, you have told us for many years now that the time is near but not yet, that we cannot rise in revolt till the Lord calls. Are you certain this is His hour?"

"My lord," she said respectfully, "I myself stood in the tabernacle of the Lord at Shiloh while the foreign dogs dragged in their idol and desecrated the sanctuary. I looked, and though the curtains were drawn it was is if I saw into the holy of holies and beheld the Shekinah of the Lord above the ark, and I heard His voice as clearly as you hear mine now. I tell you, I stood in the very presence of God, and He told me that this is the hour, and Barak son of Abinoam is His chosen deliverer!"

She had risen to her feet as she began to speak, and the chieftain and his men stared at her as if they, too, were in vision. "This is indeed the word of the Lord," he said. He, too, stood. "My lord Barak, my lady Deborah, I do not know how this thing is to be done, but I will do it. As many men from Jezreel as I can muster will join you on the ride north."

He was as good as his word, though he did indeed have to fight in the streets of his own city before his 200 men could march out three days later. Some of the men of Jezreel took swords and spears from the Canaanite soldiers they killed. The rest were poorly armed, for the Canaanite overlords had long forbidden Hebrew smiths to forge iron swords or spears. A few ancient bronze and stone weapons were all that most could muster. "I have a forge in Kedesh," Barak told Deborah. "My men cannot make weapons enough to arm 10,000—we have neither the time nor the materials for that—but we will do what we can."

By the time they crossed into the lands settled by the tribe of Naphtali, the little army had grown to a thousand strong. No longer did they skulk over the hills and through the brush: they rode on the great road north, and met no Canaanite garrisons on the way. "Jabin and Sisera have word by now," Barak said to Deborah. "They know we are mustering an army. Our task now will be to assemble our force and get to Mount Tabor before they march against us. If we command the high ground, we will have a distinct advantage."

"That is the Lord's plan," she said.

Soon they entered Barak's own territory, and messengers went out to every town and village under his protection. The time for hiding and cowering was past, he announced. Now he demanded from them the price of his protection during past years—it was time to send their sons to fight in Yahweh's army.

Deborah travelled with Barak himself to many of the towns and villages, describing to the elders what she herself had seen and heard. A full month passed from when they had left Shiloh until they finally arrived in Kedesh, and Barak welcomed her into his own home as a kinswoman and honored guest.

"Deborah of Shiloh, mother of Israel, you are welcome to our home," a voice said as she entered the courtyard, and Deborah looked around to see who had spoken. Barak and his personal guard followed behind her and servants scurried about, taking baggage, cloaks, and armor. A small boy ran across the courtyard chasing a tiny kid goat. But the center of all the activity was a woman, younger and shorter than Deborah herself, rounded with pregnancy, and dressed in a fine dyed, blue linen robe and a white head covering. Her face was serene and commanding as she approached with outstretched hands. She came close enough to take Deborah's hands and offer a kiss on both cheeks, reaching up to graze the prophetess's face. After weeks marching and camping in the wilderness with a large group of men, Deborah's first impression of Barak's wife was of how very clean she smelled.

"How pleased I am to meet my husband's dear cousin at last," Abigail said less formally. Deborah sensed, though, that these words of welcome were memorized rather than bubbling up from the heart. Abigail's dark, brown eyes did not look particularly pleased, though her smile was impeccable.

"How honored I am to be a guest at last in my kinsman's house, and to meet his wife and sons," Deborah said in as careful a voice. Barak had told her of his reunion with Abigail, and of how happy he was to be living with his sons. Beyond that, he had said little about his marriage and family, but then she had never imagined him a devoted husband. And indeed, there was a certain sense of ritual to his greeting to Abigail, as opposed to the unrestrained joy with which he embraced the two little boys who hurtled into his arms, shouting, "Papa! Papa! You're home at last! Did you bring more soldiers?"

"Yes, my sons, I brought many, many soldiers. And many more will come soon. We are going to fight a great war against the armies of King Jabin and General Sisera, and the prophetess Deborah—this lady here—has promised that the Lord God will give us victory."

Barak's younger son stared at Deborah open-mouthed, clearly impressed by a woman who received messages direct from God. But the older boy had eyes only for his father. "May I fight, Papa? I'm big enough, and I've been practicing with my sling. Abihu has been teaching me, and he says I'm a very good shot for a boy my age. Please, may I go to war with you?"

Over the boys' heads, Deborah caught the eye of Barak's wife and gave a rueful smile. "My son is the same age," she said, "and had almost the exact same conversation with Barak before he left Shiloh. It's hard to convince a boy he is not yet a man."

Instead of the understanding smile of one mother to another, Abigail looked away from Deborah, her face hard and cold as a winter morning frost. In her frown Deborah read a clear message: Abigail not only disapproved of her elder son setting himself up as a soldier—she disapproved of the entire war and Barak's role in it. Also, Deborah recognized, Abigail had sent her husband away to reason with this mad woman who imagined herself a prophetess, and had not realized he was returning at the head of an army, gambling his life on the mad prophetess's vision.

As a widowed older woman, one recognized by all as prophetess and judge, Deborah enjoyed far greater freedom than she had had as an unmarried girl or a young wife. She was free to trespass the bounds of convention to some degree, to travel with men and sit in their councils. But she was still a woman, and as a guest in Barak's household, society expected her to remain in the company of the houshold women, sharing their work and eating with them at meals. In this house, that meant Deborah spent most of her time with Abigail. And that wasn't easy. Barak's wife was polite, but she made no effort to hide her disapproval of the war or of Deborah personally. She spoke to her visitor as much as civility required her to, but she did not relax her guard and always remained remote and formal.

Deborah felt no sense of leading, no guidance from the Lord as to how she might deal with Abigail, and left to her own devices she was unsure how best to approach the woman. Surely there could be no personal jealousy in Abigail's attitude. Even if she had known or guessed that Barak and Deborah had been drawn to each other as young people, years of marriage and childbearing had occurred between those times and now, and no one could deny that Abigail was both younger and prettier than Deborah. However, no one could deny either that Barak had far greater respect for his cousin's opinion than for his wife's, and was far more interested in anything Deborah might say. *He doesn't see me as a woman at all,* she wanted to tell Abigail. *He thinks of me as one of the men—that's why he respects and listens to me.* But she had no idea whether to say so would make things better or worse, and the words remained unspoken.

It was a relief, on the third day of her stay in Kedesh, when

Barak summoned Deborah to council with him and the other officers of his army. A messenger arrived while she sat with Abigail and
her maids in the workroom, spinning wool in uneasy silence. The
lad told Deborah to come to the city gate to meet Barak and the others. Abigail shot her a look she couldn't read as she rose to follow
the boy through the busy streets of the bustling little city. As she
passed a smith's forge she heard the clear ring of hammer on anvil, a
sound that filled the air of Kedesh these days. Citizens were bringing ploughblades, pruning hooks, every metal object they owned to
be melted down and reforged into weapons to outfit Barak's army.

At the gate, the commanders met inside a bare gatehouse. Barak
sat at the head of the group, flanked by his own commanders from
Kedesh. Tribal chieftains of Naphtali and Zebulun, along with
princes of a dozen Hebrew cities sat around him.

"Greetings, Deborah," Barak said, gesturing for her to sit as the
men rose to their feet in her honor. She scanned their faces.
Although she knew most of the southern elders and chieftains, here
in the north she was less well known, but they had all heard of her,
even if few of them had ever traveled as far as the Palm to seek her
counsel. A few faces watched her warily, for some men submitted to
a woman's leadership only with the greatest reluctance. But no one
in the group would challenge her openly. They were here at her
summons, believing she carried the Lord's message.

"What news?" Barak asked four younger men who remained on
their feet when the others took their seats. They brought him word
from all corners of the 12 tribes.

"The men of Benjamin are marching, my lord," one boy
replied. "Several hundred strong, perhaps a thousand."

"We have more soldiers coming from the villages here in
Napthali and in the lands of Zebulon," another added, and a man
Deborah knew as one of the chief elders of Zebulon announced,
"You shall have every man from Zebulon who is able to hold a
sword, my lord Barak."

"Even if he has no sword to carry!" Barak said with a great laugh.
So far, the news pleased him. But he turned now to another boy
whose expression was graver. "What news from the seacoast?"

"The men of Dan will not come, my lord. And only a few have
responded from Asher. We can look for little help from the seacoast."

"The fishermen are cowards," Barak said. "The Canaanites have overrun their lands, and perhaps they are happier under Jabin's rule." He glanced around. "Any more news?"

"From the men of Reuben, the same as it was five years ago before the battle on the plains," the fourth spy announced. "They say they are coming, but they sit in council and debate and send no one. I do not think we can look for help from Reuben."

"Nor from Issachar," another one of the council added.

"What of Sisera? What is he doing?" Barak probed.

"Gathering all his forces at Harosheth," replied one of the spies. Since his conquests had pushed further south and west, Sisera had captured this city near the plains of Megiddo and ruled it as his stronghold, though he still owed loyalty to the king of Hazor. "The men heading north to meet you face little resistance on the road, for Sisera is calling every able-bodied man he has back to his own city to arm them for war."

"How soon before he will be ready to march?"

"More quickly than we can, for he is far better armed," one of the commanders answered.

"Nine hundred chariots of iron," some muttered. Sisera's chariots were the stuff of legend. His army was well-armed, fast-moving, and virtually invincible.

"They could be on the way in less than a month," a spy observed. "Perhaps in a fortnight."

Barak turned to his own commanders. "And when will we be ready?"

A grizzled older veteran shook his head. "I would be comfortable with a month to prepare, my lord. All our forces from the tribes would have time to arrive, and our men could be then adequately armed and trained. We will never have arms to equal Sisera's, but we can put together an army—perhaps seven or eight thousand men, if all the promised forces arrive—within a month."

"Too late," said a cheiftain from the city of Shunem. "In a month, Sisera's iron chariots will have time to get to Mount Tabor and capture the high ground. They could cut our forces in two, slaughter our armies from the south as they arrive, and then turn to attack us here and finally take Kedesh itself. We don't have a month."

Barak turned to Deborah. "Mother of Israel, does the Lord have any word for us?"

Sometimes she marveled at him. He spoke so readily in front of others of the Lord's word and her gift of prophecy. But privately he acknowledged his doubts, his lack of faith. Were the fires of war forging his faith more strongly, or was this entirely an act, a sham put on for the benefit of the tribal leaders? She didn't know, and she had few chances these days to talk to him alone. Again she rose to stand before the men.

"I have had no new messages from the Lord since we came to Kedesh," she stated. "But I have no reason to doubt what God has already told me: that He will give us 10,000 men, and that you must occupy Mount Tabor. If this can only be done quickly, then I would advise starting for Mount Tabor with all speed, trusting God for the 10,000."

"Well said!" Barak announced. Standing, he drew his sword from its sheath. It was a fine weapon, iron with a keen edge. He had taken it from the body of a dead Canaanite soldier years before. Now he thrust it over his head. "We march a week from today. Those men who cannot be armed with swords and spears must go with bows and slings, or with their bare hands if need be." He nodded at the messengers. "Tell those on the way not to come to Kedesh but to Mount Tabor. We will assemble our army there, and we will take that strategic position before Sisera's chariots pass through the gates of Harosheth Haggoyim." Turning to Deborah, he said, "We will do all within our power to reach Mount Tabor in time. Then we must rely on God to do the rest."

"Amen," said several of the gathered leaders.

"Call the priests and Levites of Kedesh," Deborah said. "Tell them that in six nights, before the army marches, the army and all the city will meet to offer sacrifices to the Lord and to pray for victory." The men nodded. For many years now, most of them had lived with very little in the way of public worship of the God of Abraham. Sacrifice and prayer on the eve of battle would encourage them and make it clear in whose name they went out to battle.

"Dismissed," Barak said to the chieftains and the messengers. "Go spread the word among the men. One week."

The men filed out. Deborah and Barak, following them out of the gatehouse, soon found themselves left alone in the noonday sun. On the terraces around the city the people of Kedesh were weeding and pruning the grapevines. Women and boys did most of the work now, as every able-bodied man prepared for war. Deborah scanned the narrow green terraces and the small flocks of sheep and goats grazing beneath a cloudless blue sky. Someday, she thought, all this land would be what God had promised—the land of Israel, the land of God's Chosen People. He had promised it to them, and for generations they had struggled to take hold of that promise. Perhaps this war would finally turn the tide.

"A good thought, about the prayers and sacrifices," Barak said. "It will put heart into the men. I will address them at that time, and you must do the same."

"I will. Do you have— is there a small house, or a room in some quiet house, where I might stay alone until then? I want to fast and pray, to seek guidance from Yahweh. This is the last time I will speak to the men before they leave, and if the Lord has a message for them I must give it then."

Barak, buckling on his sword again, spoke as if his mind were far away. Deborah knew his thoughts were already at the forges where the smiths hammered weapons out of every scrap of bronze and iron they could find, at the archery butts where arrows flashed to the center of targets, at the storehouses where his captains decided how much food the army could carry. "A widow in our street has a small and quiet house. You may stay there—she has a private room—and fast and pray all you want. But you need not worry that this will be your last chance to give God's message to our troops." As Deborah looked up quickly at him, he caught her eye with a swift glimpse of an old and golden smile. "You're coming to Mount Tabor with us, Deborah. I'm not going into this fight and leaving my prophetess behind."

ChAPTER 26

The military camp was quiet on the night before battle. As silent as a host of men nervously awaiting possible death could be. Barak heard low voices talking. An occasional burst of laughter punctuated the darkness. The screech of a weapon blade being sharpened. Other than that, little disturbed the darkness.

For a while he stood looking down the southwest slope of

Mount Tabor toward the plain of Megiddo. Sisera's forces had spread out along the Kishon. Their campfires dotted the landscape. He could even see the dark shapes of the chariots and their horses. The battle was entirely in his hands. Sisera could, and would, remain there forever if Barak didn't engage his forces. The Israelite army had already held its own position for a week. The Canaanites had arrived two days ago. He had considered waiting longer. Perhaps the delay would make Sisera uneasy. But now the decision was made. They would attack at dawn.

Earlier he had gone over the final battle plans with his commanders. "Our numbers are stronger than I expected," Shammah, an elder of the occupied town of Gath-hepher in Zebulon, who commanded 300 warriors, commented at one point. "Nearly 10,000."

"That is what the Lord promised," Lamach of Benjamin reminded them. He was a very devout man. Barak envied such people for their faith. Really, faith was all they had. Sisera had nearly 20,000 men with iron chariots, and every man was well armed. Many were trained warriors. Barak had no reason in the world to believe he could beat the Canaanite general on the morrow. The Israelites held the high ground—that much was true. Other than that, their only advantage was a promise from God. Someone who hadn't had much faith in years, Barak was now staking everything on a leap of faith.

In his mind he tallied his forces. The bulk of them belonged to the tribes of Zebulon, Naphtali, and Issachar. Of the rest, the next largest contingent came from Ephraim and Benjamin, probably because those were the tribes that knew Deborah best and were most likely to trust her word. A handful had arrived from the tribe of Manasseh. Half of the 12 tribes. The other half hadn't responded at all. If the tribes of Israel had stood together, he would have an army on this mountaintop tonight that could wipe Sisera from the face of the earth tomorrow.

After reviewing the battle plans for the dawn attack, he said goodnight to the other commanders. Then Barak began walking through the camp, greeting those men who were still awake, trying to find words that would encourage them.

He wasn't surprised to find Deborah doing the same. Nor was he surprised to find her berating a few men whose courage seemed weak. She had never had much time for doubters. Barak knew she disapproved of him—because he hadn't jumped at once when she told him he must advance against Sisera. Because he admitted he didn't have a great faith in God. Yet he was here, tonight. That was what counted.

They spoke for a few moments, every sentence charged with more meaning than the words themselves would suggest. In the face of the stern and somewhat forbidding woman before him, Barak saw an echo of the girl he had once fancied he was in love with. Life's pathway had been so different from what either of them had expected. Yet on this night, she had faith in him. She believed God would use him—despite his doubts, despite his fears and past failures. "You are an arrow in the hand of God," she said.

The words stayed with him long after Deborah had returned to her tent. In his own tent, his armor-bearer asleep across the entrance, Barak sat sleepless. It would be good to be well-rested for the morning, but he was facing the battle of a lifetime and could not imagining closing his eyes. Instead he stayed awake, replaying in his mind the battle plans, the conversation with Deborah, the past 20 years. He remembered Sisera's face as the Canaanite captain roughly threw a Hebrew slave boy to the ground. Tomorrow, Barak would finally have his chance at revenge.

CHAPTER 27

All she could do was watch.

Once the ram's horn sounded the signal to advance and the army began its charge down the mountainside—their momentum aided by the steep slope—Deborah found a spot to sit on a rock that allowed her to see over the dense trees covering the hillside and across the valley. Barak had assigned two soldiers to guard her. He had wanted to leave half a dozen but she had insisted against it. Every man who could be spared was needed in that valley today.

As she watched, she saw the first assault hurl itself against Sisera's forces, saw them beaten back by Barak's archers and slingers. But she saw, too, the first Hebrews fall on the slope with Canaanite arrows lodged in their chests and throats. Deborah had never witnessed a battle before. Although she was much too far away to identify individual men, she was still close enough to hear the babble of shouts and the clash of sword upon shield.

Deborah remembered one of the ancient tales of the great leader Moses. The children of Israel had fought a battle against the Amalekites, and Moses had sat on a hillside, watching and praying. As long as he kept his arms raised in prayer, the Hebrew forces prevailed. But when his arms grew tired and fell to his sides, the enemy beat back the Hebrews. Eventually he had to have helpers hold up his arms.

It sounded like a legend—hard to see how such a thing could affect the course of a battle, but the ways of Yahweh were strange. Deborah was willing to try it. She would pray, of course, for the success of Barak's army, and she often did pray with her hands raised. When she let them drop, she could see only the same confused melee of clashing forces, under the cloud of dust kicked up by their feet.

She turned to one of her guards. "How is the battle going? Can you tell?"

"Oh, yes, Mother Deborah." A Benjamite, he addressed her as people of the southern tribes often did. "The men of Zebulon have Sisera's army fighting hard. The tribe of Naphtali is approaching them now from the north, and the army of the other tribes from the south, and Sisera's troops are so much engaged with the first wave that they have little strength to spare for the other two. Soon we will have them surrounded."

"So it goes well?"

"It goes well. But their numbers are still greater."

Deborah looked down at her hands lying folded in her lap. The Lord had promised victory. Still, she kept praying.

A long hour passed. The sun climbed higher in the sky, and one of the guards handed Deborah a waterskin. Sisera's army now had to defend itself on three sides, with the stream at their backs. Despite their superior numbers, even she could see that the Israelites prevailed.

"See, there's my lord Barak's standard," the other guard indicated. He was one of Barak's own men from Kedesh. Deborah followed his pointing finger and saw a tattered fragment of red fluttering above the carnage below. "He's trying to fight his way to Sisera himself. If the general can be killed or taken, his whole army will lose heart."

Deborah knew that the young soldier, eager for battle and excited at the thought of victory, was thinking of General Sisera's death. But the words he spoke could as easily have been true for the Hebrew army. How would they fare if Barak himself fell? The Lord had called him to lead the Israelite forces. Had he guaranteed Barak's personal victory, or would He bring victory to Israel no matter what happened to their leader? With a shudder Deborah recalled the prophecy the Lord had given her. No matter what Barak was trying to do down on that battlefield, she had the word of the Lord that he would never slay Sisera by his own hand. Why was he even trying?

She recalled, too, the other part of the prophecy. The Lord would deliver the enemy general into the hand of a woman. The camp followers that had straggled along with the army—much to her own disgust—remained on the mountaintop along with a few servants, awaiting the outcome of the battle. She could hardly imagine that the Lord would use a prostitute to bring down the Canaanite general. Though, remembering the tale of Rahab and the spies, she realized it was better not to make too many predictions about whom Yahweh might use. All the same, of the few women near the battlefield today, she was His most likely instrument. And how He might employ her to defeat Sisera, Deborah had no idea.

Is there somewhere else I should be, Lord God of Israel? Something else You are calling me to do, rather than just sitting on this hillside watching and praying?

But she received no answer. The Lord told her nothing to contradict the counsel of her own good sense: the safest place to be for a middle-aged woman was well away from the fighting. If God had a plan to use her further, Deborah had to assume He would let her know about it in His own good time.

"Look! Look!" one of the guards exclaimed.

Again she stared in the direction he was pointing. Off on the western horizon, over the heads of the fighting armies, masses of dark clouds were gathering. "A storm is coming," one of the men said. "Unusual for this time of year."

The thunderstorm burst quickly and fiercely. The dark clouds hid the sun, and soon even Deborah and the guards were forced to seek the shelter of a tent. Rain poured like the River Jordan from the sky. The heat of the day cooled quickly as Deborah's damp clothes stuck to her skin. Absently she thought the rain must provide relief for the hot, dusty men below, then wondered how they could go on fighting in such conditions.

"If this lasts very long, it will make a mess of the streambed," one of her guards said.

"It'll turn the soil in the plain along the Kishon into mire," the other agreed.

"How will that affect the battle?" Deborah asked.

"Bad news for Sisera. His horses and chariots are all down in the valley. When that ground gets wet, you can be up to your knees in mud. His charioteers won't be able to move."

"The rain's holding up," the other soldier reported, peering out of the tent.

Then, as quickly as it had struck, the thunderstorm ended. Deborah emerged from the tent into the cooler air and looked down on the plain below. At first she could make no sense of what she saw, but one of the guards said, "Just as I thought. Sisera's army is trying to retreat, but they're abandoning the chariots—look!" Then she could see in the distance the infamous iron chariots—that had struck terror into so many Hebrew hearts—stuck useless in the mud of the plain bordering the Kishon.

Sisera's soldiers, on foot, were fleeing west across the plain, down the valley.

Above the confused sounds of battle the clear note of a horn rose in the air. "Retreat! He sounds retreat!" the guard shouted.

Deborah was on her feet, watching the scene below. More and more of Sisera's army pulled away and headed down the valley of Jezreel. But they did not go unchallenged. "Barak's men are pursuing them," the guard announced excitedly.

"Good for him!" the other soldier declared. "This is meant to be a complete victory. He should pursue them to the gates of Harosheth Haggoyim."

"What happens then—when they get back to Sisera's own city?" Deborah wondered.

"If enough of the army can barricade themselves inside, then lord Barak will have to besiege the city," the guard from Kedesh explained. "It will be long and slow, but I think we can prevail in the end."

Down below on the battlefield, the Hebrew army was doing its best to make sure as few Canaanites retreated as possible. Deborah felt strangely remote from events on the battlefield below. Down there, men were dying. Men on both sides of the struggle. Both God's people and His enemies were experiencing the searing pain of swords plunged into their vitals, feeling their own hot blood spilling out. All of them had wives, mothers, and children awaiting them at home. She knew Yahweh had called Barak to this war, yet at the same time it was hard to believe God took pleasure in such waste of human life. She wondered if there would ever be a better way, if Israel could ever live at peace in this land of promise.

"After them! After them!" the guards urged on the army. The original battlefield at the foot of Mount Tabor was empty now, though Deborah could see the plain strewn with the bodies of the fallen.

"Look to the north!" cried the soldier from Benjamin. There, tearing loose from the rest of Sisera's force, was a very small band of men, running from the battlefield.

"Very strange," the other said. Canaanites were deserting the battlefield both in small groups and large numbers, but all were heading west toward Harosheth. Why would a handful flee north? Perhaps they might be hoping to get to Hazor or another town held by Jabin, but why risk entering Barak's own territory and passing so close to Kedesh?

"Someone very badly wants to escape without being pursued," Deborah suggested. "Could it be Sisera himself?"

"If it is, he's a coward," the soldier from Kedesh replied. "Surely he would lead his own army in retreat."

"Perhaps not," the Benjamite suggested. "What if he's the sort of man who puts his own skin ahead of the safety of his men? He might try to run in the opposite direction, knowing that all the pursuit will be toward Harosheth. Maybe he thinks he can get to safety in Hazor or another city in the north."

"Down there on the battlefield, no one would see him escape," Deborah commented. "Surely we're only seeing it because we're up so high. Can we get a message to Barak or one of the other commanders, warning them that Sisera may be escaping to the north?"

"I'll go," the soldier from Kedesh instantly volunteered. "With your permission, my lady," he added.

"Of course. Go quickly."

She turned her attention back to the battlefield as the young soldier plummeted headlong down the rain-soaked and slippery slope of Mount Tabor. The Canaanite army was in complete rout, with the Hebrew army splashing in hot pursuit along the Kishon down the Jezreel valley. She felt sure they would follow the enemy all the way to the gates of Sisera's city. Thousands of Canaanites lay dead on the field. It seemed the Lord was truly fulfilling His promise to give Barak a great victory.

But where was Sisera? Would he perish today—and by whose hand?

CHAPTER 28

For the first time in his life Barak son of Abinoam found himself running away from a battle.

It felt wrong. Every instinct, every muscle in his warrior's body told him to be at the head of his forces, leading the charge down the valley of Jezreel in pursuit of the retreating Canaanite army. Barak was determined that not one Canaanite soldier would get behind the gates of Harosheth alive.

But he would not be there to witness the utter annihilation of his long-time enemy. At the last skirmish he had given his captains their orders. All his scouts had reported the same thing: Sisera was no longer in command of the Canaanite forces. Barak could only conclude that the small group of men Deborah had seen leaving the battlefield consisted of the general and his bodyguard. While the army retreated in one direction, Sisera himself had fled on foot in another. He'd suspected it ever since he received her message. Now he was sure it was true. And this war wouldn't be over till Sisera himself was dead. Nothing but the elimination of his general could signal to the king of Hazor and his soldiers that their battle was forever lost. And nothing but Sisera's death could assuage Barak's long hunger for revenge.

So he raced back along the trail he and his men had just marked with the blood and bodies of the enemy, back to the battlefield where today he had won a great victory, and north beyond it, trying to imagine where Sisera might have gone. Barak wanted to travel swiftly. They had captured a chariot that had not gotten mired in the mud. Now, with two soldiers, accompanying him, he started after what he could only assume was Sisera. Deborah had reported seeing a party of men on foot. Turning the chariot toward the higher and less muddy slopes, the three of them started after the band of Canaanites. Barak and his men fought to keep the chariot upright. Difficult as the going was, if the general was on foot, they would soon overtake him.

As he clung to the chariot, Barak spared a thought for Deborah and wondered if she was still on the mountaintop. No doubt she was, still awaiting word of the final victory. For a fleeting moment he remembered her prophecy. *The honor will not be yours, for the Lord will hand Sisera over to a woman.* Perhaps if he captured Sisera, he should bring him back bound for her to slay. That would fulfill the word of the Lord. Could she do it? Thrust a sword through a man in cold blood? She was a gentle woman—some called her the mother of Israel. Then he remembered the cold iron in her eyes when she told him it was time to go to battle. Yes, Deborah could execute Sisera.

But he wanted to wield the sword himself. He longed to meet Sisera face to face, and know that the slave-owner who had once savagely beaten him, the man who had hanged so many Hebrew men, raped so many Hebrew girls, was dying at his own hand. Barak might even do it slowly.

Night fell. Still Barak and his men pushed on. The rain had not been so heavy here, and the horses had better footing. He saw nothing and no one, no sign of the general's passage. Of course, he might easily miss signs in the dark. It would be more prudent to rest the horses and wait for morning light. But he hated to waste time.

When they passed a village, Barak sent his men in to ask if they had seen Canaanite soldiers fleeing on the road. A boy who had been herding goats, sleepy and confused at being roused so late, said he had noticed a small party of armed men going north earlier in the day.

"Toward Hazor?" Barak demanded.

The boy's brow wrinkled. "They didn't stay together," he remembered. "Some went toward Hazor. One went alone—the other way." He paused. "I think."

Barak frowned too. If the boy was right, the solitary individual might well be Sisera himself. He could have sent his men to Hazor to beg King Jabin for more help. But why not go there himself?

Perhaps because he suspsected Barak would pursue him. "He might assume that by traveling in another direction, alone, he'll throw me off his trail," Barak suggested to his men. "But why would he go straight toward Kedesh? It's guarded by our own men."

The two exhausted soldiers stared back at him blankly. Clearly they relied on their commander to do all the thinking in this crisis.

Barak thought. "You two continue on the road to Hazor," he said finally. "Go swiftly, and try to overtake Sisera's men before they get there. The longer we can keep Jabin from hearing about the battle's outcome, the better. But if you approach Hazor and see no one on the road, turn back to Kedesh. Don't let yourselves be captured. They will torture you to learn what you know. I will go on alone in pursuit of Sisera."

"But where will you go, my lord?" one of the men asked. "You said yourself that Sisera would not go toward Kedesh. What allies does he have, in the very shadow of your gates?"

"He has one," Barak said.

When he saw the encampment at dawn he knew it was too early yet for the flocks and herds to be on the move. Heber the Kenite's people were no doubt just waking and beginning their morning routines. Rage smoldered within Barak at the thought that Sisera might be hiding in this camp. He hated the fact that a kinsman of his own people could harbor the snake Sisera in his very bosom. Why couldn't Heber the Kenite have shown more loyalty, have proved himself Barak's ally?

Dismounting from the chariot, Barak tied the horses and walked into the camp. It was quiet. Even the servants were not yet about. Only a few goats noticed his passing.

Then he saw a small slim figure approaching in the gray dawn light. "My lord Barak!" a voice called, and he saw that it was his kinswoman Jael, Heber's first wife.

She darted toward him and knelt on the ground at his feet, a much more formal greeting than she had offered him on his last visit. He offered a hand to raise her up. "You did not meet me with such ceremony when I came before, cousin."

Jael looked up, her dark eyes glittering. He could not tell if she was joyful, terrified, or both, but she was certainly suppressing great excitement. "Then I welcomed you as Barak my kinsman, the lord of Kedesh," she said. Somehow he sensed that she was fighting to keep her voice steady. "Now I greet the victor of the battle of Kishon Valley, the deliverer of Israel."

She was the first to speak those words to him, and Barak felt a small shiver of delight, knowing he'd earned those titles and that all men would acknowledge him. But he had a more pressing business here, one so consuming that for the moment he didn't even wonder how Jael had gotten news of the battle's outcome so quickly.

"I am seeking—" he began, but her words cut across his.

"Come to my tent, my lord. I will show you the man you are seeking."

Show you the man? Could she mean Sisera? Could he be a captive here? Or could he be alive and well, lying in wait for him, protected by Heber's armed men? Was Jael leading him into a trap? Although he was sure that she would never do such a thing, he still felt a shiver of fear as he followed her toward the tent.

Lifting the tent flap, she stood aside for him to enter first. What he immediately stared at on the ground was the last thing Barak had expected to see.

Sisera, general of the forces of Hazor, ruler of Harosheth Haggoyim, oppressor of Israel, sprawled on the dirt floor of Jael's tent. Barak recognized the clothing and insignia the man always wore. He even recognized the military leader's face—what little still looked like him. Sisera lay with a wooden stake—a tent peg—driven through his temple. It had shattered bone and splattered brain tissue and blood over what remained of Sisera's head and on the ground around it. Even for a man who had just come from a day of killing, it was a gruesome sight to see, especially lying so quietly on the floor of a woman's tent.

He couldn't tear his eyes from the sight. Finally he looked back at Jael. "Tell me," he said, quietly, urgently.

"General Sisera came last night, fleeing the battle, and sought shelter here. My husband, his other wife, and his sons have gone to Hazor to trade. Sisera told me to set a guard over him and tell anyone who sought him that there was no one here. He did not give me his name, perhaps thinking that I did not know who he was, other than that he was a Canaanite lord who had survived the battle."

"But you knew him? He had visited your husband here before?"

"No, Sisera himself has never come to this camp, though his men have." She turned again to the mutilated form on the floor, a sight Barak would have imagined any woman would turn away from with nausea. "But I knew his face. I saw him before, you see. It was he who led the attack on Kinnereth many years ago when I lived there. He gave the soldiers the command to rape the women. Sisera himself—" Her voice broke off though she did not take her eyes off the dead man. "I knew his face well," she said finally, and Barak saw there was at least one other person in Israel whose desire for revenge against the man was as great as his own.

"Did he tell you of the battle?"

"I didn't ask. But I knew that if he was fleeing that you must have won, and that made me glad. And bold, perhaps." Her eyes still glittered and her cheek was fever-bright. "He asked me for water, and a bed to lie on. But he stayed alert until I brought him a drink. When he took the skin from my hand he knew he was a guest, safe under my tent roof. He knew I would honor my husband's alliance, and not send my servants to attack him or betray him to you."

Despite her strange excitement she spoke calmly as she told him how she gained the trust of the man she had betrayed. "So you gave him water," Barak prompted.

"No, milk," Jael said, in that same distant voice. "I opened a skin of milk and gave it to him. Then he fell asleep."

"So quickly?"

"He trusted me," she repeated. "And he was exhausted from the battle." She did not quite meet Barak's eyes, and he thought of the knowledge many women had of herbs and the roots of plants. Barak wondered if Jael had added anything to her skin of milk. For her story went on to show that Sisera had slept soundly indeed.

"Who did this?" Barak asked, wondering which servant's hand had wielded the peg and hammer. That man had done Israel a great service, yet he had robbed Barak of the pleasure of giving Sisera the death blow.

"I did," she replied slowly.

"What, by your own hand?"

"By my own hand." She held up her arm. "I'm a strong woman, you know. And he was asleep."

"Yes, but—" It wasn't physical strength so much as strength of purpose that amazed him: that she could, in cold blood, lay the sharpened stick against his temple and deliver the blow that broke the bone. A strong woman, in more ways than one. And fueled by a hatred as intense as his own.

Barak did not speak for a long time. "You have done a great thing this day, Jael," he said at last. "A thing I wish I had done myself. But it is as the Lord prophesied. Deborah told me that God would deliver Sisera into the hands of a woman."

"Deborah told you this?" Jael asked in wonder.

"Weeks ago, before we marched north to Kedesh. The Lord told her, though He did not tell her who the woman would be or how the blow would be struck. I thought I would kill Sisera myself. But I can see there's no value in trying to outsmart the Almighty God."

Finally, Jael smiled, a terrible smile. "At the last moment I did not think I could do it. But I did."

Just then they heard a ram's horn sound. Jael looked toward the tent door, fear in her eyes. "It's my husband. I fear he will not look as kindly upon this day's work as you do."

Jael and Barak together went out of the tent. The morning sun was just rising in the east, and they squinted into it to see Heber the Kenite and his people riding their donkeys up the hills from the southeast.

"What news, wife?" Heber called. Then he saw the man standing beside Jael. "Barak of Kedesh. You are welcome to my lands."

"That's Barak, the victor of the plains of Megiddo, my friend," he said without smiling.

"So your battle is won? I left Hazor before dawn, and no news had come from the battlefield." As Heber dismounted from his donkey, Barak could see the thoughts racing behind his calculating eyes—that it might be best to abandon his old policy of neutrality if Barak was the unchallenged ruler of Naphtali.

"Our battle is won," Barak said.

"And General Sisera? Was he slain?"

Now Barak permitted himself a smile. "Perhaps you should ask your wife what has become of General Sisera."

Heber looked puzzled, but Jael only walked to the tent and held the flap aside as she had done for Barak. Her husband went inside, then quickly backed out again. "How did this happen?" he demanded. "Did you allow Barak to attack Sisera within our very walls, after I had promised him safety?"

"I did more than that, my lord," she confessed, and told him the story.

As he listened, Heber's face clouded with rage. "What kind of creature is this, my lord?" he appealed to Barak. "This is no woman!

She is an unnatural thing, who could do such an act. And in defiance of my orders! She knew I had pledged friendship to Sisera, and vowed no harm would come to him within my tents. Now she has shamed and disgraced me!" He spat upon the ground at her feet.

"Yet she has placed you on the winning side in this battle, Heber," Barak said evenly. "Tread carefully, for you are camped now on my land—Hebrew land. Before another harvest is gathered in you will see the Canaanites utterly driven out of these lands, and you will regret you ever made a treaty with such a snake as lies dead there in your wife's tent."

Heber the Kenite glanced away. "It is as you say, my lord. You are the victor, and I will pledge loyalty to you. I have never wished for more than a peaceful and untroubled life. But the matter of my wife is unchanged. She has been disobedient and unwomanly."

"Then I will relieve you of this burden," Barak replied. "Jael, summon a servant to pack your things. I will take you, your servants, and the body of Sisera back to Kedesh. There you will be honored as one of the victors in this battle." He met her eyes. "It is better than being beaten as a disobedient wife, is it not?"

Jael's face was solemn but her eyes were bright. "Better indeed, my lord. I will make ready to come with you."

EPILOGUE

Deborah stood in the middle of the room, surveying the neatly packed and rolled bundles of clothing, her few belongings ready for another long journey. *My last long journey,* she thought, then smiled to herself. So many times before she'd believed her life was settled, that upheaval and change were safely behind her. Although she was an old woman, gray-haired and a grandmother, she was by no means on her deathbed. Who knew what Yahweh might yet have in mind for her?

Her plan, until the Lord told her otherwise, was to return south to her own lands. Back to Shiloh, at least for a visit with her children, and then on to the Palm of Deborah, where she would again make her home. Perhaps she would bring her youngest son Japhet with her. She missed the boy, though Anna's household cared for him well. But it would be good to have him by her side, all the same, as she returned to the Palm. She still had a work to do in these uncertain times. God had directed her to return to the place where she had first heard His voice, and after a year in the north, Deborah was glad to be returning home.

It had been an eventful year. Barak's decisive victory over Sisera at Mount Tabor, and the general's shocking death at the hands of a woman, had been just the beginning. Swelled by recruits from throughout the Hebrew tribes, Barak's army had swept southward, driving out the Canaanite invaders, freeing Hebrew towns and establishing the independence of God's chosen people. His latest victory was his greatest. With Ephraim and Benjamin free of Canaanite control, he had returned to his own lands in the north, then besieged and captured King Jabin's city of Hazor. The city where Barak the boy had once been a slave was now in Hebrew hands, and he planned to move his own headquarters from Kedesh to Hazor and establish himself as its ruler.

"A fine irony, after all you suffered there," Deborah told him.

"I will make a better ruler than Jabin or Sisera," he said simply.

And he was right. Barak in victory was a different man. His bitterness and anger had fallen away from him. Confident and successful, he seemed also more humble. Deborah had seen little of him since the battle at Mount Tabor. He had mostly been away fighting in the south, while she remained with his family and Jael at Kedesh. But since his triumphant return from Hazor a few weeks ago, they had finally had an opportunity to speak.

"Your faith in God all these years has finally been rewarded," Barak had admitted. "I was a fool to have doubted so long."

"You had good reasons for doubt," she reminded him. "And despite your doubts, you were faithful. You answered when God called. That is what matters, in the end."

"Will you not stay here in the north? Come with me to Hazor when I establish my fortress there. Your leadership is needed."

"It is needed in the south too—in my homeland. God is calling me to return to my old home and my old task. He is not finished with His prophetess and judge yet."

"Nor am I finished with you. You will find me coming to you with all manner of questions and problems, just as all the other tribal leaders will do."

Now as she prepared for her journey south in the company of a guard of Barak's armed men, she heard a footstep at the door of her chamber. Turning, she saw Jael. The younger woman had become like a sister in the long months they had spent together here in Kedesh. Now she quickly crossed the floor to stand before Deborah. "I have something to ask of you."

"You may ask anything."

"Take me with you. I want to go south, to remain by your side and serve the Lord's prophetess."

Deborah felt the quick leap of joy in her own heart at the words. Being prophetess and judge was a lonely life. With her husband dead and her older children having lives of their own, she longed for a companion, someone who would indeed stay by her side. Still, she cautioned Jael, "You have a place of honor here, in Kedesh, and at Hazor when Barak moves there. Would you leave that behind?"

A smile tugged the corner of Jael's mouth and for a moment she looked like a girl again. "Indeed I do have a place of honor. Did you know that Barak has offered to marry me?"

"To marry you— himself?"

"Yes. To take me as a second wife, even though I am barren and divorced. He says he offers me his name and protection in thanks for the service I did him by slaying Sisera. In fact, he will build me my own house so that I can live apart from Abigail and her children, and I will have my own servants."

"Well." Deborah knew a swift pang of jealousy that vanished almost as quickly as it arose. Barak had offered her riches and honor and a house too, but not marriage. She knew he saw her as an equal, perhaps even a superior, an older woman despite the fact that she was in fact two years his junior. But he would never have made an offer of marriage to the Lord's prophetess, the judge of Israel. High position and great responsibility carried a price—the price of loneliness.

"And even with such an offer, you will not stay?"

Jael shrugged. "I have been a wife. I have no wish to be one again, not even to my lord Barak. Although he is a good man, I would not live as second wife to Abigail, with all men knowing he took me in only out of pity and gratitude. There are worse reasons for a marriage, I suppose, but there are also better lives I might lead. And the one I choose is as your sister and servant—if you will have me."

Deborah held out her arms to embrace her cousin. "From me

you'll have no pity, but great gratitude. Come, let us go take our leave of the lord of Kedesh."

In the streets outside, people had gathered to bid farewell to the prophetess. They were singing the song written in honour of Deborah, Barak, and Jael, celebrating their victory over Sisera. The now familiar words rose in a shout of praise from the crowds at the town gate:

"So may all your enemies perish, O Lord!
But may they who love you be like the sun
when it rises in its strength."

Barak waited for them at the gate, resplendent in the rich garments of a ruler. He took Deborah's hands in his. "So you will rob me of both my warrior-women at a single stroke?" he said, his smile warm.

"Yes, Jael is coming with me."

"She spoke to me of her desire to travel to the south with you. I hope that one day I will see you both in Naphtali again."

"I hope you will come to us at the Palm to seek the counsel of the Lord."

His face grew serious. "I promise you this, Deborah. As long as I rule this land, I will do it with the Lord's counsel. He led me to victory, and I will not turn aside from that path." Still holding her hands, he knelt before her, and the people around fell to a hush. "This is my solemn vow to the Lord, and to you," he proclaimed.

Deborah opened her mouth to speak, but words fled her. Instead she felt the Lord's Spirit spreading over her, into her, speaking through her. "And this is the word of the Lord, Barak son of Abinoam," she said formally. "Long and well will you rule this land as long as you heed the voice of the One God, and worship Him truly. For 40 years you will rule this land in peace, and no enemy will arise if the people of Israel are faithful to the God of Abraham, Isaac, and Jacob. The mouth of the Lord has spoken it."

"Amen," he said, and the people standing around echoed his benediction. He rose to his feet and dropped Deborah's hands. "Go in peace, cousin."

At last Deborah found words of her own. "Stay in peace, cousin." With her servants, her guards, and Jael by her side, she set her feet on the road home.

AFTERWORD

This is the second time I have attempted to build a full-length book around the brief account of a Bible woman. The first time, I dealt with Queen Esther and faced the interesting challenges of trying to fit together the biblical story with the historical accounts of King Xerxes' court.

The story of the prophetess Deborah and the liberator Barak posed a different set of problems. The biblical account is extremely short. Essentially, it's one chapter, Judges 4, which then gets expanded upon and embellished in a poem called the Song of Deborah (possibly by Deborah herself, or perhaps just "about Deborah") in Judges 5. No other historical records of these events has survived, and this particular period in history—Israel in the time of the Judges, at the end of the Bronze Age—is far less well-known than fifth-century B.C. Persia.

I took certain imaginative liberties with this story, since the Bible tells us so little. For one thing, we have absolutely no reason to believe that any prior relationship existed between Deborah and Barak, much less that they were cousins or had ever considered marrying each other. In Judges 4 Barak's response to Deborah seems to me to indicate a level of familiarity with the prophetess that may simply reflect the fact that this tribal chieftain and the prophetess/judge had had official dealings with each other before. Imagining a personal relationship between the two simply allowed me to add some richness and depth to the story. Similarly, I grafted Jael into their family tree to provide a connection that might explain why the wife of Sisera's ally took such a decisive action against Sisera.

Again, the Bible does not indicate that Barak was ever a slave. I employed the story of his slavery and escape from Hazor to illustrate a little of what life under Canaanite rule might mean for a young Hebrew at that time, and to give Barak a personal motivation for overthrowing Sisera. In fact, the Bible gives us no indication at all about Barak's previous life before Deborah calls him to fight Sisera.

The heroes of the book of Judges seem to me more deeply

flawed, and thus more human, than the "superstars" of the rest of the Bible. Their doubts and fears (think of Gideon coming back to God again and again with his fleece!) perhaps reflect the time and society in which they lived. During the era of the Judges, Israel was not so much a nation as a loose affiliation of tribes (a situation clearly indicated in Judges 5, in which Deborah laments the unwillingness of the tribes to support each other in war). Though the Lord has promised conquest under Joshua, the reality of the situation in Judges is that Canaanite overlords frequently suppressed the tribes. They were also, to some degree, assimilated into the larger culture, tolerating the worship of Canaanite deities alongside that of the Lord. I tried to reflect all these factors in creating the world of Deborah, Barak, and Jael.

Barak, then, is a man of his time: a person who would not doubt the existence of God or the gods, but who questions whether that God intends to keep the covenant He made with Israel as His chosen people. Barak's doubt—only hinted at in his brief biblical conversation with Deborah—became for me the defining element of his character, one that symbolizes the ambiguity of Israel's relationship with God at that period.

Deborah herself is a popular figure with many women because of her unique leadership role, so rare for a woman at that time. Again, her background is mysterious. We know that she judged Israel, which implies leadership, and that Israelite tribal society accepted her as a prophetess—one who brought God's messages to the people. We don't know how a woman achieved such status in that patriarchal culture, but we find no hint that the men of Israel questioned her right to lead. In fact, Barak seems to rely more heavily on her than she would like him to!

The reference to her as "mother in Israel" in Judges 5 gave me a hint as to how she might have been seen: an older woman, whose motherly wisdom offered comfort and guidance through difficult years. Yet her words to Barak make it clear that she could be stern and did not hesitate to offer a rebuke!

Scripture describes Deborah as "wife of Lappidoth," though, since "Lappidoth" means "flame," some commentators have suggested that the Hebrew here may be a title for Deborah herself ("woman of fiery spirit") rather than indicating her husband's name. While Deborah was certainly a woman of fiery spirit, I have assumed that, like almost all women of her time, she would have been married, and I have thus kept Lappidoth as her husband and given him the sort of character I believe a man in that society would have needed to accept and support a wife like Deborah!

I drew upon the different portraits of Deborah in Judges 4 and 5—prophetess, judge, wife, mother, war leader, and possibly poet and singer—as well as some imaginative details, such as the Jewish midrash tradition that Deborah and Lappidoth made lamps for the Lord's tabernacle, to create a picture of a woman who I believe could have responded to God's call and risen to such a position in the world of the Judges. The role of a prophetess—what it means to receive messages from God and how the prophetess understands the difference between her own wisdom and God's voice—was of great interest to me, and it led to some of the book's central conflicts.

I wish I could have given more attention to the story of Jael, who could be the subject of a book in and of herself, but to keep this book from being overwhelmed I chose to focus on the two main figures and to make Jael an important but secondary character.

Two great taboos for Christian writers writing for a primarily Christian audience are sex and violence: we don't like to write about them in any detail, yet the Bible is unfortunately full of both. Writing about sexuality was a constant stumbling-block in telling the story of the harem girl Esther, while in the account of Deborah and Barak I had to deal with violence. This is a narrative of war and brutal bloodshed in a violent and bloody time. As a Christian pacificist who wholly embraces Jesus' message of nonviolence, I've always found the blood-stained book of Judges difficult. It was a challenge as an author to immerse myself in the thinking of the time and recognize how natural it seemed to people such as Deborah and Barak that God would use violence to free His people. Not only did I have to research details about late Bronze Age/early Iron Age warfare, I chose to write from the point of view of Barak himself, and thus had to describe battles firsthand. In doing so I tried to walk the line between gratuitous violence and an honest portraying of the brutality of war at that time (and, indeed, at any time).

Immersing myself in a time and place so different from my own required a great deal of research. As well as the valuable help provided by Dr. Douglas Clark and my editor Gerald Wheeler, I owe a debt to a number of books, the most-used of which was Oded Borowski's *Daily Life in Biblical Times*.

I became very fond of both Deborah and Barak during the writing of this book, and reluctantly have to remind myself that any imaginative recreation of a biblical story is just that—one person's imagination. You, perhaps, may read Judges 4 and 5 and take the same details to imagine a very different Deborah or Barak. Regardless, I hope my telling of the story has helped you to see the original in a clearer light, and has stimulated your thinking about how God leads His people through difficult times, when His purposes seem unclear and His promises unfulfilled. Though you may have moments in life when you feel like Barak, I pray that God will give you something of the hope and courage that sustained Deborah.